Extreme Measures

Marc Stevens

This book is a work of fiction. All material in this publication is the product of the author's imagination. Any similarities to places, or persons, living or dead, is purely coincidental, and should not be in any way interpreted as something else.

Cover by: Covermint Designs.

This book is dedicated to the Korean War veteran who joined the ranks of his fellow brothers and sisters on March 28, 2020.
His struggles in life are over, and he now rests in peace in the company of our creator.
I miss you Dad.

1

My mixed-race crew and I, pulled off some high-risk missions in the last few months. One of which, was capturing the supposed king of the pirates, Eiger. It was a feat that took us the better part of two years. I now stood outside of the brig on my ship the Legacy, with a scowl on my face. The Principal Investigator for the Chaalt people Sael Nalen, was giving me a summary on her interrogation of Eiger. My first officer and significant other Tria, who was also of the Chaalt race, stood holding my arm. On the other side of me was Klutch, my Tibor Troop Master. Standing next to him was the other member of my crew responsible for helping capture Eiger, Coonts of the Grawl race. The looks they were giving the Principle Investigator were going from bad to worse. Sael just explained the reason we captured Eiger wearing some frilly looking junk armor. The armor was only worn at Murlak Royal weddings, and Eiger was the groom to be. Sael went on to explain that the pirate had talked his way into the Royal family via marriage, to a pre-selected member of royal Murlak descent. The piece of scat was getting all of his murderous sins forgiven, by agreeing to give up the pirate life and turning over his massive cache of ill-gotten goods to the royal family. The booty ended up in my possession as well.

I tried to calm myself so my response would not be the oath laden tirade that was dancing about my brain. "Sael, how can we believe anything that deceitful coward has to say?"

Sael stared me in the eyes. "If it was only his word, I would doubt him as well. There is no other reasonable explanation for the armor. I have carefully inspected it, and it appears to be a genuine relic of the Murlak royal family. It is adorned with the names of every royal family member who has ever worn it. Eiger's name is now etched into it. Murlak law forbids all but the royal family to wear it."

I personally didn't care if the murdering bastard was wearing a tutu, he wasn't going to walk away free, no matter what story he cooked up. The air around us was getting fouler by the minute and we all stepped away from the Troop Master. I cast him a stern look. "Klutch! You are not helping matters!"

"Commander" Klutch said, pounding his fist together. "Let me have some time alone with him, and I will find out if he tells the truth!"

We already knew how the Troop Master conducted his interrogations. His methods might be better described as atrocities. It was questionable whether or not all the information he attained was accurate. Anyone fortunate enough to live through the interrogation, was more than willing to agree to his suppositions.

By the way Coonts was eyeing Klutch, I knew he was going to give us his two cents worth, no matter if we needed it or not. "Commander" he said looking out of the corner of his eyes at Klutch. "Perhaps if someone of greater intellect was to question the Murlak, we might gain enough insight to decipher his subterfuge."

I felt Tria squeeze my arm as I looked to the overhead slowly shaking my head. This was getting more complicated by the minute. Tria whispered to me. "If I knew capturing the pirate would cause so much trouble, I would have killed him."

I gave her a small nod of my head because when we went after Eiger, it was my intention to kill him, repercussions be damned. When the unexpected opportunity presented itself to capture Eiger alive, Tria made the decision to do so for the wealth of information he would most assuredly possess. At the time, it was the most logical course of action. It was way too late to change what happened. What was done is done. The assertion that the entire Murlak race would hunt me down if we didn't let Eiger go free, would have been a meaningless threat, if I had not made the mistake of intentionally letting a witness escape as a warning to other pirates. Every time I show a little mercy, it comes back to bite me in the ass. I was going to seriously revisit that faulty way of thinking.

Sael and Klutch were both giving Coonts a glare after his intended, or possibly unintended swipe at their IQs. I had to give the Grawl his due, because he was more or less correct. A greater intellect might clear the air and disclose how much truth was in Eiger's disclosures.

I called to Justice, the artificial intelligence that controlled the Legacy. This earned me a small grimace from Coonts. "Justice, what do you make of the Murlak's confessions?"

"Commander, after carefully analyzing the Principle Investigator's interactions with Eiger, the pirate's exhibited biometrics, indicate a small percentage of deceit when it came to questions concerning the amount of his collected wealth to be given away. The questions related to his marital affiliation with the Murlak royal family lacked any perceived duplicity. I did note, his threat that the Murlak people would hunt you relentlessly if he is not released, had a distinct edge of certainty to it."

I looked at my crew members to see what reaction they had to Justice's disclosure. They didn't seem to give a damn, one way or the other. Sael Nalen was the exception, she wore a frown on her face. I don't know what was eating at her, we have always had conflict with the Murlaks. All my past experiences with them always ended in violence. They were a lot like the Scrun, they were always up to no good.

"Why the sour face Sael? You can't possibly think that I will let Eiger walk because he was going to marry a Murlak royal."

"I have a feeling you will end the pirate's life before you can take the time to thoroughly consider all options." She said.

Her comment was for the most part correct. I was thinking I would have a discussion with Eiger. If he did not come up with some really good reasons why I should not kill him, other than it would ruin his life as a royal, he would be taking a walk in the void. I almost smiled, thinking Coonts and Klutch would be wagering on how much longer Eiger would continue to waste our oxygen supply. When in doubt about validity of hearsay, go to the source. With my crew and the Operative in tow I walked into the brig.

"Justice open Eiger's cell."

The cell wall went translucent and the door opened. Eiger was sitting on the edge of a bunk and quickly stood. His beat-up ceremonial armor and dented helmet lay on the bunk. I turned to my crew and Sael, then pointed at the benches outside of the cell. Coonts and Klutch quickly sat whispering back and forth between themselves. Sael must have heard what they were saying or betting on, and chose to sit on a separate bench. Tria on the other hand, would have none of it and stood at my side giving me her "Hell no" look. Rather than look back at Sael to see what she thought of Tria's lack of decorum. I walked into the cell with her at my side. She did after all, make the decision to take Eiger alive. The few times I have had the displeasure of speaking to the pirate, it was always on his terms. Now they were on mine.

The frown on his face, said that he never knew what I actually looked like until now. I would speak from a position of power, so he would understand in no uncertain terms just where his future stood with me. "The only reason you still live, is my first officer believes you have information we can use. If you make me feel otherwise, as sure as the stars shine in this galaxy, I am going to kill you."

The frown disappeared from his face, but the look in his eyes said he was long overdue for an exorcism. When he set his stance and tensed his muscles, the Oolaran beast imprinted into my brain, clawed its way into my consciousness from some dark hidden place. My respiration stepped up a notch, and I turned sideways to him. Eiger was now giving me his full attention. He was a couple of inches taller than Tria, who was a head taller than me. His shoulders were as broad as mine, and the muscles in his arms considerable. I was sure he didn't get to the top of the pirate food chain, by being a second-rate brawler. A small smile flashed across his furry face. He obviously thought he had better than average odds of kicking my ass. The beast was starting to push all my go buttons, when Tria did the most unexpected thing. She came around with a lightening quick kick, that momentarily changed the shape of Eiger's face. His mistake of ignoring her as a potential threat and discounting her abilities, cost him a mouthful of his front teeth. He rebounded off the cell wall and onto the floor. When he tried to push himself up from the deck, she kicked his left elbow with such ferocity it reversed in a very unnatural direction. The pirate went face down, choking on his teeth and groaning in pain. I heard a howling laughter from outside of the cell, and turned to see Klutch slapping Coonts on the shoulder, saying he now owed him an additional twenty thousand credits. Grimacing, I turned back staring wide eyed at Tria. She stood over the pirate with a look of rage on her face. Eiger was spitting teeth from his wrecked mouth and made another mistake. He reached up toward Tria with his good arm, in what may have been a gesture of capitulation. It was another bad decision on his part. She grabbed his outstretched fingers with both hands and violently jerked them in opposite directions, ripping his hand almost in half. Now the pirate was screaming.

That pushed the pause button on my interrogation. Now everyone stood staring at the mess Tria had made out of Eiger in less than two minutes. Her Oolaran muscle enhancements weren't as pronounced as mine and Coonts, but it was obvious her strength and fighting skills made her a very deadly opponent. Eiger rolled over onto his back and used his legs to push himself into the corner of the cell. A gory trail of blood and teeth marking his progress. His howls of pain subsided into non-stop groaning. Tria bent down, and I thought she might give him another attitude adjustment. She instead hissed down at him.

"I am the only reason you are still alive. My Commander would have killed you! This is the only leniency you will receive. You will answer our questions without hesitation, or I will slowly emasculate you with my boot!"

Eiger gurgled out something that sounded like a positive reply. We thought Tria might be done, but she did the most unladylike thing. She hocked up a mouthful of spittle and deposited it on Eiger's face.

"That is for the beating you and your cohorts gave me. Now we are just about even!"

Coonts, Sael and I were just a little shocked, but not Klutch, he broke into a braying laugh that instantly annoyed me. When he saw my stern look, it quickly trailed off into a snicker as he departed the brig. Coonts just shrugged his shoulders and followed him out. Sael stepped into the cell and looked down at Eiger.

"He will probably die if he is not treated for his injuries. That outcome will not net any usable intel."

To our surprise, Justice broadcast over the cell intercom system in an unusually deadpan voice. "He will live."

If that was Justice's prognosis, I was good with it. Eiger's face was now a swollen bloody mess, so I decided he should have a little time alone to thoroughly assess his future.

"Justice, his care is in your hands, we will come back later to start the interrogation process once again."

Justice commented again in the same deadpan voice. "He will be fine."

With that, Tria and I walked out of the brig with Sael following.

We were approximately eleven light years from Alpha base and holding at a jump point. We had rendezvoused with our Zaen flagged freighter full of Eiger's pirate loot. It was currently a couple of thousand yards off our stern. The Sig crew manning it, were waiting for new jump coordinates. I had decided after talking with Tria, it might be a good idea to consult with everyone on Alpha base, concerning my plans to reveal the location of our home to the Sig. Coonts was in command of the freighter, but insisted on coming aboard the Legacy when he learned we had captured Eiger alive.

"Justice, have you got any comms traffic for me from Alpha base?"

"Negative Commander, I will alert you as soon as I receive a reply."

"Since I have yet to ask you Justice, I would like to hear what you think about letting the Sig know the coordinates of Alpha base."

"Commander, I believe your alliance with the Sig has been a lot less troubling than our affiliation with the Chaalt."

While the comment rolled right off Tria's shoulders, it registered as a slap in the face to Sael. To her credit, she clenched her teeth and bit down on the rant she was going to spew at the AI. She knew Justice was right, but was not about to admit it. She silently followed us with a dark scowl on her face.

"Commander, I have a transmission from Alpha base. Jaran said to relay it to you."

"Okay Justice, what did he have to say?"

"It was not word for word, but it was basically the same evaluation that I have already given you, prior to the communication."

Sael stepped up beside me, and I could see she was on the verge of a meltdown. "Commander Myers, the sooner I return to your base and board my shuttle, the sooner you will be rid of me. I have better things to do than listen to the insubordinate scat coming from the defective AI that runs this ship!"

I was not in the mood to hear a full-blown bickering contest between Sael and Justice.

I had a lot of irons in the fire, and nursing Sael's bruised ego wasn't one of them.

"Justice, transfer Alpha base's coordinates to our freighter and tell Coonts to get back aboard and moving ASAP. Jump us home as soon as he debarks."

"Affirmative Commander, moving alongside the freighter now, and I will be ready for DEHD core operations in T-minus fifteen minutes."

Sael stormed off toward the hangar bay. I felt like I should say something to sooth her feelings, but was having a hard time thinking what that might be. At this point, I didn't think we were going to have any formal farewells or other pleasantries, when we returned to base.

Tria gave me a nudge with her elbow. "Admittedly, the Principle Investigator is a pain, but if it were not for her, we would not have the advanced manufacturing systems that give us an edge over our adversaries."

Tria was right. I also had to admit, that once Sael got over not leading our last combat mission, she was a valuable asset to our team. The loss of her ship by an apparent mutiny or defection, was tearing at her soul, and might be part of the explanation for her contemptuous split personality. We just needed some time apart. In the past, it always seemed to heal most of the anger issues she had with me. I really didn't want Sael going away mad, I just wanted her to go away. I took a deep breath and slowly let it out. Rubbing ointment on Sael's sore ass was going to be on my to-do list after all.

"Sael! Hold up a minute!"

She threw up two of her arms waving me off, and kept going. I picked up my pace and caught up with her.

"Sael, Justice is just messing with you. While there is some truth in what he is saying, I think you are taking it out of context. The Chaalt people, and you in particular, are an extremely valuable asset to us."

She finally stopped walking and turned to me. The look in her eyes said that she knew bullshit when she hears it. "A properly functioning AI does not "mess" with command authority!" she replied.

I knew this wasn't going to be easy. "Sael, Justice is still working on whether or not you are command authority."

She crossed both sets of arms and squinted her eyes at me. I knew a change of subject was in order. "Sael, you know our freighter has a huge assortment of valuable artifacts and currency aboard. There is no way for us to determine who the rightful owners are. We would like the majority of the haul to go to the Primitive Planet Protection fund. Since we wish to remain anonymous, I would like you to personally handle the donation. We are okay with it being from the Chaalt people, less of course, any handling fees your Council might assess on such a large transaction."

That wiped the steely eyed stare I was getting, right off of her face. She quickly turned away to try and hide her reaction to my statement. It gave me a sense of accomplishment, knowing I just handled the dilemma of what to do with such a large amount of blood money, and at the same time, smoothing over the friction created by Justice's guileless commentary. I turned and saw Tria nodding to me with a smile on her face. I winked and blew her a kiss. The human gesture always seemed to make her laugh. This time however, she covered her mouth and pointed behind me. I turned back around, and found the Principle Investigator in my close personal space, once again giving me a piercing stare. The look quickly disappeared, and she shook her head letting just the hint of a grin cross her face.

"Just when I lose all hope that one day you will be something more than a simpleminded primate, you prove me wrong!"

"I am not sure what you mean Principle Investigator. My only ambitions in life, are to efficiently stack scat and fornicate."

"HAH!" She barked. "Now we are getting somewhere."

I smiled, knowing she just needed to blow off some steam. It was a shame my ass was the target when her check valve reached its limit.

"Nathan" She said. "I know our relationship has been... thorny, but I want you to know I am working on it. Your command decisions are at times, compulsive and unnecessarily perilous, but I must admit the results are usually unquestionable. I am sure Tria has already pointed out, I have trained my entire life to be a leader of my people's military. To find myself in a position, where I am following an alien whose race has yet to venture any further than their own local moon, is demoralizing. For a Chaalt military officer of my rank to be taking orders from a male of such a race, is maddening! Adapting to your unique command style is a challenge I find myself failing at times, but for what it is worth, if given the future opportunity, I would follow you without hesitation."

I noticed she did not go as far as saying she would follow orders without her usual bitching and moaning, but for now, I was good with it. Tria stepped to my side and grasped my hand as my reality faded away in the bright cascading whitewash of a DEHD core transition.

2

My return to normal spacetime was accompanied by the usual data dump from Justice.

"Commander, I have no anomalous activity to report, and will make a straight in approach to Alpha base. Coonts and our freighter will be exiting hyperspace in approximately sixteen minutes. I have contacted Jaran, and he has alerted the scientists that we will be offloading the freighter's cargo for inventory."

"Thank you, Justice, as soon as we land, I want our combat armor transferred to Felix for repairs and resupply."

"Affirmative Commander, Xul has already made the arrangements"

Xul was the Legacy's Grawl science officer and artifact specialist. He like

Coonts, was another shining example of what the Grawl race could be if they were to change their current mindset. The Grawl as a rule, only cared for themselves, and concentrated on how much tech and wealth they could collect, steal, or otherwise. Since he joined the crew of the Legacy from the scientists ranks, he has taken it upon himself to be our backup shuttle pilot and battle suit maintenance officer, along with his other duties.

Justice set us down in the hangar bay of Alpha base, and we debarked to find our entire clan had gathered outside. The Grawl scientists and Felix, lined both sides of the boarding ramp, and warmly greeted us back home. All made hand contact with each of us. To Sael Nalen's surprise, they held their hands out to her as well. The neutral expression on her face slowly changed to a smile as she embraced the spirit of the moment, and made hand contact with all the members of my clan.

The scientists moved off to the artifact storage building. The large overhead door was open and several cargo transports sat ready in anticipation of the freighter's arrival.

Tria and I caught up with Sael before she boarded her shuttle. "Sael, you are welcome to stay and take part in the cataloging of the freighter's contents."

"No Nathan, I have a lot to think about and need some time alone. As you probably already suspect, I will have to make a detailed report on all of my interactions with you. I need the time to decide just how much of the report I will actually disclose to my superiors."

With that, she turned and boarded her shuttle. Tria and I stood and watched as it finally lifted off the deck and silently accelerated down the entrance tunnel toward the void beyond.

I took Tria's hand and walked toward the artifact building. She squeezed my hand. "The time she needs alone will have more to do with how she wants to spin the report, than how the events actually happened." She said.

I laughed. "That was what I was thinking as well. I am glad you said it before I did."

Justice called to us. "Commander, our freighter has arrived in system, and Coonts is requesting landing clearance."

"Bring them in Justice, let's make it a group effort to get it offloaded and sanitized, so we can send it back to Outpost 9765 as soon as possible. I have to make good on a promise to Broza and Hylet, that we would have a new freighter for them to make use of. After we get the freighter turned around and out of here, I want a report on the current state of all our prisoners."

"Roger that Commander. Freighter ETA twenty-one minutes."

Twenty-one minutes would not be near enough time for the personal debriefing I was going to give Tria. I could see Jaran and Graf standing to the side of the gathered scientists and looking in our direction. If I had to guess, I would say they were waiting for both Tria and I. The two Grawl saw us moving in their direction, and met us halfway. They greeted us again and made hand contact. Then Jaran stepped forward.

"Commander Myers, I have a report on the facility upgrades that have been added in your absence. Unless Justice's subsystem has alerted you of our work, I would like to brief you."

I smiled at the two Grawl. "Jaran, as long as we are not in the presents of guests, I would prefer that my clan members address me as Nathan."

A Grawl smile is not a pretty sight, but I had grown used to the expression and now appreciated it for what it was.

"Nathan, the scientists and I have taken the liberty of building individual quarters in the bunk hall. They are small and spartan, but now all of the scientists have a semblance of privacy, and an area to store our personal items."

I had no problem with that whatsoever. A while back, I gave Felix permission to build his own private quarters, along with the replicator building. While Felix's residence could in no way be described as spartan, it did contain a project work station in his rather large sleeping quarters. The brilliant young replicator engineer was full of ideas. He obviously felt the need to store them for future use, no matter what time it was.

"Jaran, this is your home as well as mine. Please feel free to modify it any manner necessary to make you and the scientists more comfortable."

This earned me another smile from both the Grawl scientists. "We are glad that you and the crew of the Legacy have returned safely. I will leave you now so that Graf can give you his report." Jaran said.

With that, he turned away, leaving Graf to come forward. Tria and I knew, that at some point, Justice's subsystem would have given us a full report on all base activities. I personally liked the interaction with the senior scientists. It was easier for me to get a feeling what they were thinking, and what mood my clan was in, as a whole.

"Nathan, Tria, I would like to report on the prisoner, Illam Pove. After your departure on your last mission, Pove became exceptionally violent and irrational. Since he was moved to the escape tunnel security cells, it was necessary to bring his meals down to him. Jaran and I took on the duty, so none of the other scientists would be subjected to his bizarre behavior."

I frowned, "What kind of bizarre behavior are we talking about?"

Graf held a data recorder out to me. "Perhaps it would be best if you saw for yourself."

He handed over the recorder. Tria and I stared at it in disbelief of what we were seeing and hearing. Pove was screaming and ranting that if the Grawl did not release him, Eiger would kill them all, then hunt down all of their clan siblings, and kill them as well. All the time he was doing this, he was drawing crude Grawl travesties in different poses of death, with his own fecal matter. I glanced up at Graf.

"I hope you cut off his rations to put an end to his madness."

"No, having been a prisoner once myself, and starved, I could not muster enough anger to do the same to him. I chose instead to give him a single serving of Pungo with his water ration pored over it." Graf said.

I knitted my eyebrows. "What is Pungo?"

"It is a slang Grawl term for the base protein most food rations are made of. It lacks any of the flavoring and processing that makes it an edible staple to most all races. Whenever any of the scientist and I fell from favor back on the research station you rescued us from, we were fed Pungo until we could present our masters with favorable results."

I shut the recorder off in disgust at the animalistic behavior of the Murlak. "I take it you received favorable results?"

"While it did quiet his ranting, it did not stop him from his grotesque art work. I shut down the enclosure's nano scrubbers, so he would no longer have a clean surface to work with. The walls are caked with his excrement, and he must live with the stench of his handy work."

Tria and I were appalled at what Pove was doing. Out of the corner of my eye, I saw Klutch working with the scientists unloading the freighter. I let out a shrill whistle that got everyone's attention. I yelled out to the Troop Master and waved him over.

"Klutch! I need your help!"

The Tibor stopped loading the transport he was on, and came jogging over to us. "What can I do for you Commander?"

"I need you to put Eiger in the cell next to Illam Pove."

The wicked smile on Klutch's face, said he would love nothing better.

"Klutch, I need him to arrive alive and in the same shape that he is currently in!"

My statement got us just the faintest whiff of his displeasure, earning him a grimace from the three of us.

"Troop Master! I don't mind if Eiger knows how much you dislike him. It is not necessary to prove it to us!"

With that, he gave us his usual goofy grin, and stomped off to retrieve the Murlak from the Legacy. Turning back to Graf, I gave him instructions on how I would like the matter of Pove's filthy behavior handled.

"Graf, once the Troop Master has Eiger settled into his cell, I want you to activate the scrubbers on the shared wall between them. If Pove starts with his scat artwork again, give him a few minutes, and then clear the wall so he can show off his handiwork to Eiger. That should give both of them something to think about."

Graf gave me a nod and headed to the lifts that take you to the subterranean tunnel system. At some point, I would let Pove know in no uncertain terms, he was expendable now that we had Eiger. I was pretty sure that would be a potent antidote to his prehistoric behavior. A groaning noise caught our attention. Tria and I turned in time to see a grav-gurney with Eiger strapped to it go sailing by. The groaning was coming from Eiger because Klutch had chose to ride on it. He was sitting on the pirate's legs, all six hundred plus pounds of him. He threw us a rather jaunty salute and disappeared through the doors of the lift.

I pinged Justice with my implants. "What is the status of the remaining Prule entity?"

"Commander, I have been maintaining the entity's biomass to minimal habitation standards. The Overseer has uncovered some interesting information, and has since abandoned the containment capsule. After revealing select intelligence from your foray into the former Prule Hunter manufacturing facility, the entity's reaction to the data was recorded by the Overseer as violent anger. It seems the Hivemind had determined you would lose your lives during your incursion. Now that it knows you have not, it has stopped all communications with the Overseer. The intel gathered by the Principle Investigator is now verified. The Prule fear you and the human race as a whole."

That statement put a big smile on my face. "You hear that Tria, a single human has the galaxy's worst enemy, quaking in the tin cans that carry their worthless asses around."

Tria just rolled her eyes and shook her head. "Justice, is there more to the report?"

"Yes Tria, the Overseer has also coerced an admission that we both find troubling. It seems that the Hivemind had directed the forces at the Hunter manufacturing facility to prepare a ship, and the forces necessary to seek out the planet of Nathan's birth, and destroy it at all cost. Once the planet or planets have been identified, it was to be the prime directive of all remaining Prule forces in this galaxy."

That wiped the smile from my face. I suddenly had a bout of nausea that paled my complexion. Tria was just as startled by the declaration. She grasped my arm and pulled me close.

"Nathan, the ship we destroyed at the base, was being repaired so it could search for your home world!"

I was having a hard time swallowing the repercussions of what might have happened if the Prule had managed to capture me. They no doubt had ways to extract information from prisoners. Information that could have led them to Earth. There were thousands upon thousands of Hunters just waiting to be loaded aboard that ship. If they were unleashed on Earth, all the militaries of the world would have stood little to no chance against them. My race would become extinct, just like a great many of the other primitive races that got caught up in the first invasion of the Milky Way galaxy. What was even more sobering, was the fact that a lot of the worlds that were destroyed, had military tech that was hundreds of years or more, ahead of anything the nations of Earth could field.

Justice must have felt my reaction, and tried to steady the downward spiral of my once buoyant mood. "Commander, by destroying the starship and the Prule base, you have effectively delayed any action they were taking against your home world for the immediate future."

I noticed he used the word "delayed" and not the word "stopped." With all the turmoil going on in the galaxy, I had forgotten just how vulnerable Earth was to many of the predatory races that seek out primitive planets to exploit their resources. It would be perilous to think that Earth's protected status could shield it from harm, until such time humans can successfully climb the ladder to an advanced classification. Another bleak thought slapped me in the face as well. A lot of my actions have not endeared me to a number of races far more advanced than humans. The Scrun, Quill and Murlaks quickly came to mind. Any one of them could lay waste to my home world if they knew my origins, and the location of Earth. If a large enough fleet could slip past the twenty plus thousand picket drones before the Galactic Union could respond,

Earth would be doomed. Now yet another question loomed large in my mind.

"Justice, how was the Hivemind able to transmit the orders to go after Earth, halfway across the galaxy?"

"Commander, that would have remained a mystery had it not been for the data recovery devises you brought back from the Hunter facility. The Overseer and I are still working on a complete transcript of the intelligence, but have deciphered enough of the code, to find what we believe to be references to the Fury. We also uncovered partial coordinates to other facilities. Once we can confirm the numbers, I recommend we prosecute the intel as soon as it is feasible. It may prove to be an effective way to stop the spread of information directing Prule forces to search for Earth."

I thought my crew and I would get a much-deserved breather. If Justice comes up with enough data to give us the location of the Fury, it was going to be a priority target to capture or destroy it. Stopping the propagation of the Hivemind's orders to terminate Earth, was now at the very top of my to-do list. Even if we succeed in containing the information, the Prule were just one of several races that could be potential threats to the existence of humans. I decided it would be smart to have backup plans in place in case we don't manage to find the Fury.

"Justice, please tell me you have already considered these scenarios and are working on contingencies."

"Yes Commander, the scientists and I have been working on this situation because it also applies to Alpha base as well. We have several designs for stealth attack drones. Now that it appears we have unlimited access to cutting edge materials like Containium, it would be advisable to move forward with prototype manufacturing and testing."

It was a relief to know IQs much greater than mine, were working all the angles while I was of out wrecking mayhem on the enemies of all. I wasn't aware of the project and needed a detailed report.

"Justice, I want a briefing on the project, and a maximum effort to develop it."

"Commander, I had scheduled the briefing for after the departure of our freighter, but will give you a summary now. Since encountering the predatory race known as the Quill in a neighboring star system, I have determined that Alpha Base

31

has vulnerabilities that must be addressed. It was decided by the Grawl scientists and I, that it would be prudent to have a robust defensive capability in place to ensure allied forces could reach us in enough time to prevent an invasion or destruction of this facility. Stealthy attack drones are used by a number of advanced races for defensive and offensive operations. As you already know, a large number already surround Earth and is a tripwire to alert Galactic forces to breaches of the protected planet covenant. It is the opinion of our scientists, that we are in the unique position of having materials and a knowledge of Guardian technology, that no one else as far as we know, possesses. We have the means to produce drones from the strongest known materials, and with the latest generation Guardian negation and cloaking technology. These are systems we have already proven in combat conditions, multiple times."

I could see Tria was carefully processing everything Justice was telling us. Myself, I just wanted it yesterday so we could deploy the tech sooner than later. She finally gave me a look I was very familiar with. I usually got the expression just before getting a no shitter.

"Nathan, the drones can only be part of the equation. Earth needs to be able to put up a viable defense. The only way to do that is for humans to put aside their petty differences and stand together. If they cannot overcome their primitive backwards thinking, and unite for the common good of all, your home world will perish. Your people will die divided and lost, to a future that could very well prove to be the only hope for our galaxy."

Damn, there it was again. A really smart alien telling me the human race can save our galaxy from the sickening rot that was eating away at it. I wanted desperately to believe her. When I left Earth, it was more divided than ever. The countries that really counted, were all going back to a cold war mentality. I rubbed my temples in frustration. I was really having my doubts. Tria suddenly embraced me.

"Nathan, you must go back to your home world and show them what is happening in the galaxy. Surely when they see what you have encountered, it will change their self-destructive mindset."

3

Tria was right. I needed to go back and show them what I have seen. The people of Earth needed to know what was going on in the universe. There was a very real possibility, that one day they could all be enslaved or annihilated, depending on the race that stumbled upon Earth. The odds were not getting more favorable that it would be an innocuous encounter.

"Justice, how soon can we start a production schedule for the drones?"

"Out of the five designs submitted, we have narrowed it down to two. Both are contingent on a newly reverse engineered copy of the power generators aboard the Daggers. What sets the designs apart from each other, is one uses the Dagger's anomaly weapon and the other, the latest generation beam weapons mounted on the Legacy."

"Okay Justice, from your point of view, which is the more viable system?"

"Both are viable weapons. The designs share many of the same attributes. Both will have Containium armor, Guardian negation and cloaking, and our new IST communication capabilities. They will have starship quality shields and an onboard AI battle management system along with the same interdimensional capabilities as our comms buoys. The only difference is the main weapon. What the anomaly weapon lacks in range, it makes up for in damage. The beam weapons have superior range but inflict less damage."

That gave me a lot to chew on. By the sounds of it, a mix of the two systems would be the best defense. It would come down to what weapon could be produced the fastest. Felix was already working the replicator to its limits just trying to keep up with maintenance and weapons resupply. The answer to the problem was simple, or possibly not so simple. I looked up at my beautiful counterpart and she gave me a dazzling smile.

"Tria, get on the Chaalt IST and call Sael. Find out what she will take in exchange for two more replicators."

Her smile turned to a neutral expression. I could see that was not what she expected to hear from me. I quickly tried to smooth it over.

"I will need a thorough briefing on your discussion after we get the freighter underway!"

She cocked an eyebrow at me and turned away. "HAH! You can get your briefing from Justice"

Now it was my turn to have my expression go sour. Damn! I had a feeling the R&R I had planned for later, was now off the table.

"Justice, get the plans for both the drone weapons finalized, and find out from Felix how soon we can get a production schedule."

"Affirmative Commander. I have two urgent requests to speak with you. They are from Eiger and Illam Pove."

Now my mood was really deteriorating. I didn't have time to listen to any of the scat those two could spout at me.

"Tell those Throggs to take a number!"

Justice did not reply. I was confident he knew sarcasm when he heard it. The two criminals would have to get over the fact they were not going to get a response, until I was good and ready to give them one.

I saw the Sig crew from the freighter helping unload our haul. I wanted to personally thank them for all they have done to make my last mission such a huge success. When they noticed me moving in their direction, they stopped and gave me a proper Sig salute. What must have been the two ranking officers stepped forward, and the rest went back to work. The first one introduced himself as a Senior Captain. He spit out what sounded like a phrase that I knew was his Sig name. I swear it kind of sounded like he said, "My dick's in the damn door." I wasn't going to touch that with a ten-foot pole and just smiled and nodded. The second Sig stepped forward and introduced himself as the Crew Commander and gave me another tongue twister. Both had expectant looks on their faces. If they were wanting me to greet them using their names, we would be standing here a while. The Senior Captain finally baled me out.

"Commander Myers, we would be honored if you would give us a title of endearment from your home world."

I am not sure why, but when I looked up at the almost twelve-foot-tall aliens, Poncho and Lefty landed on my tongue. It stuck in my head and nothing else came willingly to mind. I bowed in the direction of the Senior Commander.

"Poncho"

I did the same to his counterpart.

"Lefty"

They both let out booming laughs and pointed at one another repeating the new names. The shucking and jiving finally stopped. The Senior Captain put on a serious face, leaving me wonder what he had to say next.

"Commander Myers, my crew members and I, have fulfilled our obligations to the military. We are now freelance contract workers for Tam Lin, and have been ferrying freighters for her shipping service. Our contract has expired and we have been searching the open market. We have yet to find anything more lucrative than ferry pilots, so we have stayed in Tam Lin's employ beyond our contract date. We would like to offer our services to you."

The statement caught me off guard, and I wondered if Tam Lin would object to me picking up their contract. After pondering it another minute, I decided she intentionally sent this particular crew with the freighter for a reason. She was in tight with the Sig military and had access to a very large pilot pool. It was probably a small manipulation on her part, but it was nice to know she was looking out for my interest. As far as I was concerned, having qualified competent pilots was a definite plus. These guys had already proven they were pros when the chips were down. If it were not for them, the Zaens would have got their asses shot off by the pirates that attempted to board them. I already knew what Tam Lin would say, but wanted to verify my suspicions.

"Poncho, as long as you get it approved with Tam Lin and Sushi, I have no problems picking up your contracts."

They again gave me a salute and headed back to help get the freighter unloaded. I could hear them calling each other their new names. They seemed genuinely happy about the monikers. I shook my head thinking it would be nice if it was that easy to make everyone happy. Knowing not everyone was, I decided to find Tria and see if she was still annoyed with me. I hadn't taken ten steps through the Legacy's boarding hatch when Justice called to me.

"Commander, the Overseer and I have made a breakthrough in the multi-layered encryption system used by the Prule. We now have what we believe are direct references to the Fury. We are working on additional layers of encryption to confirm our conclusions. If our theories prove correct, it might also reveal the ships whereabouts."

"Did the intel come from the Hivemind or the Prule base?" I asked.

"The intelligence was recorded by one of the Data Siphon Modules used at the Hunter facility." The AI responded.

"Is the Hivemind still refusing to communicate with the Overseer?"

"The entity has not communicated since it learned you survived what it incorrectly determined, was a suicide mission to the Hunter facility." Justice replied.

That was all I needed to hear. The Hivemind was officially expendable. That piece of scat was getting a one-way ride to oblivion. Maybe it was time to go down and visit my two prisoners after all. It would save someone else the trouble of moving the Prule containment vessel to the Legacy. I made a one-eighty and started off in the direction of the lifts that would take me to the escape tunnel. I was intercepted by Coonts and Klutch. They both rushed up to me elbowing and swatting at each other, then attempted to give me a report at the same time. I crossed my arms and exhaled loud enough, they figured out I was in no mood for their clown act. Coonts stepped forward and I caught just the faintest whiff of Klutch's warrior's scent. I squinted my eyes and gritted my teeth at the Tibor. He gave Coonts a withering stare, and stalked off in the direction of the freighter. The look of satisfaction quickly disappeared from Coonts face when I locked my gaze on him. He tried to clear his throat, only to find that not all of Klutch's scent went with him. His first words came out as a cough and a gag. I did my best to act like my olfactory senses were not taking a beating. Coonts managed to finally do the same.

"Commander, the freighter is now sterilized of any evidence that could be connected to our clan. The hold is now empty and the Sig crew reports they can depart within the hour."

"Very well Coonts, tell Poncho and Lefty they can head back to 9765 when they are prepped and ready."

At first the Grawl engineer balked at my statement, but then caught on it was my new Earth names for the Sig pilots. I noticed he was looking over my shoulder. I turned and found Tria standing behind me. She was wrinkling up her nose, and looking around for the Troop Master. I quickly shooed Coonts on and grabbed her by the hand before she could comment on the caustic condition of the atmosphere. I pulled her along toward the lifts. She went along willingly at first, but pulled up short at the entrance of the tube. There was a good chance she was misreading my intentions.

She pulled her hand free from mine. "The Principle Investigator has agreed to trade for the new replicators."

Yep, a definite misread. She was obviously not over being miffed at me.

"What does she want in return?" I asked.

"Nothing, after I gave her the exclusive salvage rights to the Prule base we destroyed."

"Is that all?" I said, hoping the sarcasm in my voice was not overly detectable.

She held out a hand and pretended to pick some invisible annoyance from her finger nails. "No, I gave her fifty percent of the ship salvage as well."

I doubt that I would ever know how many billions in credits the two replicators just cost me, but knew in the future, not to piss her off before asking her to deal with the

Operative. Their less than loving relationship has caused more than its share of irritation between Tria and I. I also knew it would be an error on my part, to make the mistake of hinting that it was a decision we should have made together. Oh well, my granddad always said, easy come, easy go. I planted a fabricated smile on my face and did the only smart thing left to do.

"Thank you Tria, we really needed the additional manufacturing capability."

It was her turn to be surprised, and she didn't hide it well. "Where were you dragging me off too?"

"I was going down to find out why Eiger and Illam Pove are both demanding to speak to me. While I was down there, I was going to retrieve the Hivemind's containment vessel. Justice and the Overseer have made a breakthrough in decoding the Prule encryption algorithms. The Hivemind is no longer a useful information tool, and I was going to permanently remedy that situation."

The expression on her face went from surprise to something else. She grabbed the front of my smart cloth uniform and pulled me away from the entrance to the personnel lift. We heard a warning beep and the doors unexpectedly parted. Jaran stepped out and looked as if he had something to say.

Tria held up a finger. "We will get back with you after my briefing on the acquisition of our new replicators."

Jaran's reaction to Tria dragging me toward the large freight elevator, was a big Grawl smile. He turned and headed toward the replicator building with no further comment. After pulling me into the cargo lift, Tria called to Justice.

"Justice, take us down to the escape tunnel and lock out the lift controls."

Justice shot right back. "Affirmative Tria, will it also be necessary to terminate the feed from the security monitors?"

She pushed me against the elevator wall. My legs went to mush as she called out. "Affirmative Justice!"

The usual transit time for the elevator to drop the thousand or so feet to the escape tunnel level, was about four and a half minutes. Justice made the trip more than thirty. It was no coincidence the doors opened exactly when we got our uniforms back on. The shot of Sha' Leen Tria hit me with, along with her sexual brawling, had my legs a little shaky. I leaned back against the wall and slid down to a sitting position.

Tria seemed to think this was funny and stood over me laughing. "What makes you think that I am done with you?" she said with a wicked smile on her face.

It wasn't that I was tired, it was I no longer wanted anything to do with the three reasons I had come down here for in the first place. I reached up and grabbed her hand, pulling her down next to me. She inaccurately judged my intent once again, and started pulling her uniform back off. It was my turn to smile. I stopped her when her smart cloth had the job half completed. That would be good enough for now.

"I thought you were going to give me a briefing on the transaction you made with Sael." I said.

That comment got me a small frown and she started to close up her uniform. I put a halt to her effort. "That won't be necessary until after I determine our briefing is over."

This brought the mischievous grin back to her pretty face. She promptly sat straddle of me and proceeded to fill me in on some of the details of her conversation with Sael.

"The Principle Investigator was her usual irritable self. I was not in the mood to hear any of her superior officer to subordinate scat, so I threw out the exclusive rights to the Prule base. I am confident we will find more in the future, and the place was buried under a significant amount of rubble. They will have to do some serious excavating, so it's not like they were gaining anything the easy way."

Tria noticed I was not focusing all my attention on her briefing.

"Nathan! My eyes are up here!"

After another free-for-all, that netted me some additional dings, she put on her uniform and properly cinched it up. We lay prone on the deck to catch our breaths. Tria rolled over and embraced me. She laid her head on my shoulder and spoke softly in my ear.

"As I was saying before you interrupted me. Sael was being stubborn, and tried to rub it in my face, that strategic machinery is an extremely valuable and heavily regulated asset. I had my fill of her using her rank and authority to get her way. Rather than have her lecture me anymore, I threw in half the salvage, most of which, is antiquated and shot to pieces. The bulk of the value will be in the materials collected for recycling. She agreed to recycle our share and ship it to us already processed. Since we still have the salvage from the Hiveminds lifeboat, I didn't see the need for us to divide our attention from other goals that are vastly more important."

Tria pointing out our divided focus, hit home. Eiger, Pove and the Hivemind weren't going anywhere. I decided they did not rate another moment of my time because we had other priorities to address. The adjustment Tria made to my attitude, pushed any notion of speaking to the prisoners to the very bottom of my to-do list. I had given my word to the Zaens, we would get them a new freighter that could not be traced back to our attack on Eiger's base. It was time I made good on that promise. I also wanted to augment Earth's defenses. My next stop would be to talk to Jaran about the drones and see how fast we can get operational prototypes. Now I just had to break the news to Tria we would be making another trip to see Tam Lin. I suspected she was jealous of the Earth girl. It wasn't an unhealthy jealousy, but at times, there was a noticeable tension in the air. I was going to try and get that ironed out during our visit. Tam Lin's connections have turned out to be invaluable. The last thing I wanted, was for that to change. I gave Tria a kiss and decided there was no better time than the present.

"Tria, we need a replacement freighter. We are to the point we are not going to be able to get by without one. When the mine finally gets up and running, we will be keeping the Zaens busy on a full-time basis."

Tria looked like she was pondering my words and then said the most surprising thing.

"Nathan, we are going to need more than one. We should go enlist the aid of Tam Lin, and see what she has to offer. If it is your intention to haul Containium around the galaxy, the freighter must be heavily armed. I don't think we want to waste our time escorting every shipment."

I have always wondered if she could somehow read my mind. Any thoughts of her having issues with Tam Lin were allayed for now. It may have had something to do with Tam Lin's response to the attempt on our lives. Tam Lin took it personal when the Kasulla merchant Cralmo, slipped through the dragnet of Sig special operations troopers she had deployed to catch him. She promised to give us a call if she could uncover evidence of the Kasulla's whereabouts. I was very much interested in having a not so polite conversation with the conniving slug. Trying to kill me was one thing, but when the attempt targeted Tria as well, it rocketed the murderous Throgg to the top of a list that Eiger had once dominated.

4

On our way back up to the hanger, Justice was kind enough to give us a report.

"Commander, I took the liberty of informing the scientists you wanted an expedited production plan for the defensive drone project. Jaran has delegated Graf and a number of scientists to catalog the cargo from the freighter. The rest will concentrate on finalizing the drone specifications."

"Has he given you an estimate on when that may be?"

"Negative Commander. I suspect he was going to brief you prior to your trip to interview the prisoners."

I shook my head and smiled at Tria. She smiled back, and gave me a not so gentle shove in the direction of the replicator building. I hoped like hell, that no one would inquire about any possible intel I might have gathered from the prisoners.

As I entered the huge building where the replicator was housed, I saw Felix and Jaran standing in front of a large view screen. Both were pointing at the machine diagrams displayed on it. Out in front of them were twenty of the Grawl scientists sitting at individual work stations. It warmed my heart to know how dedicated all these aliens were to our cause. Jaran took notice of me and headed in my direction. Felix acknowledged my presence with a nod and continued his instructions. Jaran joined me, and we walked back to the entrance so we would be a distraction. I was relieved he skipped over any questions about my briefing from Tria.

"Nathan, at the direction of Justice, we are now concentrating on two designs for the defensive drone program. The scientists and I had hoped we could put both of our best weapons aboard a single design. Unfortunately, that would make the drone's dimensions exceed the size restrictions required to take maximum advantage of their stealth characteristics. We have also encountered some deficiencies in the power generators we reverse engineered from the Dagger design. With Felix's help, we are on the brink of a workable solution. The math is good, and we know we have the materials to make it possible."

I put my hand on the little Grawl's shoulder. "Jaran, I have no doubt you and the scientists will succeed. If there is anything that I can do to speed the process, please let me know."

Jaran gave me a smile. "When we get the designs programmed into a manufacturing schedule, it would be ideal to have additional replicators for the task."

It was hard to keep my cheeks from warming. "Tria has already made arrangements with her people for two new replicators. If you have an estimate on when you will be ready for production, I will do everything in my power to have them here and operational."

"I believe seventy-two hours will be enough time to overcome our design paucities. The manufacturing program will take a minimum of two-hundred hours. That should include the necessary materials preparation, and the AI indoctrination briefing."

"Thank you Jaran. I am planning a trip to Outpost 9765 to purchase two new freighters. We will be leaving when our battle armor is repaired and back aboard the Legacy. I will make it my goal to return as soon as possible so we do not delay your manufacturing schedule."

Jaran touched my hand once more and went back to his brainstorming session. I looked over at the production area next to our lone replicator. Xul was loading two easily identifiable sets of armor aboard a cargo sled. They belonged to the Troop Master and Coonts. I waved him down as he got underway. He slowed to a stop and stepped off the transport.

"Yes Commander, how can I be of service?"

"How long will it take to have the rest of our armor repaired and back on the Legacy?"

"Felix has the parts manufactured and Justice is working on them as we speak. He stated they will be complete within the hour."

"Okay Xul, I know you have not rested since our return. As soon as the rest of our armor suits are repaired and loaded on the Legacy. I want you to put two of the Containium blocks into the cargo hold as well. After that, you are officially off duty. I want you to take a rest period. We will be departing for Outpost 9765 in approximately eight hours."

The little Grawl gave me a thumbs up. "Roger that Commander."

He jumped back on the lift and moved off at a rapid pace. I loved it when the aliens in my clan used Earth adages. If it were not for the way they looked, you would not know they were from different parts of the galaxy.

I made my way back to the Legacy and met Coonts coming down the boarding ramp. He did not look happy. Since he seldom wore a happy face anyway, I let it go and inquired about the whereabouts of the Troop Master. His face went from a look of disdain to that of someone who just found a turd at the bottom of their soup bowl. It wasn't a stretch to guess why.

"Coonts, have you been taking sucker bets from Klutch again?"

I thought his large dark eyes would burst from his head. Yep, he lost another wager.

"Klutch is in the galley. He was purposely trying to ruin my appetite by discussing many of the unsavory attributes of Pungo while I was trying to eat. He finally succeeded!" He said through clenched teeth.

I somehow knew that was probably not the case, but decided it was not a topic worth wasting my breath on.

"You need to get yourself squared away and ready to go. We will be leaving for 9765 in less than eight hours. I advise you to get some rest because I have a busy agenda once we get there."

My statement seemed to brighten his outlook. He turned around and disappeared into the Legacy. I was headed for the command deck, but Tria stepped out of the lift tube stopping me short of my destination.

"Nathan are you hungry? I was going to the galley. Xul has alerted me the Troop Master has been in there awhile. I have hopes he will be done about the time we get our rations selected."

As a matter of fact, I was hungry. It would give me a chance to eat and alert Klutch of our departure at the same time. I hooked my arm in Tria's and we went back towards the galley. When we walked through the big arched entry way, we saw Klutch sitting alone. He had three empty trays in front of him and a number of credit vouchers scattered on the table beside him. When he saw our approach, he quickly scooped them off the table and into his uniform pocket.

That was all the confirmation I needed. Coonts had indeed lost some sort of stupid bet. We approached Klutch and he gave us his normal big toothy grin.

"Troop Master, we will be making a trip to 9765 to purchase a couple of new freighters. We will also be picking up supplies. You should let Xul know what rations and other items to add onto his reacquisition work sheet."

For some reason Klutch was acting strangely. He was getting fidgety and it appeared he was stealing glances at the ceiling over our heads. After the third time of him doing this, Tria and I both shifted our gaze upward. Twenty feet above our heads was a gelatinous mass stuck to an overhead structural beam. The Troop Master suddenly got up from the table and tried to walk by us. Tria shot out an arm grabbing him by the uniform, putting a halt to his retreat. Turning to the Tibor, I pointed upward.

"Klutch, what… the hell…is that?"

The big lummox swallowed hard. We caught the faintest whiff of his obvious discomfort. He finally cleared his throat.

"That would be an experiment in adhesion Commander."

Both Tria and I were now giving him a squinty eyed stare.

"Don't make me ask again Troop Master!"

For whatever reason, the grotesque looking glob lost its grip and dislodged from the beam. It hit the floor in front of us and splattered on our uniforms.

"That would be Pungo Commander."

Now I was pissed. It didn't take a genius to figure out this had to do with some kind of moronic wager between him and Coonts.

"Justice, I want the scrubber bots shut down in the galley. The Troop Master has volunteered to hand wash the entire area. I would like you to supply Coonts with two scrub brushes and a bucket of sanitizer. Inform him he is to report to the galley for extra duty."

Klutch had his usual goofy grin on his face and I was in no mood for it.

"Wipe that silly smile off your face Troop Master! If you keep pushing your luck, the hangar will need scrubbing as well!"

My comment deleted the smile from his face. Tria grabbed me by the hand and turned me around. We walked out of the galley and made a beeline for the lifts. As we were rising upward to the command deck, Tria and I burst into laughter. It wasn't what they did, that was so funny. It was trying to guess what possible conversation could have led to such a wager in the first place. We stepped out of the lift tube and went to my quarters. I was beat and needed a shower and some sleep. I was glad Tria had already bathed and went directly to bed. She had a knack for turning showers into a watersports event. After a fast shower and a warm blow dry, I crawled into bed and quickly fell asleep. I awoke six and a half hours later to Justice calling to me. I sat up in bed a little groggy and looked around for Tria. She must have risen early and decided to let me sleep in.

"Commander, the Legacy is ready for departure, and the crew with the exception of Tria, are in their quarters sleeping."

"Thank you, Justice. Could you alert Tria, I am headed to the galley for breakfast and wondered if she would like to join me."

"Commander, Tria has already eaten and is visiting with Felix and the Grawl scientists. She is ensuring that all have had an opportunity to add something to the supply reacquisition order."

The start of my day was going nothing like I had anticipated. I decided to change subjects. "How are the Grawl doing on the drones?"

"They are doing well Commander. Most of the shortcomings in the designs have been compensated for. Jaran's estimate on the engineering time line, appears to be an accurate assessment. My subsystems are processing the materials necessary to the specifications. A sufficient quantity is already available for manufacturing the prototype testing units." Justice replied.

"I am sure you already have an estimate for the number of drones that will be required to effectively defend my home world. You have yet to tell me what that number is."

"Commander, the percent…"

"Justice! I need a no-shitter, not percentages for success."

"Commander, the variables are nearly endless. I have no choice other than to make assumptions. The first being, the hostile fleet will be comprised of a hundred ships or less. Then, you must add the possibility the attacking force will be equipped with the most powerful weapons we have encountered. Finally, I added the probability, Earth will be unable to launch an effective defensive response from the surface. Those factors with no other considerations, make the number in excess of eight thousand. This estimate assumes a full response from all the Galactic Union attack drones."

The thought of breakfast was no longer appealing. My digestive track was suddenly derailed. Perhaps a sterilized percentage point would have been more encouraging after all. Justice's presentation on reality, left me with another nagging question.

"What kind of time frame are we talking about?"

"Commander, it will depend on the number of new replicators dedicated to drone manufacturing."

"Both of them, it is the main reason I chose to make the acquisition." I shot back.

"If all the materials are available, and resupply delays kept to a minimum. Operating two replicators twenty-four hours a day, will yield eight thousand two hundred drones in approximately eleven months, six days and four hours."

The answer to my question seemed a little cryptic. Justice knew what I was going to use the replicators for. I was scratching my head wondering if this was some kind of lame effort at putting a good spin on the poor numbers. If that was it, he was coming up short.

"Justice, is there something you are not telling me?"

His silence hinted that I was indeed on to something. I had made the decision to purchase the additional replicators without consulting with the AI. He obviously felt I should have. It was not out of the ordinary for me to make less than brilliant choices without first discussing them with him. As much as I found it distasteful, I would try a little strategic brown nosing to get his input.

"If you have a better recommendation, I am all ears Justice."

After a period of awkward silence, he did come up with a recommendation. It was not what I expected.

"Mentioning my production numbers during sexual combat with Tria might reveal other possibilities. It might also increase your chances of achieving a victory by fifteen percent."

I was momentarily speechless and more confused than ever. What did that load of scat have to do with my question. I couldn't make the connection to why this had anything to do with mine and Tria's sexual proclivities. While I had no problem with

Tria's instinctual aggressiveness to always be on top. The freakin evil robot apparently did. Why else would he be attaching some sort of stigma to that outcome. I knew his Oolaran programming was biased toward victory. If that were not true, I would not have survived the wilderness on Earth, let alone, the warzone our galaxy has revealed itself to be. The peculiarity of our conversation, had me thinking he was wanting an accurate accounting of the reasons I did not try harder to change what he must perceive as some sort of defeat. If that was indeed the circumstances, he was going to be waiting a long time. I got up and put my uniform on and headed toward the lifts. My clan would be gathering to see us off. I would rather occupy my thoughts with that, rather than continue this inexplicable tête-à-tête with Justice.

I stepped out of the boarding hatch and saw Tria had already bid her farewells to the gathered crowd. She was walking up the ramp, and as we met, I blew her a kiss. She laughed and said she would wait for me at the hatch. Quickly making my way into the crowd, I touched all the hands held out to me and told each good bye. Giving everyone a final wave, I stepped into the airlock as the hatch closed behind us.

"Tria, I had the strangest conversation with Justice when I woke from my sleep period. My small Earthman brain is still trying to decipher it. I have come to one conclusion; it has something to do with you."

At first, she looked puzzled. Then I gave her his drone production estimates. Her face slowly turned to a frown.

"I should have anticipated the turmoil I would be creating by asking Justice to keep something from you." She hinted.

Now I was really confused. My mind started wandering in all directions but settled on a single topic. "Tria, why would you feel the need to hide something from me? If you want me to be more dominant, I can do that. Where I come from the desire to lead just comes naturally. You want Tarzan, you got it!"

Her frown faded away and she burst into laughter. I had explained the Tarzan reference before, so she knew what I was talking about. She thought it was funny then, but now, she found the metaphor downright hilarious. She was busting a gut like Klutch. I usually found his raucous braying annoying, as was hers right at the moment. Her mirth finally tapered off when she saw the look on my face.

"Nathan, that would not be a secret I would keep from you. Justice knew what my negotiations with The Principle Investigator entailed. I was hiding the truth of what was actually gained. You may not recall, but I never said how many replicators we would receive. I just agreed when you believed the number to be two. We will be getting four replicators for the salvage transaction. I wanted a deal for a total of five, but had to make a small concession to Sael so she would stop questioning my loyalties. I wanted it to be a surprise."

The heat radiating off my cheeks could have started a fire. Justice's inuendo led to the truth, but I was pretty sure he had worded his disclosures to engineer my conclusions. There was no doubt in my mind it was his intention to bring my embarrassment level to its current peak. His brand of dry machine humor generally chapped my ass, now would be no exception. Tria made a small attempt to sooth my tarnished ego.

"Come on Tarzan, if you are lucky, Jane might take pity on you."

I had my fill of conspiracies and stalked off to the lifts. I had more important things to do than be a pawn in some game cooked up by Justice. I was going to praise Tria for her bargaining skills, but her last comment was like a piece of sandpaper on my already sore ass. Rather than continue to be mad, I would endeavor to get even. By the time it took me to reach the command deck, I had regained my composer. Tria knew differently, but decided not to add anymore salt to my wounded self-esteem. She sat at the communication station with just a hint of a smile, but refrained from making additional extraneous comments.

I sat in my command chair and called out to Justice. "Jump us to Outpost 9765!"

5

We exited our jump in the star system Outpost 9765 occupied. It was usually an uneventful straight in approach to the outpost. This time would be an exception. As a rule, Justice always went full stealth whenever we exited hyperspace after a DEHD core jump. The cautionary procedure proved prudent.

Justice called out a warning. "Commander, I am detecting a fleet of one hundred and twenty-eight vessels. The drive signatures identify them as Galactic Union warships. They are outbound from the vicinity of the outpost."

Justice highlighted the large ship formation with yellow boxes, and 9765 with a blue one. There was a lot of ship traffic in this sector, including four hundred and seventy Sig military spacecraft. Justice put green boxes around the Sig ships and circles around the balance of the return signals.

"Justice, do they have the capability to detect DEHD core transition?"

"Commander, The Galactic warships appear to be of a very modern design. I suspect they have sensors that will rival the quality of the Chaalt's latest generation instruments. If they make a turn in our direction it will verify my suspicions."

Justice made a right angle turn to clear our datum. At first, there was no reaction. Then thirty ships disappeared from the fleet formation and quickly reappeared close to our hyperspace exit point. The intersystem jump verified that their sensors were indeed good. The bulk of the fleet maintained its original course, leading us to believe it was a marginal detection at best. We watched in fascination as Justice turned their scanning sweeps into visible patterns. We were able to move with impunity in and out of the Galactic ship's detection envelopes. After more than thirty minutes of full spectrum scanning, the ships jumped back to the fleet as it moved to the edge of the star system. In a show of active coordination, the entire fleet jumped to an unknown destination.

Our freighter was still in hyper space and would arrive sometime in the next twelve hours. I immediately got down to business and put a call in to Tam Lin. The local Sig garrison commander informed me she was presently unavailable. I let him know that we were in close proximity to the outpost. He immediately made a private interior dock available that could accommodate the Legacy. Since my crew and I were on several species most wanted lists, we tried to maintain a low profile. We liked our whereabouts to remain unknown and appreciated the secrecy surrounding our presence at the outpost. Tam Lin's Sig security teams made sure no one had access to our dock area. As was his custom, Xul selflessly appointed himself to the security watch while we were debarked. When we departed the ship, Tria, Coonts, Klutch and I were met by Pasta. He was Tam Lin's personal friend and Sig envoy.

"Commander Myers! It is good to see you and your crew again. Tam Lin sends her apologies for not being able to meet you. As I am sure you are well aware, we have been visited by the Galactic Union. Tam Lin will be returning shortly. She will personally brief you on her observations of the meeting that took place between the Union fleet Admiral and the General in charge of my people's forces in this sector."

It didn't take Klutch more than a second to decide he was not going to be needed, and requested permission to go to the local Tibor Guild. I was still a little miffed at him and Coonts for their latest antics. Even so, I was not mad enough to deny him the pleasures that I could indulge in on a regular basis.

I gave him a stern look. "Klutch, just so we understand each other clearly. There is to be no unnecessary brawling, shootings, stabbings or poisonings, you got that?"

He gave me a goofy grin. "Absolutely Commander."

It was surprising that an alien with such a dense body mass, could move as quickly as Klutch does when it comes to doing something he likes. Coming from a home world with four times the gravity of Earth, made him as agile as a ballerina in the standard one gravity enjoyed by most other races. The looks I was getting from Coonts, insinuated he wanted to be elsewhere as well.

"Coonts, tell Xul he is dismissed from the security watch and take him with you. If he gives you any guff about it, tell him it is an order."

The over muscled Grawl gave me a thumbs up and went to break the news to Xul.

I winked at Tria. "It looks like it is just you and me. You want to go shopping?"

She looked at me cocking an eyebrow. I could tell she was sorting through her limited collection of Earth euphemisms. "That would be a no from me, as in hell no!"

Admittedly, our last shopping excursion ended with an assassination attempt, but I didn't think it would put a permanent damper on her sense of adventure. Before I could say anything in protest, she turned and looked up at Pasta.

"Pasta, we have come to purchase a new freighter. Do you think Tam Lin would mind if we waited in her office and looked through her ship inventory?"

The Sig must have thought the exchange between Tria and I was cute. He let out a booming laugh. "Of course, Tria. Tam Lin has made it known that her home is your home. Please follow me."

Tria grabbed my hand and pulled me along like an unruly child. Pasta took us to the private lift that takes you to Tam Lin's office. When we exited the lift, he took us into the office and walked us around to Tam Lin's massive desk. With practiced dexterity he brought up the holographic view screen.

"This will show you the vessels that are currently for sale. When Tam Lin arrives within the hour, she may have additional options available that are not listed here."

I was going to plop down in Tam Lin's throne like chair, but Tria beat me to it. This made Pasta chuckle out loud as he left the room. Tria didn't even look up from the view screen. I was forced to pull one on the large high back side chairs around next to her so I could properly see the specifications on the different spacecraft. She quickly passed over the different freighters that were in the same class as our previous purchase. We were going to go big and heavily armed this time around. Unfortunately, this rapidly narrowed the field of selections. The few that remained in the category we were interested in, looked like stripped and outdated military surplus. After an extensive search of the data base, we were convinced we would have to look elsewhere.

Our pursuit of the perfect freighter consumed enough time that Tam Lin finally arrived from the far side of the outpost. Tria started to get out of her chair but Tam Lin put a hand on her shoulder and pushed her back down.

"Don't bother Tria. Pasta told me what you were looking for. The crap you see in my commercial data base, is more or less for public consumption. I have several restricted listings that I want you to look at. Pasta could have shown them to you, but would not have access to the pricing."

With that said, she walked to the wall in her office where her private vault was hidden. She touched the wall in a few places that appeared to be random. The wall opened to reveal a large heavily armored door. She entered more access codes and the door opened. She disappeared inside and returned moments later with a familiar looking shiny bottle and three ornate shot glasses. I knew the bottle contained a liquor she lovingly called the good stuff. She came and stood next to me. I finally got the hint and vacated the chair so she could sit next to Tria. I moved another chair around so I now sat beside her. This brought just a hint of a smile to Tria's face. It vanished when she saw the sour grapes expression, I gave her in return. Tam Lin pretended not to notice and put the glasses on the table, carefully pouring three equal measures of the precious concoction.

She raised her glass. "To my comrades in arms!"

She tossed back her drink, leaving us no choice but to honor the toast and do the same. It was as good as I remembered. Tria and I set our glasses down and Tam Lin promptly refilled them. The warmth the drink imparted to my belly was just starting to kick in when she raised her glass again.

"To my new business partners, may we live long and prosper!"

Down went the second shot, leaving me wonder why her toast sounded so familiar. Tria was quick to place her hand over her glass before it could be refilled again.

Tam Lin held the bottle out. "Are you sure?"

Tria surprised me when she said, "Perhaps after we finalize our business."

The Earth girl nodded to Tria and put the bottle on the desk. She turned to me. "We have a lot to talk about and not all of it is business."

If it were not for the gentle warm feeling of well being that was seeping into my system, I would have frowned at her remark.

She leaned in front of Tria. 'First things first."

A virtual key board appeared on the desk top. She ran her fingers over it like a well-practiced piano. Several classes of spacecraft came and went as she voiced her negativity out loud. She suddenly stopped and sat back.

"This is the hull of a new Sig battleship. It has a modern star drive, weapons and shields. What it does not have, is the extensive floor plan and compartmentalized systems needed to make it a troop-carrying capital ship. What it does have is a massive cargo hold."

In order for us to get an idea of the true dimensions of the ship, Tam Lin worked a little more magic on the key board. A smaller ship appeared next to the battleship. Tria and I leaned forward for a closer look. It was a scale rendering of our currently owned freighter. I was just guessing, but it looked like the battleship hull could easily accommodate two of the freighter class ships in its hold.

I smiled at the petite Earth girl. "You already knew I would want it, or you would not have shown it to me. How much?"

"This one is not for sale because it is the newest acquisition to my shipping fleet."

She reached out and tapped a few more keys bringing up what appeared to be an identical copy. This one was missing a few large sections of its hull.

"This one will be available in about a month. It lacks the shields and weapons that mine is equipped with. The Sig people have agreed to give it to you free of charge."

Tria and I looked at each other, then back at Tam Lin. We both waited to hear the hook.

Tam Lin looked a little uncomfortable when she returned our gaze. "The Sig that have been involved in some of your adventures, have reported that the Legacy has some very exotic weaponry. They claim the range and destructive force of your weapons are a magnitude beyond anything they have in their arsenal. In exchange for the new freighter they would like you to share the technology on one of the weapons systems."

Shit! No wonder she was trying to loosen me up with her best liquor. I wasn't sure what to say. I knew I did not want to be a weapons dealer. Death and destruction seemed to follow in my wake no matter where my travels took me. It was prolific enough without me throwing fuel on that fire. I was speechless and it was not lost on Tam Lin. She could see I was wrestling with indecision.

"Nathan, you do not have to make a decision now. Give it some thought and let me know when you decide. I personally know the general in charge of the Sig forces in this sector, and he is a close friend and confidant. He is also my direct link to the Sig leadership. I have his assurances you will not lose the favor of the Sig governing council if you do not wish to share the technology."

I took a deep breath and looked over at Tria. She kept a neutral expression on her face. She was wise enough not to comment on a decision that I alone would have to make. Tam Lin finally bailed me out of the hard spot she had put me in.

"Nathan, let's move on to other subjects. I understand the freighter you brought back is no longer of use to you. After hearing the reasons why, I bought it back and gave you a credit for its worth. The crew on the other hand, want to be gainfully employed by you on a permanent basis. Pasta and I have no objections to that, and they are free to join you at your convenience. Now let's get to the subject I know you really want to hear about, and that would be why the Galactic Union was snooping around in my neck of the woods."

I was glad we had something else to talk about because I was still stuck on the Sig wanting weapons tech. I felt a foot touch mine and knew it wasn't Tam Lin playing footsies with me. Tria's touch coaxed some words from my mouth.

"Sure Tam, I was wondering if the Sig were at odds with the Union."

"No Nathan, since the Sig have joined the Union, they have a good working relationship with most of the races. Many breathed a sigh of relief that they no longer had to worry whether or not the Sig would return to their predatory ways. That is not to say they don't give the Sig a wide berth, but for the most part they no longer dread their military. It is not widely stated, but a great many believe the sudden decline in the huge number of pirate attacks, is directly related to the Sig military patrols throughout the galaxy. The Sig routinely handle countless distress calls, regardless of race."

If that wasn't Tam Lin's unequivocal vote of confidence in favor of the Sig receiving our brand of weaponry, I was a freakin Throgg's uncle. Tria was no stranger to knee deep bull crap and waded into our discussion with the intention of getting it back on track.

"So, you are saying this was a standard Union patrol or something else?"

Tam Lin turned to Tria. "They occasionally patrol out this far, but it is an unspoken rule the Sig military maintains the security around here and a large number of the surrounding sectors."

Tria's question dislodged the cat that had my tongue. "Pasta said you were observing the meeting between the Union Admiral and your friend the General."

"Yes, and by the way, my friend the General has an Earth name he is quite fond of. If you have a chance to meet him, please address him as General Bonaparte."

Tria just gave me a blank stare but I had to chuckle at the nickname.

Tam laughed as well. "I had never met a general before and I couldn't think of anything else that sounded distinguished."

I was over the awkwardness of Tam's request and was growing tired of the small talk. "What was the meeting about?"

"Yes, sorry I got side tracked. It seems several Galactic council members have been alerted to a new pirate faction that is causing considerable trouble in a number of sectors. It seems the Murlak Royals had a member of their family killed, and the whole race is apparently up in arms over it. They are not well liked by a large number of the other Union races, but they are none the less members. They have brought their grievance to the council and demand action by the Galactic military. Normally something like this gets shuffled around by the Union races and most of the time it goes away. This thing with the Royals has got the ears of a few on the council and they want it dealt with decisively. The Admiral is out rallying the Union members. He is personally putting out the word to all military officials in his authority sectors. The Murlak Royals have put up a bounty of fifty billion credits to anyone who captures the leader of this new terrorist organization."

Tria and I stared at each other. Tam Lin immediately picked up on our change of mood.

She looked at us in disbelief. "Nathan, please tell me it wasn't you that killed a member of the Murlak Royal family."

My silence confirmed to her I was the shit stirring culprit who had the Murlaks, and now the Union up in arms.

"I hope this was not some kind of terrible accident or a case of mistaken identity. The repercussions of this will not go away easily."

I was going to explain what really happened, but Tria spit it out first. Her voice had a deadly edge to it. "It was no accident or mistaken identity! We captured Eiger and the cowardly Throgg still lives!"

Tam Lin jumped up from her chair. "Eiger! What the hell does he have to do with the Murlak Royal Family?"

Tam Lin knew we were hunting Eiger, but did not know the rest of the story. I held up my hands to calm the anxiety in the air. I explained to her in detail what was really going on. When I was done, she sat rubbing her temples in frustration. She grabbed her bottle and filled our shot glasses. She took hers and downed it without a word and filled it again. This time the three of us drank, but could find no reason to toast.

I could tell Tam Lin had turned the situation over in her head enough times, she was now working on damage control.

"Nathan, I can take some of the heat off of this situation by getting the word out that the Murlak Royal family has been sheltering Eiger from prosecution. The fact they are omitting the exact details of who was actually killed, will gain us some traction when the story gets around. If they decide to come clean and claim Eiger is a royal, that should bring enough backlash from the rest of the Union members, they may eventually disclaim him. The void in the pirate community created by his demise, will be far reaching and a story that will spread like wildfire. Can I see a recording of his testimony?"

"Yes, call down to your security team in the dock and see if one of my crew has returned to the Legacy. If so, tell them to send up a recording. According to the Principle Investigator, there will be no mistaking the ceremonial armor he has with him. We will have to edit Tria and my faces out, but the ass kicking she gave him will make primetime viewing to all those who have suffered at his hands."

In a surprisingly short time Pasta called back. He let us know he spoke to Xul and was on his way with a data cube. Five minutes later Pasta exited the lift to Tam

Lin's office. The big Sig was moving quickly and he looked excited. He handed the data cube to his boss and then leaned over the top of her chair so he could see the video. Tam inserted the cube into a data port on her console. It silently digested the encryption then beeped, indicating the video was ready for viewing. Tam Lin rubbed her hands together in anticipation. She hit a button and the holo screen increased in size and began the video.

A closeup view of Eiger appeared on the screen, his beat-up ceremonial armor at his side. Tria and I entered the cell and he rose off his bunk. After a few minutes his body language changed to combative, and both Tam Lin and Pasta leaned in closer. Tria's kick was just a blur.

Tam yelled out. "Damn!"

She stopped the video and ran it back and forth a couple of times in slow motion. Pasta was slapping his hands together and calling out some Sig oaths my translator wasn't getting a read on. They both looked at Tria, she sat with her arms crossed and was not watching, she looked bored.

Tria's next kick got loud exclamations from both Tam and Pasta. "Ohhh!"

Tam played it back again. "I'll bet the dumbass never had that happen before!"

When Tria splayed Eiger's hand like she was pulling the tail from a well-done lobster, both Tam and Pasta stared at her in wide-eyed silence. Tria just shrugged it off. Tam Lin and Pasta roared their approval when Tria spit in the pirate's face.

This finally garnered a response from Tria. "That is my favorite part as well!"

6

With the show over, Tam Lin shut down the screen. "Sorry Nathan, but Tria is now my favorite badass."

I smiled and looked over at Tria. "Yeah, she's my favorite too."

Tam got back down to the business at hand. "Nathan, I want a sanitized copy of the video that can be put out to all of my information sources. This is as hot as anti-matter, and the faster it is disseminated the better. Once something this good shows up on the video nets, it will take on a life of its own. At some point the Murlak Royals will have no choice but to walk back their claims. Since the pirate piece of scat is still alive, you have a potential source of information that could clean up a large number of pirate operations."

I told her about Illam Pove and the Union council connections tied to Eiger.

"Nathan." Tam Lin said. "You have an opportunity to severe some of the links that are corrupting the Union council. The more of them you take out, the better the chances it will silence the corrupt council members that are demanding action against you."

I nodded in agreement. "We have every intention of doing just that, but have other higher priorities."

Tam Lin suddenly slapped her hand on the deck top. "Nathan, if you take out those crooked bastards, and make it appear Eiger is the one fingering them, they will crawl back under their rocks in fear of the same thing happening to them. This shit storm along with the fifty billion credit bounty, might just dry up and go away!"

That comment got Tria's and my attention. That was an angle we had not considered yet. If it gets to a point where we run out of targets, a vid of Eiger dropping a dime on his deceased associates, would be a great way to focus the ire of all the criminal elements away from us and directly on Eiger. Tam was right, we needed to start moving on the trove of information we have uncovered. I had one other piece of no so good intel I wanted to pass on to her before we left the outpost. I told her about the threat posed by the Prule and the orders to eradicate the human race. She sat stone faced for several minutes, then looked over at me.

"I have always wondered if Earth would one day face an advanced race bent on destroying us. It occurred to me a while back, that I was in a position to do something about it. Since the Sig and I are now of the same clan, they have taken it upon themselves to help protect Earth. It is why I would do almost anything to help them in return. This would include trying to influence my allies into making decisions that might run contrary to their principles."

I had to chew that over and over for several minutes. "Tam, are you telling me the Sig are protecting Earth."

She reached up and patted Pasta on the hand. "Pasta, tell Nathan what your people have been doing now for more than a year."

"Commander Myers, we have been actively patrolling the star system of your clan for more than four hundred planetary rotations. At any one given time, there is a minimum of one hundred and twenty Sig military vessels moving in and out of that sector."

Earth's chances of surviving an invasion, were turning out to be better than I thought. The odds of the Sig inheriting some of our Oolaran weapons technology, just got a whole lot better as well. I was going to tell Tam we would discuss the technology transfer and get back with her, when an alarm sounded on her workstation. She pushed a button and asked what was going on. Tria and I both heard one of Tam Lin's security officers give a report of an altercation at the Tibor Guild. They stated the report came from the surveillance team assigned to watching over Klutch. Tam inquired if the outpost security was notified. The officer said the call was intercepted and routed to him.

She shook her head and looked over at me. "Pasta will take you to retrieve your crew member. It would be advisable to hurry before someone makes a call my security net cannot intercept."

Tria and I quickly got up and followed Pasta to the lift. It rapidly descended to a garage area where Tam Lin's private transport was parked. We piled into the back with four Sig special operations troopers. The transport jerked into motion and was soon moving at high speed through light traffic. We turned onto a corkscrewing ramp that took us down several levels into the bowels of the outpost. The transport barely slowed, making everyone hang on tightly.

I put a call in to Coonts on my BS transmitter. He immediately answered, giving us a heads up that Klutch had called for help. He said that him and Xul were armored up and on their way. Now I was more confused than ever. If Klutch was calling for help, he might not be the instigator behind the trouble. It also left me wondering why I did not get an alert.

We came up on a Sig road block and was waved on through. The Sig had the area locked down tight so no one else could get involved. We pulled up in front of the Guild and baled out of the transport. We saw three heavily armed Sig soldiers in full body armor and closed helmets, standing next to another large transport. They had two bound and gagged Tibor laying on the ground at their feet. The stench in the air was horrific, making us close up the helmets on our recon armor. Pasta asked the soldiers for a sitrep. The officer in charge, reported that the transport pulled up in front of the Guild about an hour after Klutch arrived. He further stated that eight Tibor wearing light body armor exited the vehicle. They were armed with pistols and fighting knives. All but the two on the ground ran inside. There were shots fired inside the entrance then a mass exodus by the occupants of the building. Klutch and the assailants were still inside.

I called to Klutch on the BS transmitter. "Klutch, Tria and I are outside the Guild. What the hell is going on in there?"

After a minute of silence Klutch came back over my comms. He was breathing hard. "Commander! This was not my fault!"

I tried to calm my voice. "Troop Master, I need a sitrep!"

"Commander, Skoal and some of his clan ambushed me at a very inopportune time. He nicked me pretty good with a fighting knife, but I got it away from him. I am holed up with him in a latrine. His clan is getting ready to shoot their way in here if they don't hear from the Throgg pretty soon. Commander, I did not disobey your orders, but Skoal is in no condition to answer his clan."

"Hold tight Troop Master, we are coming in to get you!"

I heard a whooshing clunk behind us. Coonts and Xul uncloaked and both were carrying a spare shotgun. They handed them over to Tria and I.

Pasta gave me a warning. "Commander Myers, you must end this quickly. The comms nets are starting to get a lot of distress calls. We can't keep this suppressed much longer."

I turned to my crew members. "Coonts, Xul, take the lead!"

We ran to the front of the Guild and the entrance was partially open. A Tibor corpse was keeping the door from closing. He had been shot in the head at close range. Just inside, was another that suffered the same fate. Our audio systems picked up the sound of someone yelling in the Tibor dialect somewhere above us.

Coonts called to us on our private comms net. "Commander, my sensors have a hard lock on Klutch's BS and IST transmitters. He is not at the same location as his recon armor. I also detect five hostiles very close to his current location."

Tria asked the next important question. "Coonts, are you detecting any non-combatants?"

Coonts and Xul called back in unison. "Negative Tria!"

I responded by calling weapons free and to move out. The open floorplan made it easy for us to boost up onto the open walkways above us. Coonts and Xul went down a corridor lined with doors. The ones that were open were empty except for one. We saw a dead female Tibor naked on the floor. She was decapitated. There was an ocher trail of Tibor blood leading out of the room and down the hall. If it was from Klutch, he had sustained more than just a nick. The beast in me growled its displeasure.

Tria gripped my arm tightly and commed me over a private channel. "Nathan, calm yourself. They will pay with their lives for what they have done!"

She eased her grip and I pointed at Coonts and Xul, then down the hall. They followed the blood trail down to the next junction. It was unguarded and they waved us up. We quickly joined them and took a knee with our weapons up and ready.

Coonts called over our group comms. "Next corridor on our left, all the way to the end."

I rapped him on the shoulder and he turned to me. I drew my finger across my neck and then pointed down the hall. He nodded to me and told Xul to stay behind him. I called up Klutch's BS channel and told him to hit the deck. He acknowledged my call. His voice was weak and he was panting.

"I already have Commander."

We eased up to the next corridor. Coonts put his shotgun low to the floor and quickly stuck it around the corner and pulled it back. We got a good weapon sight view of five Tibor kneeling on both sides of the hallway. They were all armed with Tibor capacitive discharge pistols. The sidearms packed a big punch for their size. I didn't want to find out what effect they might have on my light recon armor. We heard Klutch yell out and he didn't sound good.

"If you suckling Throggs think pleasuring each other will gain you the courage to face a real warrior, you should come in here and see how it worked out for Skoal!"

That comment set a fire under their murdering Tibor asses. They all stood up to charge the door. That was as far as they got. Coonts spun up his minigun, then stepped around the corner. He hosed the killers down for close to twenty seconds. Smoke and dust rolled out of the corridor. Coonts charged forward into the cloud yelling Klutch's name. We followed close behind. The upper torsos of the five Tibor were mutilated beyond recognition. The lower halves of their bodies now laying where they once stood. The hallway was a wreck as was the door to the latrine. We stormed inside behind Coonts. Klutch was laying naked on the floor in a pool of his own blood. His blood trail led to a dead Tibor in one of the stalls. It had to be Skoal. His head was jammed into a toilet. He was drowned in the waste eating chemicals that cleansed the basin.

We tried to help get Klutch off the floor, but Coonts would have none of it. Klutch let out a low groan as Coonts hoisted the big Tibor up on his shoulders and carried him out the door. Xul took the lead with Tria and me on both sides of Coonts. We were met by Pasta and a security detail. He warned us that security bots were at the road block. He said his troops purposely overturned one of their transports and set in on fire as a diversion. Coonts decided to give his armor suit servos a work out and broke into a run. The Sig security team cheering him on as he came barreling out the door. He made it to the transport and laid Klutch gently on the floor. We piled in around him and the transport raced off at breakneck speed. Pasta passed a med kit to Tria and she went to work on Klutch's wound. He was slashed open from his shoulder to the middle of his back. The rough trip from the Guild to the transport had it bleeding profusely. Tria staunched the flow with a nano seal but warned he had lost a lot of blood. She injected him with a blood expander and looked up at me with concern on her face.

"We need to get him back to the Legacy and in a med pod as soon as possible. He is very weak and his life signs are deteriorating."

Justice hailed us over our group comms. "An evac gurney is waiting at the base of the boarding ramp Commander. I am monitoring Klutch's biotelemetry through Coonts armor suit sensors. His life signs are critical but Tria has effectively slowed his rapidly declining condition. I can repair his injuries."

We breathed a collective sigh of relief. The beast in me was still stalking my consciousness. Its deadly intentions must have been felt by those around me. Even Pasta and his Sig troopers were stealing glances at me out of the corners of their eyes. The massive gates to Tam Lin's compound were open and waiting for our arrival. A large contingent of heavily armed Sig troopers had a perimeter set up in front of the entrance. They parted so our transport could pass and then quickly closed ranks behind us. Tam Lin was standing next to the Legacy's boarding ramp as we pulled up and stopped. I could not tell if the look on her face was anger or concern. She watched as we carefully unloaded Klutch onto the evac gurney. It disappeared into the Legacy with Coonts and Xul closely following.

Tam Lin slowly approached me. She was holding her hands up. "Nathan, I know how you must feel, but you need to calm yourself and listen to what I have to say. I have a preliminary report from my surveillance team. They have collected enough evidence, that I am convinced we know exactly what took place. Please follow me to my office so we discuss this and other matters that I have been made aware of."

Tria was holding onto my arm and pulled me close. I was taking slow deep breaths trying to push the demon from my thoughts. She commed me over a private channel.

"Nathan, it will do no good to stand here brooding over what has taken place. Let's go and hear what Tam Lin has to say."

I took another deep breath and let it out. I nodded to Tria and retracted my helmet so everyone could get a read on my state of mind. Tam Lin and the Sig seemed to relax after that. We followed Tam in silence up to her office. When we were seated, she offered us another drink which we declined, so she got right to the point.

"Nathan, several months back, a number of very unsavory Murlaks were found slain on this outpost. Initial evidence implicated the Tibor mercenary Skoal, as the primary suspect."

Tam Lin was staring at me. "We both know that he was not responsible."

She was correct. Klutch and I had killed the Murlaks. I told Klutch to dispose of the bodies. At the time, I had no idea he was going to make it look like Skoal did the dirty deed. I felt it would be wise just to keep my mouth shut and hear Tam Lin out. By the look on Tria's face, I knew she was thinking the same thing.

Tam Lin continued. "Skoal was released after more than a month in detention for lack of any real evidence tying him to the slayings. It wasn't long after that, we learned from some very reliable sources, that your Troop Master was having sexual relations with a female Tibor by the name of Cholula. She was also romantically involved with Skoal. While your Troop Master and the female Tibor in question, did not give a shit what Skoal thought about their relationship, Skoal obviously did. It is our understanding; he swore revenge if he was ever to cross paths with Klutch again."

It really sucked to hear Tam Lin hinting that if Klutch had handled past events differently, today's problem may never have happened. I had a feeling she was going to spell the whole thing out for me, whether I wanted to hear it or not. And she did.

"Nathan, the altercation at the Tibor Guild, was a plot by Skoal and members of his clan, to kill Klutch and his lover for their indiscretion. You are fortunate that my surveillance team is very adept at cleaning up messes in ways that will avoid further scrutiny. As you already know, the Sig apprehended two of Skoal's clan members at the scene. Since they participated in the revenge scheme that caused the deaths of two innocent bystanders, and the female at the center of the plot, they will be prosecuted for the murders. The Sig took the precaution of moving Skoal's clan members to a secure location after you and your crew went inside the Guild. Before they were turned over to the outpost authorities, the surveillance team purposely made false and misleading statements that were overheard by the prisoners. One of which described the gruesome demise of Klutch at the hands of Skoal. They both now believe that Klutch is dead. We intend to leave it that way. Future visits to this outpost are not to include liberty for your Troop Master. He is welcome to stay in my compound, or on the Legacy, but the rest of the outpost is off limits."

Tria wanted to put this behind us as soon as possible and thought I was taking longer than necessary to reply. As my first officer, she must have felt inclined to take the high road and do it for me.

"We appreciate what you and the Sig have done to limit our exposer to this unfortunate incident, and will respect your decision."

Tam Lin looked at me. Tria's response was not going to be enough. She wanted to hear it from me. "Nathan" Tam Lin said. "This could have turned out a hell of a lot worse. Sometimes our intentions, good or bad, have repercussions. You may not think so now, but the way I see it, you are fortunate this played out the way it did. There are no longer any loose ends to tie this mess to you or your crew."

I guess instead of listening, I was thinking about how bad the air quality in the Legacy was going to be when Klutch wakes up. Finding out that Skoal's clan of murderers beheaded his girlfriend, and he was now persona non grata at the outpost, was going to severely piss him off. Tria's elbow banged off my armor, bringing my wandering mind back to the current topic. Tam Lin was giving me the stink eye. As my crews Commander, I felt it was my responsibility to take ownership of this cluster grope. What happened to Klutch was a shit deal. Him being almost killed and then censored for it, did not sit well with me.

"I have decided that in the future we will conduct our business at another location, so we do not cause you further inconvenience."

Tam Lin's expression promptly changed to one of surprise, then neutrality.

"Nathan…" She said.

I cut her off before we could revisit the subject.

"Tam, you said you had other subjects we needed to go over?"

7

Tam Lin wisely decided it was best to move on, and I was glad she did. What kind of surprised me, was Pasta's reaction to my decision. He was smiling at me till Tam looked in his direction. He quickly went stone faced. I was guessing he liked the novel idea of a commander who stood up for his subordinates.

Tam Lin finally shrugged off her surprise and got back to a topic I was going to bring up before our departure.

"Nathan, the Sig and I have assembled the engineering teams necessary to bring the Containium mine back on line. The detailed information provided by your AI, was precise enough to build the atmospheric locks for the mine shaft entrance. Once they are in place, the engineers can start the repairs and decontamination that is needed to make a safe working environment."

This was great news, but there was still the problem of manpower. It was an issue I had no answer to. My scientists were working full schedules. It would be counterproductive to pull any from my ranks of skilled technicians.

"Were you able to find qualified personnel willing to work in such an isolated location?" I asked.

"Manpower will not be a problem. I have a list of more than nine hundred former slaves who have experience in mining. A large number on the roster would have spent the rest of their lives doing just that, if you had not intervened in the Scrun's plans to sell them off to the highest bidders. What they lack in operating skills, my teams of Sig specialist will teach them."

This was excellent news. It put us a step closer to a capital source that didn't rely on the blood money collected by predatory races. I had personal reasons why we would not refrain from continuing the practice. The first being, I really liked the idea of the corrupt races funding the Primitive Planet Protection Fund. The massive influx of income we were funneling to the program, would help ensure the safety of billions of primitive life forms. I was ready to wrap things up and had one more question for Tam Lin.

"How long will it take to get the engineers on sight?"

"They are already in the star system close to El Dorado. The Sig have made other discoveries on the planetoid the former pirate base was located on. It appears the pirates had nothing to do with the base's construction. They have come to the conclusion it is an old storage facility of some unknown race. The Sig engineers were brought in because vast underground caverns have been discovered. All were vacant, but the infrastructure connecting the caverns, points to some military industrial use that has yet to be determined."

Tria and I looked at each other. The probability was high, the base was of Sentinel race origin. Rather than recap our past experiences with a long drawn out story, I decided as long as an Overseer was not involved, I would let the matter go. The chances were miniscule at best, that one would be discovered. If an Overseer AI was present, it would have revealed itself to the detriment of the pirates a long time ago. Tam Lin did not miss the look Tria and I gave each other.

"Nathan, is there something you would like to add?"

"Other than our home base was a similar discovery, no."

She seemed to accept my explanation and continued our briefing.

"After the discoveries were made, the Sig decided to expand the entire facility and make it a major military hub for their fleets that will now patrol the sector. The Union has been notified of the Sig's intentions. Because of the remote location, the Union has announced they will only make bi-annual inspections once the facility is complete and operating. The information released to them, stated it was a former pirate stronghold that was destroyed, and is now under construction. That will give us roughly a year before they will send someone around to see what the base looks like."

Tria was a little unsettled with the thought of the Union snooping around so close to El Dorado, and said so.

"Do you think it wise to have the Union going there at all?"

"Tria, the base will be up and running long before the Sig open it for Union inspection. By the time they come for their first assessment, the true size and scope of the facility will be well hidden. They will see it as just another remote Sig base, designed to counter pirate operations on the fringe of the galaxy. They will lose interest, just like they have with a large number of other Sig outposts. Inviting the Union in, also serves another more important purpose. The corrupt members of the council who knew what was actually taking place there, will warn off their pirate partners to steer well clear of this sector. The possibility of pirate interference with our operations should be extremely low."

Tria and I both nodding in agreement. Her and the Sig have been playing this game a lot longer than we have. Her insight was proving to be another bonus to our alliance. She continued with the briefing.

"Getting back to your question about the mine timeline. The Sig have the four airlocks assembled and ready to ship. The decontamination machinery was readily available, and now it is just a matter of getting the equipment on a freighter.

Everything should arrive at Venture within the next two weeks."

I gave the Earth girl a puzzling look. "What or where is Venture?"

She said something that sounded more like a noise than a word. I didn't know whether to say excuse me, or bless you.

She smiled at my confusion. "Nathan, that is the name of the new Sig base. It means Venture in their language."

I liked it. It was short, to the point, and easy to pronounce. A beep from Tam Lin's desk top had her push a button to bring up a holo screen. A Sig's face appeared on it. He alerted Tam Lin our supplies were all loaded onto the Legacy. She thanked him and signed off. I had a couple of more things on my mind before we departed.

"Out of curiosity, I was wondering about the Rugerian council member?"

Tam Lin looked up at Pasta. He nodded and turned to me. "Commander Myers, the Rugerian is grudgingly supplying us with the routes of pirate freighters. Most of the freighters are loaded with illegally obtained supplies that have lessened our need to procure them elsewhere. His name is Juda and if you wish to question him, he is still in a prison cell at Venture base."

Tria wanted to know what became of the crazy Ilor. Pasta laughed out loud at her question.

"We finally coaxed a name from the crazed Ilor. He called himself Bolus, and claimed to have the Fusra Pus Virus on his genitals. We thought his claims were unlikely, but did not want to take any chances. Since he was wearing a sealed pressure suit, we took his word for it. His behavior finally became so bizarre, we brought him here and released him at the gate to his people's Guild. A few days later, it was reported his antics got him shipped off to a Thought Reprocessing Institution. It is a shame, because he was amusing. While at Venture, we placed him in the cell with the Rugerian. After just a single day together, the Rugerian begged us to remove him. We finally did, after he gave us information on a pirate freighter route."

The last thing on my agenda was to pay for our supplies and make a down payment for the Sig's investment in our mine.

"Tam, I have two billets of Containium that weigh in the neighborhood of six thousand pounds. I haven't done the math, but I am pretty sure we should be more than square. It should cover what we owe you and the Sig for your time and monetary expenditures related to our mining business."

Tam Lin's eyes grew wide. She looked up at Pasta who had the same expression. He found his tongue and said, "Commander Myers, that should cover all the initial expenses related to getting the mine operational. Once it is up and running, we will sit together with Tam Lin to decide on a permanent agreement."

I could not ask for anything better than that. It was an ideal partnership for all parties. Tria and I stood up to leave. Tam Lin quickly stood as well. I could tell she wanted to talk about her decision to keep Klutch out of the public's eye. I waved her off.

"Tam, we are good. Let's just leave it alone."

We took Tam's private lift down to the docking area. Coonts and Xul were standing next to the open cargo bay doors. They were checking the inventory against the requisition list. When Coonts saw us coming, he met us half way. He gave me a status report on Klutch.

"Commander, Justice has assured me Klutch's prognosis is good. He is lightly sedated so the nanites can repair his wound. Justice told me Klutch would like to speak with you when you have time."

Out of the corner of my eye, I saw a freight transport moving in our direction.

I pointed over my shoulder. "Coonts, I want the two billets of Containium loaded on the transport coming this way."

He gave me a thumbs up and went back up the cargo ramp into the hold. Xul reported everything was accounted for and locked down.

I thanked the little Grawl and told him when Coonts was done, to button up the ship and prepare for departure. Tria and I headed to the med bay to check on Klutch. When we got there, we saw that he was laying on his stomach inside of a med pod. The long ugly gash on his back was now a thin puckered line. We leaned down and his eyes fluttered a couple of times. They finally focused on our faces. Before I could say a word, he started talking.

"Commander, what happened was not my fault. When I got to the Guild, Cholula all but attacked me. At the time, it seemed like obliging her was the right thing to do. She didn't say a word about still having a relationship with Skoal. Last I heard, he was in a prison cell. I had no idea I was being used to make him jealous. If he would not have been a coward, and stood face to face with me, I would have spared his life and found another to pleasure me. There is no act more cowardly than stabbing an unarmed combatant in the back."

I held my hands up to the Troop Master. "We can talk about this some other time. I know you did not intentionally start a fight with Skoal's clan."

"Commander," he said. "I did not disobey your orders."

I looked my Troop Master in the eyes to reassure him I understood what he was saying.

"I know Klutch. I want you healed up and back on duty as soon as possible. We will be going back into the belly of the beast, and I will be counting on you to lead the way."

Klutch gave us a halfhearted smile and a thumbs up. His big lizard like eyes blinked a couple of times then closed. Justice had sedated him once more. We walked out of the med bay. Tria took me by the hand.

"Technically Klutch is correct. He did not disobey your orders. I distinctly remember hearing you tell him not to shoot, stab or poison anyone. If I am not mistaken, Skoal drowned."

I rolled my eyes and shook my head at the pretty alien. She was one of the few I would knowingly let get by with omitting facts. Brawling was specifically mentioned to the Troop Master. By what I saw in the latrine, Skoal did not come up with the idea to voluntarily shove his head into a toilet. I was over the topic and told Tria so. She leaned into me and gave me a peck on the cheek. I took that as a change of subject.

Just when I thought things might get back to some semblance of normal, Justice alerted us that Sael Nalen had an IST message for Tria. She took the call and vocalized her responses. She told Sael we would be back at Alpha Base in eight hours. I frowned at first, because I knew we would be back within an hour. I did not comment, because I was still guessing at what Tria's change of subjects might turn out to be. She ended her call with Sael and told me our four new replicators would be arriving in eight hours. Sael was personally delivering them. Since Sael was the only Chaalt we were currently allowing into Alpha Base, she had no choice in the matter. While that might change at some point in the future, it wasn't happening now. It would also be a good time to brief her on Justice's findings on the Fury.

I called out to Justice. "Whenever your ready, take us home!"

Justice cloaked the Legacy and eased us out of Tam Lin's private dock. He made a DEHD core jump once we were well clear of the outpost. We materialized back in our home star system. After a cursory scan we made a direct approach and landing at Alpha Base. We were met by our gathered clan members. We went through our customary greetings and then set to work unloading our cargo. When all was stowed, they went in small groups to check on Klutch. Justice reported he would not be back to active duty for at least thirty-six hours. I decided to move him to the base's infirmary so it would be easier for the Grawl to check on his status. It also made it less likely he would demand to be released early from his recuperation period. The med bay was going to be an unpleasant place to be if Klutch found out what I had in mind.

Tria and I were heading back to the Legacy when we were intercepted by Felix. He was bubbling with excitement. The rumor we would be getting four new Chaalt replicators, had somehow got out and made it to Felix. It left me wondering who leaked the information. After stealing a look at Tria, I decided I may have been the only one it was withheld from.

"Commander." Felix said. "The production building is prepped and ready for my new replicators. With the help of the scientists, we made use of the older model powerplant that once powered the Legacy's weapons. Its rated output will allow for future expansion of the production facility, should you decide to acquire additional equipment."

I smiled at the Zaen engineer's speculation as to who actually owned the replicators. While I had his undivided attention, I decided it would be a good time to address some concerns that I had.

"Felix, are you going to be able to handle the operation of five replicators? I have a very ambitious production schedule planned. It will require you to run all four of the new machines at maximum capacity for at least six months."

The young Zaen looked confident with his answer. "Commander, I have been personally training Graf and he has proven to be a quick study. He can handle the day to day operation of unit number one. I will take on the responsibility of the four new units. When they arrive, we will install and set them up for their break in protocols. This will require a minimum of twenty-four hours to complete. Once all the initial settings have been verified, we can begin programming the defensive drone production sequences. Two of the units will be dedicated to the manufacturing of the beam weapon drone and two for the anomaly weapon model."

Tria addressed the next logical question. "Felix, there has been questions concerning the availability of the materials needed to complete eight-thousand drones. Have you already determined the quantities necessary?"

The engineer answered without hesitation. "Yes Tria. Justice has anticipated our needs. He also included the percentage of surplus he felt was sufficient to take on any unforeseen problems related to the programs. Since new data has come to light, Justice has revised his figures. We now have an immediate needs target of six-thousand drones. After that goal has been reached, we will continue production to fulfill Alpha base's defensive needs. Justice also stated the Legacy will be armed with a loadout of sixty drones for offensive and defensive engagements. It was the reasoning behind the drones having the same diameter as the torpedo weapon carried aboard the Legacy."

That was a revelation the wargaming AI had yet to discuss with me. His motives for not doing so, may have had something to do with his endless observations of Tria and my interactions. He may have decided to not bother me with the details, when I could possibly entertain his processors with some of our more unique activities. Sooner or later he would have got around to letting me know. It would be pointless to argue with him about the timing. I was sure he had already formulated some obscure reason that would make it a losing proposition.

The logistics required to manufacture six-thousand combat drones were huge. We had a large assortment of artifacts at Alpha base. The information I received from Justice, indicated all of it would be necessary in the manufacturing process. He insinuated it would not be nearly enough. Somewhere along the line, I was left out of the briefing that accounted for the extra materials.

"Felix, where exactly, are we going to get the raw materials needed to stay on your production schedule?"

"Commander, Jaran chose a scientist named Borla to take the Grawl transport shuttle to the Sig artifact storage base. Borla is a metallurgy specialist. He is meeting with Chief, the Senior Research Scholar in charge of the facility. Together they are processing all the low value salvage collected from the Prule lifeboat. If Borla or Chief find anything of interest they will set it aside. It was my understanding, the majority of the relics recovered are ancient junk. The base materials from the salvage being the only thing of value."

There was a lot going on that I didn't have a clue about. A lot of the day to day decisions I used to be burdened with, were now being delegated by my senior clan members. I was finding that I now had time to consider other projects. Tria informed Felix the Principle Investigator was delivering the new replicators within the next eight hours. He ran to the production building to ensure all was ready for their arrival. Tria decided we should talk about my new found free time as well as other topics in my cabin. She hooked her arm in mine and steered me in the direction of the Legacy.

After a private discussion with Tria that didn't involve a lot of discussing anything, I changed the subject to something I wanted. I told her of my desire to scratch an itch that was bothering me since the assassination attempt on our lives. She admitted to wanting closure on that particular subject as much as I did. I told her I wanted to take a quick hop to outpost 655. It was a black-market outpost not far from the Chaalt exclusion zone. It was run by a Coram warlord by the name of Enochey. The chances of him still being alive and running the outpost were slim at best. He did not have a lot going for him. He was not well liked or respected by his own mercenary troops. He also made the mistake of screwing with my crew. He managed to successfully bargain for his life, but I didn't let his miscalculation go completely unpunished. When we left him to his own means, evidence of our actions made it appear Enochey betrayed Eiger's clan members. From what I understood, that blotch on your criminal record usually resulted in a slow painful death at Eiger's hands. The reason I wanted to pay 655 a visit, was because it was home to a considerable number of Coram mercenaries. Since the mercenaries that attacked Tria and I were also Coram, it seemed like a good place to start. I was going to throw some credits around in hopes that someone could give us a hint at the whereabouts of the Kasulla slug that orchestrated the hit. Even a third-rate rumor would be more information than we currently had.

8

I had just about nodded off to sleep when an idea hit me like a rock to the head. Why not go down and ask Eiger not so nicely, if he killed Enochey. I know the piece of scat and his former right-hand man Illam Pove, were wanting to speak with me. Now I had a reason to get that bit of unpleasantness off my list of unlikely things to do. Tria had fallen asleep while I was contemplating my next moves. I gently slid my shoulder out from under her head and sat up on the edge of the bed. There was a good possibility she would want to be present when I questioned Eiger, but I didn't have the heart to disturb her. Thinking better of it, I made a lame attempt at waking her by whispering in her ear. I smiled when it failed to get any meaningful reaction. It occurred to me that a more earnest attempt could lead to further delays. If things went well, I would be back before she knew I was gone.

I got up and put on a smart cloth uniform and headed for the boarding hatch. The ship was quiet and nobody was on the bridge. I exited the Legacy and made my way to the lift that takes you down to the holding cells in the escape tunnel. In a case of Deja Vue, I was met by Graf exiting the lift.

"Graf, has the change in diet affected Illam Pove's behavior?"

"Yes Commander, his enclosure is now clean. Your idea of revealing Eiger's presence in the adjoining cell, has had a devasting effect on him. He now sits with his back to Eiger's cell and no longer speaks at all since requesting an audience with you."

"What about Eiger?"

"Eiger now spends his time beating on the dividing wall of the cell and ranting about Pove's betrayal. Pove cannot hear what Eiger is saying, but knows it is not endearments."

"Has Eiger stated why he wants to speak to me?"

"No Commander, he instead wastes his time endlessly attempting to bribe his way out of his cell. I have awarded his endeavors with the same Pungo diet as Pove. It has yet to have any effect on his efforts."

I nodded and waved the Grawl scientist on. I entered the lift and dropped rapidly to the subterranean tunnel. I stepped off and walked the two hundred plus yards to the holding cells. As Graf had stated, Eiger stood pounding on the dividing wall with his one good arm and screaming out unheard threats of violence at Pove. Justice, in a surprising show of mercy, had set the pirates broken arm and stabilized it with a splint. Eiger's badly swollen face and missing teeth, did not rate any additional minutes of the AI's time.

The Murlak's ceremonial armor was now in a pile in the corner of his cell. Since he was never going to be making use of it, I had a better idea for it. It would be going on my trip to outpost 655.

"Justice open Eiger's cell."

The door opened without a sound. I could now hear the threats being yelled at Pove. Eiger was screaming, he was going to slowly roast Pove's infant offspring over his ancestral fire pit. I felt a little fake news was in order.

"You no longer have an ancestral fire pit. The Royal family has already seized your compound in the Crisbarry Mountains. I suspect they have already pissed that fire out, and started a new one of their own."

The pirate jumped at my comment, and plastered himself against the dividing wall. It would be a shame if I had startled him enough to soil himself. I walked over to his armor and turned my back on him. I started tossing the pieces out the cell's door.

"You won't be needing this junk anymore." I said glancing over my shoulder."

Eiger's face contorted in rage and he took a step towards me. I threw the last piece of armor out the door and turned to face him. He took another step in my direction, which put a big smile on my face. The expression stopped him from taking another.

"If you think you have got enough gas in your tank, go ahead and jump."

I could tell he was confused by my use of a slang phrase.

"Here, let me make it easy for you. Even a coward like you should understand what I am implying."

I put my hands behind my back and closed my eyes, then turned and faced away from him.

"Come on! What is a yellow bellied Throgg like you waiting for? I am sure you used to do stuff like this all the time. It is probably how you got to be the top pirate!" I called provokingly.

After a minute, I finally turned back around to face him. He had pushed himself back into the corner of the cell with his eyes wide and staring. It took me a second to realize he was not looking at me. He was looking over my shoulder. I followed his gaze behind me, and found Tria leaning against the door frame with her arms crossed. She was wearing my very first pair of combat boots from my artifact 699 body armor. They looked ridiculously large on her. The smart fit qualities of their design, had to be getting a workout trying to make them fit. The implication of why Tria would wear them, was not lost on Eiger. Tria pointed to the dividing wall between the cells. Both Eiger and I looked in that direction. Illam Pove now had his face pushed against the see-thru wall. For unknown reasons, he now looked happy.

Tria called to Eiger. "I doubt his cheerful demeanor is based on the assumption we are setting you free."

The pirate looked over at me. "I know where there are hidden riches that can make you wealthy beyond comprehension." He pointed at Illam Pove. "Kill that traitorous Throgg and they will be yours."

Tria and I walked to the wall where Pove stood.

I called to Justice. "I need audio please."

"Audio now available Commander." He replied.

"Pove, Eiger says he will give us huge sums of hidden wealth if we kill you. I was wondering what you could offer up, if we end his life instead?" I said, looking back at Eiger.

"He lies! Your raid on Shurmosk took most all that he has ever collected. What little he might still have hidden, would be on our home world, in his clan's compound." He quickly answered.

I was always a true believer in the phrase, "You can't fix stupid." Eiger proved he was, with a capital "S". Tria and I were standing about five feet from him, with Tria being the closest. Eiger lunged out of the corner like a spring uncoiling. He was going for Tria's throat with both hands. She turned and caught his wrist before he could grab her. He had put all of his weight into his effort and Tria used that against him. She fell backwards pulling him with her. As she rolled, she pushed him over the top with her legs. He landed hard on his back with Tria coming upright on top of him. I had been down like that enough times to know she could pretty much do whatever the hell she wanted from that position.

I yelled down at him. "You are going to regret pulling that stunt!"

He managed to wrench his one good arm from her grasp and got a handful of her uniform, it was a short-lived victory. With her arm now free, she drove her elbow down into his face, splitting his eyebrow wide open. I could see bone inside the gory wound. His head rebounded from the floor and in the blink of an eye, she gave him another one across his short wide muzzle. It changed the landscape of his once protruding nose. It was now flattened and gushing blood worse than the cut over his eye. His arms went limp and he was making a gurgling noise. He wasn't dead, but probably wished he was.

Tria looked over at me. "I think he is ready to answer any questions you might have."

It was one of those rare occasions when she was wrong. When I asked Eiger if he had killed the Coram warlord Enochey, he made another really bad call. He decided to spit a mouthful of blood into Tria's face. His swollen mouth only capable of getting the spittle as high as her chin. Tria carefully wiped the mess off, and smiled. Eiger had no idea how bad of an omen that would turn out to be. Like a snake striking its prey, she drove two of her fingers into his eye and gouged the eyeball from its socket. When Eiger opened his mouth to scream, she shoved the severed orb inside. She then placed both her hands over his mouth until he was forced to swallow. He bucked and thrashed for more than two minutes, then went still. Somewhere deep in my darkest consciousness, I heard the low growling mirth of the Oolaran monster imprinted into my brain. It was applauding Tria's performance. I was now wondering if the partial weaponization she underwent, somehow infected her with the murderous phantasm that haunted me. I looked over at Illam Pove, he was no longer smiling.

Tria stood up wiping at the mess on her uniform. She looked down at Eiger one last time and shrugged. "I guess I won't be needing the boots after all."

She walked over to where Illam Pove stood staring at her through the wall. He slowly backed away holding his hands out in front of him and shaking his head.

Tria called to him, her voice sounded low and dangerous. "Now that you know what happens to fools who waste our time, you should choose your words wisely."

Pove's voice came out high and shrill. He sounded like he was on the verge of coming unhinged.

"I swear to you! I do not know of a warlord named Enochey!"

The deadly vibes radiating from Tria, made me grab her by the hand and pull her in the direction of the lift. If she questioned Pove in her current state of mind we would lose any chance at gathering useful intel from the pirate.

On our way to the surface we did not speak. I wasn't even sure what to say. Tria's breathing finally slowed and her hostility seemed to ebb as well. By the time we stepped out of the lift she was back to her normal composure. We saw two of the

Grawl scientists leaving the artifact building. It looked like they were going to move in our direction. They suddenly changed course when they noticed Tria's oversized boots and the blood on the front of her uniform. I could only imagine the rumors that were going to be making the rounds. Justice would see to it Eiger's body would be consumed by a measured dose of nanites. Soon it would be like the pirate was never here. The rumors would be confirmed.

Justice called to us. "Commander, a small freighter escorted by two Chaalt battleships have entered our system from hyperspace. I have an IST transmission coming in from the freighter. It is from the Principle Investigator. Would you like me to hold it, or put it through?"

"Give it to me Justice."

Sael came right on. "Nathan, I request permission to dock. The compact dimensions of the freighter should allow it to pass through your access tunnel."

I called to Justice before I replied. "Justice, we have never had a freighter in our dock before. Will it fit without damaging the atmospheric locks?"

"The clearances are acceptable Commander. I will project a navigation beacon to aid their approach. I foresee no problems if they carefully follow my directional cues."

I replied to Sael. "You are cleared to dock. Please have your Captain follow the navigation markers and the approach velocities recommended by Justice."

She gave me a curt reply. "Acknowledged, ETA sixteen minutes!"

The last time Sael delivered a replicator she used a really big cargo shuttle. I guess she did not want to waste the time it would take to make four trips.

"Justice, set up the briefing room. I want you to give Sael the intel we currently have."

"Commander, The Overseer and I are confidant we have a reference to the Fury. We are still working on the numbers that were translated into the coordinates of the Prule Hunter facility. We have enough similar matches to piece together partial destination points. We are still trying to fill in the blanks enough to surmise an actual location."

"Do you have anything solid I can give Sael?"

"We are close Commander, but still lack several of the numerical characters necessary to pinpoint a precise location. I will notify you the moment we are successful"

Tria squeezed my hand. "I will meet you in the briefing room."

I was guessing her present appearance would have Sael asking questions Tria did not feel like answering. At some time during the briefing, Eiger's fate would have to be mentioned. It would inevitably lead to ridicule, because Eiger could have turned out to be a valuable information asset. Granddad used to tell me, what goes around comes around. Eiger nearly beating Tria to death while she was his prisoner, has now come full circle. Unfortunately for Eiger, Tria completed the job. I was not going to cry over a little spilt milk, or in this case, a lot of spilled pirate blood. I had sworn, sooner or later, I was going to kill that son of a bitch. Tria saved me the trouble by doing it sooner. The upside of Eiger's untimely demise, was that Illam Pove had a ringside seat. It would give answers to any questions we might ask of him, a certain amount of credibility.

I saw the entrance tunnel lights flare to life. My eyes went wide at the sight of Sael's freighter coming down the tunnel. It filled the passage to its entirety. What Justice had described as acceptable clearances, was actually mere feet to spare. I was puzzled why Sael would choose a ship that size? Replicators were very large pieces of equipment but they wouldn't fill the hold of a freighter that size. I waited for it to come to a halt and lower the cargo ramp. Standing inside the huge opening was Sael Nalen. She was decked out in her red recon armor and had a no-nonsense disposition when she started barking orders. Gravity sleds loaded with billets of encapsulated materials started making their way down the ramp in a convoy led by Sael. She stopped in front of me and held up a hand to halt the procession.

"Commander Myers, where would you like us to store these materials?"

I was speechless. I had no idea we would be getting anything other than replicators. Apparently Tria had not revealed the true extent of her bargaining. She had said she wanted it to be a surprise, and it was turning out to be a big one.

Sael grew impatient. She leaned forward and spoke quietly so I would be the only one to hear her.

"I am sorry if I interrupted your scat stacking session, but I have better things to do than watch you decide which of your orifices you wish to pick at."

If I was not so surprised by Tria's non-disclosure, I would have had a witty comeback to throw back at Sael. I instead turned and saw the gathering crowd of my clan members. I whistled and held up my index finger. Jaran separated from the growing assembly and quickly made his way over to me.

I smiled at Sael's souring expression. "Excuse me for just one second."

She didn't answer, but did cross all her arms and fume.

That was acceptable as an affirmative reply. I leaned down to Jaran and he stepped closer.

"Jaran, did you know we would be getting supplies from the Chaalt?"

"Yes Commander."

"Do you also know where they are going to be stored?"

He nodded. "Yes Commander."

I now knew Tria's subterfuge was part of a much larger conspiracy. Rather than contemplate the true proportions of its enormity, I instructed Jaran to take charge of the supply convoy. I turned back to Sael and extended an arm in the direction of the Legacy.

"Sael would you please follow me to the Legacy. I would like to give you a briefing on intelligence we have uncovered."

Her frown disappeared and she followed me toward the Legacy. I took another glance back at Jaran to see where he was directing the supplies to be stored. The convoy was headed for the replicator storage warehouse. I was just about to the boarding ramp of the Legacy and Sael hissed at me.

"What is the matter with you? Were you not aware I would be bringing samples of materials collected from in and around the Prule base?"

I waited until Sael was at the top of the ramp and reached out and grabbed one of her hands, pulling her inside.

Sael pulled her hand free. "What kind of game are you playing on me you primate!" She snapped.

"Sael, I was not told in advance about the supplies."

Sael stopped her bitching and gave me an incredulous look. "Why would Tria purposely withhold that information from you?"

I wasn't about to give Sael the details on how much Tria had manipulated her during their bargaining session. I was just now becoming privy to the actual value Tria had gained for assets we really could not immediately make use of. Tria was ensuring we would not have a materials deficit when the defensive drones went into production. She was as determined as I was to help defend Earth. I could only smile at the revelation. My expression angered Sael.

"What are you smiling about! Your subordinates are purposely hiding important information from a superior officer. You would be foolish to not address this inappropriate behavior, regardless of who is instigating it!"

I wanted to laugh out loud but knew that Sael would freak out about it. I tried my best to put a neutral expression on my face. I was having a hard time keeping a straight face when I finally replied.

"Yes Sael, you are correct. I am going to have to discipline Tria."

Sael crossed both sets of arms and squinted her eyes at me. "You have no intention of doing anything about this breach of conduct?"

I was glad I caught myself before saying Tria was a bad girl and would get what was coming to her.

"Sael, I will address the issue. Let's go to the briefing room and discuss the real reasons I wanted to talk to you."

9

Sael followed me in silence. Her body language was stiff and abrasive. I hadn't seen her wear her red recon armor for a very long time. She had told me things back on her home world were not good. Certain members of the council were questioning her command. It made me wonder if she decided the betrayal of the Fury's crew warranted a return to her former Kala Mor Dee style of leadership. I hope I was wrong. Sael could be a real pain in the ass, but Kala Mor Dee was an insufferable bitch.

Sael and I had just made it to the bridge and Justice pinged my implants. It was one of those rare occasions went the AI added emotion into his dialog. He also added a tad too much volume. I stopped in my tracks and involuntarily put my hands over my ears.

"Commander!" Justice said. "The Overseer and I have made a breakthrough!

We have decoded a complete set of location coordinates."

Sael almost collided with me. I could tell she was going to say something unpleasant. She stowed the comment after seeing the surprise on my face.

"Nathan, what is happening?" She asked

I commented to Justice instead. "Justice, save it for the briefing room so all can hear."

Sael again ask me. "What has happened!"

Rather than answer, I took her by a hand and took off at a jog to the briefing room. Sael followed without hesitation. When we entered the briefing room, Tria, Coonts and Xul looked up in surprise at our hasty entrance. I pointed at a chair and Sael sat down with a frown on her face. I stood at my place at the head of the table.

"Give us what you got Justice."

"Commander, the Overseer and I, have successfully deciphered enough of the Prule machine code to give us the location of a Prule installation."

The expression on Sael's face went from a frown to something different entirely when she heard Justice's next statement. So, did everybody else's.

Justice continued. "We have a reference to the Fury and the location of a Prule base. The location is already known to us."

Everyone but Sael Nalen was shocked to silence. She stood up and yelled at me in a very unladylike voice. "What does Justice mean by that! You already knew of a Prule base that could be harboring the Fury, and decided to not tell me!"

I now regretted telling Justice to wait until we could all hear his report. He did me a solid by saving me the trouble of telling Sael to shut the hell up. He cut off her rant before she could continue.

"Principle Investigator, you are making inaccurate assumptions. If you will be so kind as to listen, you will better understand my intelligence report."

I cast a stinky eye to Sael and she promptly sat down. I could practically feel the heat coming from her side of the table.

"Justice you will not be interrupted again. Please continue."

"Commander, the coordinates exactly match the known location of the Scrun fleet we encountered close to one of our transponder destinations. We may have concluded incorrectly that the base we observed was under construction. There is now evidence suggesting it was an excavation site and not a newly constructed slave depot. There are two references to the Fury. Until we get a better understanding of the Prule machine codes we can only speculate on their meaning. Our previously recorded data gives little credibility to the theory that the Fury would be at the site. We do however, have two sets of matching data that reference the Fury, and our decryption algorithms have confirmed they contain location coordinates."

Sael looked like she was going to start ranting again. I told Justice to display the video recordings. That seemed to placate her disruptive behavior. A view screen appeared on the briefing room wall. It showed the blue-green planet surrounded by the wispy white haze of its atmosphere. The Scrun ships suddenly appeared as red boxes. More than a hundred surrounded the planet. Three of the hostile return signals were much larger than the rest. The biggest boxes disappeared from the planet's orbit. The video distorted and then blinked to reset. When it did, a closeup view of three unidentified ships filled the screen then quickly receded from sight.

Sael jumped to her feet. "Justice! Stop the video!"

She got withering stares from all of us.

She looked at us with shock on her face. "Justice!" she said. "Run that back again!"

Justice obliged her and reversed the video. The large ships came back into view. When one of them filled the wall screen she yelled stop again. Sael got up and walked to the screen and studied the image for several seconds. She turned back around with a look of disbelief on her face.

"Those are Heckler warships!"

I looked over at Tria and she shook her head negative. Turning back to Sael I asked the question everyone was thinking.

"Sael, who are the Heckler, and why would they want to be an ally of the Scrun?"

Sael did not answer, and sat back down. She looked bewildered, and put two of her hands on each side of her face. My curiosity was quickly being quashed by my rising anger at her silence.

"Sael, I asked you a question."

The Principle Investigator finally looked up at me like she was noticing me for the first time. "Nathan, I don't think the Heckler are allies with the Scrun. I cannot be absolutely sure, but do not think it is possible based on the intel that I have access to."

Tria stood up with a frown on her face. "Principle Investigator, if you have information on those warships, you need to share it with us. The purpose of this meeting was to share intelligence with you that is currently unavailable to anyone else. Data should flow in both directions!"

Sael Nalen's gaze finally locked on me. "Nathan, those ships are possibly older than the Legacy. The Heckler is another of many races that disappeared more than two hundred Earth years ago. Chaalt research scholars are just now scratching the surface on intel related to the race. We have very little of their language to translate. We know they were called the Heckler and not much else."

Coonts and Xul were talking quietly together. Coonts held up a hand and all eyes shifted in his direction. I asked him if he had something he would like to add.

"Yes Commander." He said. "Xul and I have a theory. We believe the Heckler ships were discovered by the Scrun. It is how the Grawl came into possession of the Legacy. It was accidently discovered by asteroid mining surveyors, and secretly transferred to a Grawl facility. There is the very real possibility the Scrun stumbled upon the ships while searching the Prule base. We also believe there are no Prule present at the base. It is just another theory, but if the Prule were there, we believe the orbit of the planet, as well as its surface would be littered with the wreckage of those unfortunates that made the initial discovery."

Everyone sat back down to digest the Grawl's theories. I decided Justice was doing the same thing and was holding his opinion until asked. I called to him.

"Justice, I would like your input. What is your take on the new data?"

"Commander, I concur with Coonts and Xul's assessment. It would be foolhardy not to presume other races have not discovered military artifacts. We are already aware of the fact there are hundreds if not thousands of hidden military installations throughout the galaxy. We can only speculate on what might be hidden in the caches, but the reality of the situation is clear. The contents regardless of what it might turn out to be, will inevitably be the property of those who discover them first."

Justice's unfiltered appraisal was all I needed to validate Coonts and Xul's premise. If the theories being floated about the room proved correct, I could live with the idea we were not facing a new advanced predatory race. What I did find unsettling was the idea of the Scrun finding advanced military tech. As much as I hated to admit it, if it was indeed the Scrun operating those ships, I envied their discovery. It had me wondering about the AIs operating the ships.

"Justice, what is your evaluation of the AIs operating the Heckler ships?"

"Commander, when we first encountered the Heckler spacecraft, I speculated the aggressiveness of the AIs was a product of a predatory race's programming. I have since reevaluated my hypothesis and added the new information parameters provided by the Principle Investigator. My revised evaluation suggests the programing was designed to do battle with the Prule. I also believe the survival algorithms of the AIs have determined the Scrun are not Prule surrogates, therefore they would be acceptable inheritors of the abandoned technology. There is also the possibility the AIs have defaulted to programming that would determine any enemy of the Scrun, as a possible ally of the Prule."

I scanned my crewmates faces to get a read on their reactions. All seemed bothered by the intel except Coonts. The corroboration Justice gave to his and Xul's theory went straight to his head. He sat with his overly large chest muscles puffed up and was admiring his arms as he flexed his muscles. To have brawn and brains, was inflating the Grawl's ego to cringeworthy proportions. I rolled my eyes and glanced over at Sael. It looked like she was now brooding over our exchange of ideas.

She looked back at me. "Nathan, if the Fury is in The Scrun's hands, the possibilities are frightening. If they manage to unlock the secrets of the technology aboard that ship, it will elevate the Scrun's military competence to extremely dangerous levels. This information will be toxic if it is disclosed to my people's military council. They may choose to declare all out war on the Scrun. While many races might think it is a good thing to confront the slavers, the repercussions of dividing our military on yet another front, could be disastrous to our already slowing growth and economy."

Sael was only looking at the problem through her eyes. She needed to get a galactic view of the bigger picture.

"Sael, the technology aboard the Heckler ships is comparable to that of the Legacy. The weapons are on par with the Legacy's. That already makes the Scrun much more dangerous adversaries. Do you have intelligence on the full weapons capabilities of the Heckler ships?"

"Very little Nathan." She answered. "What I can tell you, is that my people salvaged a large fragment of a Heckler ship. In our examination of the wreckage, we found the remnants of the ship's primary weapons. Careful analysis of the components, revealed advanced architecture that has formed the design basis for several weapons that are still in use on some of our older classes of warships."

"Okay Sael, based on what you know about the Scrun. What is the likelihood of the them having talented enough scientists to reverse engineer Heckler technology or the Chaalt tech aboard the Fury?"

I could practically see the gears in Sael's head grinding up my question. She looked like she was getting ready to say something when Coonts and Xul both put up their hands at the same time. All eyes shifted to them. Xul deferred to Coonts. Whatever they were thinking, the conclusion came to them both at the same time.

"Commander." Coonts said. "The Scrun have not advanced to the level of scientific proficiency that would be required to reverse engineer tech of the complexity we are discussing. It would take them a decade or more to capitalize on the finds. They would have to have help from another more advanced race. Only two come to mind that are capable of taking on a task of this magnitude and actually producing results in the near future. Of the two, only one would consider working with the Scrun."

We already knew who Coonts was referring to without him spelling it out for us. Since the Chaalt would never work with the Scrun, that only left the Grawl. It would not just be any Grawl, it would have to be some lowlife like that long dead piece of scat Drayen. According to the Grawl scientists in my clan, there was an overabundance of greedy corrupt Grawl swayers, just waiting for chances like this to come along.

Justice called to us. "Commander, I am carefully studying the single high-altitude image that was taken of the Scrun base when the Legacy passed low over the planets atmosphere. The light cloud cover and less than optimal sensor aperture angle, gives little detail to the extensive installation. I have enhanced and sharpened the image as much as possible. I would like to show you my findings."

An image appeared on the viewscreen. It was blurry and slightly distorted, with scale markers to the top and sides. The complex was eight miles wide by five miles deep. It sat on a very pronounced peninsula that jutted upwards several thousand feet above the ocean that surrounded the single continent. The rest of the small planet was covered in blue green ocean. We could see several shallow lightly colored mounds beneath the surface of the water but no other land features. Justice changed the picture angle, and we could now make out four large construction cranes towering above the city like complex. Each was sitting at the edge of a dark oblong shadow. The Scrun were indeed excavating or building unknown structures below the surface. What really caught my eye was the jungle that bordered the back of the base. The trees dwarfed the cranes that stood more that a thousand feet over the few buildings that dotted the area. The scale markers indicated the forest was at least three thousand feet tall. Justice changed the angle once more showing us the aft view as the Legacy was moving away from the target. He highlighted three very distinct dark shadows in the gigantic tree line at the edge of the complex. They were identical in length and width. The scale markers verified they were all more than a mile long by roughly a half mile wide. The three Heckler ships would have fit perfectly into the indentations.

Tria looked over at Sael Nalen and quietly commented on the surreal scene. "The Heckler ships could have been hidden for hundreds of years by the dense forest growth."

Sael stood up and walked back up to the screen. "How old is this image?"

Justice answered. "Three months, nineteen days and seventeen hours."

Sael grimaced. "It would have been nice to have the intel back when you encountered the Heckler ships."

I shot right back at her. "It would have been nice to have more intel on what was going on, when we bailed your asses out of that fiasco at your research facility."

Touché, Sael stiffened at my rebuke. She turned to me. Her lips formed a thin flat line, and she acknowledged my comment with a nod. She turned back to the viewscreen. She pointed at the buildings in the image.

These are large defensive weapons emplacements. If they are of Prule design, it will make it very difficult for assault troops to land anywhere near the base. Did they respond to your incursion?"

"No, this was taken when Justice jumped us to the center of the Scrun ship formations. At the time, we were trying to avoid engaging the Heckler ships. I was thinking that if we did not fire on them, they might balk at deciding we were hostile combatants. I was later proven wrong. Justice, play the rest of the video."

Sael watched in fascination at the methods used by Justice to break off the engagement. She had a small smile on her face right up until the Heckler ship's spread out and salvo fired all their defensive weapons. The picture distorting and resetting widened her eyes.

She looked over at me. "Were they able to strike the Legacy with that strategy?"

"No, but trying did reveal valuable information on the AI's defensive tactics. Justice was able to get a lot of data on the ship's capabilities and deficiencies. In a one

149

on one, or two on one engagement, the odds would lean in favor of the Legacy. In a two or more engagement, the odds would go to the Heckler. If you add the one hundred or so Scrun ships to the equation, we decided retreat was the wisest option."

Justice ended the video and Sael sat back down. She looked impressed with what she saw.

"I now understand why you chose to withhold the data. My next question is what are you planning to do about it?"

I thought about it for a second. "That depends. Part of me wanted to assemble a task force of my trusted allies, and strike the hostile fleet. If that were possible without losing a large number of friendlies in the process, we would attempt to subdue and capture the base intact. With the new intelligence that has come to light, it could possibly turn out to be a blood bath. I am not willing to gamble the lives of my allies on some hastily contrived adventurism. With that said, it also doesn't mean that I am not considering other options."

Sael gave me a piercing stare. "When you said your trusted allies, I hope you were referring to the Chaalt military."

I gave her a stone-faced reply. "Among others."

Sael winced at my comment. I was sure the implication did not sit well with her. She tried to justify her statement.

"Nathan, if you plan to go up against the Heckler ships and what could now be a large Scrun defensive fleet, you will need the help of my people. The Sig may be able to assemble the numbers necessary to get the job done, but at what cost? Their ships are not advanced enough to win a protracted engagement."

Sael didn't know it, but she just made up my mine to go ahead and share some of our weapons technology with the Sig. Their ships may not be the equal of the Chaalt's, but their weapons would soon be in the near future.

10

Rather than get angry at Sael's declaration of superiority, I turned my back on her and took a slow deep breath. I knew she was desperate to be the one to find the Fury, but pissing on my boots wasn't the way to go about it. If she thought I could only carry out a successful operation with the exclusive help of her people, she was wrong. My next statement would let her know in no uncertain terms, it was a return volley for her intentional slight at the capabilities of my crew and that of the Sig.

I slowly turned around and in a calm voice gave her a piece of my mind. "Sael, we did pretty damn well against the best defenses your people had to offer when we went into your prized research center. If I remember correctly, we did it without the help or support of your military."

The sting was obvious on Sael's face, it just wasn't accompanied by the report of the slap. It had the desired effect and conveyed my displeasure in a way she absolutely understood. She sat in silence wringing both sets of hands and staring down at the table in front of her. The briefing room was dead quiet.

Sael finally looked up at me. "Nathan, I apologize. You have proven on more than one occasion, that you are capable of succeeding when others, including my own military have failed. What I should have done, was ask you what your plan of action will be, and if I am allowed to accompany you?"

That was not what I expected to hear. That's not to say it wasn't welcomed, it was just surprising coming from Sael's mouth. I was a little lost for words and was formulating a response when a loud booming voice from the corridor answered for me.

"We are going to go there and kick the scat out of those Throggs, and if the Fury is there, we are going to take it from them!"

All eyes went to the doorway where Klutch stood. He pounded his fist together. "Commander, I am healed and ready for duty, when do we leave?"

Tria and I couldn't help but smile. The Tibor could not have chosen a more opportune time to join us. The awkward silence hanging in the air was now gone. Coonts got up and ran around the table. He looked Klutch over carefully. The exposed dark gray skin of the Tibor's arms, neck and head had spots that were dabbed with nano gel. They were the telltale signs the Troop Master had undergone a nano lamination procedure to his epidermis. The alien technology drastically toughened the skin and made it impervious to most blunt force punctures. It was just one of the many phases of the Oolaran weaponization process that Tria, Coonts, and I had undergone. In my case I had received the whole enchilada, including some very questionable survival imprinting. Tria, Coonts, and now Klutch, only had a select few levels of the enhancement program. I actually wasn't aware Klutch was even a candidate for the procedure.

Coonts was poking at the spots, asking if they still felt like lava burning under the skin. Klutch nervously glanced at me out of the corner of his big lizard like eyes. He swatted Coonts hand away, and quickly changed the subject.

"Justice said you carried me out of the Guild on your shoulders. You should have let me die, because it is the only way you are going to get out of paying the twenty thousand credits you still owe me!"

At least the big buffoon said it with a smile on his face. Coonts acted like he was mad until he turned away. Then he put a big Grawl smile on his face that quickly disappeared when he sat back in his chair. Coonts used his foot to kick Klutch's chair away from his. Klutch laughed at him and pulled it back to the table right next to him, and sat down as if nothing happened. Sael was now the one that was speechless. She had to have been wondering where Klutch was at. Now she knew part of the story, but not enough of it to quit giving me the inquiring looks. I didn't plan on bringing up the subject. I instead tried to blow Sael off, by marginalizing the story with a much too simple explanation.

"Klutch slipped in a latrine and hurt himself."

That removed Klutch's goofy grin, but added a fragrance to the briefing room that could have melted an unlit candle. Xul got up and let me know if he was needed, he would be in the artifact building. Tria apparently didn't like my explanation any better than Klutch, and elbowed me none to gently in the ribs. Justice did us all a favor by kicking the air purifiers up a couple of notches, bringing some relief to the assault on our olfactory senses.

Tria decided to add a little legitimacy to my explanation and assuage Klutch's wounded pride. "We were at Outpost 9765 when Klutch was targeted for an assassination attempt. As you can see, it failed."

While Tria's additional commentary took some of the skeptical look off Sael's face, Klutch's next comment made her eyes almost bug out of her head.

"Tria." Klutch said. "Since we seem to be discussing recent events, I heard a rumor you whacked Eiger. Since I was not fortunate enough to be there, I would like to hear the details of how it happened."

I elbowed Tria. "Yes Tria, we are dying to hear about that!"

Sael stood up and leaned across the table toward Tria. "Eiger could have given you information on pirate strongholds throughout the galaxy. Why would you kill him?"

If that wasn't bad enough, the freakin evil robot decided to make it a show and tell session. He put the video up on the screen. Tria glared at me and left the room. Coonts, Klutch and the Principle Investigator crowded together to watch the screen. I sat back in my chair and closed my eyes, massaging a dull ache forming in my forehead. This briefing was fubar and getting worse by the minute.

As soon as Coonts saw the oversized boots on Tria's feet, he nudged Klutch. In a low voice, he said. "The twenty I owe you says she kicks his head in."

Of course, Klutch took the bet. I don't think he actually cared if he won or lost, he just wanted to see Tria do it. What happened next, momentarily left their mouths gaping.

Klutch started braying out loud and slapped Coonts on the back. "Now you owe me forty thousand!" he laughed.

Coonts had an expression that implied he had just waded through Throgg scat. Sael turned to me. She had a look indicating she was going to start in on me. I poked a finger at her and left the room in search of Tria. I was done with this circus. It occurred to me it would be a good idea to find out if Tria was actually mad at me. If I was lucky, she was just acting like that, as an excuse to bail out before Sael could start chewing on her ass again.

I found Tria in the galley having a warm beverage. I ordered one for myself and sat down beside her. "That went well didn't it."

She gave me a grin and nodded. I could tell we were good. "About as well as most we have had with Sael." she said.

She was right about that, so I changed the subject. "Klutch is trying to hide the pain of his procedure. Do you think he is mission capable?"

Rather than answer me, Tria called to Justice. "Justice, what is the status of Klutch's recovery?"

"Tria, before I sedated Klutch to repair his battle damage, he insisted I should perform the nano-weave procedure on him. Since his request would also aid in his recovery, I took the liberty of going ahead with the enhancement. As you are well aware, the recovery time is relatively fast. But the pain of the adjustment period, lingers for more than a week. His injection wounds will heal within twelve hours, but the Troop Master may be what Nathan would describe as "crabby" for the next seven to ten days."

That was good enough for me. I knew just how to keep the Tibor from being an irritable pain in the ass. Put him back in the field so he can focus his pain on our enemies.

I asked Tria, "What do you think about doing a recon of the Scrun's new base?"

I could tell she had been contemplating the subject. "After the missile barrage you left as a parting gift, I suspect the Scrun will reinforce the orbitals and take additional measures on the ground to protect their find. Sael's assessment may also be correct. The Sig will take considerable losses if we go in guns blazing."

Sael's ears must have started burning, because she came walking into the galley. I suspect Justice alerted her to our whereabouts. She was walking straight at us then made a detour to the drink fountain. She chose a water then came over and sat across from us.

"Certain unnamed members of your crew are suffering from brain rot." Sael said with a straight face.

I looked up from my coffee and grinned. "Yes, we fear it is progressing much faster on the crew than the command staff."

Tria cocked an eyebrow at me. "Speak for yourself!" she said.

159

This got polite chuckles from the three of us. Sael's face turned serious. "Is Klutch exaggerating, or are you really considering going into that death trap alone?"

Tria's voice had an edge to it when she shot back her reply. "You should know by now; it is what we do best!"

Sael did not like the curt reply and her expression showed it. I held up my hands to the both of them. "Ladies, lets dial it back a notch. Sael, to answer your question, yes, I am considering taking direct action against the Scrun base. I just don't think my Troop Master is one hundred percent ready for a mission of that difficulty."

Sael took a sip of water then looked me in the eyes. "The longer we wait the more difficult it will be."

The word "we" was not lost on Tria or I.

"Sael" I said, "I think whatever was done to improve and protect the base, would have been done right after our first incursion. My mindset, is that the longer we wait, the more the Scrun will start getting comfortable with their defenses. It has been our past experiences, that the lack of action on our part usually encourages the slavers to think their preparations will be enough to dissuade another visit. By not striking the

Heckler ships, we may have sent the misleading message, that we fear them, and fled to keep from being destroyed. While there is a small percentage of truth to that statement, the fact of the matter is, nothing points a finger at us as the aggressors. All of our past engagements were decisive and the outcome was always the complete destruction of the target. We have never made a strategic retreat until now. So again, I reiterate, they have no idea who was messing with them."

Sael carefully processed the facts I presented to her. She finally nodded in agreement. "Yes, I believe you have a valid point, but I think you are considering another mission. May I ask what that might be?"

The Principle Investigator was as perceptive as Tria. I wondered if I should mention what was currently chafing my posterior.

Tria spoke up for me. "It is a personal matter, and I don't think it would warrant taking any of your time."

Sael pursed her lips and looked back and forth at both of us. I really couldn't add anything useful to Tria's statement that wouldn't otherwise require answering more questions.

The Operative in Sael asked another anyway. "Will it involve killing lawless Throggs?"

I had a feeling she wouldn't leave it alone, so I gave her a vague reply. "Possibly."

She quickly threw out another. "Would it have to do with the attempt on the Troop Master's life?"

I had a feeling this was going to lead into another argument with Sael and I already had my fill of that. I shook my head no, and was going to say so as well, but Tria placed her hand on my leg and ran it well north of my knee, then squeezed. I blurted out an involuntary "yes" instead. My cheeks took on a rosy complexion, and I smiled at Sael through gritted teeth.

I guess Tria thought that Sael would not be interested in a private vendetta. She was proven wrong when Sael glared at us, then offered up her services, regardless of who the targets may turn out to be. I suspect Sael thought we were trying to get rid of her so we could do the Scrun mission on our own. That was only half true. We were wanting to ditch the Senior Operative, but were wanting to avoid being crass by saying it to her face. The rock was now being shoved further up my ass by a hard place. I saw what I thought was an out and took it.

"Sael, I am sure you need to get that freighter back, so your council don't start getting the idea we stole it from you."

For reasons unknown to me Sael looked shocked. She crossed two of her arms and placed the other two on the table. She started drumming her fingers while giving Tria a seriously ugly look. Tria rolled her pretty emerald green eyes upward and then turned to me.

"Nathan, the freighter is ours to keep. The Principle Investigator felt that the value the Chaalt people received from our trade, justified a reasonable increase in our returns. She was kind enough to include it in our compensation package."

Sael saw this misunderstanding, or more likely underestimation on my part, as gross insubordination on Tria's. I wish I had not made the mistake of telling her I would handle the matter accordingly. Rather than have her start bitching again, I took disciplinary action.

"Tria you are confined to my quarters until further notice!"

At first Tria looked surprised, then she got up and turned away to leave. When she was facing away from Sael, she winked and blew me a kiss. It didn't take but a second for Sael to decide she was being played for a fool. She got up and stormed out of the galley, voicing out loud her IST transmissions. She called her battleship overhead, then gave the freighter crew two minutes to assemble and prepare to teleport out. I called to her before she made it the down tube.

"Sael! I will IST you when we are ready to move on the Scrun base. You have my word!"

She spun and gave me her response. It wasn't just a single middle finger; it was four of them. I wondered how long it would take her to figure that one out. It wasn't as long as I hoped.

This was shaping up to be one hell of a day, and I was ready for it to be over. I heard a ruckus coming from up the corridor and new the sound well. Coonts and Klutch were having a profanity laden discussion that I did not want to hear any part of. I headed for my quarters at a dead run. I passed by them quickly enough, I only got looks of surprise, and not questions. They shrugged it off and went back to haranguing each other.

When I got to my cabin it was dark inside. Before I could summon my implants to give me some light, I heard Tria call to me in an alluring voice.

"Tarzan, Jane is sorry if she embarrassed you."

I woke more than eight hours later, well rested and hungry. To my disappointment I found myself alone. At least I would start a new day with a smile on my face. I pondered the previous day's proceedings. It would be difficult deciding which event was more gratifying, the windfall trade with the Chaalt, or finally getting to be king of the jungle. A few more seconds of deliberation made me laugh out loud and pound on my chest with both hands. I took a hot shower and put on a fresh uniform. Once I had a cup of Justice's dishwater coffee, I would be ready for whatever the day could throw at me.

I walked into the galley and found my crew. They had already eaten and were quietly conversing among themselves. I got a tray and sat next to Tria.

After exchanging greetings, I got down to business. "Has Tria given you a run down on my plan to pay Outpost 655 a visit?"

I got a positive response from them all. I took a couple bites of artificial scrambled eggs then pushed my tray away. It wasn't because they tasted all that bad, it was because the food processor could not add the peppers and onions my grandmother used to put in my eggs when I was young. I washed it down with more coffee and turned to the Troop Master. The visible places where he was injected with the nano weave compound were almost completely healed. He looked well, but I know he had to be uncomfortable. I also knew what a tough bastard he was.

"Klutch, are you ready to get back to breaking scat and taking titles?"

He smashed his fist into the table hard enough his food trays rebounded off the table onto the floor. "Yes Commander! I am growing fat and weak like a certain other member of the crew. I am done with laying around and doing nothing."

The barb directed at Coonts, made him swell up his chest and start flexing his oversized muscles. I had to get these clowns back out into the thick of things before they started rubbing me the wrong way. Sael was bad enough, but I always have the option of sending her home. That wouldn't be the case with these two, they were a product of my own making, and I had to live with them.

I called to Justice. "Is the Legacy ready to depart?"

"Yes Commander. The weapon stores are at capacity and your battle suits are all in the green. Xul has the Eagles prepped and ready to load on your order." Justice answered.

"Okay Justice, have Xul load the Eagles and prepare to get underway to Outpost 655."

"Roger that Commander, the matrix is charged and DEHD core operations are available."

11

Justice DEHD core jumped us to the edge of a nebula that skirted the space Outpost 655 occupied. It was familiar territory and we used the same stealth tactics we adopted the last time we visited the location. Justice made a stealthy pass by the outpost so we could get good scans on the area of operation. There was only light ship traffic, and the orbitals were vacant of parked spacecraft. Apparently, the site was no longer a hotbed for black market commerce. Justice gave us a report that gave us insight as to why.

"Commander, the majority of detected comms traffic is in the Murlak language. Our last visit, recorded the comms as predominantly Coram. I surmise there has been a major shift in the governmental landscape, and the new ruling party appears to be Murlak."

My crew and I were on the bridge at our normal stations. We were all observing the outpost from the unrestricted scrutiny of the view dome. Justice highlighted several Murlak assault shuttles parked on a ramp outside of the marketplace. It was not far from where Enochey's office used to be. If Justice was correct, the place was now a Murlak outpost. Everything we were seeing, was also substantiating that theory. If that turned out to be the case, the odds of Enochey still being alive were minute.

Klutch slapped his hands together and rubbed them. "Commander! If I remember correctly, Enochey was in power at the behest of Eiger. If Enochey is not running that zoo, then it means Eiger's clan has taken over. That makes all of the Throggs on that scat hole pirates. Unless our rules of engagement changed while I was in the med bay, they are all targets of opportunity!"

My crew members all turned to look at me. The looks of anticipation made the beast lurking in my brain, growl out its desire to kill my enemies.

I called out to Justice. "Alert Xul to prep Eagle one for a mission."

His reply made me smile. "Commander, Xul is going over the prelaunch check list and will be ready for departure by the time you arrive."

My crew was up and moving before I could even say gear up. Coonts and Klutch ran off the bridge. Tria waited at the downtube for me to catch up.

"Is there something troubling you Nathan?" she asked.

"I don't know that I would describe what I feel as troubled. It has more to do with priorities than anything else. I had hopes of getting information on the whereabouts of Cralmo or the Coram mercenaries that helped him escape. If this turns out to be a Murlak pirate base, it defeats the purpose of coming here. If one of us were to be injured, I would have regrets for choosing to continue in light of the intel we have uncovered."

"Nathan, they are pirates. They are using this location to shelter their activities. If we let them continue to operate unhindered, the blood of their victims will be on our hands."

Tria was right, and she had history on her side to prove the point. I had on a few occasions let criminals walk only to find out afterwards, they were murderous cowards that killed innocent beings without provocation. I had sworn more than once, that I would not let that happen again.

Tria slapped me on the ass hard enough to sting. "If we keep standing around, Coonts and Klutch will leave without us!"

I smiled and pulled her against me then kissed her. She embraced me and then stepped into the downtube. She gave me a long wet one as we tumbled slowly downward to our destination. We righted ourselves at the hangar deck and stepped off in time to see Klutch go running out of the ready room. His braying laugh echoing down the corridor. The profanity that followed him was all I needed to confirm Coonts had taken another sucker bet. He came scrambling out of the ready room yelling something about Klutch being a cheating Throgg. The balance of his profane oration suddenly caught in his throat when he noticed Tria and I. He promptly closed his helmet and disappeared into the hangar. Sitting next to my locker was a large mesh bag with Eiger's ceremonial armor inside. Justice already surmised I was going to take it with me. Tria and I quickly stepped out of our uniforms. We were in the process of putting on our suit liners when Justice gave us a sitrep.

171

"Commander, I have intercepted comms traffic originating from below the Sitch fighting pits. The language is in Murlak but has referenced the Coram."

"What are they saying Justice?"

"The Murlak is ordering the Coram on the other end of the communication, to clean the fighting pits in preparation for today's Sitch competition. The Murlak has also stated that high ranking members of Eiger's clan will be making a visit to the outpost to compete in the upcoming event. The Murlak is threatening the Coram with violence if the area is not spotless."

I looked over at Tria and a grim smile crossed her face. "Do you still doubt our purpose here?" She asked.

We stepped up into our battle armor. Justice's armor subsystem closed and secured them. My HUD came online and showed my weapons were all in the green and the suit's check list did the same. Justice gave us a rundown on the additional hardware and munitions he included in the strike team's loadout.

"Commander, the storage unit you refer to as your ass pack, is loaded with two large anti-matter scuttling charges and three Data Siphon Modules or DSMs for short. If the opportunity should arise, I encourage you to place the device on any computer systems you might encounter while on the outpost. I redesigned the DSM units you will be taking on this excursion. These units will not have to be recovered. They will send an encrypted data burst to your armor suit as long as you are not operating in heavily shielded areas. They are also protected by a molecular acid anti-tamper system. Should someone attempt to remove them, the acid capsule will burst and consume the equipment or combatants within a six-foot radius. I have included safety features that will disable the charge that sprays the acid in the event strike team members are in close proximity of the device when it is tampered with. Should that scenario occur, the acid will dissolve the module onto whatever piece of equipment it is attached too."

I loved the fact that Justice war gamed non-stop. He was always working on some new toy to include in our arsenal. Tria and I ran to the hangar. We saw Coonts and Klutch standing on the ramp that was extended from the rear of the assault shuttle. They were going over each other's armor and loadout. Justice had broadcast the sitrep on our group comms. The two had quit clowning around and were back to concentrating on the business at hand. I looked up at the cockpit window of Eagle one and saw Xul setting his switches in preparation for departure.

I called to him. "Xul, are we good to go?"

The little Grawl turned and gave me a thumbs up, then closed the helmet on his Zaen armor. Tria and I went over our kits. As we walked up the ramp, the Troop Master and Coonts tugged and slapped at our armor, double checking to make sure the ammo packs and our weapons were secured for combat. We walked into the back of the shuttle and strapped into our seats. Xul closed the door and engaged the stealth systems. He called to Justice over our group comms.

"Justice." Xul said. "We are ready for departure!"

Justice replied. "Optimal approach vector coming up in six-minutes."

I felt Justice grab onto the shuttle with the tow beam. He picked us up off the deck and we heard the telltale thud of Xul retracting the landing struts. The timer in my HUD counted down as I watched the exterior pressure monitor on the bulkhead drop in pace with it. In exactly six minutes the atmospheric pressure dropped to zero and the big hangar doors rapidly opened. Justice had the Legacy's hangar door pointed away from the outpost when he launched us into the void. Xul made a hard turn back toward the AO and accelerated to sub-light. Everything went eerily quiet when he shut down the star drives to coast the rest of the way to the objective. We were thirty minutes out at our current velocity. A view screen on the hull came to life with a magnified picture of the outpost. The glow of the atmospheric retention field distorted the surface features. I had my doubts that much had changed since our last visit. A red blinking circle lit up on the outpost's exterior. Xul made a small course correction and the circle turned green. Our destination was a large protrusion on the rocky surface. It was where our previous visit had logged the location of the subterranean Sitch fighting pits.

Justice called us with another sitrep. "Commander, a gunship of Galactic design has just transitioned into our area of operations. It is broadcasting encrypted code to the outpost. The code is known to me. It is an algorithm that was used by

Eiger and his pirate fleet to communicate. I will update my files and compare the messages to the partial translations that already exist in my data base."

"Roger that Justice, I think the comms are going to confirm the guests have arrived for the Sitch competition."

The way things were starting to develop, it sounded like we were going to be crashing a party. I was hoping someone would bring a cake, because I haven't had a bite of one since my nineteenth birthday.

Justice called to us again. "Commander, I have deciphered the Murlak communications and identified the captain of the gunship as a high-ranking member of Eiger's clan. He has identified himself as Gorgin. He has stated there are additional Murlak in transition to this location. One of which is Theodess, who is a lower house clan member to the Murlak royal family. The other is one of Eiger's siblings, Rastus."

Hot damn! Things were really starting to get interesting. I ran a bunch of new scenarios through my head. My machinations kicked out a new course of action that would be doable under the right circumstances.

"Justice, can your sensors give me a head count."

"Commander, I am detecting two hundred and sixty-six combatants wearing weapons with a power source. There is another twenty-nine in the Sitch pits, who appear to be unarmed and have no detectable power sources on them. This number may change if the target area has shielded areas other than Enochey's former office. The sensor data I have collected, shows the heat sources in the Sitch pits have lower body temperatures than the armed combatants. While this could possibly indicate a lack of clothing or a much cooler climate in the Sitch pits. That probability has a much lower percentage of accuracy than my theory the sensor returns are the surviving Coram that used to inhabit the base. If I add the information revealed in the communications, I further speculate the Coram are being used as slave labor by the Murlak."

The evil alien twin that prowled my subconscious thoughts, was applauding their misery. That part of me said the Coram got what they deserved for attempting to turn Coonts and Klutch over to Eiger. The Earthman still residing somewhere inside of me, didn't care for anyone being a slave, no matter how screwed up their moral compass was. It also made me wonder if Enochey was among them.

I made a call to the cockpit. "Xul, change of plans. Veer off and put us in a holding pattern."

"Roger that Commander, changing course and holding." Xul responded.

My crewmates gave me some dirty looks but held their tongues. Before I could ask Justice if he had overheard an ETA on the other arrivals, he called to us.

"Commander, I have another contact that has transitioned into our AO. I have no data on the ship design. It is smaller than a gunship class starship and is now sending encoded comms that match those transmitted by the Murlak gunship."

The party was going to happen soon and we were already dressed for the occasion. The plan I was putting together in my head was starting to gel. Justice called again with a translation of the messages.

"Commander, the ship has now been identified as the personal transport of Theodess. He will be making a direct approach to the outpost and a private interior dock is being made available to him."

Two down, and one to go. As soon as the last guest arrived, I was going to make sure they wouldn't be leaving.

"Xul." I called over our comms. "Follow that ship to its dock and find us someplace to hide until the other Murlaks arrives."

He quickly replied. "Affirmative Commander, altering course now."

I watched on the monitor as we turned in pursuit of the Murlak ship. It was making a slow leisurely approach and Xul had no problems maintaining our distance with our maneuvering thrusters. We entered the atmospheric retention bubble that surrounded the outpost and slowed so we would not close the distance between our ships. We were heading directly at a shear rock face that had three large hangar doors on it. The one on our right opened, and the ship slowly entered. On top of the bluff, well above the doors, sat two large storage tanks that held unknown contents. Xul masterfully pulled the nose of the shuttle up and over the top of the tanks and reversed our direction before setting us down in between them. We now had an excellent view of a large portion of the outpost. There was very little movement on the surface. We saw four different roving patrols. Each consisted of two Murlaks wearing medium body armor. They had beam rifles and sidearms. All had their helmets open and were carrying on conversations like they didn't have a care in the world. An evil grin formed on my lips. The bastards better enjoy it while they can.

My IST beeped and we all looked at each other at the same time. Justice was not taking any chances on using our standard communication network. He grouped commed us on our private IST system.

"Commander, another Murlak gunship has arrived, and is making its approach to the outpost. Communications confirm it is the arrival of Rastus. ETA twelve minutes."

I unstrapped and stood up. "Okay let's get ready to do our thing!"

My strike team stood with me and we closed our helmets. We gave each other one final inspection. Justice gave us another alert.

"Commander, the gunship has taken a stationary position next to Gorgin's ship, and they are both launching shuttles."

"Roger that Justice, let me know where they are headed."

I formed up behind Klutch and next to Tria. I felt Coonts rap me on the back of my ammo pack. I did the same to Klutch and he held his hand over the ramp release.

"Say when Commander!" Klutch commed.

"Commander, the shuttles are on a course that will take them directly to your location." Justice warned.

"Roger that, we are holding!" I replied.

Klutch suddenly disappeared in front of me and his blue outlined avatar appeared in my HUD. "Stealth systems on and in the green!" he called.

We did the same and acknowledged our systems were working to specs. I visually verified what my HUD was confirming. The strike team was cloaked and our negation equipment was activated.

Justice gave us a final sitrep. "Commander the center hangar door has opened and both shuttles are lining up for a final approach."

I rapped Klutch twice on the shoulder. "Go Troop Master! Let's follow them inside before the door closes."

Klutch hit the ramp release and the artificial lighting of the outpost flooded the inside of Eagle One. He boosted hard for the edge of the bluff with me, Tria and Coonts in formation with him. We nosed down over the cliff face in time to see the trailing shuttle just start to enter the opening. Klutch kept us high over the rear of the shuttle. We entered the opening against the rocky overhead. Klutch steered us to an observation point nestled amongst the large atmosphere scrubbers and duct work hanging from the ceiling. The hangar door closed and the equipment we were using for cover, roared to life. So far, so good. No alarms and the fools below us were carrying on like this was just another party night.

It had been years since I was last here. The Coram that used to be in charge, was at least smart enough to have alert and watchful patrols in locations throughout the outpost. The Murlak now running this place must be thinking his numbers would discourage anyone from messing with them. Complacency has a tendency to make you lazy. It might also end up being a word used in the epitaph on your headstone.

At the dock furthest from us, was a very large heavily armed Coram shuttle. I knew this because we owned a smaller version of it. Next to it sat the two pirate shuttles one behind the other, and below us, was the sleek hull of Theodess's ship. A ramp extended from the hull and a procession of guards marched out on either side of a

Murlak with a large assortment of adornments on his chest. We assumed this was Theodess. Two Murlaks came over from the shuttles. I had my HUD magnify and record their faces. The two had to be Gorgin and Rastus. They waited to meet Theodess at the base of the ramp. They gathered and exchanged pleasantries. The Murlak wearing the fancy uniform swung his arm up and beckoned toward his ship. The cargo doors parted and another ramp extended. A handler came forward pulling four Sitch that were tethered together. The bizarre cone shaped creatures were wearing bright shiny chainmail body armor. I heard Rastus yell out an order. A large doorway on a side wall opened and two Coram attempted to run to where Rastus was standing. The process was difficult because they were both wearing leg shackles on their big grasshopper like legs. The chains clinking out a cadence with each step they took. Rastus kicked one of them and shoved the other in the direction of the Sitch. They went as fast as possible to the handler and both took the tethers from him. With the handler in tow they pulled the Sitch along toward the big doorway they had come from. When the Sitch were inside,

Gorgin yelled out more orders. Four more Coram came hobbling out of the entrance and went to the two Murlak pirate shuttles. The ramps on the shuttles came down and the Coram disappeared inside. Several minutes later they came out pulling more Sitch. These were wearing dark armor with some kind of insignia emblazoned on their flanks. The Coram pulled them toward the tunnel. Apparently, all the arriving dignitaries had brought Sitch to do battle in the pits. I guess having a mindless beast doing your bleeding for you, was all the rage. I presumed the callous bastards giving the orders, never had the opportunity, or knew what it felt like. We were going to change that.

12

When the Sitch were out of sight, the doorway was secured behind them. Gorgin and Rastus escorted Theodess to the far end of the dock and through another doorway that had a sign over it that translated to "spectator seating" in Galactic standard. That must have been the signal for the crews of the three ships to debark and go inside to find a seat. Seventeen crewmembers of the royal transport, and six more from the two pirate shuttles made their way to the spectator entrance.

I called to Klutch. "Troop Master, let's take a look inside Theodess's transport."

I pointed at the pirate shuttles. "Coonts, secure those shuttles. I don't want them leaving here under their own power."

"What about the Coram gunship?" he asked.

"Leave it for now, we are going to have a busy schedule as it is." I replied.

He threw me a thumbs up and moved off to take care of business.

"Move out Klutch!" I said.

This would be a fast trip down, because the ship was almost directly beneath us. We made the necessary adjustment and cut our gravity thrusters. We freefell the hundred or so yards in a few seconds and arrested our falls mere feet off the ships hull. We would not be using a hatch just in case there were boarding alarms. The sleek contours of the ship did not hint as to where the bridge might be. As was usually the case, we were going to improvise.

"Klutch, I don't care where you do it, make us a hole."

Tria quickly made a suggestion. "Somewhere forward!" she said.

The Troop Master ran toward the front of the ship with Tria and I close behind him. We were scanning in all directions in case someone didn't like the outcome of a Sitch match, and came back to brood about it on one of the ships. Klutch held up a fist and we stopped about a quarter of the ship's length to the nose. Her leaned over and gave us a good portal the first try.

I grabbed the back of his ammo pack before he could jump first. "If you don't see us by the time the portal starts blinking, join up with us."

The look on his face did not convey a pleasant acceptance of my order. He gritted his teeth and nodded without comment. I was glad the atmosphere scrubbers were still roaring away above us. I jumped in with Tria at my back. We found ourselves in a large passageway. We were fortunate it was empty. Tria was facing the opposite direction from me.

"Nathan, I can see the bridge just ahead and it is unoccupied. I do not believe they would leave the ship docked at a pirate base without someone standing watch at the hatch."

I turned and followed her forward so we could both take a look at the bridge. Klutch came dropping into the passage behind us with a thump. He saw our position and called to us.

"Commander, I'll go aft and secure the machine spaces."

The look on the Troop Master's face said he was in the mood to kill something, so I waved him on.

Coonts gave us a report on our IST net. "One hostile down in shuttle two. I am moving to shuttle one now."

"Roger that Coonts. When you are done, I need you to keep surveillance over the area until we join back up with you."

"Affirmative." He replied.

Tria pulled a DSM out of her equipment pack then pointed into the bridge. I nodded my approval thinking I should have thought of it first. Just outside of the ship's bridge was a set of up and down gravity tubes. I peeked into the one with the prominent down pointing chevron over the entrance. Tria came back from the bridge and we stepped in together. It was a short drop of about twenty feet. When we stepped out onto the deck below, we were almost exactly that same distance to the boarding hatch. Leaning against the opening was a Murlak in a dark gray uniform that had a single metal displayed on his chest. His beam rifle was slung over his shoulder and his helmet was on a nearby console. He was busy eating a green fruit or vegetable that was about the size of a grapefruit. It must have been good, because he was gnawing away at it like there was no tomorrow. The thought crossed my mind to let him finish, because for him, that would indeed be the case.

I started to draw my fighting knife and move in his direction. Tria stepped in front of me and held up an index finger. I stopped as she carefully walked up to the Murlak. She was maybe a couple of feet from him when he quit chewing on his snack and squinted to where Tria was approaching. Our suits could not give us perfect invisibility in bright light. The results were very good while standing still, but movement gave minute distortions to the return picture seen by others. This must have been the case, because the Murlak's eye grew large. He dropped his munchie and opened his mouth to yell. Tria rapidly closed the gap between them and backhanded him hard in the face. His head bounced off the edge of the hull and he went down like he was poleaxed. His head no longer had a natural shape to it. I was going to call Klutch and ask if he had found anybody else aboard when he came jogging up the corridor.

"Commander, I found two techs in the machine spaces. What they were doing to each other had nothing to do with the ship's maintenance. I stashed their bodies under the drive couplings. I also strapped a couple of grenades to the energy transfer switches. If the pilot engages the gravity drive, the switches will go boom. Repairs could take a day or longer"

Coonts called out an alert. "Commander! Two pirates and a member of Theodess's crew just exited the spectator entrance. They are moving at a rapid pace in my direction. I cannot be sure, but I think they are going to board shuttle number two. If they look in the shuttles hold, they will find their comrade's body."

"Roger that. Let them board then make sure they don't leave. I am sending Klutch to back you."

"That won't be necessary Commander, I can take care of the problem!" Coonts replied.

His statement irritated me. "Coonts! that was not a request!"

"Affirmative Commander, holding for Klutch." He acknowledged.

I turned to Klutch. "Troop Master give Coonts a hand. I want the job done quietly with no dicking around. You got that?"

"Yes Commander. Give the dick a hand and no Coontsing around."

Tria gave Klutch a healthy shove out the boarding hatch before I could put a boot in his ass. A beep in my HUD was accompanied by a message the DSM had just uploaded the data collected from the ship's computers.

Tria grabbed my hand. "Nathan we should remove the siphon module and reuse it."

We went to the bridge and Tria pulled the module and put it back in her kit. She suggested we make a quick search of the ship. It was a good idea. You never know what you might find. Tria took the lift and went up a deck. I took the other and went down. I found the crew quarters and galley. I gave the crew quarters and officer's cabins a cursory inspection. Not seeing anything of interest I moved on to the galley. I saw nothing to warrant wasting any more time. As I headed for the exit, my eyes locked onto the contents of two good size crates sitting on a table. Both were filled with what looked like cupcakes. Apparently, his royal assness was going to have a celebration when the contests were over. I picked one up and inspected it. The icing on top was a little sloppy but all in all it looked pretty good to me. Since cake used to be a favorite of mine, and I hadn't tasted any in years, I had to know.

I asked my suit subsystem "Are these edibles?"

"I detect no toxins and assume they are considered palatable by the Murlaks." The AI replied.

I thought what the heck. I opened my visor and took a bite. The icing was sickening sweet and the filling was like jelly made of anchovies. I spit it out. I should have known the Murlaks would have poor taste and threw it back into the crate. I heard something behind me and quickly closed my helmet and turned around. Tria was coming up the passage. I grabbed one of the cakes and held it up.

"Look Tria, the Throggs made cupcakes for a party."

She cleared her war mask from her visor and squinted at me. I guess she had no idea what a cupcake was.

She swatted it from my hand. "Nathan. that is Torba. The topping is made from the sweetened fatty muscles of a deceased crustacean's anus. The filling is the contents of its decomposing entrails. The Murlak feed them to their Sitch as a training treat. Come, I have found Theodess's cabin"

As much as I wanted a tooth brush and some mouthwash, I nodded to her and followed. When I got back to the Legacy, I was going to talk to the evil robot about my subsystem's response to my enquiry. The maniacal machine knew just because something was not toxic, didn't necessarily make it edible as well. The AI claiming that Torba were palatable to the Murlak was now suspect.

Tria waved me to the lift tubes. We jumped in and were whisked to the very top of the ship. When we exited, we went aft again. Tria pointed at the entrance to Theodess's private quarters. It had a small upraised flat panel about the size of my hand on the right side of the vault like door. On the left, was a key pad lacking any numbers or letters on the keys. The chances of us randomly discovering the codes, was very unlikely. I was going to call the Troop Master and find out if him and Coonts were done screwing around.

Justice's battle suit subsystem let me know, not having the code was not an issue. "Commander, the data siphon module has recorded the first officer's emergency access code."

Justice highlighted the key sequence and Tria entered it. The door opened, revealing the suite took up most of the deck. It was admittedly opulent as compared to the rest of the ship. We didn't touch anything until we looked in the sleeping quarters. Against one wall was a sizable vault and it did not have any visible means of opening it. My suit subsystem didn't offer up another miracle code, so we were going to have to use our skeleton key of choice. I tried calling Klutch but my comms was being blocked by some very sophisticated shielding. Tria and I retreated back the way we came. When we stepped back into the lift tube, our comms came to life with Coonts reporting in.

"Commander, Klutch and I are on overwatch awaiting additional orders."

I called back to him. "Coonts hold your position and send the Troop Master back to our location."

His acknowledgement almost made me laugh. "Thank you, Commander!"

A few minutes later Klutch showed up and we led him back to Theodess's suite. Out of curiosity, I inquired as to what the Murlaks were up to.

"Commander, the pirates had a drug deal going with Theodess's first officer. My guess would be they didn't want Theodess knowing anything about it. The pirate Coonts killed in the second Murlak shuttle, was preparing the drugs so they could be quickly transferred to Theodess's ship. I think they wanted it to appear as thought everyone was watching the Sitch competitions. The Three Throggs Coonts and I whacked, snuck out to do the deal. They thought they could get it done and blend back into the crowd before anyone noticed they had slipped out." Klutch explained.

He handed over several credit vouchers. "They won't be needing these anymore." He said.

We walked through Theodess's cabin and into his sleeping quarters. I pointed at the vault and Klutch nodded with a goofy smile. He activated the portal device and got a hole big enough for Tria and I to step inside. There were trinkets of every description hanging on racks. I assumed it was Theodess's personal jewelry. We also found small-stacks of Containium bars and other valuable minerals. We pocketed all of them including a sizable stack of credit vouchers. The Primitive Planet Protection fund was going to receive another windfall in the near future. I saw a very ornate decanter sitting on a shelf with matching tumblers. I picked it up and shook it, verifying it had liquid contents. I pulled the stopper and sniffed it.

While I wouldn't say it had a pleasing scent, I couldn't say it smelled all that bad either. I filled a tumbler almost to capacity, and tossed it back. It was actually pretty good, but burned all the way down. It managed to cleanse most of the taste of dead crab ass out of my mouth.

When Tria turned around, and saw what I was doing, she gave me an incredulous look. "Nathan! What are you doing?" she yelled.

She grabbed the bottle from me and sniffed at the contents before throwing it to the floor. "You are fortunate that is not toxic!"

It seemed that I was just lucky that way. The portal started blinking so we ended our search and stepped out of the vault. Tria was still giving me strange looks, so I waved at the Troop Master.

"Klutch, let's join up with Coonts, move out!"

We followed the Troop Master out of the ship and under the nose of the first pirate shuttle. Coonts was perched on the landing strut and jumped down to join us. I pointed to the access doors where the Coram had taken the Sitch. We ran across the dock to the large metal doors. Tria, Coonts and

Klutch took a knee with their weapons pointed at the spectator entrance. I tried the latch on the doors with no luck. They were locked from the inside. I put some muscle to it. Even with the suit assisted servos, all I managed to do was bend the outside handle out away from the door. This was getting us nowhere. I was going to move to the spectator entrance when Klutch made a suggestion.

"Commander, you should try knocking."

I gave him a skeptical look, but went ahead and tried for the hell of it. I rapped on the door three times then stood back to see what would happen. After a couple of minutes of nothing, I was ready to move on to the other door. As I turned away, I heard the loud clank of a bar latch being thrown open. The door creaked open about a foot and a Murlak wearing a battle helmet stuck his head out. He looked puzzled right up until Klutch slammed his shoulder into the door pinning his neck. He let out a yell that was promptly cut off when I grabbed his head and savagely twisted it a hundred and eighty degrees. Klutch let his weight off of the door and the guard's body fell out of the opening. The Murlak now had a wonderful view of his ass. The Throgg probably

197

thought guarding the Coram was the worst thing to ever happen to him. He was never going to know just how wrong he was.

Klutch jumped over the body and bolted through the door. Tria and I went after him while Coonts took up a position covering our flank. We found ourselves in a poorly lit tunnel and our audio pickups were assaulted by the sounds of a roaring crowd. One side of the tunnel was lined with metal barred cells. The first five had Coram sitting and laying about the floors. Several of the Coram jumped up and stood at the bars when they saw the body of the guard sliding across the rocky floor from the doorway. A murmur started among the prisoners and was growing in volume.

Tria ran to the cells and uncloaked momentarily. "Keep quiet if you want to live!" her battle suit translator called out in the Coram dialect.

The prisoners immediately went quiet. "Is Enochey among you?" Tria asked.

One of the prisoners called out in a low voice. "He is removing the dead Sitch from the arena. He will be at the arena entrance with the other two guards."

I moved to Tria's side. "Is the Coram shuttle in the dock void worthy?" I asked the prisoners.

One of the prisoners from the next cell bulled through the gathering at the bars. "Yes! If I had the help of some of the others, I can have it ready to launch in a very short time!"

I grabbed the corroded bars of the door and pulled until I got a warning light in my HUD. The latch broke and the door opened. Tria and Klutch helped me, and we popped the doors on the other cells.

"Commander!" Coonts called. "I have two Murlak leaving the spectator entrance. It is Gorgin and Rastus, and it looks like they are headed for the shuttles. What are your orders?"

"Tria, give Coonts a hand. I want them alive. Hold them in one of the shuttles, we will be done here shortly." I told her.

I warned the Coram prisoners to wait until Klutch gave them the all clear, before going to their shuttle. I told them they were not to leave until I gave them clearance, or my ship would shoot them down. They had no problems with that scenario, as long as they had a chance of getting the hell out of here.

One of the Coram called to me. "You must not kill the guards until the next match has begun. Once Enochey has pulled the dead Sitch from the arena and the victor is put in its cage, they will release others for combat. The guards and Enochey will not be missed until the match ends."

"How many matches have taken place?" I asked.

"The first has just ended. Enochey and the guards will be at the front of the tunnel very soon!" The Coram answered.

I ran the clock in my head and reviewed the timing. We had been inside the dock for just over an hour. It would have taken maybe fifteen- or twenty-minutes, for Theodess and company to get settled before the first match started. I figured we had thirty minutes at the most, to wrap this up before the next match ended.

Klutch interrupted my planning. "Commander, I can see Enochey at the entrance to the tunnel!"

I looked toward the arena, and sure enough I could see Enochey with a harness strapped around him. The harness had a length a chain that was hooked to a dead Sitch. Enochey was no longer the obese alien I remembered. He was now so thin I hardly recognized him. The crowd was booing and jeering his efforts at pulling the dead combatant from the arena. One of the guards was leading a bloody chainmail clad Sitch along with a tether, while the other kicked and berated Enochey. The crowd was throwing all kinds of crap out of the bleachers onto him, some of which was also hitting the guards. If Enochey was getting this treatment for the past few years, he had paid dearly for his betrayal.

13

Enochey finally dragged the dead Sitch into the tunnel. He fell in a heap wheezing from the effort. The Murlaks did not cut him an inch of slack. The guard that had been kicking him, had something stuck on the side of his helmet. He took it off and slammed it into Enochey's back. The Coram clinched his teeth and stifled his grunt of pain.

The guard raged down at him. "You will clean that scat off my helmet! If you were not so slow it would not have happened!"

The other guard put the Sitch he was leading into one of the cells and came over to where Enochey lay on the rocky floor. He pulled his helmet off and drew it back to slam down on the Coram. I wrapped my arm around his neck and lifted him off the ground. It choked off the foul words he had for Enochey. I took his helmet, and as his partner turned toward me, I crushed his skull with it. He went down in a heap next to Enochey. The Coram's mouth gaped wide and he pushed himself away from the corpse. He rolled over and gawked in terror at the other Murlak who appeared to be floating in the air. I jerked my arm to my chest, snapping the guard's neck, then let him fall to the ground.

I uncloaked and stared down at the pitiful wretch that lay at my feet.

"There is always the chance this would have been your fate, even if you had not betrayed my crew, and broke a contract with me."

At first the Coram stared terrified and bewildered at my war mask, then understanding creeped into his brain. He started pushing himself back away from me.

"YOU!" He screeched. "After all this time you have come back to kill me?"

"No, Enochey. I did not come here to kill you. It looks like death would have been better than the way the Murlaks are treating you."

The noise from the bleachers was taking on a note of nastiness. The crowd was growing restless and impatient. I reached down and pulled the Coram upright.

"Now that I know you are alive; I have a use for you. It remains to be seen if you are ready to change your deceitful ways. If you decide you are, I will see to it you get out of here alive. I don't have a lot of time to explain, so you need to make up your mind now."

Enochey shook his head affirmative and then held up his hand. "Wait! This will buy us some time to escape."

He went to a control console and I watched him enter a sequence of commands. The pens holding two of the Sitch, opened and the beasts trudged out into the arena. The crowd roared their pleasure. The Sitch turned on each other and started flailing away.

Tria called and let me know they were holding Gorgin and Rastus. I told her to send Coonts for Eiger's armor. It took a second for her to acknowledge my order.

"I will relay the message." She replied.

I called Klutch. "What is the status of the Coram shuttle?"

"The prisoners are in terrible shape and are working as fast as they can. They have the powerplant on line and are working on the gravity drives. I am trying to help, but there is little I can do to speed the process.

It is going to take another fifteen to twenty minutes to run the checklists and make sure this thing is void worthy."

"Roger that, I will go to plan "B". Let me know as soon as they are ready to launch."

Klutch sounded skeptical. "I didn't know we had a plan "B" Commander."

"I always have a plan "B". Just get that shuttle ready to launch, and I will get back with you."

Enochey pulled off his makeshift harness and threw it to the ground. He looked up at me. "Not long after you left me here, I thought things might get back to normal, but Rastus came and informed me that Eiger's take of the outpost profits would increase to forty percent. That drove all but a few merchants from the market place. When the word finally leaked that Cesil was killed on my watch, Rastus came back with more than two hundred crack pirate troops, and attacked our garrison for not defending his clan members. Most deserted me as did the rest of the population that once called the outpost home. Those that fled, took every available transport after the initial attack. That left the rest of us trapped and badly outnumbered. I tried to negotiate with the pirates, and surrendered myself in exchange for my remaining troops lives. They agreed, and when we laid down our weapons the pirates slaughtered all but the few you see with me."

"If all of the transports were taken, what about the shuttle in the dock?" I asked.

"It was owned by another warlord named Oleg. He was one of my clan siblings and came to do business with me. The Murlaks convinced him to land. Him and most of his crew, were slaughtered, and the shuttle was hidden in the dock." Enochey replied.

"So, you are telling me there are no civilians on the outpost?"

Enochey looked surprised by the question. "No, there are only pirates. This place was once one of the most profitable black markets in the sector. I know that must sound distasteful to you, but we did have our principles. We sold weapons and supplies, but never drugs. Of course, there were small quantities being traded secretly among some, but when they were discovered, they were banished. Now this outpost is one of the biggest manufacturing and suppliers of illicit drugs in the quadrant."

That explained the strange events going on with the drugs and Theodess's crew. The first officer was smuggling drugs back to the

Murlak home worlds where they were most probably banned. The plan "B" I mentioned to Klutch now had legitimate roots, and was quickly turning into a plan of substance.

I called Tria. "Is Coonts back with Eiger's armor?"

"Yes Commander, what should we do with it?" Tria inquired.

"Tell Coonts that I don't care how he does it, but I want that armor on Rastus. When he gets that done, he is to make Gorgin and Rastus put the drugs they sold to Theodess's first officer, along with the dead bodies, in the royal transport's cargo hold, and wait for me there."

"Roger that, I have a quick question?"

"What would that be Tria?"

"I heard Klutch grumbling something about a plan "B" Is there something you would like to tell me?"

"It will all be self-explanatory very soon. I am sending Enochey your way. Please keep an eye on him until I finish here."

"Nathan, do not let that monster in your head, talk you into doing something stupid!"

Tria promptly killed the comms connection. I could not blame her for being a little testy. In the past, I had done some very questionable acts that could have led to my death, and possible serious injury to the members of my crew. We have been fortunate that those occasions for the most part, worked out in our favor.

I turned to Enochey. "You are to go out of the tunnel, and a member of my strike team will meet with you. I want you to open all three of the dock doors. If you chose not to follow my orders, I will leave you on this scat hole."

Enochey nodded and ran as best he could up the tunnel. I looked out into the arena. The two Sitch in the pit were bloody messes, and still going at it. I looked over at the next contestants. The pirate Sitch wearing black armor with a coat of arms emblazoned on it, was closest to me. I pulled one of my anti-matter scuttling charges from my ass pack. I set it for remote detonation and reached through the bars, shoving it securely under the Sitch's armor.

"Sorry Betsy, but your about to be the bearer of really bad news." I mumbled under my breath.

I went to the control console and entered the same switch sequence that Enochey entered. The cells opened and the two new Sitch contestants marched forward into the arena. The crowd went quiet for a second, then some started booing and hissing, while the majority of others cheered the foursome on. Whoever the controllers were, they decided to make the best of it, and the two new combatants started beating the hell out of each other. As I turned and ran up the tunnel, the fervor of the crowd changed for the better. Plan "B" was now set to go.

I called Klutch for a sitrep. "Troop Master, is the shuttle ready to launch?"

"Close enough Commander. They have a major fault on one of the gravity drives, but the Coram say they can get underway with just one if they have to. Once they are clear of the atmospheric retention field, they can engage the star drives."

"Roger that, tell them to prepare to get underway. Enochey will not be joining them. They are free to go on my signal, and advise them to make it someplace very, very far away."

"Okay Commander, they want to know what the signal will be?"

"They will know when it happens. Meet me at Theodess's ship."

"On my way Commander!" Klutch replied.

My next calls were going to start the ball rolling and there would be no bringing it back. "Xul have you got a copy?"

"Yes Commander, what are your orders?"

"I want you to clear the area and hold at the far side of the outpost until I call you. Be aware, a Coram shuttle will be departing shortly and they will be in a hurry. Please feel free to eliminate any pop-up ground targets."

"Affirmative Commander, moving now." Xul acknowledged.

I boosted hard for the tunnel entrance to the docks. Landing at the entrance doors, I stopped long enough to pick up a set of shackles the Coram once wore. I pushed the door open and stepped out, carefully holding the lock bar so it would fall in place when I pulled the door closed. My crew was waiting in the open cargo bay of Theodess's ship, and all were looking in my direction. They got a warning in their HUDs when I armed the anti-matter charge.

My HUD warning system went from red, to orange to yellow, when I landed on the transport's ramp. That was good enough for me, but my crew felt differently, and gave me the stink eye. Gorgin and Rastus were sitting on the drug crates eyeing us nervously. Eiger's helmet was at Rastus's feet, and his face a swollen bloody mess. I looked over at Coonts, and he tossed his hands up like he had no idea what happened to him. Enochey, aside from looking like warmed-over scat, seemed to have found his will to live. I handed him the shackles and his mouth fell open. I told him to put them on Rastus, and his expression quickly changed. Now he looked jubilant.

Rastus yelled at Enochey as he came forward. "If you put those on me you Coram piece of scat, I will roast you alive over my ancestral fire. This madness will come to a halt very soon. I have more than two hundred well trained troops…"

I chose that moment to detonate the charge. There was a tremendous thump and the whole complex bucked under our feet. The tunnel door to the pit was blown from its hinges, and hurled through the viewscreen of the pirate shuttle. The cockpit started smoking and burst into flames. Rocks and dirt dislodged from the overhead and came showering down. The pilot of the Coram assault shuttle, accurately determined the massive explosion was his cue to get the hell out of Dodge. The shuttle took off like it was shot from a cannon.

When the clouds of dust finally settled, we saw that Enochey, Gorgin and Rastus were all hugging the deck. Tria cleared her war mask and shook her head. She had a look of annoyance on her pretty face. I smiled back and shrugged my shoulders.

Justice commed me a warning on my IST. "Commander the two Murlak gunships are getting underway. I believe it is their intention to stop the Coram shuttle from departing the area."

"Destroy the gunships Justice, then make sure we are not interrupted before we finish our business here."

"Affirmative Commander, engaging now." The AI acknowledged.

Rastus and Gorgin got to their feet. They both had looks of rage on their faces. Gorgin hissed between clinched teeth. "Our gunships will kill you all for the murderous act you have committed!'"

Justice's timing could not have been more perfect. There was a star bright flash that lit the entire dock and took several seconds to fade. It was quickly followed by another of equal intensity.

I pointed up and over my shoulder. "I sure hope that wasn't the gunships you were going to use to kill us all."

We could hear weapons fire echoing from somewhere outside of the docks. Xul was most assuredly putting the final touches on a seriously bad day for the Murlak pirates.

I called to Justice. "Can your scanners identify the drug manufacturing facilities?"

"Affirmative Commander. Scanning for telltale emissions... I have detected three potential targets. All three are emitting chemical gases associated with the manufacture of a variety of illicit substances."

"Thank you, Justice, transfer the targeting data to Eagle One."

"Transferring now Commander." He said.

I looked over at Enochey. He quietly stood staring at me, most probably wondering about his future. He knew he didn't have a ticket out of this place without catching a ride with me. It probably crossed his mind more than once, that this could be his end, if I decided he was of no use.

I pointed at the shackles. "I believe you were going to make use of those." I said with just a hint of sarcasm.

Enochey reached down and snatched the manacles off the deck. He hurried over to Rastus and clamped them on his wrist. Gorgin spit at Enochey as he backed away.

The Coram was so used to the vile act, it did not faze him. A high order explosion somewhere in the distance made us all flinch. I looked over my shoulder in time to see large pieces of a building raining down somewhere close to the former marketplace.

Xul called over our group comms. "Target one is destroyed. Vectoring for target two."

Another tremendous blast shook the docks and the Murlaks went prone again. Enochey was now immune to the spectacle, and gawked at the flying debris.

Xul called out a warning. "Commander, the third target is close to your location. I would not classify it as danger close, but I would caution you to take cover if you have not already done so."

"Roger that, wait one." I called to the Grawl pilot.

Tria, Coonts and Klutch heeded the warning, and stepped farther back into the cargo hold. I put a hand on Enochey's shoulder, and pulled him along with me.

"Okay Xul, let her rip."

His response made me smile. "Ripping now Commander!"

The Murlaks were pushing themselves up off the deck when a massive thunderclap shook the dock and showered it with flying debris. Gorgin and Rastus were knocked back into the drug crates, overturning them. The contents scattering across the hold.

Xul called again. "All targets eliminated and the area appears clear. I am standing by for further orders Commander."

The smoke from the burning shuttle was getting thicker by the minute. The front half of the pirate shuttle was a raging inferno and there was a good chance it might explode. It was time to wrap this up and make good our escape.

"Meet us at the dock behind the Murlak royal transport, we are almost finished here."

"Roger Commander." Xul replied.

Gorgin and Rastus got to their feet. Gorgin again spit in Enochey's direction.

"Our clan will avenge this outrage. All your siblings will be hunted down and dismembered. Their heads will adorn the walls of our waste stations!" the pirate yelled.

I had heard just about enough of the belligerent fool's endless scat. I reached down to the corpse of the ship's First Officer, and drew his sidearm from its holster. I held it out to Enochey who misconstrued my intentions. He stepped back with a look of dread on his face. I flipped the weapon over in my hand, and held it out to him grip first.

"Enochey, do you have something you would like to say to Gorgin?"

The Coram slowly reached out and took the sidearm. The look of fear faded from his face. He turned to Gorgin, who was still adding to his list of threats, but promptly stopped when the weapon swung in his direction. We would never find out if the pirate was attempting to apologize for his rant. When the Murlak opened his mouth to speak, Enochey shot him in it. The top half of the Murlaks head blew off, spraying the bulkhead and Rastus. I was going to commend the Coram for his marksmanship, and retrieve the pistol. Before I could, he turned and did the same to Rastus. Apparently, Enochey had a lot to say, and developed a stutter while doing it. That wasn't exactly what I wanted to happen, but what was done was done. There was no denying the look of satisfaction on Enochey's face. He calmly walked over and cleaned the grip of the pistol on the dead First Officer's uniform, then placed it in the corpse's hand.

The indifferent looks I got from my crewmembers, said they were good with the outcome. It would require me to alter my plans slightly to offset the demise of Rastus. After thinking about it for a few more seconds, I decided the outcome did take care of any loose ends that could point to us as being the culprits behind the misfortune that befell the outpost. The Murlaks will obviously wonder, but the confusion of Rastus wearing the royal armor and the drugs aboard the royal transport should cloud their determinations.

I called to Justice. "Can you corrupt the ship's AI so there will be no records of our presence?"

"Yes Commander. I will need one of your battle suits to make hand contact with the bridge master computer."

I pointed at Coonts and he gave me a quick nod and ran to the lifts. We heard the approach of Eagle one and turned around to see the boarding ramp lower on the cloaked shuttle. I did not have to tell Enochey he would be coming with us. As soon as the ramp touched the dock, he ran aboard. The royal transport's lighting started flickering like a strobe light and a loud hiss was coming from the PA system. Coonts came running from the lifts and gave me a thumbs up. We boarded Eagle One and took off in a steep ascent to rendezvous with the Legacy. Justice pulled us into the hangar with the tow beam and turned hard away from the outpost, quickly leaving it behind.

14

I ordered Justice to make a standard transition to outpost 9765. He informed me it would take more the twenty-seven hours to reach that destination. I was good with that because I had questions to ask Enochey. I also had no intention of revealing any of the Legacy's capabilities to him. First, we needed to clear the air concerning his past transgressions against us. Enochey must have been thinking the same thing. Since Enochey was already familiar with Coonts and Klutch's species, there was no point in hiding their identities because they were already known to him. Tria and I on the other hand, were not ready to disclose ours to the Coram. As soon as Coonts and Klutch retracted their helmet's, the Coram immediately started begging for their forgiveness. Klutch surprisingly was first to grant his wish.

"For someone whose has been a prisoner as long as you have, and still able to demonstrate the sidearm accuracy you displayed, is commendable. You have my forgiveness for your betrayal, but be warned, if you ever pull that scat on me or the members of my clan ever again, I will pull your limbs from your body and flail you to death with them. Are we clear?" the Troop Master said in a menacing voice.

"Yes!" Enochey said. "You have my allegiance, and I swear to you, I will never betray your trust again."

Coonts was not so easily swayed by words alone. He wanted consequences in case the Coram chose to have another lapse in judgement. I could tell his think tank had come to a boil, and he was using his considerable IQ to come up with contingencies.

Coonts pulled Tria and I aside and whispered to us. "Commander, what if we were to fit Enochey with one of our IST units. They are tamper proof, and it would allow us to monitor his whereabouts and conversations at any time. It would be the perfect way to keep tabs on his whereabouts if you choose to release him. We tell him it is a tracking device that is capable of killing him if he decides to go back on his word. He will never know if it is actually a fact or not."

Justice weighted in on the conversation. "Coonts, the IST units can easily be altered to cause death on command, or death by tampering. It would only take alternate programming of the nanites in the IST's anti-tamper systems. Instead of only dissolving the IST implant, they could also be programed to attack the host."

That little revelation was and eye opener. We now wondered if the Chaalt did the same with the units they implanted in our heads? Justice quickly quashed that line of thinking.

"Commander, there is no need to worry if the Chaalt have installed weaponized ISTs into you or the other members of our clan. I thoroughly examined the Chaalt design architecture when I chose to reverse engineer the technology. The nanite programming will only become active after the host is deceased, or their brain function is reduced to an irreparable vegetative state."

Hearing it from Justice was good enough for me. Now I had to decide if I really wanted some of our best tech to be installed in someone of Enochey's questionable background. Tria and Coonts both made up their minds and thought it was an excellent idea.

"Nathan" Tria said. "We should tell Enochey that the price of an allegiance with our clan, is a weaponized tracker. If he refuses the offer, we will know he cannot be trusted."

Tria had a valid point and Coonts was nodding in agreement. I could find no faults in their reasoning. It would be like having an insurance policy against future treachery. We walked back over to Enochey.

"Enochey" I said. "I am going to give you two choices, but you have to decide now which it will be. Choice number one, is to let us implant a weaponized tracker in you. It is to insure you are not going to betray us again. If the AI controller detects duplicity, the device will permanently incapacitate you. I know this may sound distasteful to you, but we do have our principles." I said with just a hint of sarcasm.

When the look of shock and fear subsided from the Coram's face, I continued. "There are advantages to having the device. When your allegiance is no longer in question, you will benefit from a very profitable alliance. When I say profitable, I mean more than any of your illicit business ventures combined. I would also like to point out, choice one includes the same protections enjoyed by all members of my clan. If you are being targeted with violence, unless it is a simple misunderstanding, those responsible, will be subjected to the same fate as the pirates at your former base of operations."

Enochey sat wringing his hands and nervously fidgeting. I knew from looking at him, he was wanting to know what the other choice would turn out to be. He just couldn't summon the intestinal fortitude to ask. I saved him any further distress.

"Your second choice is a lot less complicated, but still comes with its own perils. Choice two, would be no tracker, and you get a quick trip to an outpost of our choosing. Once there, you will be kicked out the airlock to fend for yourself. What's it going to be?"

We were surprised by how quickly he made up his mind. In less than a minute, he swallowed once hard, and said choice number one. Coonts escorted him to the crew quarters, and instructed him to shower. We would supply him with a smart cloth uniform that would accommodate his Coram physique. The odor permeating the rags he wore, was comparable to that of an infuriated Tibor.

Justice commed me on a private channel, and said he would implant the IST unit after Enochey was cleaned up. Once it was installed, I would no longer have any reservations about revealing my uniquely human facial characteristics to the Coram.

When I last saw Enochey a few years ago, he was more than two hundred pounds heavier. Now it was easy to see many of his skeletal features. I doubt if he had a decent meal in years. I would see to it he had one, before asking the questions I hoped he had answers too.

Tria and I shed our armor and went to my cabin to get ourselves ready for the upcoming questions and answers session. Tria piqued my interest when she was speculating on how Enochey might be able to help us gain intelligence that we would have difficulty gathering ourselves. She suggested getting him a new ID chip and a new name, then setting him up as a wealthy trader on outpost 9765. We have always had a surplus of saleable artifacts. Having someone besides the Zaens to peddle our wares, would give us another legitimate income stream. It might also turn out to be the store front, Tam Lin hinted that we would need to sell our Containium. If we set him up close to the Coram Guild, we might also find out what the mercs are up to on a real time basis. This could give the former Warlord a new lease on life, and us, a deep cover agent feeding us information on what the shadier races were up to. I would have to clear it with Tam Lin, but didn't foresee it being a problem as long as we shared the data.

Justice pinged my implants and updated me on Enochey's status. He said he had implanted the IST, but was treating the Coram for malnutrition, intestinal parasites, dislocated bones, a fractured clavicle, stomach ulcerations, fungal infections, infected lacerations and partial blindness in one of his eyes. The treatments would require Enochey to remain in the infirmary for another six hours so the nanites and other medications could work their miracles. Enochey's treatment at the hands of the Murlaks was horrific. I wasn't quite sure how he survived all this time. What it did tell me, was that Enochey was one tough son of a bitch.

I ran the raid on the outpost back through my brain, and wondered if I should have done something differently. Killing several hundred pirates would be considered a worthy deed by most all races. Intentionally killing a Murlak royal, something Tam Lin advised me to avoid, was not. Giving the Throgg an unexpected meeting with his maker, somewhat troubled me because of the additional furor it was going to stir up on the Murlak home worlds. Now, after hearing what was done to Enochey over the years, it bothered me about as much as a minor bout of gas.

Since I now had a few hours of down time until Enochey would be released from the med bay, I decided to catch some shut eye. For a change, Tria felt the same way and we fell asleep thinking we would get up in about four hours. We awoke to Justice telling us that Enochey was now in fair condition, and was released from the med bay. My implants failed to wake me, and I noted we had slept for six and a half hours. It was hard to find a reason to bitch about actually getting more sleep than intended. Tria and I showered and went to the galley, only to find Coonts and Xul talking quietly outside the entrance.

When we asked them what was going on, Coonts hooked a thumb over his shoulder. "Take a look for yourself Commander." He said.

Tria and I peeked around the corner. Klutch and Enochey were sitting across from each other at one of the tables. Enochey had one empty tray beside him and was tearing into a full one like a starved wolf. Klutch was chuckling and carrying on a conversation with the Coram. We thought the Troop Master's eating habits were a little primal for our tastes, but Enochey's was down right savage. Klutch pushed one of his heaping trays across the table to the Coram, and Enochey thanked him.

I heard Klutch ask the Coram when the pirates found out. We had no idea what they were talking about, because we missed that part of the conversation. Enochey stopped eating long enough to let out a barking laugh. His sudden hoot, sprayed bits of food down the front of Klutch, who didn't seem to notice. The Coram told Klutch, the Throggs finally noticed the cook's prison cell no longer had an overabundance of scat piled up in it. Klutch started braying and beating his fists on the table. Enochey said the pirates beat six of his fellow prisoners to death.

He stood up and pointed to his side. "They broke four of my ribs and my jaw, then almost blinded me before I stopped laughing."

"Klutch stood up. "I will bring you another tray."

Enochey patted his belly. "No Klutch, I have been dieting in hopes a female will find interest in me again." He said with a sarcastic chuckle.

I was just a little miffed. It was a hell of a lot harder for me to get on a first name basis with Klutch when I first met him. I recalled he was trying to kill me at the time. Tria took me by the hand and pulled me through the entrance of the galley. Coonts and Xul quietly followed. When Enochey saw us approaching he started brushing the food from his uniform and trying to clean up his spot at the table. He was staring at us trying to put our faces to any of the species he was familiar with.

He drew a blank with me and said, "Mr. Myers?"

"As you were Enochey. We can talk when you have finished." I said.

He studied us for a few more seconds, then sat back down and went to work on his trays with a vengeance. Tria and I turned away, we would eat at another time. When Enochey saw the looks he was getting from Coonts and Xul, he wiped off the table and bench with his sleeve. He waved the two Grawl over to sit next to him. They kindly refrained and instead walked back out of the galley. Tria and I went to the drink dispenser. I poured Tria some water, and was getting a cup of artificial coffee when Klutch walked over to us.

"Commander, I don't think Enochey is the Throgg we though he was. I know he tried to get me and Coonts killed, and he did break a contract with us, but he paid for his mistakes, and has the scars to prove it. When he told me, he was sorry for betraying me to the pirates, I believe him. I think we should give him a chance to prove himself. For what it is worth, he has my vote."

Hearing that come from Klutch meant a lot. He was not known to be very forgiving. As a matter of fact, with the exception of myself, I had never known him to forgive anyone that tried to kill him. Now I was wondering if the Troop Master had a softer side to him. The Klutch I knew, was blood, bombs, and blasters if you tried screwing with him. This was definitely different. I already knew that Tria and Coonts wanted to give him another chance. As far as I was concerned, it was now unanimous.

I heard a loud gurgling belch and turned to see Enochey throw up his hands. "Sorry Mr. Myers. I have not had a reason to use my table manners in a very long time. That will never happen again!"

I shook my head and followed Tria to the table next to Enochey's. There was no way we were going to sit near the mess he and Klutch had made. I pointed for him to sit across from us. He brushed his uniform off one final time, and sat down. Klutch surprised us when he went around the table and sat next to Enochey. I was starting to think the Tibor genuinely liked the Coram.

He was still giving Tria and I close scrutiny. "I do not mean to be rude by staring. I know it is an ill-advised habit of the more primitive races, so please forgive me. Your companion looks very much like some of the Chaalt warriors that occasionally passed through my former outpost. Since you lack the proper number of appendages, I will assume your race is somehow connected to that lineage. As for you Mr.

Myers, I have never seen an alien quite like you. Your tech insinuates that you come from a very advanced civilization. May I ask what race you might be?"

When I didn't answer, he held up his hands. "I am sorry. I will not broach the subject again. I realize that I have not endeared myself to you by many of my past actions. If you will give me the chance, I will do whatever it takes to make it up to you. The Troop Master has told me you have questions, and he would not elaborate on the topic. I am keenly aware, you could have asked me whatever you wanted back on the outpost, and then left me to die, so please, ask me anything you like. If I have the knowledge you seek, it will be yours."

I was glad to change the subject of racial backgrounds, and wanted to get down to business. "Do you have knowledge of the Coram Guild on Outpost 9765?" I asked.

Enochey looked surprised by the question. He started scratching at his small seashell shaped ears. "I have been there twice that I remember, and it was a long time ago. If I recall correctly, the Guild Keeper's name was Tavor."

I nodded because Tam Lin had told me the Guild Keeper's name, back when Tria and I were attacked. She also stated, that he was no longer there after the Coram shuttles made a hasty exit from the outpost. She assumed he was with the group that helped Cralmo escape capture.

Tria asked the next question. "Do you know a Kasulla named Cralmo?"

Enochey stiffened at the question but answered without hesitation. "Yes, there are very few in the black-market business who do not know of Cralmo. He is a very wealthy, and very ruthless, merchant of fine minerals and artifacts. If he cannot purchase what he desires, he hires others to take it by whatever means necessary. Unless I am mistaken, he sold valuables at 9765 as well."

"Yes, he did." I said. "I bought an artifact from him as a gift for Tria. He tried to have us killed so he could take back our purchase. We would like very much to talk with him about the mistake he made."

"I assume, when his attempt to reacquire your artifacts failed, he fled the outpost. I also surmise he had the mercenaries at the Coram Guild help him make his escape." Enochey said.

I had to commend the Coram. He knew how to put two and two together, and get four without anyone's help. "You are very perceptive, and yes, that is exactly what happened." I said.

"Mr. Myers." Enochey said. "If it were anybody else but you asking such questions, I would tell them they were on a fool's errand. Cralmo can be a very dangerous adversary. He has enough wealth to afford the most accomplished mercenaries' credits can buy. If he thinks you are a real threat to him, he can go into hiding, and he will not be found."

I didn't like the direction this conversation was going, but I wasn't about to give up yet. "Enochey, are you telling me you don't know where we can find Cralmo?"

"Not exactly Mr. Myers. While I may not know the whereabouts of Cralmo, I know someone who might. There is another Coram Warlord who is much more accomplished in his exploits than I could have ever been. He is wealthy, intelligent and a remorseless killer with no scruples. His name is Glock. If it was a Coram mercenary operation that helped Cralmo escape, Glock would know about it. They were close associates and business partners, before they both grew to be independent operators. You do not want him as your enemy."

I looked over at Tria and smiled. I felt a little vindication for venturing to outpost 655. Aside from saving Enochey's life, and the lives of what few soldiers that survived the pirate occupation, we might have actually turned up a lead on Cralmo.

"Where can we find Glock? I would like to have a conversation with him on where Cralmo might be hiding."

"Mr. Myers, I don't mean to sound patronizing, but I just told you Glock is one of the most dangerous mercenaries that I know of. He doesn't live on an outpost. He lives on a small asteroid that is known to my race as, "Helriks Hiff.""

Our translators defined the Coram words Helriks Hiff, as Death's Door. When the words had no effect on our demeanor, Enochey persisted.

"I know you are very capable soldiers, and you have achieved things that I thought were impossible by such a small fighting force. Eiger and Glock are allies of convenience. You don't want them both hunting you. Sooner or later, one of them will find you. When they do, they will bring the brunt of their forces down upon you and your clan. In the case of Glock, we are not talking about a hundred or so slovenly soldiers, we are talking about very motivated and highly paid crack mercenary troops. If you add to that, the sheer number of pirates Eiger can summon against you, we are talking about overwhelming odds." Enochey declared.

Klutch broke out in laughter. Enochey turned to him frowning. "Klutch" he said, "I am serious. This is not a laughing matter!"

"That Throgg Eiger, will never be anyone's problem again!" Klutch laughed.

Justice took that as his cue to put the video of Eiger's final moments up on the big galley viewscreen. Klutch told his new buddy to turn around and watch the show. When it was over, Enochey sat staring at Tria in disbelief. She just shrugged her shoulders in a show of indifference, then leaned forward to Enochey.

"We still want to knock on death's door." Tria said with an ominous edge to her voice.

15

Enochey gave us the location of Glock's base of operations. As it turned out, Klutch said he had heard of it before, but had no idea it was called Death's Door, or that it was now Glock's stronghold. Back when the location was first revealed to him, it was a hideout for mercenaries on the run from their illicit activities and executions.

We told Enochey that was all the questions we had for now, and he should get some rest. He was very agreeable to actually getting to sleep in a bunk, after years of laying on a filth covered cell floor.

When Justice notified us that Enochey was asleep, we DEHD core jumped to the vicinity of Outpost 9765. We called Tam Lin and informed her of what had taken place. As was expected, she was less than thrilled that a relative of the Murlak royals was now deceased. I told her there was no witnesses that could point to us.

Her response was not what I would consider favorable. "Nathan" she said. "You wiped out the entire freakin outpost! That usually only happens when two or more factions are feuding. When things like that happen, there are a lot of bodies from all the warring participants. Since that is not going to be the case, and the deceased are all Murlaks, who's face do you think they are going to put with the carnage? They sure as hell won't fall for that crap bit of ambiguity you left behind!"

I had to admit, when Enochey blew Rastus's head off, it foiled my original plan of having him on video declaring Eiger dead, and he was making himself the new leader of the Murlak pirates. Him wearing the royal armor while making his claims, seemed like a nice touch of legitimacy at the time. Now, there was the possibility it might backfire and be interpreted as a flaming arrow pointing directly at me. Was I going to lose any sleep over it, no! Was it going to stir up a scat load of additional trouble, probably? Did I really care, hell no!

When Tam Lin cooled off, I told her of my plans to set up Enochey as a spy under the guise of a Coram merchant. She seemed intrigued by the prospect of having a new source of information, and agreed to the idea. I inquired whether my Containium advance would cover the Coram's new ID chip. She assured me it would. She let me know that when her Sig strike team entered Cralmo's former place of business they did considerable damage to it. Since the Throgg was no longer around to make use of his property, she greased the correct palms, and the ownership of the premises was passed onto Haras. It was recorded as auctioned for delinquent outpost fees. Repairs were made with the intention of selling it for a considerable profit. Now it would appear as being purchased by a wealthy Coram merchant. What made the location even more desirable was its proximity to the Coram Guild. Both were on the same level of the outpost.

When Enochey awoke, we let him eat his fill. When he was done, we told him we were temporarily turning him over to a new handler. When he found out about getting a new ID chip, he decided that having a weaponized IST was not such a bad thing after all. The perks he was receiving far outweighed the inconvenience of knowing he could be killed at a moment's notice. We still did not alert him to the communication capability of the IST. He thought it was only a tracker. At some point, I may need to have a long-distance conversation with him, and he would officially be informed.

When two Sig showed up on the Legacy's boarding ramp to escort the Coram, he freaked and thought he was doomed. It took several minutes of assurances from Tria, me and Klutch to convince him they were not going to incinerate and eat him. He finally got used to the idea that the Sig were my allies, and now that he was part of my clan, he was an ally as well. I sent a message with Enochey's Sig escort. It was an invitation for Tam Lin and Pasta to join us on the Legacy. I wanted to have a meeting to discuss our past and present endeavors.

Since I was still a little pissed about Klutch being blackballed from the outpost, we would have our meetings aboard the Legacy. It was part of my one for all, all for one leadership strategy. Pasta and Tam Lin showed up about an hour later. It wasn't hard to tell Tam Lin was upset with my decision not to put my boots on the outpost. I knew that would change very shortly with the news I was going to give her.

The exterior boarding hatch on the Legacy could easily let Pasta's twelve-foot-tall frame pass through. The interior hatches were not so accommodating, at just over nine feet tall. Pasta had to duck through them all, and then be careful of what may be hanging down from the overhead. We had a table from the science lab brought to the briefing room as a bench for Pasta to sit on. When all were settled, I started the meeting by telling Tam Lin and Pasta about the intel Enochey gave us on Glock. Both found it interesting, but wondered as much as I, if the Warlord would turn over information on Cralmo. After I commented on our past abilities to loosen the tightest lips, Tam Lin snorted in disdain and used Eiger as an example.

"Nathan" Tam Lin said. "I can't take a single thing a dead alien would say seriously."

Tam's sarcasm was duly noted and possibly warranted. Pasta was a lot more receptive and wanted in on the action. He said he could pull one of Sushi's task forces from El Dorado long enough to do the mission. Tria liked the idea of having backup if things took a turn for the worse. That scenario was less likely with a dozen squads of Sig special operations troops watching our backs if we had to go in and make a personal visit. I would make an attempt to ask for the information on Cralmo nicely. Depending on the response, I would take the appropriate action.

As much as I disliked dealing with Sael and her bi-polar mood swings, I would reach out to her. She had already volunteered her services, and when it came to blood-letting, she was a pro. If the cause was worthy of her time, she was as game as we were, and would take on all comers. We finalized our plans and I moved on to the final reason I wanted to speak with Tam Lin and Pasta.

"Justice, have you prepared the data cube I requested?"

"Yes Commander, the armament upgrade package is complete. It includes hull armor upgrades as well as shield and weapons enhancements."

An arm extruded from the overhead and placed a data module on the table in front of me. Pasta and Tam Lin were both surprised when I picked it up and held it out to them. I guess they thought I had decided against sharing our weapons tech. It did cross my mine, but the Sig's willingness to go into harms way on our behalf, and their proven allegiance to our causes, changed my way of thinking.

"I am counting on you to use this technology wisely. Please, do not make me regret this decision." I said solemnly.

Pasta took the data module from me. "Nathan Myers, I can assure you that will never happen. Since making an alliance with your clan, we have seen first-hand your pursuit of justice for all. Your willingness to protect those who cannot defend themselves is the noblest of causes. The leadership of my race has instructed my people and the military to re-align our moral codes so they closely parallel yours. We no longer wish to be looked upon with trepidation and scorn for our predatory past. We have come out of the darkness and into the light. My people have no intention of ever going back."

Hearing that coming from Pasta was good. Hearing it from his superiors would have been better. Tria and I had discussed the matter of weapons with Justice. He knew the capabilities of the Sig warships. We decided to give them upgrades that were considerably better than what they had, but not the latest technology we were currently using. What they didn't know would not hurt them. I was sure they have noticed our transit times were miniscule compared to theirs. I wondered how long it would be before they would make inquiries about our jump tech as well.

Pasta let me know it would take a day for the task force to prepare for combat operation and to get underway. He selected a location that would put the fleet a short jump from the mercenary stronghold. The distance they had to travel to get there, was considerable. Once the fleet jumped from Venture, the twenty-two ships would be in hyperspace for more than eighty-five hours. Before Tam Lin and Pasta departed, Pasta told me to expect our new battle freighter to be ready in about three weeks. Once it was void worthy, we would still have to arm it with our weapons and add defensive shields. Pasta made sure it would be kept in the atmospheric dock until our upgrades were complete.

I wasn't sure how Xul was going to take it, but I was going to reassign him to other duties. He had adapted well to our mission profiles, and was an excellent assault shuttle pilot, but he still lacked the hardcore combat training the rest of my crew underwent. His new duties would not be without its hazards. I wanted him to be the Captain of our new battle freighter and take charge of all future shipping operations. When I pulled him aside and told him I was reassigning him, I could tell he was not happy. That changed very quickly when I told him he was now the Captain of our new freighter and in charge of shipping. His first order of business was to take our Chaalt freighter and load it with the armaments and shield equipment necessary to get the battle freighter up and operating. Once that job was complete, he was to bring it back to our moon and park it in the large crevasse south of our base. We would upgrade the star drives and install a jump core that was based on the Legacy's standard jump drive. It would cut down on the freighter's transit times by half as compared to the Sig designed unit.

When the Legacy was well clear of the outpost, Justice DEHD core jumped us back to Alpha Base. I adjourned our meeting and told Tria I would be along shortly and we would finally get a meal together. It was the first time I found myself alone. I wanted to have a discussion with Justice about a certain event that took place back on Outpost 655.

"Justice, I think you were aware the Torba I tasted was not for consumption by the Murlaks, yet you let me eat it anyway. Why would you do that?"

"Commander, I have observed you taste things I know are not consumable and yet you still continue to do so. Since you refuse to discuss my inquires about the behavior, I assumed you might be trying to broaden your horizons."

Freakin evil robot! I decided to move on to other things that actually warranted my attention. I made my way out of the Legacy and waded through the members of my clan, touching each of there hands. The last hand touched was young Felix's.

"Felix, are the new replicators up and running?"

"Yes Commander, I have started the drone production schedules on three of the four machines. I was given an updated priority requisition sheet and allocated units one, and five, for the additional weapons and shield emitters needed for our new Sig freighter. We already have several weapons and shield equipment in our inventory as spares for the Legacy. I will need an additional fourteen hours to complete the new order. Once that is done, we can get back to our normal production schedules for unit one, and drone production for unit five."

I saw Xul headed my way and went to meet him. "Commander" Xul said. "The spare weapons and shield equipment are being loaded now. Once Felix's completes the load out, I will depart for the Sig shipyard. I surmise it is your intention to turn our Chaalt freighter over to the Zaens?"

"Yes, they are becoming impatient and a nuisance to Tam Lin. They are just one of the reasons I want you to make a stop at Outpost 9765. Once there, pick up the Zaens and take on the Sig crew that used to man our freighter. They will now be your new crew, and under your command. Tria has assured me that Broza and Hylet will have no problem handling a ship the size of our Chaalt freighter. The defensive systems are automated and it has a very good jump drive. They will be able to fend for themselves. After you get to the Sig shipyards, send the Zaens on their way."

"Roger that commander, I should be departing within the next sixteen hours."

I called to Justice to see if he had already ditched the Chaalt AI. "Justice, have you commandeered the freighters systems and replaced the AI with one of your subsystems?"

"Yes Commander. I also took the liberty of installing one of our IST units in a discreet location on the bridge. We should be able to track the freighter and make contact with the Zaens if the need arises."

Justice was extremely possessive, and would never allow another AI that was not part of him, to be entrusted with our care or operate any of our equipment. The performance of his systems to date, were nothing short of amazing. Other than his sense of humor, Justice had my complete confidence.

I called to the AI. "What is the status of the Legacy? I want to reconnoiter Glock's stronghold before we knock on his door."

"All munitions are at maximum capacity and all ship systems are optimal. The battle suits are resupplied and combat ready." The AI replied.

"Okay Justice, pull the Eagles out of the Legacy's hangar and load the Daggers. Give the crew a warning order. I want to leave within the next two hours."

"Affirmative Commander!"

I had every intention of permanently removing the last remaining Prule entity from Alpha Base and was sidetracked before I could get the job done. I now had a little free time and would finish what I set out to do. While I was there, I would ask Illam Pove what he wanted to say to me before he witnessed his former boss's demise. I saw Coonts and Klutch come out of the replicator building and they were heading to the Legacy. When they noticed I was going to the lifts that take you down to the escape tunnel, they altered their course in my direction. There was no point in going down without them, and I didn't feel the need to order them to find something else to do. We dropped the thousand or so feet without Coonts and Klutch so much as saying a word. That told me they had already made some kind of wager when they first saw me going to the escape tunnel lift. While I did find that it made me a little irritable, the two would serve another purpose. Their presence would make Pove believe he was about to receive another interrogation by the Troop Master. As we walked by Pove's cell, Justice cleared the walls of the enclosure. Klutch helped reinforce Pove's worst fears, by holding his fingers up to his mouth and gnashing his teeth together. I shook my head, but did not comment on his behavior.

We went to the cell at the end of the block. Justice opened the door and we walked inside. Klutch decided we were there for another reason.

"Commander, is this going to be a group effort to feed the biomass?"

As much as I would have liked to tell Klutch yes, I informed him no.

"No Klutch, I think the Hivemind entity has outlived its usefulness, there will be no more efforts to sustain the biomass."

"Justice, open an audio channel to the Hivemind."

"Communication channel open Commander." Justice replied.

"I have decided you are no longer useful to me, and your existence no longer necessary. Your race is a scourge on our universe and it gives me great pleasure killing each and every one of you I find. Your traps and subterfuge have wasted enough of my time. Now it is time for you to answer for your crimes against all races." I said with finality.

"If you end my existence, you will never learn the locations of the other Prule bases which continue to operate. There are thousands of my race still active in this galaxy and they are preparing for our glorious return. Our Supercarriers would have returned to Andromeda by now. We took immense amounts of technology from the species we conquered. The technology will be vastly improved, and used to aid us in wiping out the biological infestation that plagues this cesspool of a galaxy!" The Hivemind seethed.

"Hah!" I scoffed. "It sure looks like that is working out well for you! Not only have the races of this galaxy kicked your asses back to Andromeda, we sent an invasion force to help your enemies wipe you out!"

"You speak madness! I do not know how you have managed to escape your demise, but my race will sterilize this galaxy of all the useless primitive life forms such as you. Your only useful purpose is a source for biological material. We are the superior race, and bio-machines will rule the universe!" The Prule ridiculed.

The Hivemind had a way of getting under my skin, and managed to push all my buttons, in all the wrong order.

"Justice, how much moisture is required to keep the biomass hydrated?"

"Approximately two ounces a week Commander."

"What is the volume of the containment vessel?"

"It was originally designed to contain and sustain several hundred entities Commander. The liquid reservoir that supplies the biomass is capable of holding one point two gallons. The feed tube is metered to prevent over saturation."

"Justice, please open the reservoir filler cap and increase the metering in the feed tube to maximum."

"Coonts, Klutch, I changed my mind. I will need your assistance after all. According to the Hivemind, we are only useful for our biological materials. I think it is time we should donate our fair share."

When we finished, there was a puddle making its way across the cell floor, and stretching toward the door. I was personally satisfied with our results, and praised Coonts and Klutch for a job well done. Klutch was laughing and mocking the words of the Hivemind. We turned around and saw Tria standing in the doorway with her arms crossed. She stepped to the opposite side of the doorframe so her boots would not get wet. Klutch offered up an excuse before I could come up with an intelligent comment for our behavior.

"Sorry we did not invite you Tria, but as you can see, the containment vessel appears to be overfilled. Perhaps if you come back later you can contribute as well." The Troop Master said smiling.

Tria shook her head and made an unflattering noise with her mouth. "If that is the manner in which you are going end the other Throgg's life, I will applaud your efforts, but think it is doomed to failure." Tria said sarcastically.

16

We walked over to Illam Pove's cell and stared in at him. He was cowering in the corner and spouting unintelligible gibberish. I knew he was frightened by Klutch, but was absolutely terrified of Tria.

"Before Eiger made his fatal error, you wanted to speak with me. Now is your chance. I hope for your sake, you are not wasting my time!" I said in a menacing tone.

It took Pove several seconds to compose himself. He knew the only way to survive would be to give us information. He surprised us by his next statement.

"You have been played for fools. The Ilor that was in the cell block back at the pirate base, was not the mentally deficient lunatic he made himself out to be. He did what was necessary to protect himself from interrogation. If you would have questioned him in the same manner as the others, you may have found out he is one of Eiger's closest allies. He has many aliases, but his real name is Canik. He is cunning, shrewd, and a master of manipulation. He knows how to survive and has done so a great many times when all others have died. He is a ruthless and merciless killer, second only to Eiger when it comes to committing atrocities. You do not have to take my word for it. If the Sig have not killed him, or he has not managed to escape, you should find out if I tell the truth."

I hope the shock of what Pove revealed, didn't register as a billboard plastered with our dumbfounded looks. Tria took my hand and pulled me away from the cell. Coonts and Klutch quickly turned away as well. On our way out of the tunnel we met Graf. He was carrying Pove's Pungo ration.

I stopped him as he nodded to us and started to pass. "Graf, as long as Pove continues to act civilized, give him regular Murlak rations until further notice."

He looked surprised, but acknowledged my order. "No problem Commander, I will see to it now."

"Justice" I called. "I need you to launch a jump buoy to our deep space comms relay. Send a message to Tam Lin and ask her to make an immediate inquiry to the Thought Reprocessing Institute that Bolus was shipped off too. Tell her I need to know the Ilor's status yesterday."

"Affirmative Commander, launching jump buoy in one minute."

If what Pove told us was true, I held out little hope that the Ilor would be found at the Institute. The extent of his deceit was hard to swallow. Now there was a possibility that many of the criminals like the Rugerian, would be warned and go into hiding, making it extremely difficult for us to take action against them. To make matters worse Bolus had a closeup description of our armor, weapons and bodily dimensions. He also knew the Sig were our allies.

"Justice" I called. "Cancel the buoy and prepare to get underway. I want to make a DEHD core jump back to Outpost 9765."

"Affirmative Commander. The energy matrix is charged and ready for DEHD core operations. The Legacy is ready to launch on your order."

When we exited the lift, we ran across the landing pad to the Legacy. I saw Jaran flagging me down and stopped long enough to explain our sudden departure. He let me know that he would be in contact via IST if something needed my attention. I ran up the boarding ramp as Justice was retracting it. As soon as I entered the hatch it closed behind me and Justice took off at high speed down the entrance tunnel. We had barely cleared the planet our moon base orbited, and Justice DEHD core jumped us within comms range of the outpost.

I put in a call to Tam Lin and Pasta answered. I quickly filled him in on the intel we had. His language took a turn for the worse. My translator was getting a workout trying to decipher the venomous swearing coming from the comms transmitter. He put me on hold for more than a minute. A groggy sounding Tam Lin came on. She was swearing in sentences, and I had no problem understanding the nature of her expletives.

When her anger subsided, she composed herself. "Nathan, I have a trusted Ilor contact in the marketplace. I will give him a call and have him make some inquires at the Ilor Guild. I am going to need some time to get this sorted out and for my contact to get back with me."

"Roger that, we will be standing by."

I killed the connection. Now we would be forced to play the waiting game and I was never any good at it. We gathered in the galley and tossed around a few scenarios. None of them were good, nor would they net us any answers. After more than an hour, Tam Lin called back and she only left us with more questions.

"Nathan, we have a problem. My contact has yet to leave the Guild or make any attempts to call me. Pasta is assembling a strike team and they are making plans to go into the Guild to find out what happened to my contact. This is going to turn to shit very quickly, because the Sig will be entering the sovereign property of the Ilor."

"Tam don't do that. Let me and my team go in. It will keep the Sig out of any conflict with the Ilor, and there will be no connection to you. We will go in cloaked and be out before anyone knows something has happened."

"Nathan, the outpost is still reeling from the deaths at the Tibor Guild. I really need this to be done as quietly as possible."

"Don't worry, we got this. It's what we do."

"Okay Nathan, I am putting my trust in you. My contact's name is Kenna, and he won't be hard to recognize. His clan enjoys decorating their atmospheric suits with flamboyant colors. As far as I know, he should be the only Ilor at the Guild with a flashy suit. Please don't turn the Guild into a warzone."

"Roger that, we are on our way. ETA fifteen minutes."

I turned and shouted to my crew. "Armor up!"

We raced to the ready room and geared up. I cautioned everyone that we needed to keep the collateral damage to a minimum, and no unnecessary weapons fire if possible. I got solemn nods from each of my team members.

Justice called to us. "Commander I have the Legacy's stealth systems engaged and we are holding over the atmospheric draft tubes that pass through the outpost. I have mapped the location of the Guild and will guide you to that location."

We ran to the Legacy's hangar door and got into our combat formation. Justice killed the lights in the hangar and rapidly opened the door wide enough for us to jump. We went out quick and freefell into the draft tube. Justice pulled the Legacy up and away from the outpost so he wouldn't pose a navigation hazard to any departing spacecraft. We slowed our descent with measured burps from our gravity drives. My

HUD flashed a directional beacon when we came to the level the guild was on. We made a hard turn and went horizontal, chasing the navigational cues. Justice put a flashing yellow box in our HUDs. The Guild was just ahead. It was a two-story building with high walls surrounding it. We circled it once and Klutch called out an alert.

"Commander, there is a covered entrance at the back of the building with a ground transport parked under it. If it is a loading dock, we should be able to gain access from there."

"Okay Klutch, lead the way."

Klutch took us down and we landed on either side of the rear entrance. The transport was unoccupied and had its rear cargo door in the open position. Klutch pointed at one side of the freight door. I moved to it while he took the other. Tria took up a position at the base of the loading ramp. Coonts was at the front of the transport watching for unexpected company. I wasn't sure how we would get inside. We could possibly set off an alarm or other device warning that the door was being used. My scanners were not giving me useful information on the interior of the building. The walls and doors were well shielded and I was sure they had devices to monitor the dock. Whatever the Ilor were doing here, they wanted it to remain their business only. There was a window on each of the sliding doors. I leaned around and took a look. There was a heavy mesh imbedded in the window. Not only did it prevent scanning, it obscured the view of anyone wanting to take a look at the interior.

I was going to tell Klutch to make a hole, but the doors suddenly parted. We plastered ourselves against the wall of the building, and I told my team to hold tight. Two Ilor stepped out wearing holstered sidearms. They took a quick look around then one waved over his shoulder. Another Ilor rapidly moved out the doorway with a gravity sled in tow. There was an Ilor strapped to it, he was wearing a brightly colored pressure suit. He wasn't moving or broadcasting any alarm on his vocal transmitter. All three, along with the sled went into the back of the transport. Two more armed Ilor came out of the entrance and joined the others, closing the door after them. The transport lurched away from the dock at a leisurely pace. We boosted away from the building and followed at a safe distance.

I called Tam Lin and gave her a sitrep on what was going down. She was furious that she had sent her contact into a trap. I told her I would follow and keep her updated. She informed me they now had security drones over the site and had them under surveillance. The transport picked up speed and headed for the ramps that went toward the surface. Tam Lin called back, and alerted us that a large Ilor cargo shuttle was docked at a freight terminal, and was requesting departure clearances. She passed on the location and said she didn't think it was coincidental the ground transport was going in that direction.

Coonts called over our group comms. "Commander, we should attempt to stow away on the shuttle and see where it takes us. There is a possibility we may find Canik at the shuttle's destination point."

It wasn't just a good idea; it was a great one. I called to Justice. "I need you to locate that Ilor shuttle at the freight docks. It is probably warming up its drives for departure."

"I have a hard lock on the shuttle Commander, and it has activated its drives in preparation for departure." The AI replied.

A red box appeared in our HUDs and started blinking. We boosted hard for the target and set down between several freighters about a hundred yards from the busy freight terminal. We moved quickly underneath the parked spacecraft on the ramp, until we were beside the target shuttle. Its large cargo hatch was open, and several armed Ilor stood just inside. We boosted above them and entered the rear of the cargo bay against the overhead. It was a simple matter to find cover amongst the atmospheric generators and duct work. We settled in to wait.

Several minutes went by and a commotion started below us. The transport came barreling up the shuttle's ramp and drove directly into the hold. The cargo door closed and the guards went to work securing the transport for takeoff. The back of the transport opened and the Ilor who kidnapped Kenna stepped out. They were met by another Ilor wearing a black pressure suit with silver colored bands on the sleeves. He appeared to be congratulating the team that brought Kenna. I doubt that he was going to feel that way when we decided to make our presence known.

We could feel the shuttle lift off and accelerate. The equipment we were hiding around came to life with a low roar. We got atmospheric warnings in our HUDs indicating the air in the shuttle was now suitable for Ilor to breath, but far too exotic for our consumption. We heard three blaring reports from a klaxon and the Ilor started shedding their pressure suits. I got my first look at what an Ilor looked like. I was surprised to see that their features looked very similar to a bald Orangutan. The noted difference, was their arms were shorter, and legs longer than the simian counterparts I was comparing them too. They pulled one-piece jump suits from lockers and put them on. They all seemed very much at ease, but still strapped on sidearms. These guys were not the harmless traders that Ilor were generally known to be.

My stomach flip-flopped and I was just a touch dizzy. I knew the feeling well. The shuttle jumped to hyperspace. I did not know if Justice could track the shuttle once it transitioned. When we arrived at our destination, a signal from our IST units would give Justice our location. A DEHD core jump would have our backup within striking range in a matter of minutes. Two

Ilor went inside the cargo compartment of the transport. A couple of minutes later they dragged Kenna out by his legs and stripped off his pressure suit. He was still not responsive, and I assumed he was drugged. They would not have gone through this much trouble if he was dead. My suspicions were confirmed when a hatch to the hold opened, and an Ilor wearing a light gray uniform stepped out. He was carrying a small box in his hand and walked over to Kenna. He had the guards roll Kenna over on his face and he kneeled down beside him. He took an object from the box and pushed it against the middle of Kenna's back. The response was almost immediate. Kenna rolled over and sat upright. He looked around bewildered. The guards pulled him to his feet and walked him to the bulkhead and shackled him to piping on the wall. Kenna was pleading with them to release him. They laughed at him and said he should have minded his own business.

My stomach flip-flopped again. We were in hyperspace for maybe thirty minutes tops. If this was the destination we hadn't gone far. My team and I was wondering what would come next when we felt a jostling shake. It was another feeling I was familiar with. It was the none to gentle grasp of a tow beam. We were being pulled aboard another spacecraft. My strike team was maintaining strict comms silence. I could tell they were getting antsy and it was contagious. Hanging around doing nothing was eating at me as well. Not knowing what was happening outside of the hull was making it worse.

A grinding thump let us know the shuttles landing struts were lowered. It was followed by the much bigger thump of us setting down on a solid surface. Just when I thought things couldn't get any more tense, the ship we just landed on made a jump to hyperspace. We had no idea where we were going, and no idea what we would be facing when we got there. Uncertainty was creeping into my brain when I felt a small tug on my leg. Looking back, I could see the outline of Tria behind me. Her touch was reassuring. I again wondered if she had the ability to read my thoughts. I smiled and thought about Tarzan. It was disappointing when I didn't get a reaction.

Several minutes passed, and I assumed they were adjusting the atmosphere in the landing bay. The rear cargo ramp finally lowered and we saw three Ilor wearing their customary sealed pressure suits. They were accompanied by a slightly shorter alien wearing what I knew to be a Grawl cloak suit and a Scrun. The mixed races had me thinking we were on a pirate ship of unknown origin. We could see the noses of two other shuttles within a hundred feet of the boarding ramp. The tight spaces hinted that we might be on a ship roughly the same size as the Legacy. It would have been nice if we could take a look around and get our bearings. Politely asking for a tour, was unlikely to get us a heartfelt welcome and a warm embrace.

The mixed-race group approached Kenna. He was slumped against the bulkhead. He could neither sit or stand upright because of the manner in which he was shackled. He again begged to be released. An Ilor from the group stepped forward. His pressure suit had two gold bands on the sleeves and the front of it had adornments displayed on it. I had no idea if he was the Captain of the ship or a pirate of rank.

"What is your interest in Bolus? No one has ever expressed any concern for his welfare until you came along."

"He is a fellow llor and his behavior concerned me. I only wished to see if his condition has improved." Kenna explained.

"That is an interesting statement, considering Bolus has never seen or met you before. We think it is more likely that you were sent by the Sig or others to find out where Bolus might be. Your life expectancy is going to be very short if you do not give us the answers we seek." The llor threatened.

Things were about to go to shit if they attempted to harm Kenna. I held out little hope of getting him out of here alive without shooting the place up. I was ready to go weapons hot when the llor doing the talking, stepped up to Kenna. I was relieved when he pulled an encryption key from his belt and touched it to Kenna's shackles. They popped open and the llor fell to the deck. The gangly Scrun came forward grabbing Kenna and dragging him out of the shuttle.

We eased down from the overhead machinery and slowly followed until we at were at the shuttle's tail. I gave the hangar a quick look. Behind us and facing the hangar door was a control room with a large clear window. There was an llor standing inside, looking out into the landing bay. I reached out and touched Coonts, getting his attention. I pointed at the control room and he quickly moved off in that direction. Looking back around I noticed the bay was cramped and the three shuttles made for close quarters. The hangar was smaller than the Legacy's and I wondered about the size of the crew. Based on what I knew about the Legacy, less than a hundred seemed like a reasonable guess.

There was very little room in between the three shuttles. The only open area of any size was directly out in front of a hatch and it was deserted. If we were going to take action, now would be the time to do it before anyone else decided to join the party. The group of pirates stopped in front of the big hangar door. The Ilor leader called out a command and a shimmering field appeared in front of it. It was an atmospheric retention field and it didn't take a genius to figure out what was going to happen next.

The senior Ilor barked out another order. Kenna fell to his knees and pleaded for his life as the hangar doors parted. The group crowded in around Kenna.

The two Ilor that accompanied their leader, each took one of Kenna arms and pulled him upright. They dragged him to the opening and held him there.

The senior Ilor punched Kenna hard in the face with his right hand and again with his left. "You are going to die if you do not tell me what I want to know. Who sent you to find Bolus? Was it the Sig or the alien that is called the Demon Warrior?"

Kenna's lips were split open and bloody, but he still managed to grin. "Your matriarch is uglier than a Throgg and I was forced to put a sack over my head so I could not see her face when she pleasured me."

I was as surprised by Kenna's taunt as the pirates. I called to Coonts on my BS transmitter. "Take the control room now!"

Tria, Klutch and I landed behind the pirates as they started beating Kenna mercilessly. When the pirate leader stepped back to admire the work his crewmates were doing to Kenna, I smashed my fist into the back of his helmet, driving him forward on top of Kenna. The other pirates were startled by his sudden fall, and attempted to pick him up. Klutch rammed his shoulder into the Scrun, giving him a one-way tour of interdimensional space. Using his momentum, he kicked his short tree trunk leg up, and his armored boot made solid

269

contact with the Grawl's facemask, fracturing his helmet, and giving him an unhealthy dose of the Ilor atmosphere. The two remaining Ilor were shocked to see the Grawl rebound off the hangar door and fall to the deck convulsing. Tria drove her fighting knife into the Ilor closest to her and shoved him out the door. She spun and grabbed the other by the neck and in the blink of an eye stabbed him four times before sending the corpse to join his partner. The deed was done. Now we needed to figure out how to get the hell out of here.

17

Coont's used his BS transmitter to give us an interesting report. "Commander, the equipment in this control room is labeled in Galactic standard. As far as I am aware, the Galactic Union is the only military that uses a generic language on their warships. I believe we are aboard one of Eiger's Union gunships."

"Roger that Coonts. Deploy a DSM and wait for further orders."

"Acknowledged." Coonts replied.

I wanted to send an IST data burst to Justice. I knew he would receive it, but would be unable to get a lock on our position until the pirate gunship exited hyperspace. Tria picked up Kenna and threw him over her shoulder. I pointed to the back of the shuttle that brought us here and Tria took him inside. Klutch boosted to the top of a shuttle and watched the access hatch to make sure we didn't get any unexpected guests. I grabbed the pirate leader by his pressure suit and dragged him up the ramp into the shuttle. Tria put Kenna down and checked his wounds. Other than a bloody face and numerous cuts and bruises, he would live. We heard him moan and he rolled over.

Tria and I uncloaked. Kenna's first look at my war mask was unsettling and he called out an Ilor oath. "I have been discarded by my maker to rot with those who inhabit the darkness!"

I dropped the pirate leader next to him. "Not yet my friend, we came to get you out of here."

Kenna's eyes found their focus and got wider. "You are the Demon Warrior! How is it possible that you found me?"

"We don't have a lot of time. We still have to find a way off this ship. You need to put on this Throgg's uniform. I will find you another helmet."

Kenna quickly complied with my request and I gave him a helmet from one of the lockers. I took the pirate and shackled him to the bulkhead where Kenna once was. When he awoke from his little nap, he would answer my questions or I would remove body parts until he did.

272

Klutch called out a warning. "Commander, three hostiles just came through the hatch. They look like part of the team that took Kenna."

"Thanks, Klutch, hold your position."

He sent back a curt reply. "Holding!"

Coonts called next. "They are definitely moving in your direction Commander."

I acknowledged Coonts and turned to Kenna. "Go out and wave to those Throggs. I want them in the back of the shuttle."

Kenna nodded and went out on the ramp. Tria and I could hear the pirates arguing amongst themselves. One of them yelled at the others. "Go relieve yourselves! You smell like those insufferable Tibor's on B deck!"

That comment was going to degrade the exotic atmosphere to the quality of smog. I would have to talk with Klutch about securing his suit vents. He knew better, but apparently thought it would not matter now that we were killing pirates.

Kenna yelled down at the three pirates. "Quit messing around and get this corpse out of here!"

That shut the pirates up, and they hustled up the ramp. Kenna turned his back to them. The leader of the snatch team asked if he got any useful information. "Did the sniveling piece of scat know anything about the coward the Murlak are calling the Demon Warrior?"

Kenna replied with a single word. "Yes!"

The pirate gave a barking laugh. "Hah! Now we will make that Throgg pay for interfering with our business. Where can we find him?"

Kenna slowly turned around. "You won't have to find him, he found you."

Tria took that as her cue to smash the two underling's heads together. The noise of their skulls violently colliding made their commander turn around in horror. His mouth opened to scream and I choked it off when I lifted him off the deck by his neck. I was going to get some answers one way or the other. The pirate in my grip was thrashing wildly trying to breath. It was a waste of time. He finally went limp in my hand and I let him fall to the deck. He was still breathing so I told Kenna to strip off his uniform. I gave him the encryption key to the shackles.

"Lock him to the other." I ordered.

Kenna quickly complied and I turned to Tria. "We will not have a use for those two."

She nodded and threw the two pirates into hyperspace. Kenna called to me. "The ship's Captain is awake."

I went back into the shuttle's cargo bay and stood over the pirate Captain. I did not like the defiant look he was giving me. Tria came up the ramp and saw the look as well. She decided a little motivation would speed the questioning process. She stomped the unconscious pirate's foot flat. His eyes popped open and he started screeching in agony. Kenna went over to a control panel on the hull and closed the shuttle's cargo door. The screams of the pirate shackled to the Captain promptly ceased when he passed out from shock. The cargo hold was now deathly quiet. The look on the Captain's face changed, but still didn't give us the impression he would willingly answer our questions. It didn't seem as if he gave a shit what happened to his subordinates. Tria put her boot on his foot and slowly started crushing it. We now had his complete attention.

"What do you want from me!" he yelled.

"Where is Canik?" I demanded.

"I do not know!" He replied through clinched teeth. "He went into hiding when he heard someone was inquiring about Bolus."

Tria applied more pressure with her boot and the pirate screamed until she let up. "Where were you taking Kenna?" She asked.

"To our base! He was to be tortured until he no longer had useful information. The information is valuable to Canik. He sends comms buoys from different locations daily. They contain information on where to send our reports. When Kenna outlived his usefulness, his remains were to be dumped back at Outpost 9765 as a warning to anyone looking for Bolus."

If Canik was the mastermind Pove made him out to be, the Captain's admissions had the possibility of being true and correct. Waiting around for a buoy to show up so we can try to track it was a fruitless plan. We were supposed to be reconnoitering Glock's stronghold. The Sig would be on station at a jump off point in another fifty hours of so. They would be expecting to hear from us shortly after they arrive. I suddenly felt my stomach gyrate. The shimmering gray of hyperspace flashed a blinding white, and a starfield became visible through the opening in the shuttle bay doors. The pirate ship had transitioned out of hyperspace and was slowing to a stop. It changed my mind about throwing the pirates into the void.

"Tria, send an IST data burst to Justice so he can get a lock on our location."

She opened the hold and ran to the open landing bay doors. Coonts called out a warning. "Two hostiles down, and I am getting lots of comms traffic up here. The DSM dumped to my suit and I have it stowed. Should I hold this position Commander?"

"Can you lock down the hangar to buy us some time?"

"I can Commander, but if I do, the anti-boarding security systems will set off alarms all over the ship."

That was probably going to happen at some point, we just didn't need it happening now. "Hold your position, Justice is on the way."

Events were happening faster than I would have liked but there was little I could do about it. My thoughts were confirmed by a call from Klutch.

"Commander, seven hostiles just came through the hatch. They look like the shuttle's crew. What are your orders?"

"Light up anyone else that comes through, things are going to turn to scat very quickly."

I was once again proven correct when the shuttle crew slowed their approach. They were talking among themselves. Apparently, they thought they should see some sign of their comrades and started calling to them. When they didn't get an answer, they drew their sidearms and advanced cautiously. When Kenna saw Tria and I cloak, he took it upon himself to try and help. He stepped out on the ramp and waved to the pirates.

"The prisoner has escaped and has a hostage!" He yelled to the pirates.

To make matters worse Coonts called out a warning. "Commander, the combat information center is reporting an unusual energy discharge close to our position. They have not received a reply from the Captain and demanding an explanation from the control room personnel."

The pirates broke into a run toward the shuttle with their weapons ready. I pulled Kenna back inside and pushed him to the deck.

"Take cover and do not move!" I shouted at the Ilor.

I called back to Coonts. "Can you drop the retention field and decompress the hold?"

"Not with the hangar door open Commander. There are safeguards to prevent that from happening!" Coonts replied.

"Coonts." I yelled. "Do me a favor and use your wonderful IQ to figure out something quick! They will be sending in the troops any time now!"

Tria and I opened fire with our needle guns dropping five of the pirates. The rest returned fire into the rear of the shuttle. Klutch opened fire with his tube launcher, blowing the last two pirates off the ramp.

I called to Kenna. "Can you pilot this shuttle?"

Instead of answering the question, he told me the pirates had killed the Captains subordinate. Looking to my rear, I saw the pirate Captain had pulled his underling in front of his body. Kenna was correct, the Ilor pirate had a large hole in his chest. I didn't have a problem with the pirate Captain being shackled to a dead body and again asked Kenna if he could pilot the shuttle. This time I got a positive response. I told him to close up the shuttle and prepare to

279

get underway. Tria and I ran down the ramp as the hold started closing. An alarm started whooping and my respiration kicked up another notch.

Klutch called out another warning. "Incoming troops!"

His exclamation was rapidly followed by several jarring explosions. Tria and I took cover behind the nose gear of the shuttle Klutch was shooting down from. We could see the entry hatch was open and a flood of pirates were pushing past the bodies of their fallen crewmates. They were holding thick transparent blast shields in front of themselves, and firing in all directions trying to find a target. I opened fire low to the deck scything down several of the shield bearers. It barely slowed the torrent of attackers.

Tria called out a warning that turned the blood in my veins to ice water. "Nathan, we have hostiles to our rear!"

Tria poured minigun fire into a pirate crawling out of a hatch on the hangar deck. She crouched and ran to the hatch and fired pointblank down into it, then tossed a grenade in for good measure. She jumped away and went prone. The back blast from the grenade blew upward into an open service panel on the belly of the shuttle.

Smoke started gushing from it and fiery droplets rained to the deck. The blast and subsequent fire attracted a lot of attention. We started taking direct fire out of the hangar entryway.

"Coonts! What the hell are you…"

There was a large explosion from above us. It was followed by the grunt of Coonts bouncing off the side of the shuttle we were sheltering under and hitting the deck between them. I was going to chew his ass but a piercing alarm sounded and the atmospheric retention field disappeared. The hangar explosively decompressed, sucking everything not secured to the deck out into the void, including us. My suit AI took over and righted my flailing exit from the hangar. We had a lot of company and not all were deceased. The pirates were wearing void capable armor. I swung my arm around to target the pirate closest to me. To my surprise, he disintegrated into a puff of gore. The red hostile indicators in my HUD were disappearing one by one. Leaving just three blue icons scattered out in the clouds of debris. Our backup had arrived.

I called to my strike team. "Is anyone injured?"

Tria, Coonts and Klutch all replied they were good to go. They made course corrections and quickly formed up with me.

Justice's voice came over our comms. "Commander, I find your habit of repeatedly getting lost somewhat disturbing. If I were not concerned for the crew, I would discontinue my efforts to constantly come looking for you."

"Very funny Justice! Do you have anything useful to report?"

"Yes Commander, the Union gunship you previously occupied is bringing its star drives online. What are your orders?"

"Do not let them get underway! We have a friendly aboard and we need to get his shuttle out of the hangar."

I spun around and looked back at the Union gunship. The upper decks started going to pieces as Justice raked it with rail cannon fire from close range. We had battled Union gunships before, and Justice knew exactly how to disable the ship without blowing it to hell. The pirate ship's shields flickered to life then failed. Justice sent another burst of cannon fire into the heart of the ship taking out the CIC, insuring there would be no retaliatory fire. The ship was defenseless and slowly spinning end for end, spewing its life support out into the void.

We boosted hard for the mortally wounded vessel and ducked inside as the open hangar door came around to meet us. The freight shuttle where we left Kenna was still locked to the deck. The rear of the freight hauler had sustained serious damage. If the pirate was still in the hold, it was questionable whether he would have survived without a pressure suit. We maneuvered through the bodies and debris littering the hangar. There was a glow coming from the front of the shuttle. We landed on the nose and locked ourselves down. The cockpit lights were on and we could see Kenna through the view screen. He was sitting in the pilot's seat and had his hands over the face of his helmet. I knew what was probably going through his mind. He thought we were either dead or abandoned him. Klutch beat on the hull three times hard. The Ilor dropped his hands from his helmet and jumped up out of his seat. We uncloaked and turned on our external lights so he could see us. I pointed at the airlock on the side of the shuttle and he disappeared in that direction. Coonts, Klutch and Tria cloaked and moved off into the hangar to make sure we were alone. The exterior airlock was still functioning and the hatch opened. I stepped inside and the hatch closed behind me. I got a sub-optimal pressure reading in my HUD, confirming the shuttle was indeed leaking atmosphere. The interior hatch slowly cycled opened.

Kenna seemed genuinely shocked that I was standing there. "I thought I was doomed to die here." He said. "I confessed to my maker in hopes he would take me and I would not suffer a slow miserable death."

"As long as you don't give your maker the same epitaph you gave the pirate Captain, I think you will live a charmed life."

Kenna barked a laugh. "I felt my end was near, and I did not want those Throggs to know how scared I was. It was the only thing I could think of saying to make them kill me swiftly."

"Is your pressure suit still functioning properly?" I asked.

"Yes, the pirate Captain had very good tastes, and the quality of his pressure suit is no exception." Kenna anxiously replied.

Tria called me on her BS transmitter. "Nathan, there are no survivors in the cargo hold and we have established a defensive perimeter."

"Roger that Tria, I am sending Kenna to you. Take him to the Legacy, I will be along shortly."

I turned to Kenna and pointed to the airlock. "My crew will take you to my ship."

The Ilor spared no time leaving. When he was gone, I went to the cargo hold and found the frozen bodies of the two pirates amongst the debris. I dropped the ramp and found Coonts and Klutch still standing guard at the rear of the shuttle. I pulled the bodies along with me, neither of them questioned my motives for bothering with the dead pirates. I suspect they already knew my intentions. When we cleared the hold doors of the pirate gunship, Justice pulled us into the Legacy's hangar with the tow beam.

Justice gave me an update on where the pirate gunship was taking Kenna. "Commander, when I entered this system, there was another frigate sized vessel of Union design on a course that would have brought it to our current location. When I attacked the gunship to prevent it from getting underway, the frigate veered off and transitioned to an unknown location. I have made deep space scans along the frigate's reciprocal course, and identified a possible target several degrees off of that vector. I have also detected seven additional transitions from different locations around the suspected target. I surmise the target is a pirate base of operations and the occupants are in the process of fleeing."

"Jump us in close to the target Justice, and let's take a look."

"Affirmative Commander. Be advised, they will not be able to identify the Legacy, but will be able to detect our intersystem transition. I will immediately clear our datum, but they will know we have arrived."

"Roger that, jump when you are ready."

My stomach momentarily felt like it was in rebellion and the feeling passed. Justice put a view screen up on hangar bulkhead. An image appeared and I had to take a closer look to determine what I was seeing. Justice increased the magnification making the image sharper. My team and I studied the target. The Troop Master was first to voice his opinion.

"The fools are using a salvage dock as their base. I only recognize the largest hull of the three. It is older than sixty solar rotations and a precursor to the Murlak Warbringer series of battleships. I have no idea what the other two hulls used to be."

I looked at Tria and Coonts. "Do you have any input you would like to add?"

Coonts shook his head negative, but Tria had seen such things before. "I have witnessed many races repurposing derelict ships. It is an extremely hazardous way to live, but some have no choice. It looks like the pirates have been operating from that pile of scat for a very long time. It would be a shame if they were forced to relocate someplace else."

That was my thoughts as well.

18

Justice moved in toward the pirate base. The closer we got, the more forlorn and decrepit the place looked. It was leaking gases and other contaminants from several cracks and severed piping. It was debatable whether it was intentional or not. There were lights visible here and there and it made me wonder how many pirates were still aboard. I was considering putting a torpedo into the scat pile and getting on with the mission we had set out to do, but something on the junk pile caught Klutch's attention.

"Justice bring us back around and slow our approach" The Troop Master called out.

"Affirmative Troop Master."

I wasn't sure what he had seen. But the concern on his face made us all look closer. "What are we looking for Klutch?"

x

"I saw a blinking light Commander, and just need to see if that is all that it was."

As the Legacy reversed course and slowed Tria called out. "There! I see it! All stop Justice!"

"All stop Tria." Justice responded.

I saw a couple of blinks a few seconds apart and then nothing. I turned to Klutch and Tria. "It stopped. It was probably something arcing against the hull."

Tria looked at me. "Not if it repeats itself. Give it another minute." She said.

I squinted my eyes at the spot where I had seen the light. There was nothing and I was going to turn away, when it started blinking again. Coonts called out this time and he looked surprised.

"That was nine. I counted nine!" Coonts said excitedly.

Tria and Klutch were both nodding in agreement when there was another single flash. I was going to ask them what was going on when we got another single flash and then nothing. My crewmates all turned to me. Tria told me the significance of what we were seeing.

"Nathan, it is a universal distress code. Someone down there in that wretched mess, is signaling for help."

"Commander." Klutch said. "It would be very unlikely if it were the pirates signaling. Justice said he detected seven transitions. My guess is the pirates fled when we slagged the gunship. I doubt if those Throggs would have taken the time to bring their slaves or prisoners. The more likely scenario, is they left them all to die on that pile of scat. If the pirates return and find this dump still intact, they will just move back in and carry on with business as usual"

I let that sink in. "Justice, what are your scanners telling you?"

"What the pirate base lacks in the most basic of aesthetics, it does not lack in scan shielding. I surmise it is the reason it still remains operational to this date. I have a weak detection on a power source in the largest derelict hull, but cannot pinpoint any heat signatures indicating the location of lifeforms. I concur with the Troop Master's hypothesis, and it has a ninety-seven percent probability of being correct."

"Alright, change out your ammo packs and let's go down and take a look." I called to my crew.

Kenna was standing by quietly. I told him the AI of the Legacy would show him to the crew quarters and that he should make himself comfortable. He was having a hard time coming to grips with us going into the pirate base.

"Do you have additional troops on this vessel?" He inquired.

"No." I replied. "We will return shortly."

"How can you be so sure? You have no idea what could be waiting for you. You should wait until you have backup. I am sure the Sig would help if you were to call them."

I knew the Ilor was afraid he would be abandoned once again if we did not return. "I tell you what, if we don't return, the ship and everything in it is yours to keep." I said with just a hint of a smile.

That seemed to placate the Ilor. He no longer had any reservations about us leaving. I left him standing there inspecting his new surroundings. I met up with my crew in the ready room. They were locking fresh ordinance packs onto their armor and checking each other's gear. Tria had already replenished her suit, and stood waiting to help me with mine. I ejected the partially spent packs onto the deck and she snapped new ones into place.

She cleared her war mask and smiled at me. I blew her a kiss and she laughed. "You should not say things like that to an Ilor. They are traders and merchants above all else. He now believes he has a verbal contract with you, and may no longer wish us a safe return." She said with a twinkle in her eyes.

"With an AI like Justice, who do you think would be getting the better end of the bargain?" I said sarcastically.

She laughed again and slapped me on my armored ass. "We are running behind schedule. We should have Justice send a comms buoy notifying the Sig strike force we have encountered problems and they should remain at the jump off point until further notice."

"Justice…"

"The buoy is on its way Tria." The snide AI responded.

I rolled my eyes in irritation. "Justice get us as close to the source of the signal as possible."

"Moving now Tria."

I hoped by the time we returned the AI would find something else to focus his superior intellect on. Coonts and Klutch were already waiting at the hangar door. Tria and I went over our gear one last time and we moved into our combat formation.

The hangar door opened just far enough for us to exit. We engaged our cloaking and negation systems.

I rapped Klutch on his ammo pack. "Take us out Troop Master!"

Klutch jumped out into the void and we quickly followed. He nosed us down toward the three derelict hulls. We could see the makeshift support beams, gantries and hull plates that held the floating junkyard together. It was obvious there was no planning to the hodgepodge of constructed connections joining the hulls. They were at every possible angle, and there were at least a hundred on this side of the largest hull. Some were so small they would have to be crawlways or vents. Others were big enough to drive a transport through. The place was a maze that only the inhabitants could comprehend. We had no problem finding the source of the signal, because it was repeating itself again. Klutch zeroed us in on the light source, it was over a collapsed airlock. The hull around the entrance was buckled inward, pinning the hatch into the severely warped opening. It was unusable, but obviously the external lighting was not.

I commed Klutch. "Make a hole Troop Master."

Klutch chose a spot next to the damaged airlock and got a good hole first try. We went through the portal quickly and found ourselves inside a dark unused storage area. It had no atmosphere but did register a very light gravity reading. We used our HUDs in no light mode to find another hull to breach. Klutch activated the portal device again with good results. We moved rapidly though the portal and found out the hard way, you don't know what is on the other side till you get there.

We were not alone. Klutch jumped right into the middle of several armed combatants. At first, they were stunned by our appearance. When the Troop Master landed in their midst, cloaking no longer mattered. They all started shooting. It did not matter that they couldn't actually see us in the dim lighting of the corridor, they knew something strange just happened and they already had twitchy trigger fingers. We took multiple hits damaging the cloaking qualities of our suits and making us visible targets. Klutch managed to get his hands on one of the combatants and shoved him into Tria. Without hesitation she threw the pirate out of the portal and Klutch promptly closed it. She turned and opened fire with her needle gun, sending showers of shards and bright sparks down the corridor. Coonts and I opened up to our right, engaging the targets highlighted in our HUDs. The incoming fire stopped almost immediately. We had blundered into a group of eight pirates. Less the one Tria sent out into the void, we had six KIA, some by their own careless weapons fire. Two were Ilor and the rest were Murlak. Now that the shooting had started, I wanted the pirates to know who was coming for them so we ceased cloaking.

Klutch had shielded a Murlak pirate from the high velocity shards that had ricocheted in all directions. The bloody flesh wounds on his extremities indicated he still didn't escape the barrage unscathed. He was having a hard time figuring out what just happened, and kept asking how we got here. Klutch spun him around and pushed him to me. I grabbed the pirate and lifted him off the deck. I leaned down giving him a closeup view of my war mask. He immediately shut up and started thrashing wildly trying to pull away from my grip. He finally gave up and went limp in my grasp.

The pirate was dirty and disheveled. His armor was a mishmash of thrown together pieces from many different origins. He and his dead crewmates were obviously the lowest ranking wretches on the so-called pirate base. It would be pointless to inquire about Canik.

"Do you know who I am?" I asked ominously.

"Yes, you are proof that the stories we have heard are true, and not just the lies of cowards who are afraid of their own shadows."

"Do you want to live?"

"Yes!" He pleaded. "More than anything!"

I set the pirate back on the deck. "How many are still on this base?"

"No one knows!" He said in disgust. "We found out the ones who made themselves our leaders, fled taking every available transport. They only took those who had wealth, and left the rest of us to our own fates."

"Are there prisoners being held here?"

"Unless a prisoner can prove their worth as a slave, or make a valuable hostage, they are thrown into the void. Food and water are strictly rationed. To those of us who are less fortunate than others, we get very little. The slaves that maintain the base get even less." The pirate responded.

"How many slaves are there?"

"I heard at one time there was forty-two. They are Grawl that came from a mining survey ship. When they discovered this base, their curiosity sealed their fate. They have been in this place since before I came here, and I have been here for a long time. A few were culled because their skills were not useful. Some depressurized their suits when they were sent outside to make repairs. It has been said, those that did, were hoping the rest would receive more rations. It was a foolish mistake. The twenty-seven that remain, are worked harder and get even less than before." The pirate said matter-of-factly.

I suspected the Murlak was marginalizing his place in the food chain. It crossed my mind that it was someone like him, who determined how the slaves were treated and fed. I now wondered how long the slaves have been signaling in hopes that someone would come to their aid. There was always the remote possibility some might have, only to be killed or captured when they investigated the signal.

"Take us to the slaves and I will set you free."

The pirate pointed up the passage. "Come, they are not far."

Coonts and Klutch had gone back down the passageway behind us and set up a rear guard. "Commander." Coonts called. "Klutch and I are detecting some strange noise propagations."

Tria was behind me and watching my back while I interrogated the pirate. She called to them. "Do you have any movement?"

"Negative, the noise has now stopped." Coonts reported.

"Join back up with us, we are preparing to move." Tria ordered.

Coonts and Klutch came running up the passage several minutes later. Klutch commed me. "I don't know what we heard Commander, but someone was up to something and I don't think it has anything to do with a warm welcome. I rigged the passage with a couple of grenades. It will give us a warning if they are trying to flank us."

We had no choice but to keep moving forward. I pulled my shotgun from its clip and we formed up behind the pirate. I gave him a nudge with my weapon. He moved up the passage at a fast pace. I didn't like it and told him to slow down. He slowed somewhat, then jumped around a corner and disappeared. My suit scanners detected him moving rapidly downward and then he was gone. We cloaked and formed a defensive perimeter at his last known position. Tria pulled a large piece of debris up off the deck and found the small tunnel the pirate had dropped down. She pulled a grenade from her kit and threw it down the crawl hole. It did not detonate. We had to assume the pirate was leading us into a trap and everything he told us was now suspect. That seriously pissed me off. I hated being played for a sucker. First it was Canik and now this asshole. The only thing worse than that, would be to let the Throgg get away with it.

We would be moving blind in a maze of passages. I had a bad feeling the pirates have played this game countless times to the detriment of the opposing players. My HUD still had the signal marker highlighted. We would work our way around its location and if we didn't find anything soon, we would port out and have Justice pick us up.

299

We came to an open area that was roughly twenty by thirty. There was trash scattered everywhere and pieces of cloth and other things hanging from wires and pieces of pipes. They were makeshift dividers separating piles of dirty blankets on the deck. This was someone's sleeping quarters and I didn't think the pirates, no matter how low on the totem pole they were, would live like this. That gave a little creditability to the story about the slaves. Coonts stayed put and the rest of us fanned out to look at the hovels for clues. Another interesting fact came to light after a cursory search. There was exactly twenty-seven.

Tria commed me. "Nathan, I found some markings on the deck underneath some of the rags."

Klutch and I moved to where Tria was kneeling on the deck. She had shoved the blankets and rags aside and was pointing at some scratches on the deck. Upon closer inspection I could make out three chevrons that pointed at the wall. It looked like there was part of a word etched into the floor as well. It wasn't legible enough for my translator to make any sense out of it.

"Coonts." I called. "Come take a look at this."

Klutch turned and went back to watch the passage behind us as Coonts joined up with Tria and I. He kneeled down and rubbed at the deck with his hand.

"Commander, I cannot be absolutely positive, but it partially resembles the Grawl word for prison or prisoner."

We suddenly heard a loud grinding creak and a resounding clank of metal slamming into metal. Klutch called out a warning. "Commander! A large hull plate just dropped into the passage behind us. We are trapped in here."

Klutch's warning was followed by a tinkling noise that was getting progressively louder. Tria yelled out over our comms. "INCOMING!"

We were driven violently into the deck by a huge blast that was quickly followed by another. Two raking volleys of shrapnel pelted our armor. Klutch was the first to recover and crawled over to Coonts. He started dragging him toward our position. Tria and I were laying in a heap against the bulkhead and I was sprawled on top of her.

"Don't get comfortable Tarzan, we need to go on the offensive." Tria said with an edge to her voice.

Coons told Klutch he was unharmed, but couldn't find his shotgun. We were rattled and our armor took a beating, but were combat capable. The rags on the deck and the makeshift dividers were blown to small pieces of scrap, and all of it was burning. The questionable atmosphere was filling with dense black smoke.

"Klutch, make a hole!" I commanded.

The Troop Master stood up and projected a portal on the wall. It was a good hole and we quickly ran through. Klutch closed it behind us, only to find we were not alone once again. Sitting in the corner of the room, was twenty-seven emaciated Grawl huddled tightly together. They had wrapped themselves in trash and rags trying to stay warm in the near freezing temperature of their prison. They had their hands pressed tightly over their ears and eyes pinched shut. Two more loud resounding thumps came from the adjoining chamber. They were followed by the disconcerting sound of shrapnel ricocheting off the dividing wall. Dust and dirt rained down from the decrepit overhead piping and machinery. I suspected the prisoners had heard what was taking place in the adjoining chamber, on more than one occasion.

We uncloaked and Coonts went to them. He started speaking in calm low tones in hopes of not terrorizing them, his attempt failed. They shrunk back in fear and refused to speak or even look at him. He lost his temper when he didn't get a response and yelled at them in frustration. "If you want to leave this place alive, you need to answer my questions!"

One of the group finally raised his head and said in a shaky voice. "We do not know how you gained access to this place, but we cannot not help you escape. You will be captured and you will die, just like all those before you. If you do manage to escape, and the pirates think we aided you in any way, they will take their revenge out on us." The Grawl pleaded.

Coonts was irritated at the Grawl's statement. "We don't want you to help us escape, we want you to tell us where we can find the pirates!" Coonts yelled.

This seemed to snap some of the Grawl out of their fear induced stupor. Several pointed to a wall across from us. One found the courage to say what the others would not. "There is a passage behind that wall. It is how they access this chamber. They have armed guards outside at all times."

Klutch went to the Grawl that spoke to us. "Can you show me exactly where the guards will be?" He asked.

The frail Grawl looked up at him. "The guards will be gone by the time you get the hull panel lifted. If that happens, they will kill us all. If you survive, I hope you will avenge us."

"I do not want to move the panel, just show me where." Klutch said.

19

The Grawl slowly stood and walked to the wall of the chamber. He looked back at us and shook his head. He still didn't believe we had a chance of getting out of this alive.

The Grawl touched the wall. "The guards will be here. You have raised an alarm, so there may be more than one. Do not let our deaths be in vain."

As if to reinforce the Grawl's statement, two more blasts shook the chamber we had previously occupied. The pirates still thought we were trapped, and were taking no chances.

Tria and I stood on either side of Klutch, and Coonts formed up behind us. I pointed at the wall and Klutch activated the portal device. We ran through, and found that the little Grawl knew exactly what he was talking about. I collided with a Murlak, knocking him to the deck. He was not alone. There was a Tibor with him. He had a shocked look on his face right up until Tria sprang on him and pummeled him with fist, knees and elbows. His armor held up against the blows, but not the Chaalt climbing hooks. The Tibor's facemask splintered exposing the pirates face to her onslaught. I grabbed the stunned Murlak and clamped my hand over his face. My overzealous grip and servo assisted strength, crushed his helmet along with his skull. It was all over in less than twenty seconds. Coonts came through the portal and reconnoitered the passage. He called back saying he had no contacts. He picked up the rifles the pirates had laying on a table and we dragged the bodies back through the portal. Klutch closed the opening and took the sidearms from the two dead pirates.

The Grawl were staring wide eyed at our technology and how swiftly we killed the pirates. We dumped the dead bodies next to the overflowing buckets of waste they were forced to use when they needed to relieve themselves. There was a murmur throughout the group of prisoners. Most were saying we had sealed their fate.

The Grawl who showed us where the pirates were, turned and called to the gathering. "Would you rather die serving the pirates, or do something to avenge our crew? I would rather die fighting, than live another moment as a slave." He shouted.

I looked at the frail Grawl. "What is your name?"

He looked up at me. "I am Kevel, the first officer of the Grawl survey ship, Explorer 1774, and these are my crew." He said. "The captain and seventy others died when our ship was disabled and boarded by pirates. At one time there was forty-one survivors, now we are all that remains."

"Do you know your way around this base?" Tria asked.

"Yes, I know it well, inside and out." The Grawl said with confidence.

The facts presented by Kevel gave some truth to story the pirate told us. Just because he gave me some legitimate numbers, didn't necessarily mean I believed the rest of the crap he was trying to feed us. I needed to find a way we could get the prisoners safely off the base without getting them all killed. If we went on the offensive, and used all the weapons at our disposal, there was a very good chance we would decompress the base in the process.

Anyone not wearing an atmospheric suit, would perish soon after.

As if he was reading my mind, Coonts asked the next question. "Kevel, do you still have serviceable pressure suits?"

"Yes." He said. "There is more than enough for our numbers. I can take you to where they are kept. They are stored near the outer access hatch on the far side of this hull. It is a considerable walk from here, and we will have to pass through the pirate's crew quarters and living spaces to get there."

"How many pirates will we encounter, and do they have heavy weapons?" Klutch inquired.

Kevel pointed at the rifles we took from the guards. "Those are the heaviest weapons I have seen inside the hull. There are anti-ship systems on the exterior of the base in several locations. Not all of them are operable due to a lack of maintenance. The number of pirates is unknown. Before they locked us down, I heard our captors say a ship was destroyed near this location. This caused significant panic among the pirates. We also heard that the pirates who had access to the shuttles and transports, took them and fled. Seeing you here, no longer makes me speculate as to why."

We had kindled a fire inside of the prisoners. They were now all standing and talking excitedly among themselves. This was the hope they needed to carry on. We passed out weapons to the most able bodied of the group. We each carried a Tibor capacitive discharge pistol in our kits. We used our suit AIs to disable the onboard ID chips so they could be used by others. Justice had designed the chips so when they were disabled, the IFF could target anyone but us. We passed them out with a warning on their destructive capabilities.

Klutch called the group together. "You are no longer slaves!" He shouted. "If the pirates come for you, kill them all or die trying. Avenge your fallen comrades because there is no honor in dying a coward. We will come back for you! If you see the portal, you will know it is us. If anyone else attempts to enter, you know what must be done!"

The Troop Master had a way with words. The Grawl were now as ready for life, as they were for death. It was time to move out and get some payback for all those who had lost their lives at the hands of these predators.

I leaned down to Kevel and cleared my war mask so he could see my face. I could tell he was puzzled by the origin of my race but made no inquiry.

"Kevel you must stay behind me. When we engage our cloaking systems, you will need to hold onto my munitions pack and my armor will shield you. If we encounter the pirates, go prone on the deck against the closest wall and do not move."

The Grawl looked skeptical, but nodded affirmative. I showed him where to hold onto my pack and we cloaked. Klutch made a hole and we went back out into the passageway. It was still dimly lit and vacant.

Kevel whispered to us. "All the way to the end of this corridor and then we go left."

We went about a hundred feet and there was a short ladder that went up onto a narrow landing. Klutch slowed and cautiously looked up. He spoke quietly to Kevel. "Where does this lead to?" He asked.

"That takes you to the chamber above our sleeping space. There is always someone monitoring us from that location." The Grawl replied.

I group commed my team. "Klutch, you and Coonts stay here with Kevel. Make sure nothing happens to him while Tria and I are gone. We will be back in a few minutes."

I knew they both wanted to bitch about it, but they held their tongues. Tria and I boosted onto the narrow walkway. We sidestepped our way down until we reached a passage large enough to walk through. We went another sixty feet and heard someone talking in the Murlak dialect. He was questioning someone else, and the topic had to do with us. They were wondering if we survived the grenades. Apparently, the smoke from the fire was obscuring their view. Another voice that I recognized, said we had armor and it looked very formidable. The voice belonged to the Murlak Klutch had spared. I peeked around the corner and saw two Tibor and three Murlaks. The two Tibor had military grade armor and large rifles of an unknown capability. With the exception of our former guide, the other Murlaks had a decent mix of assorted plating adorning their bodies and sidearms on their hips. That made the Tibor our primary targets. They had their face masks open and were taking turns looking into a pipe that must somehow observe the chamber below.

One of the Murlaks said he only had one grenade left and it was incendiary. The Tibor pointed out the chamber was already burning and the smoke was thick enough they couldn't see if we were dead or alive as it was. The Murlak with the most well-kept armor turned and backhanded the pirate we had temporarily captured, knocking him into the wall.

"How did they get into the base! I cannot believe they just appeared without anyone knowing they were here." The pirate shouted.

"I swear to you, we ran into them. They have very advanced cloaking. One second, we were walking down the corridor and the next we were in a firefight with them. I do not know how they got here!" The slovenly Murlak pleaded.

"You also say the alien that leads them is the so-called Demon Warrior! I think you are a liar and a spineless coward who ran when confronted by a few mercenaries!" One of the Tibor pirates scoffed.

Tria and I decided we had heard enough. We pulled our shotguns and stepped into the chamber. The pirates turned when they heard the faint sound of our boots on the deck.

We uncloaked and I set the story straight. "Your comrade is neither a liar or a coward. It would have been foolish not to run. We make it a habit of killing every pirate piece of scat we encounter." I said in the Tibor language.

The shock on the pirate's faces was priceless. The two Tibor were the first to go for their sidearms. Tria and I shot them in the face with penetrator slugs from about six feet, popping their heads like ripe melons. The explosive slugs blew their helmets apart, killing the pirate closest to them and severely wounding the other two. Tria reached down and took the incendiary grenade off the dead Murlak. As we walked back out of the chamber, she armed it and tossed it over her shoulder. We jumped back into the passage and rejoined our team.

"We met back up with our tour guide." I said sarcastically.

The flashing blast and fire from the passage above us was all Coonts and Klutch needed for an explanation. We formed up and Kevel grabbed onto my armor. We cloaked and set off at a fast pace down the corridor. The end of the passage was coming up quickly when a group of pirates came around the corner at a dead run. Klutch gave them an entire magazine of explosive buckshot. That probably did the job but he commed us a warning.

"Grenade out!"

Tria and Coonts crowded in close to Kevel, pushing him close to my ammo pack. The little Grawl sensed what was about to happen and clamped his hands over his ears. The blast from the grenade sent shrapnel pinging throughout the passageway. Klutch ran forward and took a look at his handywork. He set a grenade for anti-personnel and tossed it down the right-side corridor and waved us up. We went left, and Kevel told us to take the third passage on our right. Coonts left a gift from the Chaalt people floating near the overhead at every hatch and hallway we passed. We slowed when we reached the third passage.

I turned to Kevel. "How much farther?" I asked.

"The exterior hatch is at the end of this passage. You will have to traverse a large open area with very little cover. It is the crew quarters and living area where the pirates spend most of their time. Our pressure suits are stored in a locked storage container on the right side of the hatch." The Grawl answered.

Klutch was looking down the passage and said he could see doors on either side of the corridor. "I can see two hatches between here and the crew quarters, where do they lead?" He asked Kevel.

"The hatch on the right closest to us, is a latrine. The one on the left is a small galley." The Grawl replied.

We slowly moved up the passage to the latrine. Klutch ducked inside and came out a second later, shaking his head negative. We started moving again when we heard a blast from our rear and screams of agony echoing down the corridors. It was followed by two almost simultaneous blasts then silence. Coonts went back to the junction of the passages, and took a look back the way we came.

He commed us. "I see at least six dead and no movement."

The pirates should have figured out by now they weren't alone. I didn't know if they ever had a boarding that didn't go their way. We were leaving enough evidence in our wake, they should be able to figure out this one wasn't.

Klutch interrupted my thoughts. "I have movement to our front Commander!"

He put a period on his statement with a three-round burst of high explosive down the passage in front of us. He bounced them off the far bulkhead so they would detonate in the living area. A lot of debris blew out into the passage and some of it was body parts. To our surprise a rifle and two pistols bounced out of the galley entrance. They were followed by a call of surrender in the Murlak dialect.

Klutch called out in Murlak. "Step out into the passage with your hands on your head!"

Two Murlaks and a Tibor stepped out of the galley. I was standing behind Klutch and saw his suit vents lock into the open position. Justice once told me that Tibor never surrender, or turned their backs to a fight. This Tibor was an exception, and Klutch wasn't taking it very well.

He bellowed out in rage at the Tibor pirate. "You dishonor your clan, and are a disgrace to our race!"

He shot the Tibor dead center with a high explosive round, blowing him to pieces and killing the Murlaks instantly. We were

316

sprayed with gore and entrails from the blast. I had a caustic retort for the Troop Master, but would have to save it for later. He screamed out several oaths, and boosted up the corridor, sending streams of minigun fire indiscriminately into the pirate's living quarters. I pushed Kevel into the latrine and told him to stay put. Tria, Coonts and I charged into the demolished living area. Klutch's minigun had run dry and he was standing in the smoldering ruins, looking for more targets. Coonts ran to Klutch and pushed his arm down. He called to him on a private channel. I could not hear what he was saying but whatever it was, seemed to do the trick. They both moved off in the direction of the exterior hatch.

I gave the area a quick search and discovered two badly dismembered bodies. Tria came up behind me and tapped on my ammo pack. She pointed down at the deck across the room. I followed her and saw a bloody trail through the debris, it led to a low wall. We both cautiously moved to it and peeked over the top. There was a Murlak on the back side and he was tying a tourniquet around the stump of a severed leg. His face was pinched and his teeth gritted. He was trying to keep from screaming out in pain as he twisted the tie wire to staunch the blood spurting from the ragged wound. There was a pistol on the deck next to him. I pointed my shotgun at the pirate while Tria walked around the wall. She kicked the pistol out of his reach. He slumped back and held up his hands in surrender. I felt no pity for the pirate. I knew the pain and suffering his ilk passed out to the weak and defenseless. His kind was a scourge on the universe and he would get no mercy from me.

Coonts group commed us. "Commander, I have Kevel at our location. He has identified the locker where the pirates keep their pressure suits. The locker would be difficult to break into it without damaging the pressure suits in the process."

"Roger that, I am working on a solution." I commed back.

Tria pulled the pirate off the deck and shook him like a rag doll. "Where is the encryption key for the locker that holds the Grawl atmospheric suits?"

"I do not know what you are talking about!" The pirate said through clinched teeth.

If the fool thought that would satisfy Tria's question, he was going to regret his arrogance. Tria dropped him on the deck and he howled in pain.

"It is not hard for me to guess what you would have done to a prisoner if they lied to you. Since I am not a pirate piece of scat like you, I will give you another chance to revise your answer. However, that doesn't mean there will not be consequences for your insincerity." Tria punctuated her statement by stomping the pirate's hand with her armored boot. He was now screaming in agony. She put the barrel of her shotgun against his remaining foot.

"I expect a truthful answer. You have until I count to five to give me one, or I will choose an alternate method to obtain the correct response. One…Two…Three…"

The pirate pointed across the room at several storage lockers on the bulkhead. "It is there, in the second one closest to the hatch." He panted.

I went to the locker and opened the door. There were nine encryption keys hanging on hooks. I took them all and waved to Tria. We ran to meet Coonts, Klutch, and Kevel. I handed the keys to Kevel and he took two he was familiar with, and dropped the rest on the deck. He opened the locker and grabbed as many suits as he could carry.

Coonts and Tria did the same, taking the remainder.

I turned to Klutch. "Move out Troop Master!"

Klutch took the lead and I brought up the rear. It quickly became obvious that Kevel could not maintain the pace with the load he was carrying. He refused to drop any of the suits, so I snatched him up off the deck and carried him. We rapidly approached the last junction to the passage that would take us to the Grawl holding cell. The explosive report of a Tibor pistol made us stop in our tracks. Someone was trying to get to the prisoners and it wasn't hard to figure out why. The pirates wanted hostages. We heard a pirate yelling out to the Grawl in the Murlak language. He was telling them to throw down their weapons or they would all be killed with grenades. We had more than two hundred yards of open passage to traverse in order to reach the cells. Klutch held his shotgun low to the deck and used the HUD targeting to see what the pirates were doing. Klutch's video gave us all a view of the smoky corridor. The pirates had the hull plate that sealed the Grawl prisoners inside, partially lifted. There were three bodies on the deck outside of the enclosure and three more live targets huddled down the corridor. The Grawl were putting up a fight. Klutch, Tria and I had enough gore on our suits to render our cloaking almost useless. Coonts was the exception, because he was to our rear when Klutch gave us a dousing of pirate guts.

"I can handle this Commander. They will never see me coming." Coonts said.

I waved him on and told him we would back him if things went wrong. He cloaked and boosted near the ceiling of the passage where the most smoke had collected. I smiled when I heard a Grawl in the prison cell taunting the pirates and calling them cowards. Another yelled, and told the pirates the Demon Warrior was coming for them. The pirates must have changed their minds about taking hostages. One drew his arm back to throw a grenade and I saw the flash of a Tibor fighting knife. The arm and grenade fell at the feet of the pirates. The smoke in the passage parted as Coonts came boosting back toward us at maximum velocity. The grenade detonated, cutting off the screams of the pirate. Two were killed outright and one was prone on the deck groaning in pain.

20

Coonts reversed direction and went back up the passage. The groaning from the wounded pirate abruptly ceased shortly afterwards.

Coonts commed us. "All clear Commander."

"Roger that, we are on our way." I acknowledged.

We gathered up the pressure suits and moved down the passage at a pace that kept Kevel in the lead. I could hear Coonts calling to the Grawl prisoners, telling them we had returned. They all started crawling under the partially lifted hull plate. They were dragging two wounded Grawl with them. They had suffered leg wounds from the pirates shooting under the panel. One of the Grawl was missing a foot and had a makeshift rag tourniquet around his ankle. The other had and ugly wound to his calf. Neither complained about the pain they were in. Tria treated their wounds with nanite gel and stabilized them as best she could. She applied battle dressings and helped them into pressure suits. Coonts and I did the same while the Troop Master took a defensive posture at the junction of the passage.

The Grawl did integrity tests on their suits and reported all were good to go. Coonts and I picked up the wounded and put them over our shoulders and we moved as fast as the slowest Grawl could travel. They were in terrible shape, and hanging on by sheer guts alone. As we passed by Klutch, he tossed grenades to our rear and then quickly passed us by. He went to the next junction to make sure it was clear and then called us up until we reached the final corridor.

Klutch held up a fist and we stopped. He commed me. "Commander, there is an unarmed wounded Murlak dragging himself up the passage, what are your orders?"

"Let him go Klutch, its time we got off this piece of scat. Make sure the area near the hatch is secure, we will be there as soon as possible." I replied.

He acknowledged my call. "Roger that, I am moving to the hatch."

323

As we came upon the Murlak, our group split up and went around him. No one said a word to him. A few did take the time to open their facemask and spit on him as they passed. Klutch reported the area near the hatch was secure and we made our way to his location. Kevel took his remaining encryption key and used it to disable the security lock on the exterior hatch. We crowded into the atmospheric lock and Kevel bled the pressure down until it was safe to open the outer door. We held up our hands to hold the Grawl in place before they could all jump to what they considered safety.

"Justice, do you have a copy?"

"Yes Commander. Be advised, I have severely damaged a gunship of Union design in an attempt to disable it. The ship transitioned into close proximity of the pirate base, and left me no choice as to my course of action. The probability is high, there are still survivors aboard. I have also disabled two shuttles attempting to escape the wreckage. The status of the occupants is unknown at this time."

"Roger that, I have twenty-seven Grawl who need immediate medical attention. If you have a lock on my position, move in close so we can evacuate them to safety."

"Moving now Commander, ETA forty seconds." The AI replied.

Forty seconds seemed like an eternity to the Grawl. They were just feet away from freedom, and we were holding them back. They started crowding in closer to us when the Legacy uncloaked twenty feet from the hatch. The Legacy's hangar door was open and Justice turned on the exterior flood lights. Tria and Coonts went across first and then Klutch and I stood aside. The Grawl picked up their wounded and jumped into the void. Their momentum carried them across to the hangar where Coonts and Tria waited to assist them. Justice had evac gurneys lining up as they touched down on the deck. Any that were having difficulty were quickly snatched up by the tow beam and pulled inside. When the airlock was empty, Klutch and I jumped across. Justice turned the Legacy sharply away from the base and closed the hangar doors. I found Kevel assisting his crew members. His was helping them out of their suits and onto the gurneys. When he was the only remaining Grawl, I told him to shed his suit and lay on the last gurney. As it started to move away,

I asked Kevel if there was anyone other than pirates on board the station.

"Not anymore." The Grawl answered.

"Justice, when we are at a safe distance, I want you to torpedo that scat hole."

"Affirmative Commander, but be advised, the remains of the Union gunship are well within the minimum safe distance, and will most assuredly be destroyed." Justice warned.

"What about the shuttles?" I enquired.

"They are far enough from the target they will not be destroyed outright, but may suffer critical damage from the scatter of high velocity debris."

This little adventure was taking considerably more time than I thought it would. We stumbled onto to a well-established pirate operation, and as far as I could tell, it wasn't on anyone's radar. Now we had a number of interesting leads that would take even more of our time to properly prosecute. This was rapidly blooming into a full-blown intelligence gathering mission, and I felt it would be counterproductive to halt the raids. I had no doubt the news of what was happening here, was spreading quickly. My gunboat diplomacy and no mercy policies, were becoming widely known among the pirate community. We needed to gather as much information as possible before the leaders of the clandestine operations went into hiding in another sector.

Tria, Coonts and Klutch gathered around me. Tria cleared the war mask from her helmet. "Our findings at this location are significantly more important than revenge on Cralmo. It would be an error on our part to not take as many high-ranking pirate prisoners as possible." She said matter-of-factly.

The looks on Coonts and Klutch's faces told me the three had already discussed the matter.

"Justice hold off on the torpedo attack and take us to the nearest shuttle."

I looked at my strike team. "What are you waiting for? Resupply your munitions and let's get ready for some boarding missions."

We went to the ready room and saw that our loadouts were waiting. Justice had queried our armor AIs and knew exactly what we needed to bring our ordnance back up to capacity.

"Commander." Justice called. "We are cloaked and in close proximity to the first shuttle I disabled. I have been actively jamming the comms from both shuttles, and have destroyed two jump buoys launched from the remains of the gunship. I took steps to insure they no longer have that capability."

"Roger that Justice, hit the shuttle with tight beam comms, and tell them to put their weapons in the airlock and surrender. If I do not have a positive response in two minutes we will board and they will all suffer the consequences."

"Message sent Commander." The AI replied.

The two minutes were up, and there was no response from the shuttle. We were going to do it the hard way. I have had more than my fair share of examples on why you should never trust a pirate, several recently. They had more than enough time to booby trap the airlock or barricade themselves in. The pirates always seemed to think help would arrive, and they would be miraculously saved from demise. It was somehow hardwired into their pirate brains, and couldn't be any farther from the truth.

In all the time I have been sticking it to the pirates, no one has ever come to their aid. They turn their backs and run as hard and far as possible, in hopes that misfortune will not catch up with them as well.

We stacked at the hangar door as Justice maneuvered directly above the shuttle. We stepped off the deck and Klutch led us down. I held up a fist and my team stopped just over the top of the spacecraft. I used short burps of my gravity drives to position myself where I was looking down on the airlock hatch. I reached out and slammed my armored fist on it three times and then rejoined my strike team.

"Make a hole Klutch!" I commed.

He lined up the portal device with the ships cockpit and I gave him a thumbs up. He triggered the device and we had a good hole. He jumped through with Tria, Coonts and I right behind him. The cockpit of the shuttle was tight quarters to begin with, and it was even more so now. There were two pirates wearing battle armor and holding rifles directly in front of us. They had their backs to us and Klutch wasted no time insuring they had no chance to turn their weapons on us. He grabbed the first pirate by the back of his armor and yanked him violently backwards stripping the rifle from his hands. In one smooth motion he turned and shoved him into my arms. Not wanting to waste the inertia, I jerked his sidearm from its holster and pushed him up and out the portal. Not missing a beat, Klutch used the rifle as a club on his next victim. He drove it down on the helmet of the second pirate hard enough to make him drop his weapon and stumble backwards. He got a quick trip out of the portal as well. Klutch closed the hole so we could get down to business.

I called to Justice. "I need you to corral those two with the tow beam until we finish here."

"Affirmative Commander." The AI acknowledged.

The cockpit door was closed and barricaded with several pieces of equipment. It had me thinking the two pirates hiding up here were upper management. We would find out soon enough, if we found additional troops in the shuttle's hold. We tossed the equipment aside and readied our weapons. Klutch opened the hatch and took a peek below. There were five pirates wearing void armor and one was sitting behind a nasty looking mounted weapon. They were all focused on the airlock. I noticed the one on the mounted gun had void armor of a different design. He also had a large pistol in a holster on his side as compared to the others.

I group commed my strike team. "Klutch, I want the one on the big gun alive, the rest are expendable."

The Troop Master boosted hard across the hold and plowed into the pirate on the mounted gun. He was driven from his seat and into the bulkhead. Klutch smashed his fist into the pirate's helmet and then yanked his oversized pistol from its holster. He stuck his shotgun barrel against the pirate's facemask.

Tria, Coonts and I opened fire into the backs of the remaining pirates. The penetrator slugs detonated on their armor, knocking them forcefully to the deck. We were on them in a heartbeat, shoving our weapons against the junctions of their armor and helmets. The job was finished with another slug that blew their helmets apart.

The odd survivor threw his hands up. "I surrender!" He yelled in Murlak.

Klutch yelled back at him. "It's a little late for that!"

A bright bluish arc of light flashed from the back of the hold and the pirate's armor burst into flame as he crumpled to the deck.

Klutch had shot the pirate with the oversized sidearm he had taken from his prisoner. We gathered near Klutch's victim, and looked at the results of the weapon's strike. There was a four-inch hole burned through the pirate's armor and flames were still spurting from the scorched opening. We had never encountered a weapon like that before. I wondered what it would have done to our battle armor if the pirate was given the time to use it.

Klutch group commed us. "I don't know where the Throgg got his weapon, but I am keeping it!"

I was wondering the same thing because the rest of the pirates had standard issue Murlak beam pistols. We gave the hold a quick search and didn't come up with anything of interest.

"Klutch make a hole, we have more stops to make." I ordered.

Tria took his prisoner and the Troop Master made a hole on the hull. Tria gave the baulking pirate a hard kick in the ass sending him head first into the portal. We rapidly followed and regrouped outside the shuttle. Justice snatched up the pirate who was tumbling end over end on an outbound trajectory, with the tow beam. He pulled him none to gently into the other two pirates and whisked them to the entrance of the hangar. We boosted to the group and jerked them through the atmospheric retention field. Pulling our shotguns, we herded them like cattle to the brig. Each got their own cell. Justice killed the lighting and blacked out the cell walls, isolating them from the outside world. He bled off the atmosphere to dangerously low conditions so they would not take off their armor. We didn't know if they had additional weapons hidden inside their suit liners. Justice would monitor them closely in case they decided to decompress. They would not be getting off that easily.

"Justice are you detecting additional weapons on the prisoners.?"

"Yes, Commander, all have various small arms hidden under their armor. I have contingencies that will encourage them to disarm."

"Okay Justice," I called. "Dust the shuttle and move to the second one."

The AI commed me back. "Target one destroyed Commander. Moving to the next objective."

When we were above the shuttle, I had Justice send a message that was slightly different than the first we had sent. This message stated I wanted information, not blood. Anyone who surrendered, would have a choice as to which they could give me. I gave them two minutes to comply. We jumped and boosted to the back of the shuttle in preparation for an opposed boarding. A minute and fifty seconds later, Justice commed us the hatch on the shuttle opened. He reported eight pirates emerged and identified them by their void armor. There were three Murlaks, two Scrun, a Tibor, and to everyone's surprise, a couple of Sig.

The pirates had a huge and diverse network of lawless individuals. It would be foolish to think we would not encounter other races who would join them in hopes of gaining wealth, or in some cases notoriety.

"Justice, secure them with the tow beam, then uncloak and show them the business end of our rail cannons. We are going to search the shuttle."

"Affirmative Commander, be advised, I have detected a breach in the anti-matter containment vessel on the remains of the pirate gunship. Unless damage control teams contain the breach, a catastrophic detonation is imminent."

If it turned out the pirate crew on the Union gunship was inept at damage control, we would not be boarding it in search of intel. Turning to Klutch I pointed at the shuttle's hull. Klutch nodded and triggered the portal device, giving us a good hole. We went in guns ready and found that the pirates did indeed abandon the shuttle. After a cursory search that turned up nothing, we were going to exit the shuttle through the airlock.

Tria grabbed the back of Klutch's armor before he could open the hatch. She was looking through the observation window, and warned Klutch she saw something she didn't like. The Troop Master took a good hard look through the window and waved the rest of us off.

"Commander, one of those Throggs rigged a charge on the airlock. If the hatch is accessed from the outside it will explode." Klutch warned.

"Can you disarm it?" I asked.

"Yes Commander, it is a simple IED and if I had to point to the pirate responsible, I would say it was the Tibor. This particular trap is taught to every young Tibor in the early stages of military training. If done correctly, whoever armed it has the ability to remotely detonate or disarm it." Klutch replied.

"I have an idea Klutch. Can you safely rig the device so it cannot be disarmed or triggered?"

Klutch cleared his war mask from his helmet. "Not a problem Commander, I recommend that you, Tria, and Coonts, wait outside of the shuttle at a safe distance."

I looked at Tria and Coonts. Both gave me a negative response. I turned back to Klutch. "We are waiting Troop Master."

Klutch gave me his usual goofy grin, and activated his war mask. He used the emergency manual override to access the airlock. Cautiously approaching the boobytrap, he studied it from every angle, then quickly made his adjustments. He gave us a thumbs up and closed the hatch back behind him. I had him make another hole and we slipped back out into the void.

Justice called with another warning. "Commander, I have scanned the pirates for weapons. One of the Sig and one of the Murlaks, have grenades concealed inside of their armor. They all carry an assortment of small arms and bladed weapons as well."

"Roger that Justice, disengage the tow beam."

"Acknowledged Commander."

When the pirates felt the tow beam release them, they spread out into a defensive semi-circle. The way these guys were behaving, had me thinking they were mercenaries, and not run of the mill pirates. They did not seem overly afraid, and I suspected their responses were drilled into them by a military disciplined leader, possibly the Tibor. This was looking a lot like a been there, done that scenario, that may have bailed them out of this situation before.

We cloaked, and moved over the top and past the suspected mercenaries. We stopped halfway between them and the Legacy. The blackness of the void, was helping the degraded cloaking capabilities of our damaged armor. They seemed genuinely surprised when we uncloaked, and they saw the visage of our war masks. That usually scared the scat out of most pirates, but not these guys. None of the eight made an attempt to flee towards the shuttle. All turned to face us while slowly moving apart from each other. These guys were pros, and I wondered what they were doing here. Someone would have to have deep pockets to afford mercs with balls the size of this crew. It dawned on me, this may have the appearance of a surrender, but I suspected they just didn't want to be trapped in the shuttle.

21

A star bright flash in the distance made us all turn in that direction. Justice didn't have to comm the obvious. We knew what remained of the gunship, just went permanently bye-bye. The mercs spent the next thirty seconds or so looking back and forth at each other. It was the first indication they might be getting a little rattled. Apparently, the gunship might have been their intended fallback position if they had to abandon the shuttle. That option was now off the table. It also finally garnered a response from the mercs.

The Tibor moved several feet closer to us. It verified my assumption of who was in charge of the crew. He commed on an open channel that was quickly picked up by our suit AIs. "You said you wanted information, but we have yet to hear a question."

I commed Justice on a secure channel. "I don't have a use for the two who have grenades."

Justice targeted the Sig and the Murlak with the rail cannon. In a show of precision shooting, he blew the heads off the two mercs, sending their corpses spinning rapidly off into the void. The two shots were no small feat. They were a second apart, and it was with basketball sized projectiles. The mercs closed the gaps in their line, and held their hands out to their sides.

The Tibor hailed us again. This time, it sounded like his voice had a hint of exasperation to it. "You said you wanted information rather than blood! Ask your questions!"

We turned our backs and headed for the hangar. I called to Justice. "Bring them aboard."

Justice corralled them with the tow beam and dumped them on the deck at our feet. I could tell it seriously pissed them off, but there was little they could do about it. They jumped to their feet and stood back to back in a tight circle. They were definitely mercenaries.

I decided to get the formalities out of the way first. "What is your name Tibor?"

"I am Trask, the patriarch of clan Myrik." The Tibor replied.

Klutch commed me on a discreet channel. "Commander, I have heard that name before. If it really is Trask Myrik, he has been associated with several high-risk mercenary missions. I also heard a rumor he was killed. It had something to do with going after another group of mercenaries, that encroached on one of his employer's territories."

I thanked Klutch for the heads up. I decided I would use the information to test the waters, and see if there was any truth to what the mercenary was saying.

"I heard a rumor you were killed by another group of mercenaries." I said to the Tibor.

"HAH!" The Tibor barked, and his armor vents locked open. "The news of my death is an exaggeration. It would take more than twenty Jintau warriors to kill me and my strike team! We took some casualties, but killed all of Blarta's assassins. I personally emasculated Blarta for his trespasses, and presented his genitals to my employer. The coward went into hiding afterwards, and spread that ridiculous story in hopes no one would believe what I did to him."

It seemed the mercenary was not only telling us the truth; he was bragging about his exploits. The scent the Tibor was stinking the place up with, was really pissing Klutch off. His suit vents locked open as well. I was sure Justice wasn't liking the overabundance of contamination in the Legacy's pristine environment. Our battle armor always went to a default setting when we were in a breathable atmosphere. One of the defaults was to ensure we could smell. It helped make us aware of our surroundings. Tria, Coonts and I made sure our olfactory sensors were in the closed position. Puking in your helmet, was at the very bottom of a long list of things you do not want to do.

"Your line of work must be getting scarce. I personally would rather starve to death than work for pirates." I taunted.

Trask bristled at my statement. "We don't work for pirates! Those Throggs can't afford the quality of our services."

No matter what armor you put on a Tibor, it is not hard to guess what race they are. Their unique dimensions are a dead giveaway, and Trask singled out Klutch, pointing a finger at him. "We also don't hide our faces behind masks like cowards either!"

The dumbass could have said just about anything else, but calling the Troop Master a coward, was a very dangerous mistake. I thought sure Klutch was going to shoot Trask in the face for his slight. I tried to calm his anger with another question. If we got the right answers, it might help ease the tension, or dissuade the Troop Master from doing something nasty to the merc.

"Then why are you here Trask? This whole sector is brimming over with pirate scat, and you are right in the middle of it." I spat in reply.

That shut the merc up, and he didn't give me the impression he was going to answer.

I attempted another tact. "I guess we could always look up Blarta, and present him with your genitals." I said with a deadly edge to my voice.

The mercenaries went into fighting stances. I had a feeling we were going to have to kill them, and carry on with the prisoners we already had in detention. Before I could make up my mind, Klutch did the damnedest thing. He popped the seals on his armor and stepped out of it. He drew his fighting knife from the leg sheath.

Everyone seemed to freeze. Tria and Coonts gave me a look like they were going to stop Klutch. I waved them off. The mercenary went out of his way to piss off Klutch, and I decided to let the prick reap what he had sown.

Klutch yelled out at Trask. "I can shoot you down like a pirate Throgg, or you can face me in combat and die with what little honor you still have."

Trask stared at Klutch standing in front of him wearing nothing but his suit liner. He started shedding his armor and drew his fighting knife.

"I did not become the senior officer of my team, because I am second best at fighting. You had better shoot me now, because when I am done cutting on you, you will wish you did." Trask bellowed.

Klutch spit on the deck and yelled back at Trask. "I was not awarded a Troop Master's commission, because I let suckling Throggs like you beat me in hand to hand combat."

That comment wiped the sinister grin from Trask's face. He realized he had underestimated Klutch. I have been in combat with the Troop Master enough times to know just how good he was with his fighting knife. When you add the Oolaran edged fighting technics to his already deadly skills, I had no doubt, Trask was going to pay dearly for running his mouth.

I didn't know what was going through Trask's mind at that moment, but he charged Klutch like a bull. He brought his arm back like he was going to take a round house swipe at him. At the last second, he dropped to the deck, attempting to slide into Klutch's legs, and stab him low in the guts. Klutch leaped over him, and Trask's blade missed its mark. Klutch landed and spun around as Trask quickly got back to his feet.

"I have had more than my share of cowards pull that stunt on me. You would be no exception!" Klutch goaded.

Trask came charging back in, slashing at Klutch's face. Klutch ducked the slash, but got kicked in the face. He spun away from Trask and shook off the blow. They turned and faced each other again.

Klutch spit blood from his mouth, and laughed at Trask. "I had a female do that to me once. She was a fine beauty, and her scent was alluring. Her price was just too high, and I wouldn't let her pleasure me. I know you are wanting to do the job for free, but I do have my standards. She had one thing going for her, that you do not, she could kick harder."

Trask screamed out a Tibor oath and charged again. Klutch was waiting for it this time. He deflected the knife blow with his blade, and side kicked Trask's leg, dropping him to a knee. He spun and unloaded the hilt of his knife into the back of Trask's head, knocking him face first onto the deck. Klutch could have had the mercs back as he struggled to stand, but chose to insult him instead.

"I think you lied about Blarta. I think it is he, who owns your insignificant genitals."

Things rapidly escalated. Klutch was standing with his back to the Sig, and his attention focused on Trask. The Sig reach down and grabbed Klutch's arms. The move caught him by surprise. Trask saw he now had an opportunity that was unlikely to come again. He jumped up from the deck and threw his fighting knife at Klutch. The Sig wasn't prepared for Klutch's fighting reflexes, or the weight of his unique body mass. The Troop Master kicked his legs out, pulling the Sig forward and down with him. Trask's fighting knife pierced the Sig's armor between the neck and shoulder joint as he stumbled to the deck. It did not penetrate very deeply but had to hurt like hell. Tria, Coonts and I pointed our weapons at the remaining prisoners. They stepped back; arms held out from their sides. Klutch got back to his feet, and turned on the Sig who was on the deck trying to dislodge the knife from his armor. The Troop Master drove the fighting knife in with his foot, killing the Sig instantly. He then turned and stalked toward Trask. To the mercenary's credit, he stood his ground. That's not to say he wasn't trying to talk Klutch out of killing him.

He held his hands up to Klutch. "It was not an honorable battle, and you have proven you are my master. I apologize and will answer any questions you have!"

Klutch slashed the fingers from both his hands. It happened so fast; the knife was back at his side before the fingers made it to the deck.

"I know you will!" He said in an ominous tone.

Klutch smashed the hilt of his fighting knife into the mercs face knocking his front teeth out. A second blow sent him sprawling to the deck. He reached down and grabbed the merc's suit liner and pulled him up so their faces were inches apart.

"If I have any doubt about the answers you are going to give us, I will neuter you and turn you over to Blarta."

Klutch dropped Trask back to the deck and stepped back up into his armor. He went to the corpse of the Sig, and grabbed it by the feet. Looking over at the remaining prisoners he gave them a horrific grin and drew his finger across his neck. He dragged the Sig to the atmospheric retention field and shoved the deceased merc into the void with his boot.

Klutch must have took exception to Trask bleeding all over the deck. He jerked him up and dragged him to the hangar door. He took the mercenary's arms and pushed his fingerless hands through the atmospheric barrier. The shock of his hands being in absolute zero didn't register for about ten seconds. Then he started screaming in agony. Klutch held him there for another twenty or so seconds then let him collapse on the deck, blubbering. His hands were frozen black stumps that no longer bled.

"If you do not answer my questions quickly, your feet will be next. Why have you come here?" Klutch yelled down at Trask.

"We were sent to retrieve an Ilor named Kenna. He was being held by the pirates." The merc ground out through broken teeth.

"Who gave you the orders?"

"Another Ilor named Canik. He offered us five-million credits if we brought back Kenna alive, and five more, for the heads of the pirates who double crossed him." Trask lisped.

That gave us a lot to chew on. We were under the impression the pirates worked for Canik. The remaining prisoners were getting pretty fidgety, now that Trask was answering questions. Coonts and Tria backed them up to the hangar door and held them there at gun point. I took a knee next to Trask.

"I don't know what kind of scat you are trying to feed us, but we know the pirates work for Canik."

"The pirates in this sector work for no one but themselves. They have been selling information to Canik. He paid them, and they broke the deal by demanding more. When Canik refused to pay, the pirates moved Kenna from Outpost 9765, and said they were going to kill him. They brought him here because they thought Canik would be powerless to do anything about it. They underestimated Canik and his allies. Canik told the pirates he changed his mind, and would pay. He sent us instead. We had orders to make an example out of the pirates."

Now I was thinking the pirates abandoned the makeshift base because they thought it was Canik coming after them. The merc's side of the story did have some credibility. The information the pirates wanted from Kenna, would have been valuable to Canik.

"Who was on the first shuttle that attempted to escape?" I demanded.

"We picked them up at Carsoon Shipping. They are supposedly the personal emissaries of a Grawl named Genda Binar. It was obvious to us they are assassins. They stayed to themselves and spoke very little. I was told they were seeking information on the whereabouts of a freighter Captain related to Binar, and a Rugerian they refused to give us any details about. Canik ordered us to turn Kenna over to them if we recovered him alive. When you attacked our gunship and disabled it, the assassins killed the ship's Captain and several officers who were trying to escape in a shuttle. They commandeered it and fled. We did the same with the remaining shuttle."

Hearing Genda Binar's name piqued our interest. He was one of our future targets, and someone that was tied directly to the corrupt members of the Galactic counsel.

I only had one more question I needed the mercenary to answer. "Where is Canik hiding?"

"I do not know. Our orders come from a jump buoy that transitions to a predetermined set of coordinates that we frequent. Canik would not be foolish enough to let anyone know where he is hiding. We have always thought the stories the pirates were spreading about you, were the lies of cowards. Now that I know they are true, I see why Canik fears you."

I looked down at the piece of scat. I was done with him, and no longer wanted him soiling my ship. "If you can get into your armor, you are free to leave with the rest of your crew."

"Our shuttle is disabled we will be stranded here!" The merc pleaded.

"Not our problem. You got three minutes to get into your armor on and off my ship. At the end of that time limit, you are going out the door, in your armor or out, it makes no difference to me." I stated in no uncertain terms.

The merc yelled at the Scrun and Murlaks. "Help me into my armor! You cannot get back aboard the shuttle without me!"

The two Scrun came forward and grabbed Trask. They carried him to his armor and started cramming him into it. They were not being gentle, and Trask was crying out in pain. The Murlaks decided the others didn't need their help, and all three, turned and jumped into the void. The Scrun managed to get Trask into his armor, and dragged him to the hangar door. The three minutes was up, and we raised our weapons. The Scrun jumped out the door, dragging Trask with them.

I watched as the hangar door rapidly closed. "Justice, torpedo the pirate base and make a standard transition back to Outpost 9765."

"Affirmative Commander, weapon launched." The AI responded.

Justice put a view screen on the bulkhead. We saw the glow of the torpedo's drive as it left the Legacy. There was a small flash as it transitioned to the heart of the pirate base. A white-hot dot appeared on the screen. It grew until it blotted out the picture and then finally ebbed back to the blackness of the void. Justice changed the video feed to the pirate shuttle that was a thousand yards to our stern. He zoomed in so we could see the mercenaries. They pushed Trask to the shuttle hatch and he reached out to open it. There was a sudden flash. One second the mercs were there, the next they were gone, and the shuttle minus half of its port side was tumbling to an unknown destination.

Our transit time would be just over five hours. That was more than enough time to figure out what Genda Binar's assassins knew about the whereabouts of Canik. We went to the brig. Justice cleared the cell walls, and turned the lights on.

I called to the prisoners. 'Step out of your armor and throw all your weapons on the deck."

There was no reaction from the three. I guess they were showing us how tough they were. Justice said he had contingencies. I wasn't sure what they were, but had no doubt they would be effective.

"Justice, please encourage them to follow my orders."

The walls between the cells cleared and the mercs were looking back and forth at each other. The mercenary in the middle cell suddenly held his arms out and started rubbing on them. His armor looked like it was turning darker. He suddenly grabbed his helmet and started screaming. Pieces of his armor seemed to melt away and he fell to the deck. His face melted to the bone and then his skull deteriorated as well. We had seen the effects of a weaponized nanite attack before, it was not pleasant to watch. The other two mercenaries started shedding their armor like it was on fire. One of them was a Murlak and the other had a sealed suit liner with an atmospheric rebreather on it. He was a Rugerian.

The remaining Murlak had two knives and two small pistols strapped to his torso. He threw the weapons to the deck. "You have committed high crimes by using weaponized nanites! The Galactic Union will hunt you down!" He shouted.

Klutch put his face against the cell. "Who's going to tell them? It won't be you!"

That shut the Murlak up, and he backed away from the cell wall, with his arms extended out in front of him. The Rugerian had knives, spikes, vials of unknown substances, and pistols strapped to his suit liner on every appendage. His weapons made a sizable pile at his feet. This guy was a regular doctor of death, and obviously someone's number one problem solver. I was now wondering why he did not put up more of a fight when he was captured. He also seemed very calm for someone who just saw one of his crew eaten alive by nanites.

22

We walked up to his cell and stood looking in at him. Out of curiosity, I called to him. "What is your name?"

"I am called by many names, but prefer to be called the Collector. It is the least pejorative of the many I have been labeled with."

I frowned, and wondered if this was some kind of game, he was playing on us. "Well Mr. Collector." I said sarcastically. "You don't seem to care if your team lives or dies."

"Those amateurs are not my team. They were the most tolerable of my choices." He replied.

I was caught by surprise at the Rugerian's response, and wasn't quite sure what to say to that.

Tria now had a question. "If that is the case, why are you with them?"

The Rugerian stepped closer to the cell wall and looked directly at me. "They were a means to an end and expendable assets. They have served their purpose and although inept, they managed to get me where I am now. I was told there was a very real possibility I would end up in this unenviable position."

Talking about intrigue. This guy had a set of nads that rivaled the Troop Master's.

"Yet, you still took the mission?" I asked.

"I was told if I did this, I would not have to work at my unique profession ever again. There are a lot of things I have done in my past, that I am not proud of, and I will not be looked upon with favor by my maker for most of them. I have yearned for the chance to change that. An opportunity was presented to me that few in my field have ever been offered. A retirement that didn't include mandatory death. I know many things that members of my trade traditionally take to their graves. Be it by an impossible mission, or outright assassination. Assets such as I, never get to retire on our own accord. I would be the first that I am aware of, that has been offered a reasonable chance to try."

Coonts knew where this was going. "So, what is your message?" The Grawl asked.

The Rugerian looked down at Coonts. "You are very astute, and although you have some very interesting dimensions, I surmise you are a Grawl."

Klutch was still pissed at Trask, and was in no mood for amnesty. He had a way with words, and his threat would be no exception. "Give us the message, or I will cut your head off and scat down you neck, until your corpse's dimensions properly convey the reply we will be sending back to your masters."

The Rugerian looked over at Klutch. "HAH! The Rugerian laughed. "Trask was a brainless hack for underestimating you. I have no doubt about your sincerity in carrying out your threat. I would never be foolish enough to take on a Troop Master in hand to hand combat. If I could not kill you from some far away perch, I would not risk it at all."

Klutch respected the answer and his tone changed as well. "What message do you have for us?"

"It is simple enough." The Rugerian said. "Stop what you are doing and name your price. It does not matter what the amount will be, it will not be considered unsurmountable. My employers are willing to give you a percentage of their gross national incomes, to cease and desist. I am not here to tell you that you are a problem that can't eventually be dealt with. I am telling you, that if you take the offer, you will no longer be hunted, and will be wealthy beyond comprehension."

I knew we would eventually have an impact on the races whose illicit activities we were putting a damper on. I never realized just have much we were hurting them, till now.

It was the Rugerian's turn to look surprised. I guess he must have thought we would jump all over the offer. We stood silently looking at him through our war masks. He stared back at us, taking in every detail of the horrors emblazoned on our helmets.

His face was easily visible through his helmet and it turned to a frown. "Is your voice translator functioning properly? Did you not hear what I just said?"

"I understood perfectly." I said bluntly. "You stated that the races you represent, want to continue to kill and enslave all the defenseless species they encounter. They also want to steal artifacts and treasures rightfully belonging to others, and they want to do all this without interference from my strike team. If that is not the proper interpretation of your offer, feel free to correct me if I am wrong."

Justice extruded arms from an overhead hatch in the cells. He collected the weapons and armor off the deck while the two prisoners were focused on us. The hatch closed without making a discernable sound. Neither one noticed what had transpired, because they were too busy staring at us with wide eyes and gaping mouths. The Rugerian was trying to come to grips with the implications of what I said, and how I said it.

He was starting to get rattled and blurted out. "It is obvious you have very formidable technology, but even the most advanced tech can't protect you forever. I am offering you trillions in…"

I cut him off. I had heard this scat on a number of occasions. It left a bad taste in my mouth the first time I had heard it, and it wasn't any better now.

"We don't need wealth, and we don't keep credits tainted with the blood of the innocent! We take whatever we want from your employers, and use it to protect the victims of their crimes. You made a grievous error thinking you could come here and convince us to take a bribe from the scat you work for. Where I come from, they call it irreconcilable differences. The only thing that can change our differences, would be for your employers to immediately cease all illegal activities, release all those who were forced into slavery, and to give reparations to all they have harmed and robbed of their rightful property."

The Rugerian was physically shaken. He could not believe what he was hearing. He spun and looked down for his weapons. I knew he couldn't have used them on us, so he was going to use them on himself in fear of what we might do to him. His fear was justified. When the fool took the mission, he was convinced no one would turn down such an offer. He also made the miscalculation of believing he would have no problem returning to report his success.

The Rugerian turned back to us with a frantic look. "I will pass your message on to my employers."

Tria answered for me. "No, we will give them our reply in person."

We turned our backs on him and Justice blacked out the cell. We moved to the next enclosure. I knew we probably wouldn't find out anything groundbreaking from the merc, but was going to ask him questions regardless.

The mercenary had his hands and face pushed against the cell wall. He was desperate and it showed.

"I was going to let the Troop Master expend the rest of his anger on you. His frustration at not having a properly skilled opponent to kill, is not a welcome distraction."

Klutch took this as his cue to show off some of his knife juggling skills. He was spinning his fighting knife like a baton and tossing into the air and catching it. I found his twirling display impressive. Coonts stood to the side with his arms crossed, shaking his head. He apparently thought Klutch was a showoff.

After a pause to let the merc ponder his future, I continued. "Where is Canik hiding?"

"I do not know!" The merc pleaded. "He transfers credits into our accounts and we receive his orders from jump buoys."

I had heard this multiple times and I believed him. Canik was covering his tracks, and would not be foolish enough to give the information on his whereabouts to his expendable minions. I moved on to the next question.

"Where can we find Genda Binar?"

The merc answered without hesitation. "At Carsoon Shipping, freight hub eight, tower number one. He occupies the top three floors, fifty-eight through sixty."

That verified information we already had. I wondered if we could find him there, or it was just his business offices. The mercenary had very limited information and I was done with him for now. We walked away and Justice blacked out the enclosure.

On the way to the ready room, Klutch and Coonts stopped Tria and I outside of the entrance. The two were discussing something on a discreet channel all the time I was talking to the Rugerian. They retracted their helmets and were ready to reveal the ruminations of their conspiracy. I had other things on my mind, and would make them wait a little longer to give me their two cents worth.

I held up a finger. "Justice." I called. "What is the status of the Grawl surveying crew?"

"Their conditions are improving. I decided it was best to sedate all of them before treating their wounds and assorted illnesses. Many had bones that had been broken and improperly set. The surgery needed to repair them, would have required sedation anyway. They are receiving concentrated nutrients to treat their malnutrition, and I have already manufactured a prostatic foot for the Grawl who suffered the amputation. I am confident all my patients will make a full recovery."

I knew Justice was well versed in caring for Grawl, and had no doubt about his prognosis. That just left the Ilor. I was surprised he was not waiting in the hangar to see whether or not we would return.

"What about Kenna? I haven't seen him since we left for our mission."

"Commander, the Ilor's curiosity was taking him near restricted areas of the ship. I also took exception to him constantly questioning me on the fate of my crew. When he went to the galley and requested me to feed him, I added a sedative to his ration slurry and pumped it into his feeder port. He should awaken sometime after we arrive at Outpost 9765. It would not have been necessary, if someone had not told the Ilor the Legacy would be his possession, in the event of your demise."

I wondered when Justice was going to needle me on that issue, and decided to change the subject. Tria and I retracted our helmets and turned to face Coonts and Klutch. They promptly stopped their childish behavior and pretended to be waiting patiently for Justice's report to end.

"What are the two of you up too?" I asked, cocking an eyebrow.

Klutch pointed to Coonts, but got a healthy shove forward by the Grawl before he could open his mouth. He gritted his teeth and narrowed his big lizard eyes at Coonts. The scent in the passage was taking a turn for the worse, and it was becoming difficult to ignore. Tria was getting pissed and it showed on her face more than mine.

Klutch cleared his throat. "Commander, I, I mean we," He said pointing back at Coonts. "Would like to make a suggestion."

I rolled my eyes and shook my head wondering if this wasn't related to a bet between the two. "Okay Klutch, let's hear it."

"Commander, what do you think about taking the deal, and killing the Throggs anyway."

I took a deep breath and let it out. The look on Coonts face said their suggestion was definitely tied to a bet. Not wanting to confirm or deny their proposition, I threw up my hands and waved them off. I had already considered that scenario. In a moment of better judgement, I decided it was more likely to be a way to lure us into a trap. We had caused a huge amount of trouble for a number of criminal organizations. Some of which, had the backing of the leadership of their respective races. I didn't believe for a second, they would forgive and forget that easily. Even if we did go that route, how would we collect without exposing ourselves to possible retribution. I had the entire human race to worry about.

Coonts looked at Klutch out of the corner of his eyes, and then up at me. "Is that a yes or a no Commander?"

Tria already had her fill of the stooge routine, and decided I was thinking too hard on the subject. She took me by the arm, pulling me inside the ready room. Coonts and Klutch slowly followed us, arguing, elbowing, and swatting at each other like twelve-year-old siblings. When Tria and I stepped out of our armor we didn't bother to put on uniforms. We hurried out of the ready room in our suit liners. We didn't want to spend another second listening to the conversation going on between Coonts and Klutch. When we were out in the fresher air of the corridor, Tria took my hand and asked me what I was thinking. I smiled because I thought she was going to give me her opinion rather than ask for mine.

"I think the message from the Rugerian proves we are making a difference. You once told me I was put on this path by my maker. To be honest, I had serious doubts. Now after hearing what the Rugerian had to say, I believe more than ever, that change is possible. We are going to continue hurting the lawless Throggs until they are forced to find a different source of income."

I guess that is what Tria wanted to hear. When we got to the lifts, she jumped in the tube pulling me with her. On the way up, she embraced me tight enough to pop my back, then whispered in my ear. "Tarzan, we still have over three and a half hours before we arrive at Outpost 9765."

I gave her a smile and muttered "Hot damn!" under my breath. It isn't every day that you can turn down trillions in wealth, and then get rewarded for it.

Tria and I woke to the sound of Justice giving us a thirty-minute warning we would be arriving at our destination. Being King of the Jungle has a tendency to make me sleep soundly, and Jane must have needed the down time as well. We took a fast shower and put on fresh uniforms. As we stepped out into the passage, we could hear Coonts and Klutch just ahead of us in the command center. The two were still having a boisterous conversation. Tria just looked at me and smiled. I was sure she was going to tell me once again, the two were just blowing off steam, and it was harmless comradery. I was still just a little miffed at their Pungo antics and personally wanted a little peace and quiet.

When we entered the bridge, the volume of their conversation did appreciably fall to a less irritating decibel level, but did not subside.

"HEY!" I called to them. "Can that crap, or you will be eating Pungo instead of wagering on it!"

That seemed to do the trick, and the two closed their mouths for a change. Coonts however, still wanted a verbal decision on the amnesty deal. Before we could make it to the lifts, he called out to me.

"Commander, have you decided what the outcome of the Rugerian's offer will be?"

"Coonts, I know you want me to settle a bet between you and Klutch. It cannot be lost on you how much I find it irritating you have included me in your wagering schemes. I caution you both to wisely reconsider ever doing so again. The answer to your question is both a yes and a no. Yes, we will continue killing all the murdering, lawless Throggs we encounter, and no, we are not taking their blood money."

The Grawl must have decide it was a win for him, and he let out a whoop. A heated argument ensued, and before I could get really pissed at the two, Tria shoved me into the down tube and quickly followed. When we reached the galley deck, she stepped out, pulling me along with her.

"Nathan, let it go. It is harmless, and they could be up to much worse."

Tria was right, and other than being involved in their annoying game, there was no harm and no foul. That didn't necessarily mean they would get off that easy either.

When we walked into the galley, I called to Justice. "Coonts and Klutch are on a Pungo diet until further notice."

The AI responded with an affirmative. Tria and I ate breakfast without much conversation. I guess she thought I was being a bit too harsh. A second cup of Justice's dishwater coffee took the edge off my frustration, and eased my penalty shot, to just their next meal.

Our exit from hyperspace gave my rations an unwelcome churn but it quickly subsided. The comms net lit up with traffic from Tam Lin.

Justice put the call through. "Nathan!" Tam Lin said excitedly. "What the hell happened? You have been gone for almost three days. When the Legacy suddenly jumped to hyperspace and we hadn't heard back from you, we were tossing around some pretty grim scenarios."

By the time I explained what had transpired, Coonts, Klutch and Kenna joined us in the galley. Tam Lin was speechless. When she found her voice, she told us they had our usual private dock available and would wait for our arrival. I explained to her that we needed to make a quick stop at the Ilor guild to drop off a message. She inquired as to what message. I told her about the connection between the pirates and the Ilor guild. She was pretty shaken by the information because her intelligence network knew nothing about it. When I told her, our message would be dumping the bodies of the Ilor pirates on the Guild's door step, she insisted that we let her Sig operatives do the deed. As long as they got the message, I was good with that.

23

I had Justice set up our conference room for a meeting with Tam Lin. To our surprise she said both Sushi and Pasta would be attending. Justice made seating available for the two twelve-foot-tall aliens. When they arrived, they made arrangements to take Kenna off our hands. Tam Lin said he would be relocated to another outpost with a new ID chip. I informed her I needed Enochey for a temporary assignment. She was good with that because they were still working to get his store properly outfitted. She was also still working on a good background for Enochey's new cover name.

I inquired what that might be and she gave me a silly smile. "Nathan." She said. "What name do you associate with, when you think of spying?"

I haven't been away from Earth as long as Tam but really couldn't come up with a good answer to her question.

She shook her head. "Nathan, are you going alien on me or what? It only makes sense to call him Bond!"

It was a no brainer and I should have guessed. "Just Bond?" I said.

"No, Bond Connery!" She replied with a chuckle.

I just shook my head and smiled. How fitting. Now that his cover name was official, we would no longer call the Coram, Enochey. He had a new ID chip and a new life from this point forward. My crew gave me blank stares but nodded in agreement.

"Tam, would you please have Bond Connery report to the Legacy."

I thought about it a little longer and told her to wait. I reached into my uniform and pulled out a handful of credit vouchers.

I pulled one out at random and gave it to Tam. "Give this to Bond and send him to Osa's fine wearables. Tell him to have a complete wardrobe made up. I don't give a crap what it cost. Just tell him to be aboard the Legacy within the next three hours."

Tam Lin took the card and nodded. "Consider it done." She said.

I knew Bond would have no problem getting the job done in the time I was allotting him. Once Osa had his bodily dimensions, it was just a matter of picking out the materials and putting them into his fabrication machine. As long as he wasn't very picky, he would be outfitted in no time.

Klutch was talking to Sushi and Pasta. By the looks on their faces, he must have broken the news to them about the Sig mercenaries. I could tell it troubled them. I heard Pasta tell Klutch, they got what they deserved.

Sushi gave me a report on El Dorado. "Commander Myers, I am happy to report the repairs to the mine are well ahead of schedule. The atmospheric locks are in place and the environmental scrubbers are functioning at maximum capacity. The cleanup phase will be complete within the next forty-eight hours. Tam Lin is still sorting out the work crews and working on the operational shifts. Once that is done, we will stock the mine with enough supplies for a startup and shake down of the three work shifts. The crews will work for a period of thirty days, and then have thirty off when a fresh crew relieves them. If this system works well, it will be made permanent at the end of the sixty-day shakedown."

I was all smiles at the way the job of getting the mine back on line was being handled. I still haven't heard anything on the ownership splits, but had complete faith in my partners. I told my three guests about the prisoners we were holding. Sushi had no problem taking them back with him to Venture. There was plenty of empty cells and around the clock monitoring. I told him they could expect additional company in the near future, if our next missions went well. This made both of the Sig troopers give me big toothy smiles.

We again went over everything that had taken place over the last seventy-two hours. Each member of my team helped answer the many questions put to us by the Sig and Tam Lin. When we were finally done, Tam Lin had a good picture of what was going on in the Ilor Guild, right under her nose. The pirates had operations that spanned the known galaxy and most had their own agendas. It was becoming clear now that Eiger was gone, the pirates were forming new alliances or going their own way. It was now obvious that Canik was not filling the leadership position just yet. He still had a lot of work to do, and we were not going to make it easy on him during the process. The subject finally shifted to the operation against Glock, and Pasta took over the briefing.

"Commander Myers, I ordered the strike fleet to jump away from the star system they were holding in. Your disappearance troubled the onsite Commanders, and they requested permission to relocate. They felt if the fleet lingered any longer, it would tip off the mercenary forces to our intentions. We have hopes if the fleet was detected, it would be interpreted as another random patrol by my people."

I applauded the onsite Commander's decision. My unexpected delay threw a wrench into the planning and timing of the operation. We would have to reset the timetables and start over again. For now, I was going to push the Glock operation to the back burner. It was now my desire to pursue the newly developed intel we had collected. We were all in agreement that our latest data was time sensitive, and we had a rapidly closing window of opportunity to capitalize on it. The longer we waited, the more likely our targets would go into hiding before we could make an attempt to capture or kill them.

I was going to lay out a rough sketch of what I had in mind. Between my crew and allies, I hoped they could add to the strengths of my plan, and point out any glaring weaknesses.

"Now that we have an asset that is a complete unknown, I want to use him to gain access to our targets. It is my intention to set up Enoche... I mean Bond Connery, as a wealthy merchant. That is something we have already discussed, and in fits right into my plans. I propose outfitting Bond with his own transport and enough valuable artifacts to get the proper scrutiny, and send him to Carsoon Shipping's Hub Eight. Once there, he will make it known he wants to discreetly ship property to secure location on the fringe. It is hoped this will come to Genda Binar's attention and will possibly gain Bond a meeting with him. If we make the cargo appear to be valuable enough, we just might get lucky and Genda will want to be part of the operation."

Tam Lin raised a finger to me. "I assume you are going to use Containium as the bait?"

"Yes, the unprocessed ore we found when we first entered the mine."

Sushi smiled and held up a hand. "In the initial cleanup of the site, we stockpiled more than six hundred and seventy tons.

We planned to process it as part of our preproduction shakedown. I can have it put into storage cubes and, transferred here within the next forty-eight hours."

Coonts had a suggestion that would lessen the possibility of losing a large quantity of the ore, should the plan backfire on us. "Commander, it would be wise to make any samples that Bond may have to present as proof, be actual Containium ore. The cargo itself should be waste rock from our mining site sprinkled with small amounts of ore. That way, if we are double crossed by Carsoon Shipping, they will only end up with a small fraction of the value they believed they would gain."

I liked the idea of planning ahead for treachery. There was the very real possibility that was what we were going to get, no matter what plans we had in place.

"Sushi." I said. "Send us two hundred tons of waste rock. Put it in storage capsules and sprinkle the tops of each with a few handfuls of ore before sealing them."

Sushi nodded and got up to leave. He said he needed to get back to the mine so he could continue overseeing its reconstruction. He took the credit voucher I gave Tam Lin and said he would give it to

Bond with my instructions. I got up and bowed to the Sig and told him we would keep him appraised of our operation. He returned the gesture and left us to our planning.

Tria had a small frown on her face. "Tria, is there something I am overlooking?"

"Yes Nathan." She said. "If you want this operation to have any chance at all of attracting Genda Binar's attention, you are going to need a legitimate pickup point for the ore. I mean that the ore needs to be at a well-established mining location. I know of a few that might be a possibility, but they all have their own shipping fleets. Bond is going to need a solid cover story in order to convince Genda Binar to send a Carsoon freighter, to pick up ore from a site that already has the ability to ship it."

Tria had a point. Genda Binar wouldn't soil his hands on something like this if it even remotely looked like something was amiss.

A voice from the corridor called to me. It was our newly minted agent, Bond Connery. He was holding a credit voucher out in front of him. "I apologize for interrupting your meeting. Your AI instructed me to come here. I was given this credit voucher, and the Sig that gave it to me, said it came from you Mr. Myers. He told me to spend it however I wished on a new wardrobe. When I asked what denomination was on the card, he said he didn't know. My background being what it was, made me suspicious of where the card came from. When I had the card scanned to find out its worth, it had a value in excess of fifty million credits. You had warned me that any duplicity on my part could lead to permanent incapacitation. I thought it might be prudent to discuss the matter with you rather than find out the card was stolen, and suffer the consequences."

I had to smile. Bond's survival instincts verified my belief he would hold up his end of our agreement. They would also serve him well on the mission I was planning for him.

I pointed to the table Sushi had vacated. "Take a seat. We were going to brief you when you returned to the Legacy. The voucher did indeed come from me and it is yours to keep. We have a mission for you and I wanted you to have attire that has nothing to do with a uniform."

Tam Lin and Pasta decided there was nothing they could add to our discussion.

"Nathan, if you need any support from me or Pasta, let us know before you leave the outpost." Tam Lin said as she was leaving.

When they were gone, Bond extended his large hind legs and sat down. "I couldn't help but overhear your first officer point out some of the deficiencies in your planning. I know that you are familiar with my past. I have been party to several operations that sound similar to what you are proposing. Since the mission you are discussing will ultimately require my services, I would like add my input in the planning. If of course, that is agreeable to you."

I again smiled. The Coram was as sharp as ever. He may just prove to be a very valuable asset. I filled him in on what we were trying to do and how he fit into the plan. He sat for a minute scratching at his small ears.

"You are on to something, but are going about it the wrong way." Bond said. "You might find what I have to say distasteful, but my past experience in such matters makes me uniquely qualified for this mission and how it is planned. I know of Genda Binar and more importantly his employer, Bren Carsoon. With the proper support, I see no problem achieving your goals."

The Coram had our attention. "You obviously have our support or you wouldn't be here. If it is credits you are referring too. We will give you the best support credits can buy. Tell us what you need, if it is within reason, it's yours."

Bond clapped his hands, rubbing them together. He gave us an evil grin. "I have had more than my share of being gouged by Carsoon Shipping. The black market would be nothing without a means to safely ship less than reputable goods throughout the known galaxy. Carsoon is the shipper of choice when it comes to such matters. The astronomical prices they charge persons such as myself, is the reason they have expanded into the conglomerate they presently are. Between Carsoon and the pirates, profits were marginal depending on the products being sold."

Showing mercy to some of my past foes usually ended with regret at some later date. This was the first time I genuinely felt that was not going to be the case. If the former warlord demonstrated his sincerity in helping us right the wrongs we continually stumbled upon, I would see to it, he would never again have to resort to corruption in his pursuit of wealth.

"Okay Bond, let's hear how you would handle the job." I said.

He looked at each of us to insure we were listening. "If you are interested, I could give you some historical information related to your targets. Sometimes it helps to know your opponent's background, before you engage in a conflict with them."

That was a surprising statement coming from the Coram. I had once called him a dumbass and meant it. I assumed he was an uneducated Throgg that only knew how to lie, cheat, and steal. At the time, I also assumed it was the only reason he had risen to his position of Warlord. If this was a side of him, I had overlooked, I was curious just how wrong I was.

"Please feel free to enlighten us." I said.

He stood up and locked his hands behind his back and started pacing back and forth like a teacher giving a lecture. "Carsoon's eighth shipping hub is located on the planet Bowdra." He said. "It was discovered by the Grawl more than seventy-five years ago and settled by small numbers of the hardier of their race. You see, while the planet does have an oxygen atmosphere, its location in relation to the local star is a bit too close. For the majority of Grawl it is well out of their comfort zones. The day time temperatures soar to over one-hundred and forty degrees."

Coonts was the one now frowning, and held up a hand to Bond. "Are you sure you have the correct data? I have heard of a place mentioned by members of my race, that sounds exactly like the planet you are referring too. The only difference is the name."

Before Coonts could say the words, Bond said them for him. "Scowmarned Charp!"

I was now fairly fluent in the Grawl language, and knew the words meant something like, "Unbearable heat."

Coonts gave Bond a nod of acknowledgement and the Coram continued with his oration. "The planet in its early forming stages, was highly volcanic. When it finally cooled, the lava tubes solidified, leaving behind a large number of natural tunnels and massive caverns. The Grawl that chose to stay, used the tunnels and caverns to shelter from the sweltering heat on the surface. They eventually built underground settlements and mined the lava tubes for the plentiful minerals encrusted in them. This went on for roughly twenty-five years. In that time the value of the mined minerals declined and the population did as well. What Scowmarned Charp lacked in environmental advantages, it made up for in location. It was perfectly located in the exact middle of several trade routes that were grossly overextended. In steps a Grawl named Bren Carsoon, he is ambitious, greedy, and ruthless. He is also fresh from a relief mission that made him a rising star among the elite of his race. When I say the elite, I don't mean Grawl who believe in sharing with the less fortunate. I mean Grawl who rose to power by whatever means necessary."

The look on Coonts face was slowly turning to a scowl. He didn't want to hear what we all knew was his races biggest shortcomings. He decided to steal a little of Bond's thunder.

"Commander, I have researched the subject and Bond is referring to a relief convoy that Bren led through a war-ravaged sector of the void. Back then, the Sig were still making war on any race who attempted to interfere with their conquests. The Murlaks were making an attempt to retake a region of the void they claimed was theirs. The Sig disagreed, and made the whole sector an exclusion zone. The two fought some very bloody battles over the territory. What both sides didn't know, was that my race had a secret artifact research center on one of the planetoids in that sector. It was the site of a large artifacts cache. The first attempts by members of my race to evacuate the scientist and artifacts, met with disaster. The fools refused to abandon the artifacts and were being preyed upon by both sides. Bren Carsoon led a relief convoy into the heart of the sector and covertly extracted the remaining Grawl and the artifacts. He was rewarded handsomely for the feat and gained fame for his daring exploit. Now, can we get back to the best way to execute our upcoming mission?"

Bond pretended like he didn't notice Coonts irritation. The rest of us were giving him frowns for his interruption. I for one, was interested in Bren Carsoon's background and the history of the planet our target was located on.

"Bond, please continue your briefing." I said, while casting a stink eye at Coonts.

"Yes, of course." Bond said clearing his throat. "I will shorten my treatise for those who are already aware of the history of Bren and his company. So, to take up where I left off, Bren Carsoon saw Scowmarned Charp as a means to shorten the length of several trade routes. He gambled most all of his wealth and that of several undisclosed investors, and bought the planet. It was originally supposed to be a mining venture. It was well known the minerals being processed at the three largest sites were marginal in value. It was the pretense that the planet's price was based on. What happened next, infuriated a large number of Grawl government officials, who agreed to the sale and compromised on the price. Bren immediately started construction on a shipping terminal in the guise of expanding the mining operation. All concerned took him at his word. Two and a half years later, it was discovered he was operating a huge shipping warehouse and freight transfer business out of the location, and raking in billions in credits. The Grawl could do nothing about it, and those who were connected to the deal, lost their prestige as well as their jobs."

Tria held up a finger. "When was the name of the planet changed to Bowdra?"

"Not long after the operation went public, Bren's life mate went missing. She was found dead and her body horrible mutilated. The corpse was dumped at the newly christened Hub Number Eight. Her name was Bowdra. Out of spite, and in a show of defiance to his enemies, Bren saw to it the planet's name was officially changed, so it would bear his life mate's title. I personally think his hate for those responsible, made Bren the ruthless leader he is to this day. Any who openly oppose him, is found in the same condition as his former life mate. Even though it is known Bren Carsoon can order the deaths of anyone he chooses, he does so with airtight alibis. I think it has a lot to do with the shipping magnate's future political ambitions, rather than his concern for possible prosecution." Bond answered.

With the exception of Coonts, we were impressed with the Coram's background data. I think we had grossly underestimated his intelligence. There was no more doubt in my mind about Bond's future with us.

24

Coonts stood up from his chair. It was my guess he had intended to lead our discussion and Bond stole the show. I was proven correct when he started poking his finger into the table top to emphasize his point. "While Bond's historical data is interesting, and Bren may make it onto our list of targets, we are here to discuss Genda Binar and Canik!"

Bond held his hands out to Coonts and sat back to listen. We turned our attention to the Grawl. I tried my best to keep the irritation of his interruptions out of my voice.

"Coonts, if you have a plan of action, let's hear it. If you don't, I expect you to keep quiet till you do. Unless of course you have something constructive to add, other than proof your ego is as blown out of proportion as your muscles."

My statement took some of the wind from his sails and a few unwelcome snickers from the Troop Master. At first, Coonts acted as if he was lost for words. He had me thinking he was making up his plan on the fly, much like I was guilty of, on more than a few occasions.

"Commander," Coonts said. "I do have some knowledge of Scowmarned Charp. It is admittedly very dated, but I can update our planning once we gather intel from the AO. I know there were three sites on the planet that contained the majority of the population. As bond has pointed out, the largest is now shipping hub eight. The other two sites are close enough to that location, they may be part of the shipping complex, depending on how much it has expanded. I am going to assume they are, because of the time that has pasted since the original data was conveyed to me. I was thinking we should insert Enoch... Bond, into the area and have him take up residence in one of the habitat complexes. It was my hopes to find a residence close to Genda Binar's living quarter's in tower one. If we are successful, it will give us a means to study the tower and its security. Once we establish that Genda is indeed in the tower, and his exact location, we use our technological advantage to gain access and capture him alive if possible. I believe he will have the information needed to capture Canik."

I had to give it to Coonts, his plan was more or less what I had in mind. It also lacked any of the details that made me think he had thought the plan through to completion. Tria, Klutch, and I, looked over at Bond to see what he thought of Coont's plan. His squinty eyed expression displayed his skepticism. He noticed he was the object of our attention, and slowly held up a hand.

Coonts followed our gaze and a scowl appeared on his face. "Yes Bond, is there something you would like to add?" Coonts said with just a hint of anger.

"Yes, Mr. Coonts. All the residence closest to the two business towers are wholly owned by Carsoon shipping. They are occupied by Bren's employees. Unless you know of a way to get me a job there, without going through a thorough background check, we will have to come up with another more viable approach."

You could almost see the steam rising from the over-muscled Grawl's head. It was all the proof we needed to confirm he was throwing something together willy-nilly. He probably would not have gone down that road were it not for the fact it was how I handled most missions, once our boots were on the ground. Since we would be initially putting Bond Connery's life on the line, I was going to need a plan with a lot more substance than something cooked up in the spur of the moment.

Bond cocked an eye at Coonts. He was keenly aware what was at stake if we were to make a haphazard misstep. It probably crossed his mind, that Coonts may have considered him expendable.

"There is a chance that a Grawl rather than a Coram, might be better suited for this mission. Perhaps we should consider inserting you, Mr. Coonts, into the shipping hub and see if they will consider you an acceptable candidate for employment. Your unusual physique may convince them you have spent your entire existence breaking big rocks into little ones at some obscure mining site. This may, or may not be considered the proper credentials for a job, but it will be better than what I can come up with." Bond said in a dead pan voice.

Klutch thought that was the funniest thing he had ever heard. His lowkey snickering blew up into his usual full-blown braying.

"Klutch, knock it off!" I pointed at him and then to Coonts. "You two clowns can go elsewhere until we are done planning the mission, or you can shut up and make sensible contributions."

That put a zipper on the Tibor's mouth and made Coonts take his seat. I looked back at Bond, and he lost the ear to ear grin he was giving Klutch.

"Bond, I know you have a plan so let's hear it." I said brusquely.

Well Mr. Myers, I know this might not sit well with everyone, but the simpler the plan, the more likely it will not draw the scrutiny of a complex affair. So, this is what I would do. I will go to the common areas of hub eight. That is where everyone mingles. Freighter crews, passengers, Carsoon employees it makes no difference who you are, you will end up in the common area sooner or later. The reason I say this is because you can do whatever you want there. You can eat, drink, rent a temporary living space, buy supplies or buy companionship, everything there is for sale as it was at my former outpost. A large percentage of the proceeds, finds its way back to Bren Carsoon, so he doesn't care what goes on. As long as no one starts any trouble, and his employees show up for work on time, it's business as usual. It has been like that since the freight hub opened, and I don't think it has changed since the last time I was there."

"What was the security like the last time you were there?" Tria asked.

"Remote observation is prevalent everywhere. A lot of it is in plain sight so everyone knows that someone is always watching. It would be foolish to think discreet monitoring wasn't taking place as well. Roving security was light when I was there. It was done by mixed races, and all were lightly armed. When it came to muscle, it was all automated. I'm talking security bots with shields, heavy armor, and weapons to match. I saw them break up a large brawl at a drinking establishment. The security bots went into a crowd of more than a hundred. They used high voltage and gas to subdue everyone. They hauled all the unconscious bodies to an undisclosed location. I heard those responsible went missing. The rest were released several hours later. They were dumped in the street until they came to their senses and vacated the area." Bond Connery replied.

Klutch finally got serious and asked the next question. "Do you have any idea how many security bots we would be facing if we started shooting the place up?"

"Unknown Klutch, I saw twelve from where I was viewing the altercation, but there could be hundreds. I know the weapons they had mounted on their armor, were larger than my what gunners used to carry. There's a possibility they could bring down a shuttle if they wanted too."

Coonts lost his scowl and asked a sensible question. "What was the response time of the bots, and do you have an idea from where they came from?"

Bond gave Coonts an appreciative look. "Excellent question Mr. Coonts. The brawl was huge. Something like that doesn't happen all at once. I would say that it definitely took more than twenty minutes for the security bots to arrive, and all came from the direction of the business towers."

Now we were getting somewhere. Bond's intel had me thinking the security bots were located at the business towers and any threat to that location would be quelled quickly and decisively. I suspected the death of Bren's mate prompted him to take steps to insure the same would not happen to him. Bond's guess at the number of security bots may be closer to a legitimate number than we would like. It was doubtful if Bren was at hub eight, but if he was, he would want ample security. Getting into a pitched battle with a large number of heavily armed bots was not something I was looking forward to. It could lead to excessive collateral damage if we were forced to use our beam weapons to defend ourselves.

"Okay Bond, let's get back to your plan. What have you come up with?"

"I am going to need a transport and credentials for a mining surveyor that will pass moderate scrutiny. Then I am going to need a sample of the ore you mentioned earlier. And finally, a secure location to store the decoy containers of waste rock."

The Coram's requests were all easy, and I wondered when we would get to the hard part of the mission. I had Justice open a comms channel to Tam Lin. In less than a minute she replied.

"What can I do for you Nathan?" She asked.

"Tam." I said. "Can you get me some fake credentials for Bond. They need to be for a mining surveyor and look good enough to pass inspection."

"I can get you a well-worn badge and legitimate credentials from the Sig. It would be a simple matter to change the ID chip numbers and photo. Then he would be carrying the real deal with valid locations stamped in it. Is there anything else Nathan?"

"Yes Tam, I need a secure location to store a couple of waste rock containers."

Bond called to me. "A transfer warehouse with good security, doesn't matter where!"

I turned and gave him a thumbs up. He wasn't sure what that meant exactly, but nodded affirmative. I saw Klutch lean over to him and explain it was a cultural thing.

"Did you get that Tam?"

"Yes, Nathan I heard him. It won't be a problem as long as the location can be a Sig owned storage facility."

I looked back at Bond Connery. He had a smile on his face and was holding both of his hands up, with thumbs extended downward. I gave him a small frown. Klutch reached over and turned his hands upward, making me chuckle. I told Tam Lin that would be perfect, and I would get back with her soon. Justice closed the comms channel.

"Okay Bond, what else are you going to need?" I said, thinking the list would get longer.

"Only time Mr. Myers. Perhaps a seven-day period. Less if my lying deceitful ways have not failed me."

I was glad he said that with a smile. Now we just needed to know how he was going to go about getting an audience with Genda Binar. We did have a lot of irons in the fire. Other than the Scrun mission, we could put everything else on hold for an extended period of time.

We were all staring at the Coram in anticipation of an explanation of how he was going to execute the mission.

Coonts finally had his fill of waiting and jumped up from his chair in exasperation. "Tell us how this is all going to work!" He blurted.

"I am going to purchase some middle-class clothing and will take the transport to hub eight. Once there, I will rent temporary living quarters. After I have secured a residence, I will purchase intoxicants and hire the services of the highest priced companion that is compatible with me. I will then drink, brag and fornicate for however long it takes to attract the proper attention." Bond said with a big enough smile to show off the new teeth that Justice had given him.

You could have heard a pin drop. Everyone with the exception of Klutch, was giving the Coram an incredulous look. The crazy Tibor was shaking his head up and down and giving Bond a big grin. He must have seen something in the plan we had yet to decipher. When Bond did not see the expression on our faces change to something more pleasant. He decided it might be a good idea to further explain his actions.

"Mr. Myers, I am going to use the prostitute to spread the word to his or her handlers that, I am going to be a very wealthy surveyor in the near future. After a few days of companionship, I will pretend to be intoxicated and show off the ore and leave it where it can be accessed. I will then act as if I am unconscious. If the prostitute is as astute as the many that frequented my former base, a small sample of the ore will be stolen. It will undoubtably end up in the hands of someone who has the ability to figure out exactly what it is. When that happens, I will not have to find Genda Binar, he will find me."

Bond's explanation managed to close our gaping mouths, but still didn't clear the uncertainty from our faces. The Troop Master was still shaking his head like the inappropriate bobble trinket I used to have on the dashboard of my old Chevy truck. He acted as if he knew the plan all along and looked at us with wide eyes and a big goofy smile.

"It's brilliant!" Klutch declared.

Coonts threw his hands into the air and stormed out of the conference room. I turned to Tria. She was rubbing her forehead. "You care to share your thoughts with me?" I asked.

"No!" Tria said, and then got up and walked out of the room.

Bond came and stood beside me. "Mr. Myers, I can see that some of your crew questions my methods, but I can assure you this will lead us to Genda Binar. He will want the Containium for his own. He will even hide the information from his employer, Bren Carsoon. You have to trust me on this. I know firsthand how greed affects one's ability to make rational decisions. When I reveal that I have stolen two hundred tons of the ore, and have it hidden in a warehouse. Genda will pull out all the stops to acquire it. When that happens, let whoever is sent to recover it, take it. It will just be a matter of following it, until it ends up in Genda's hands."

The more Bond talked, the more he convinced me his cockamamie plan might just work. "Have you thought about what might happen to you? It is your life you are gambling with."

"You put a tracker in my head so you can keep tabs on me, right? When you are sure we have Genda where we want him, pull me out. Besides, what could they possibly do to me, that the pirates have not already done. All I ask, is if they start cutting me up really bad, and you can't get me out, kill me with the tracker."

That was one of the ballsiest things I had ever heard come out of anyone's mouth. Bond Connery was a tough bastard and just proved it to me in spades. If he lived through the mission, he would never want for wealth ever again. The look Klutch was giving me, said in no uncertain terms, I should come clean on the tracker's capabilities. After what Bond just said, I didn't have the heart not to.

"About the tracker." I said to Bond. "It has some very unique qualities, and what I am about to tell you is one of our most highly guarded secrets. The device we put in you is not weaponized. It could have been, but I chose to take you at your word when you said you were no longer a criminal. The device is called an IST, which stands for Interdimensional Signal Transmitter. It gives us the ability to have real time communications with you most anywhere in the galaxy as long as you are not in a heavily shielded ship or structure. We can track you, and if the IST channel is open, we can hear everything you say. The AI that sent you here is named Justice. He will instruct you on how to properly operate the device."

The Coram stood staring at me with wide eyes. He seemed genuinely shocked by what I said.

"Mr. Myers, I am not sure what to say. The information you are giving me is astounding. I will guard your secrets with my life, but want you to know, if I were in your position, I would have used a weaponized tracker on you if I had the technology." Bond admitted.

"When we went to Outpost 655 and found you were alive, I was sickened by what the pirates were doing to you. It made me wish that I had ended your life. That was the moment I decided you more than paid for your sins against us, and I was going to free you. Since that time, I have had a chance to get to know you and like what I see. You have already proven to be resilient and intelligent. Those are qualities that make you a perfect candidate for my organization, and I want you to be a permanent member of my team. We need someone on the outside, who can covertly give us information we cannot collect on our own. You would be the right person for that job. If you take the offer and make a permanent obligation to our cause, you will receive the same compensation all members of my organization enjoy."

Bond squinted his eyes at me. "I take it you mean we keep the wealth we take from the criminals you target?"

"At one time we did, but now it is no longer necessary. We give all the wealth we take from criminals and transfer it to third party, who in turn sends it to those who are in need. As a matter of fact, we are now one of the biggest contributors to the Protected Planet Fund." I said with pride.

Now the Coram's eyes were bugging out. I guess the concept of giving wealth away was still new to him. It was going to take an adjustment period for him to accept that premise.

"When this mission is over, you will never be in a situation where you will need to scrape together credits for a project. You will have unlimited funding. Our discoveries have given us unimaginable wealth, and technology that few can rival."

Klutch slapped Bond on the back hard enough to wipe the stunned look from his face. "My Commander is not scatting you. More wealth passes through our hands than some developing civilizations."

"I am ready to start the mission." Bond mumbled.

I smiled at the Coram. "Take the credit voucher Sushi gave you, and purchase what you need. The balance on the card is yours to keep. I will arrange for you to have a well-used transport. We will get started as soon as you are ready."

Bond almost bowled Coonts over as he ran out of the room. The Grawl walked into the conference room frowning at me. "Is he running away because you put a halt to his stupid plan?"

"No Coonts, he is going to prep for the mission, and we are going to let him run with his plan. It's his ass on the line, so I hope for his sake he knows what he is doing."

25

I left Coonts in Klutch's company and went across the hall to my cabin. I closed the door on the sound of the two calling each other derogatory names. I found Tria napping. Shedding my uniform, I crawled in bed next to her and she rolled over to face me.

"Are you really going to let Bond run his own mission?" She asked.

"I don't see why not. As I pointed out to Coonts, he will be risking his own life if his plan falls apart. Do you think he has ulterior motives?"

"No, I just fear he is ill prepared for what may happen if he has to fend for himself until we can extract him." Tria said.

"He survived for years under the worst of conditions and endured abuse that should have killed him. He more or less told me he no longer fears death, he just doesn't want to be mutilated before he dies. I am going to do whatever it takes to make sure that won't happen. If we have to go in shooting to extract him, he will have no problem figuring out we are coming to his aid."

Tria gave me a kiss. "I hope that it does not come to that."

We woke two hours later when Justice alerted us Bond Connery was on his way to Tam Lin's shipping docks. He would be boarding a utility transport and departing for his mission. He also reported our Grawl guests were now in fair condition and all were in the galley consuming nutrient heavy rations. I wanted them to know they would be free to go. I was going to contact Tam Lin and arrange for a transport to take them back to the Grawl home worlds. Tria and I showered and put on fresh uniforms and made our way to the galley. To our surprise Coonts was standing on a table in front of the group of former prisoners. He was telling them about the Grawl scientist we had rescued, and that they now worked for us. Tria and I stopped outside the galley to listen.

Kevel stood and approached the table where Coonts stood. "Coonts." Kevel said. "All but a few of my scientific scholars survived our imprisonment. The rest are maintenance specialist or surveyors. Your offer of a new home and permanent employment is very attractive, but our skill sets may not be suitable for your needs. We have decided we wish to stay together. If it were not for the support we gave each other, we would not have survived the brutal conditions we were forced to live in. Unless we can be employed as a group and remain together, we wish to go elsewhere."

Tria and I walked into the galley and Coonts jumped down from the table. We stood with him and a murmur passed through the group of Grawl. I suspected they had never seen a human before.

I held up my hands and they quieted. "I am Nathan Myers, and this is Tria." I pointed at Coonts. "With Coonts, and my Tibor Troop Master's help, we are the ones who freed you. The first thing I would like to do is commend whoever rigged the exterior lighting on the pirate outpost. If it were not for your distress signal, we may have destroyed the base without further investigation."

One of the Grawl stood up. He had a prosthetic leg from his knee down. He was the Grawl wounded in the shootout with the pirates. A cheer went up among the Grawl. Tria, Coonts and I clapped, showing our appreciation and support for the Grawl's efforts to save the crew. They seemed surprised at first by our clapping applause, but quickly took it for what it was meant to be.

Kevel put his arm around the Grawl's shoulders. "This is Delmar, he was our ship's maintenance specialist. It was his idea to trace the individual circuits that led to the damaged airlock. He knew they passed through our hidden prison cell. He singlehandedly located them in the short periods of time that light was on in our enclosure. With the help of others, we isolated a live circuit and ran a conductor to the exterior light feed. Each time we were locked in the hidden cell, we took turns grounding the circuit to send the distress signal."

I bowed to the Grawl. "Delmar, I want to personally commend you for saving the lives of your crewmates. If it were not for your efforts, you may have all perished from my retaliatory strikes on the pirate base."

Klutch walked into the galley and heard what I had to say. He came over and stood with us as we again applauded the efforts of the Grawl surveying crew.

I held up my hands again to quiet the gathering. "I can assure all of you, I have a place in my organization for you, and can guarantee you will remain together. If it is agreeable to you, I will take you to my base of operations, where you can be among others of your race that Coonts spoke of. After meeting and speaking with them, if you decide you do not wish to stay, I will make arrangements for you to be returned to your home worlds."

This got me the desired results. The Grawl cheered once more, and several even clapped their hands together this time. The crew and I left the galley and went to the brig. We would be deciding if we were going to keep the prisoners or turn them over to the Sig. I wanted to question them again.

"Justice." I called. "Have you decoded any of the DSM data from the pirate gunship?"

"I am still processing the data Commander. The Galactic Union uses a coding algorithm unlike any we have encountered before. It also appears that dated information is randomly scrambled and stored on different memory cores selected by the ships AI. There is the possibility the older data can only be retrieved and reconstructed by the AI. I will alert you if I have a breakthrough on the most recently recorded data."

That didn't sound promising. I would like to know who was responsible for making Galactic military hardware available to the pirates. I knew if I found out, I was going to have a very short conversation with them. It would be a good question to put to the Rugerian assassin.

As we entered the brig, Justice cleared the cell walls. Both the prisoners were on their bunks. They quickly got up and stood at the cell wall. Both looked disheveled and could have used some sleep. Being in their current situation, I doubted if I could have slept either.

"I have determined you both have very limited usefulness to me. My allies the Sig on the other hand, said they have methods to obtain information from you that I would find distasteful. Unless you can give me very specific reasons why I should not turn you over to them, they will be here to collect you shortly." I warned.

The Murlak mercenary was the first to break his silence. Justice blacked out the Rugerian's cell and killed the audio so he would not know what was said. There was a chance we could get the Rugarian to verify what we were being told by the Murlak.

"I know many things my employers would not like to be known." The mercenary exclaimed. "All I ask in return for the information is my freedom. If you drop me at any outpost, I can guarantee you will never see me again."

"If I were to turn you over to the Sig, I can guarantee you will never be seen again." I replied with a sneer.

That comment got a quick response from the merc. "I beg you not to turn me over to the Sig! Our orders from Canik, were to coordinate with the other mercenaries hired to collect Kenna. Once Kenna was in our hands, he was to be turned over to the Rugerian assassin. The rest of us were ordered to kill all the pirates at their base. We were specifically told to make an example out of them. After we completed that mission, we were told to jump back to a location near Outpost 9765 and link up with a strike team that was preparing for an operation at the outpost."

That was very interesting information. The two mercs had no idea we were already at 9765. Before I could ask, Tria beat me to it.

"If what you say is true, what are the coordinates of the rally point."

The pirate gave us the location, and stated that he and the Rugerian were the only ones with that information. We would make an attempt to have the Rugerian confirm the intel. Stepping away from the cell I called to Justice. He muted the audio so the prisoners would not hear what I had to say.

I had him open a comms channel to Tam Lin, she immediately answered. "Nathan, I was just getting ready to call you. We got Bond Connery his documents and a utility transport. He has departed the outpost and your ore is in transit to a Sig freight holding facility. It should arrive in two days. Is there something else I can help you with?" She asked.

"Tam, we just got intel from one of our prisoners. He says there is an operation going to take place on the outpost. It involves an unknown number of mercenaries. I think you and Pasta better come over and hear it for yourselves."

413

"Are you sure Nathan? We don't have any intelligence indicating an imminent threat." Tam hurriedly replied.

"Tam, I wouldn't have called unless I thought the intel was legitimate."

Tam and Pasta showed up fifteen minutes later. Pasta was wearing his battle armor. I told them what the prisoner had to say. They seemed skeptical, but Pasta passed the information on to the Sig garrison. They took the precaution of issuing orders that grounded all outbound ship traffic. He said his troops were on alert and were dispersing to security stations throughout the outpost. I had them sit outside of the brig and listen in. I walked back over to the Murlaks cell.

"It appears you are telling the truth so far. My AI has verified the location you gave us is very close to Outpost 9765." I said.

"I am trying to prove to you it will be worth your time to give me my freedom." The Murlack implored.

The Murlak was sounding more desperate by the minute. His fear of the Sig was justified. They loathed criminals and pirates as much as I did and their interrogation methods mirrored ours in many ways. The big difference was they always killed the prisoners unless they had some intrinsic value other than information.

"If you think giving us some small amount of obscure information will win your freedom, you are sadly mistaken. I want verifiable information before I will consider not turning you over to the Sig." I threatened.

The Murlak was quick to reply. "Once we were at the rally point near Outpost 9765, I was ordered to relinquish the command of any surviving members of my team. A Scrun mercenary named Ortulla Corva would take overall command and lead us to our next objective on the outpost."

"What was the target?" Klutch demanded.

"I do not know! That was information known only to Ortulla!" The Murlak pleaded.

I had Justice black out the cell and mute the audio. We walked out of the brig to where Tam Lin and Pasta stood anxiously waiting.

Tam Lin had a look of anger on her face. "I think I am the one responsible for what is happening. By sending Kenna into the Ilor Guild asking questions about Bolus, I let Canik know we were actively looking for him. He now knows this outpost is somehow connected to you and your team."

415

Pasta was keeping his security teams informed of our findings. They were in turn, passing the intel directly to General Bonaparte. Pasta suddenly put his hand to the side of his head and looked down at me with a concerned look on his face.

"Commander Myers, there are seven of my people's warships that patrol the sector around the outpost. They jumped to the coordinates the prisoner gave you, and report that there is no unidentified spacecraft in that location. General Bonaparte has taken overall command, and is reviewing the logs for all inbound ships. For the time being, he is ignoring the large number of small transports and shuttles. His focus is on freighters and shuttles large enough to easily conceal a strike force. He is reporting that four hundred and twenty ships fitting those parameters, have landed in the past six hours. Of the ninety-two commercial docks on the outpost, only two have reported any problems. Both had to do with contraband, and the captains and crews are being held in our custody." Pasta said.

Coonts was running the timing through his oversized brain. He gave us his thoughts. "Commander, the pirate frigate that jumped to hyperspace soon after our rescue of Kenna, must have reported our attack on the mercenary forces. That event more than likely caused the mercenaries running this operation, to move up their timetable. Without considering any unknown factors that could increase or decrease the time it took for the intel to propagate; I would guess the hostiles had several hours if not a day to start their operation."

"Do you still have security drones up near the Ilor Guild?" Tria asked Tam Lin.

"Not currently." She replied. "General Bonaparte has all the security feeds from around the outpost monitored. If there was something going down, he would be the first to know."

Pasta called the General and asked for a sitrep of that location. Several minutes passed and he reported no unusual activity. The General decided to send in the squad that was observing the Guild, and have them report their findings. Again, we waited, wondering if the mercenary prisoner was telling us the truth or the operation was called off. After more than twenty-five minutes, The General called Pasta saying the squad could not raise anyone at the

Guild. He was sending in additional troops and a breach team to investigate.

"Pasta." I said, looking up at the big Sig commander. "Tell the General my team can do the breach. We are already familiar with the compound. It will keep his troops from looking like trespassers in the eyes of the Ilor if it turns out nothing is amiss."

Pasta relayed my request. He shook his head negative. "No, Commander Myers. The General says this is a matter for outpost security. It would not look good if it was discovered that an unknown group of combatants was allowed to breach a consulate on the outpost. Security on the outpost and in this sector, is his responsibility. He says he will keep us informed."

I knew it was the General's call and he was right. We had no choice but to honor his orders and wait to see what his breach team finds when they get inside.

Twenty minutes later, Justice called out a chilling alert. "Commander! I have just detected a large anti-matter detonation in the location of the Ilor Guild."

Tam Lin and Pasta were staring wide eyed after hearing the report. "Justice." I called. "Get us as close to the site as safely possible."

Pasta called to the docking officer and had him open the hangar door. Justice launched then gave us another unsettling alert. "Commander! Four small shuttles just departed one of the commercial dock areas at very low level. I am intercepting reports they did not have launch clearance and are flying toward restricted areas of the outpost."

Pasta called out a warning to us. "Commander Myers, you must be careful you are not engaged by the outpost defensive weapons. Once activated they will engage all unidentified vessels flying into restricted areas!"

Justice put up a view screen on the bulkhead. He put red boxes around the shuttles as they streaked across the outpost just over the tops of the buildings. We were shocked to silence as they spread out and nosed over into the outpost. There were four large scale detonations that blotted out the viewscreen. When it reset, we saw four large craters and massive fires.

Pasta turned to me shocked at what we just saw. He dropped any military decorum. "Nathan, they just took out my garrison and the outpost security station. The other two went down in the market areas close to Haras. It is where my off-duty troops gather for recreation."

Klutch was standing close to Pasta and grabbed him by the hand with both of his. "Pasta, was General Bonaparte in the garrison when it was attacked?"

The shocked expression on Pasta's face disappeared and he focused on Klutch. "I am not sure Troop Master. He may have been going to the Ilor Guild."

The Sig turned to me. "Commander Myers, you must get me back to the dock so I can help with the rescue operations. If Canik is responsible for this act of terrorism, he may have just killed thousands of innocent bystanders." He exclaimed.

I called to Justice and told him to take us back to Tam Lin's private dock. Tam Lin was screaming cuss words and swearing revenge. My crew and I were silent. It probably crossed everyone's minds the suicide attack was directed at us. We headed straight for the dock, flying low through thick dark clouds of smoke rising up from the raging fires in the impact zones. Tam Lin and Pasta departed without speaking. Both were in shock at the devastation we overflew on the way to her docking area.

Justice called to us as we rapidly departed the dock. "Commander, I recorded some unusual background signals when I intercepted the comms traffic reporting the low flying shuttles. The signals appear to be on the same carrier wave as the freighter dock control tower. After carefully analyzing the signals I have determined they came from two different transmitters that are sharing the same antenna. The second transmitter is in close proximity to the control tower. The unique signals were being continuously transmitted right up until the shuttles impacted their targets. I find it very noteworthy that they terminate at the exact time of the shuttle's impacts. This new information makes me speculate the shuttles were remotely piloted to their destination points."

It took a second for that to sink in. That would mean it wasn't a suicide attack after all. It also meant there was a chance that Ortulla and his terrorist were still somewhere on the outpost, because Pasta had all the departing traffic grounded. There was also the chance the hostiles would have made their escape on outbound flights. The information from the Murlak mercenary may not have been timely enough to stop the attack, but it was in enough time to cut off Ortulla's escape. Anyone attempting to depart without clearance, would be shot down by the outpost defensive weapons systems.

The Legacy was still cloaked and our stealth systems engaged. I had Justice move us to the freight docks and hold us low over the edge of the warehouse district that was closest to the control tower. I thought seriously about giving Tam Lin and Pasta a heads up on our findings. I finally nixed the idea. They were going to have their hands full with the large number of casualties from the attack. The information would only complicate their efforts. I would give them a sitrep if we found something worth reporting.

Looking into the eyes of my crew, told me they were wanting payback as bad as I did. "Armor up!" I shouted.

26

We ran the short distance to the ready room, finding that Justice already had our armor crates open and ready. We put on our suit liners and stepped up into the tools of our trade.

Now, all we needed was a target to focus our ire on. I was hoping Justice would come up with some additional information. "Justice, have you got a lock on that second transmitter?"

"Negative Commander, there has been no additional transmission signals to gather directional intel from. Logic dictates the hostiles would abandon the device and seek shelter elsewhere."

Justice put a view screen up on the ready room wall and we gathered around it. He put an overhead view of the area on the screen and then a large circle centering roughly on the control tower.

"Commander it has been eighteen minutes since I recorded the signal. I have centered my search pattern on an area near the control tower. I have to assume a stealthy departure from an unknown number of combatants. The area inside of the circle is a best guess scenario for the distance the mercenaries could have traveled in any one direction. The area increases in size for every minute that passes."

As we watched, the circle grew, encompassing more of the outpost and increasing the size of the search area. It was maddening to watch and gave me a feeling of both frustration and helplessness at the same time. The circle suddenly became a misshaped blob.

"Commander." Justice said. "I am eliminating areas that would lack adequate cover. I am assuming the mercenaries are heavily armed and would not discard their weapons during retreat. If this is in fact the case, they will want to stay in cover and disperse so they will not draw undue scrutiny."

The search area became more of an elongated blob. It was moving out into the warehouse district. Things were becoming more difficult by the minute. The outpost was multi-leveled and Justice put a three-dimensional depiction of the search area next to his original search zone. It was already to the depth of two levels and slowly spreading to a third.

"Commander!" Justice called. "I have intercepted a distress call from among the six thousand forty-two that are being broadcast. The call came from the warehouse district to the rear of our location. The call is reporting two dead bodies have been discovered."

Justice put the source of the call on his search area. It was in the middle of the elongated part of his escape pattern and still on the surface of the warehouse search area. He was definitely working in the right direction.

"Justice, move us over the location of the call!" I ordered.

Turning to Coonts and Klutch, I pointed out at the hangar doors. "You two jump here and search out from the area where the bodies were discovered. Stay cloaked and be careful not to run into any civilians. Tria and I will jump at the leading edge of Justice's search area and work back toward you. If you encounter someone suspicious, detain them by whatever non-lethal means is necessary. We need someone to question. Move out!"

Coonts and Klutch cloaked and ran to the hangar door. Tria and I were right behind them. They jumped as soon as the door was open enough to accept Klutch's wide frame. Justice suddenly accelerated and stopped in the blink of an eye. The buildings below us blurred and then we were stationary once again. Tria and I cloaked then jumped. Tria accelerated ahead of me and was moving rapidly down to a low rooftop overlooking a trash strewn ally. We landed as softly as possible and looked to see if there was any movement below us. Our scans turned up nothing. We dropped into the alley and Tria commed me. "Nathan, I will go to the far side of this building and work back toward Coonts and Klutch. Give me thirty seconds and you should do the same."

I smiled, and acknowledged her suggestion. You could take the pretty alien away from her military, but you damn sure couldn't take the captain out of her. We worked in a zig-zag pattern, following the maze of alleys back the thousand or so yards, that separated Coonts and Klutch from our current position.

Coonts called out suddenly. "Commander! I just picked up a faint power source forward of my position. It does not appear to be from a weapon, I think it is from a cloaking suit! I am moving into position to intercept the scan return. Klutch is paralleling the target and will try to cut off any attempt to escape in his direction."

"Roger that, Tria and I are moving toward you. I want the target alive if at all possible!"

Coonts called back a curt reply. "Acknowledged!"

My suit AI put Coonts and Klutch's locations in my HUD. Their target appeared as a yellow blinking dot. It was moving forward in a stop and go progression. The target was being cautious and watching their back trail before leapfrogging forward. This had to be one of Ortulla Corva's terrorist. They had advanced cloaking and good quality shielding around their power sources. The range to the target Coonts was tracking, was inside of a hundred yards. We would normally have got a detection at three times that distance.

"Coonts commed us on the group channel. "Commander, the target is not emanating any weapon power sources. I suspect this was intentional and the target is armed with fueled or detonation accelerated projectile weapons."

I acknowledged Coonts call. Our armor was impervious to most hand held weapons that used explosive expansion as a projectile accelerant. Anti-matter was one of the few things that could be a serious threat. It was extremely hard to shield in a small projectile. Most other types of shielding that could hide anti-matter from our sensors, would make the diameter of the warhead the size of a football. As long as the terrorist didn't have exotically shielded anti-matter munitions such as we carried, being shot was not a desirable outcome, but it wasn't going to be an issue.

Just when it looked like our target was boxed in, Klutch called out an alert. "Commander, I have a power source detection that just popped up in my HUD. It is to the right of my position, and I am moving to intercept!"

Shit! We were going to have to split up. "Tria!" I called. "Back up Klutch and I will keep moving toward Coonts."

Tria commed me a quick reply. "Changing vectors now!"

My HUD showed Tria's blue icon peel off and move for the second yellow blinking dot that appeared close to Klutch's position. I concentrated on the yellow dot that Coonts was rapidly closing on. He was now within a couple hundred feet of the target. I picked up my pace trying to close the distance. The target was now less than a hundred yards from me. It made a sudden turn that put the blinking dot at the end of the alley to my right. I stopped and kneeled at the head of the passage and waited. Unless they ducked into an open doorway, the terrorist would have to pass directly in front of me. I opted to use a call from Tria's playbook. Pulling my shotgun from its clip I gripped it by the barrel and drew back for a full roundhouse swing. The target's icon was now about seventy-five feet from me and slowing. Coonts was at the opposite end of the alleyway and coming up behind it. The terrorist had nowhere to go.

As the target cautiously slowed to a stop at the head of the alley, it was less than five feet from me. My suit scanners gave me excellent definition on the cloaked combatant. He was Scrun and was wearing a bulky exoskeleton. As he turned to move away from me, I smashed my shotgun down on the junction of his shoulders above his faceplate. He stumbled forward and his cloaking flickered on and off.

Coonts called to me over my comms. "Stand clear Commander!"

He boosted up the alley with his gravity drives and smashed into the Scrun at considerable velocity, driving him into the wall of the building next to us. The wall partially collapsed, burying Coonts and the Scrun in rubble. Coonts reared up out of the debris and smashed his fist into the back of the exoskeleton over and over. Sparks and smoke flew from the Scrun's armor.

"Coonts!' I yelled. "Stop, or you will kill him!"

"Commander, he must not communicate with other members of his assault team!" Coonts yelled back at me."

I hadn't even thought of that. I just wanted to apprehend the piece of scat. "Justice! I need an immediate evac!"

"Commander, my scanners have located additional targets. Do you want to intercept them as well?"

"Negative! I need this prisoner isolated as soon as possible!"

The words had hardly left my mouth when Coonts and I, along with the prone body of the Scrun, were jerked upwards out of the debris by the Legacy's tow beam and dumped on the hangar deck. I heard Tria shouting over the group comms net. She was calling to Klutch, telling him she wanted the prisoner alive. Justice moved to their location and a few seconds later, Tria, Klutch and another Scrun were laying in a heap on the deck next to us. Justice closed the hangar door and moved away from the outpost at maximum velocity. Two medevac gurneys were rapidly approaching us.

"Justice are the Scrun still alive?" I called out in a panic.

"Justice's response brought my heart rate down several notches with his reply. "Yes Commander. Both are unconscious from blunt trauma. My initial scans reveal they have numerous broken bones and dislocations, but will survive with minimal medical aid. I will strip them of their gear and set the most serious of their fractures. They will be stabilized enough to interrogate, and I will administer stimulants that will keep them lucid throughout the process."

431

Justice was going to make sure they would not pass out from their injuries. The AI was mirroring my lack of pity, and lust for revenge. He was using his choice of free will, to ignore any programmed morals he may have had.

"Justice, open a comms channel to Pasta."

"Commander, the equipment necessary to communicate with Pasta or Tam Lin must have been damaged in the attack. Our normal lines of communication are no longer functioning."

"Pasta will have a backup of some kind, see if you can find an alternate channel."

"Affirmative Commander. I have identified an active military network being utilized by the Sig. Access will require a brute force intrusion."

Hacking an ally's military network during a state of emergency, was usually not considered a friendly act. I hoped I was not going to seriously piss off the Sig, but felt the information I had, would justify the means.

"Do it Justice. Pasta's channel only."

I was shocked by how quickly Justice did the deed. In less than two minutes he called to me. "The channel is now open Commander."

"Pasta, this is Nathan Myers, I need to urgently speak with you."

Pasta came back with a hurried response. The irritation quickly fading from his voice. "Nathan, I can give you a sitrep but don't have time for a full briefing. We have several thousand dead and thousands more wounded. Tam Lin and I have set up a triage in the remains of Haras. More than half of my garrison have been killed. The only survivors were the troops that deployed around the outpost prior to the attack. Of those, we have more than three hundred wounded and an unknown number still missing. General Bonaparte was found alive near the Ilor Guild but is in critical condition. It would be best for you to stay clear of the outpost until further notice. I have taken command in the General's absents and have issued a full military lockdown. No spacecraft of any origin is allowed to leave the outpost, and all inbound ship traffic is being quarantined at a holding point by battleships from my people's fleet. The rest of the fleet has moved in close to the outpost's atmospheric retention field and sending down all available medical support and troops to police the outpost."

"Pasta, I am sorry I had to have my AI hack your comms feed, but I urgently needed to tell you we have captured two Scrun we believe took part in the attack on the outpost."

"WHAT!" The Sig yelled. "Where are they now?"

"I have them in the brig aboard the Legacy. It is my intention to question them and find out where they were going when we captured them."

"You captured them on the outpost?" Pasta said with surprise.

"Yes, in the warehouse district near the freighter docks. Justice discovered the carrier signal the terrorist used to remotely pilot the shuttles to where they crashed and detonated. He then surmised an egress route they would have to take to avoid detection. When he intercepted a report of two dead bodies found in the warehouse district, we started searching there." I explained.

Pasta was quiet for more than a minute. Then said in a saddened voice "We have had so many reports of dead or dying we cannot begin to investigate them all. I had assumed the attack was a suicide mission."

"Pasta." I said. "I believe the terrorists planned to escape during the havoc created by their attack. When you grounded all the outgoing ship traffic prior to the attack, I think you unknowingly cut off their escape. If my theory is correct, they have to be somewhere on the outpost. It will be just a matter of making the prisoners tell us where."

There was rage in Pasta's voice when he replied. "Bring them to Tam Lin's private dock Commander Myers. They are going to tell me where the rest of the terrorist are hiding, one way or another."

Justice traversed the outpost in seconds and landed in Tam Lin's dock. Several minutes passed and Pasta showed up with several troopers marching behind him. Tam Lin was bringing up the rear of the formation. Justice dropped the boarding ramp and they quickly came aboard. There was fire in the eyes of the Sig, and I knew the prisoners were going to regret not having a chance to kill themselves before being captured.

My crew and I escorted the Sig contingent to the brig. Justice opened the cell doors containing the Scrun. Justice made sure our other prisoners could see what was happening. Pasta had two of his troopers drag the Scrun from the gurneys they were lying on. The Scrun groaned out in pain when they hit the deck. The Sig dragged them all the way to the open hangar door, and threw them down the ten plus feet to the dock floor. Now the prisoners were screaming. Tam Lin looked a little pale and Tria took her by the hand and led her away. The Sig jumped to the dock deck and surrounded the two Scrun. Klutch decided the short trip to the deck wasn't enough abuse to loosen the Scrun's tongues. He leaped out of the hangar door and landed on the legs of the Scrun closest to him. The screams coming from the prisoner were bone chilling. Pasta and his troopers stood stone faced.

Klutch turned to the other Scrun and pulled him up from the deck. His face was inches from the terrorist's faceplate. "If you tell us where the rest of your team is hiding, you will die quickly. If not, your interrogation will take a very long time." He punctuated his statement with a stomp that flattened the Scrun's hand.

Now both the Scrun were screaming in agony. Klutch held his hands out to Pasta like he was awarding him with a present. Pasta and his troops crowded in around the two and took turns asking questions. When they didn't receive answers, they started stomping on their appendages. The bloodcurdling screams were echoing off the cavernous dock's walls. One of the Scrun finally gave Pasta the location of their intended rally point and how many were involved in the attack. There were thirty hostiles and they came in on a Carsoon owned medium freighter. They were hiding inside of shipping containers. The shuttles used in the attack were offloaded from the freighter as well. As far as we knew the ship that brought the terrorist was still at the docks and probably loading legitimate freight for an outbound flight. The Scrun's escape and evasion fallback position, was in the outpost's shipyards. There were several abandoned freighters that were being cannibalized for their hull plates. The rally point was in a large fragment of a freighter in the back of the scrapyard. Now that we knew where to search, at some point we would have other prisoners. Pasta decided he was not going to honor Klutch's promise of a quick death. Killing his troops was one thing but the deaths of thousands of innocent bystanders was another. He had his soldiers throw the two Scrun in the fires that were still burning where his garrison once stood. Without their armor and life support systems they would be roasted alive in their pressure suits.

I had Justice dump the Scrun armor and weapons on the dock floor. I told Pasta and his troopers about the energy shielding and cloaking capabilities of the suits. This was several technological steps above anything we had encountered before. It gave the hostiles a marked advantage over the combat armor worn by the Sig. The weapons they carried were small solid fuel rocket launchers. The projectiles had special alloy armor piercing tips and high explosive payloads. The Scrun carried three-hundred of the eight-inch thumb sized missiles, in ammo packs mounted on the sides of their exoskeletons. Their sidearms were auto loaders with barrel diameters larger than my old ten-gauge shotgun. They fired a caseless high explosive frangible munition. Neither weapon radiated a detectable power source, further enhancing their cloaking capabilities. Everything about these Scrun was different. We had gone up against hit teams who had specific orders to kill us, and they weren't nearly as well equipped as these guys. I was thinking the best way to find out about this specialized team, was to capture Ortulla alive. The longer we waited the more likely the terrorist would move to another location. I know I would, if a couple of my troops failed to show up at the rally point.

Pasta walked over to me after examining the Scrun equipment. I was going to make an attempt to convince him to sit this out and let me go after the terrorist. To my complete surprise he agreed with me.

"Commander Myers, if it were not for your efforts, we would still think this was a suicide attack." Pasta said. "For now, I can't spare anyone from the rescue operations until a relief fleet jumps into the system. They are still more than twelve hours away in hyperspace. When the fleet arrives, I will personally board and arrest the crew of the freighter that brought the strike team, but it is obvious I am ill-equipped to track down Ortulla."

I told him I wanted all the civilians evacuated from the area. Pasta said he had already called for all available civilians to help with the rescue and firefighting efforts. He told us to be cautious, but doubted if any civilians would be in the scrapyard.

He reached out and put his big hand on my shoulder. "Good luck Commander Myers, and good hunting. I am counting on you to avenge the innocent, and show my surviving troops their comrades did not die in vain."

27

Klutch and I boarded the Legacy. We found Tria, Coonts, and Tam Lin sitting in the ready room. Coonts and Tria were explaining to Tam Lin the events that led up to the discovery of the Scrun terrorist. She was still shaken by the attack on the outpost.

Tam looked up at me. "Did Pasta find out where the rest of the Scrun are hiding?"

"Yes, we are going to go after them."

"Nathan, I can't help but think I am responsible for what has happened. I should not have sent Kenna to investigate the Ilor Guild. My actions made us a bullseye on Canik's target list."

"Tam, if I hadn't requested information on Bolus you would not have sent Kenna to the Guild. Dwelling on our past actions will not change what is happening. When we rescued Kenna, we captured a Rugerian who went as far as saying he allowed himself to be taken prisoner. He said he was given a message to deliver to us. The message stated that if we quit interfering with the illegal activities of several races, they would make us rich beyond our wildest dreams. The terrorist attack may have been the result of us declining the offer. We are some of the most despised and hunted aliens by all corrupt races. Now that I have refused the offer, I fear this is just the beginning of their all-out efforts to stop us."

Tam Lin was shocked at the revelation. She was speechless and her pallor reflected her dismay. "Shit Nathan! I knew you were stirring up trouble for the pirates and a few others, but I had no idea just how far they would go to kill you."

"Tam, this is a tactic used by all terrorist. They think if they can inflict enough collateral damage, they can break the will of the people who are supporting the efforts to stop them. It would be best if you went back to Haras and helped with the wounded. You do not want to be further associated with what we are going to do to these criminals. Since coming to the stars, my moral and ethical values have been degraded to the point they are almost non-existent. After what has taken place here, it is going to be an eye for an eye from now on. I am going to kill those corrupt sons of bitches on a scale that they will never recover from."

Tam Lin stood up to leave. She looked at each of my crewmates and saw the determination in their demeanor. Klutch smiled at her and flexed his big arms while cracking his knuckles. That seemed to relieve some of her trepidation, and she gave me a small halfhearted smile.

"Good luck Nathan, I want you to know I will always help you any way I can, no matter the consequences."

She walked to the boarding ramp and stepped off the Legacy. I watched her disappear into the smokey haze of the still burning fires.

"I called to Justice. "Take us over the target area. I want full scans of the scrapyard. We need to know what the terrorist are up to."

"Affirmative Commander, moving now!"

"Make sure your munitions are at capacity. We are going to get some payback!" I yelled at my crew.

Justice put a viewscreen on the ready room wall. We had a close-up view of the target. He highlighted three faint power sources in locations high up on the scrapped hull, that was the target given to us by the Scrun prisoners.

"Commander, the three power sources I have highlighted, are undoubtedly lookouts. I have run a number of scenarios, and all have arrived at the same conclusion. If escape is no longer possible, the hostiles will not be taken alive. I further surmise the target will be rigged with suicide munitions. The hostiles will attempt to lure any pursuers into the freighter and detonate the charges in hopes of taking as many with them as possible. If you are to succeed in this mission, you must identify Ortulla's location, and use our technological advantages to remove him, before they detonate the devices."

"Damn, is that all?" I said sarcastically.

"Commander, your goal to capture Ortulla is achievable. The negation systems in your battle armor, have already proven to be undetectable by the Scrun battle suit sensors. You will have to bypass the sentries and concentrate on locating Ortulla. In the event the Scrun are using devices similar to those used in the shuttle attacks, they will be anti-matter in nature. If you are in close proximity to any such devices, your sensors will identify the threat depending on how well they are shielded. If you are allowed enough time to scan the devices, I may be able to show you how to deactivate any anti-tamper triggers that will undoubtedly be present."

I personally didn't want anything to do with disarming anti-matter charges, and hoped I would not get the chance to try. The more I thought about it, it made better sense to just kill the bastards. A precision shot from the Legacy's beam weapons would take care of the problem without risking my crew's lives. I was going to run the idea by my team when Justice called out an alert.

"Commander, there are two ground transports leaving the scrapyard entrance, and I have just detected the powerplant of a small freighter coming online in repair bay number six. If the civilians in the area responded to Pasta's emergency orders, that would make the detected activities highly suspect."

"Have you detected any movement at the freighter hull?"

"Negative Commander, the detected power sources have not moved."

"I need some recommendations Justice!"

"I can only speculate Commander, but now that the scenarios have changed, there is a very real possibility the terrorist are going to make additional attacks on the outpost."

I needed to make some snap decisions, and I needed to do it now. The ground transports could be loaded with explosives.

"Tria, you and Coonts take the transports. If it looks like they are headed for population centers, stop them by whatever means necessary. Klutch you're with me. We are going to find out what is happening on the freighter."

We cloaked and ran to the hangar door. Justice opened it wide enough for us to jump and we went out together. Tria and Coonts peeled off and dropped down to roof top level and boosted hard for the transports. The yellow triangles in my HUD that represented the targets suddenly split up. They were now going in opposite directions. Tria and Coonts split up as well, and their blue icons rapidly gained on their targets. Klutch and I dropped to just off the deck. The Troop Master weaved us in and out of the large pieces of derelict ships strewn throughout the scrapyard. As we approached the massive repair dock, Justice called out another warning.

"Commander, there are eleven cloaked targets working on the cradle locks holding the freighter in place. It appears they are attempting to manually disengage the maglocks, and disconnect the umbilical's in preparation for departure."

"Roger that Justice. Be prepared to strike the freighter if we fail to stop it getting underway."

"Affirmative Commander standing by."

I was a little confused by what the terrorist were up to, but it wasn't hard math. If the intel from the two prisoners was correct, we had the other twenty-eight hostiles accounted for. Based on an assumption there was a single operator aboard each of the ground transports, we still had three holding in the scrapyard and the other twenty-three were working on getting the small freighter ready to depart. That made me think the scrapyard freighter was a trap meant to draw us in. The sentries were in positions that were easily detectable. When that didn't garner the response, they thought they would get, they moved on to other contingencies. The transports had to be distractions designed to give the freighter enough time to clear the repair dock and jump to hyperspace. Tria verified my suspicions with her alert.

"Nathan! I think the transport is heading for the defensive weapons tower closest to the repair dock. What are you orders?"

Coonts called as well. "Commander, Tria's report is correct. My target is headed directly for the weapons tower at the far end of the repair dock."

"Stop them without damaging the cargo boxes if possible!"

I got two quick acknowledgements. "Klutch." I called. "Do you know where the bridge is located?"

"I cannot be positive Commander; I have never been aboard a freighter of this design. It has to be somewhere forward."

"Pick a spot and make a hole Troop Master!"

The medium sized freighter consisted of a giant framework that carried portable shipping containers in between the mushroom shaped forward command spaces, and the rear box like structure that housed the star drives. Klutch chose the largest of the three seven-hundred-foot-long tubes that created the spine of the vessel. We landed on the tube just behind the forward module. Klutch got a good hole first try and we quickly jumped in. The center tube Klutch had chosen was a service tunnel. It was crammed with pipes, wires and ductwork of every conceivable configuration. We worked our way to the forward bulkhead where we found ourselves facing a series of large circular pressure doors. Each had a round viewscreen in its center, and we could see there was three consecutive doors. They were designed to hold back the void in the event of a breach. I pointed to the first door and Klutch gave me a thumbs up. He activated the portal device and we rapidly passed through the opening. He closed it and did the same to the next one. We were now looking through the viewscreen of the final pressure door. We could see a corridor that went forward to a hatch at the end, and I assumed that was the bridge. There were four hatches on one side of the passage and three on the other. All were closed and no hostiles were in sight.

My IST beeped an incoming message alert. It was from Tria.

"Nathan, Coonts and I have disabled the transports. The Scrun operators were killed when we destroyed the driver booths. Our suit sensors detected anti-matter emissions propagating from the cargo boxes but no other telltales indicating additional Troops. Justice has warned us to leave the area. He believes the Scrun would have taken the precaution to rig the charges to detonate if we tried to gain access. He has also warned us the charges may have failsafe timers. I have contacted Pasta and he has assured me there is no civilians in the area around the defensive towers. Justice is going to use the Legacy's tow beam and attempt to pull the remains of the transports out into the void."

"Excellent work Tria. Klutch and I have gained access to the freighters service tunnel and are approaching the bridge. I need you and Coonts to get back here as soon as possible and take up an overwatch position. If the Scrun working on the lockdown cradles start to board before I call you back, I would appreciate it if misfortune was to befall them."

"Roger that Nathan. I am sure Coonts and I can come up with something. ETA seven minutes."

I pulled my shotgun from its clip and slapped Klutch on the ammo pack. He activated the portal device and we stepped out of the service tunnel. He closed the hole behind us and pulled his pistols. We went to the first hatch on our right and hit the access button. The door slid open with a hiss revealing three rows of bunks lining the walls and a common area with tables in the middle. It was unoccupied. We closed the hatch and went across the corridor. It was another crew area and was deserted as well. The next two were toilets and a cleansing area. Still no hostiles. That left three hatches and the odds of all being vacant were not good. The last one on the left was a small galley, it was empty. Two to go and then the bridge.

Klutch and I were so focused on the hatches in front of us, we were both startled when we got a pop-up target warning from behind us. The tubes on either side of the service tunnel were fore and aft gravity transport tubes. A Scrun wearing a large bulky looking exoskeleton stepped from the tube. We were cloaked and almost perfectly invisible in the subdued lighting of the corridor. I still froze for an eyeblink in time. Klutch did not. He boosted hard at the Scrun. He was so close to me when he took off, the gravity fields from his drives knocked me off my feet, crashing me to the deck. Only the deaf or the dead would have missed the clatter. Klutch smashed into the Scrun, driving him into the bulkhead making yet another loud crashing noise. The hostile collapsed in a heap at his feet. The Tibor always thought more was better and boosted to the overhead. He cut off his drives, falling with his full mass from twenty plus feet onto the Scrun's body. It sounded like a head on car wreck when he landed.

Before I could make a comment worthy of the commotion the Tibor just stirred up, the hatch at the end of the corridor opened behind me. I whirled around as two Scrun came charging out with their rocket launchers up and ready. If that wasn't bad enough, the hatch across from me opened. A Scrun with a pistol leaned out of the opening. The two charging out of the bridge were on me so quickly, a collision was inevitable. I grabbed the barrel of the first one's launcher as he slammed into me. Twisting sideways, I pulled the barrel of his weapon around with me, and managed to get it pointed at the faceplate of the Scrun with the pistol. My adversary did me a solid, and chose that moment to pull the trigger on his launcher. His rocket hit his comrade's faceplate dead center and detonated. The Scrun on top of me and his compadre took the brunt of the blast, but I was still smashed violently into the wall. I was seeing double and entangled in the bodies on top of me, one of which was still moving. I no longer had my shotgun in my hands and didn't realize I had lost it. I jammed my needle gun into the arm joint of the Scrun that was flailing around on top of me. He was screeching out some nonsense my translator couldn't come to grips with. He got a two second burst of high velocity shards that shut him up and flipped him off me.

There was a warning siren blaring and along with my double vision, I found both extremely annoying. I was making another attempt to get to my feet, when I looked up at a gore covered Klutch running at me. I reached out to him for a little help and he batted my hand aside. He instead put his big armored mitt in my faceplate and shoved me not so gently back to the deck. I heard him unload an entire magazine of explosive buck shot. The trip hammer thumping and jarring choruses of explosions was followed by more alien screeching. I again tried to get my feet under me when something exploded very close to us. Klutch and I found ourselves once again sprawled out on the deck. This was not a good thing, because I doubted if our suits were still capable of cloaking after the beatings they just took. I had a feeling we had great big bullseyes plastered all over us. There was one small ray of sunshine on this otherwise dark day. While I was swimming around in Scrun guts, I found my shotgun underneath one of the dismembered corpses. I rolled over on my ammo pack and looked into the bridge. There was a Scrun leaning against the hatch and he only had part of an arm. He was using the other to raise his launcher at us. I rewarded him with twelve penetrator slugs for his efforts. The explosive blasts blew him apart, sending his remains across the bridge and out the freighter's shattered observation windows.

My ears were still being assaulted but it was not by explosions. Klutch was rapping on my shoulder and yelling cease fire. Tria was calling over the comms net trying to get a sitrep. I grabbed Klutch's hand, letting him know I got the message. I filled Tria in on what just happened, and told her to take out the Scrun working on the maglocks. She informed me that when the shooting started, all eleven of the Scrun working on the ship cradles were on their way to flank us. When they piled into the airlock, her and Coonts threw a couple of grenades in with the murderous bastards as the hatch shut. She reported the airlock was no longer functioning and she thought the same was true for the Scrun as well. I told her to come forward until she found the blown-out observation screens. There was more than enough room to crawl through the opening. Klutch reported we had five dead Scrun and three that were alive, but just barely. The self-sealing qualities of their pressurized combat armor didn't hold up well to the multiple barrages of schrapnel we introduced them too. If we didn't stop the leaks soon, they would die for sure. I was hoping against all odds that one of the Scrun that was still breathing was Ortulla.

Tria and Coonts appeared at the shattered observation screens and crawled inside with us. I called to Justice. "I want you to take out the Scrun in the scrapyard, then move in close to our location so we can medevac three wounded hostiles. We need to stabilize their conditions long enough to find out if one of them is Ortulla."

"Affirmative Commander, commencing attack."

We turned so we could see the scrapyard in the distance. After several seconds, I was beginning to wonder if Justice decided it wasn't a good idea to blow up the scrap hull. To our complete surprise, two partially wrecked ground transports came falling out of the sky from somewhere under the atmospheric retention field. There were two almost simultaneous flashes and then the shock wave rolled over the repair docks, rattling the freighter under our feet. Pieces of junk were raining down everywhere. Several hit the freighter with resounding clangs as they careened off the hull and dock fixtures. When the scat stopped falling, the Legacy moved to the front of the freighter. The hangar bay suddenly appeared in front of the viewscreens, and three evac gurneys floated through the ragged openings. We dragged the Scrun onto the gurneys and Justice brought them back aboard the Legacy.

We still had four terrorist that were unaccounted for, according to what the prisoners told Pasta. They were somewhere back in the machine spaces. They no doubt knew some bad mojo had gone down on the bridge. I wanted to take additional prisoners if possible, but it wouldn't break my heart if they ended up dead. It would save someone the trouble of killing the terrorist bastards at some later date.

Justice interrupted my ruminations. "Commander, I am detecting fluctuations in the anti-matter containment fields on the star drives. I speculate the remaining Scrun forces are trying to breach the containment fields with weapons fire. If they succeed, there will be a detonation that will destroy this ship and the repair bay as well. I advise you to evacuate and let them continue with their efforts."

Rather than crawl back out of the shattered viewscreens, I had Klutch make a hole and we made a dignified exit out onto the freighter's hull. Justice pulled us into the hangar bay with the tow beam.

"Justice, can you help the Scrun meet their maker without blowing the freighter to hell and back?"

"I can make an attempt Commander, but cannot guarantee the anti-matter fuel cells will not explode in the process."

"Please give it a try, at your discretion"

Justice brought the Legacy's shields up and fired six long burst of rail cannon fire into the rear compartments of the freighter. The spaces just forward of the star drives took on the appearance of swiss cheese. I was going to make a comment to that effect, when the entire rear of the freighter sheared away and rolled off the ship cradles.

"I detect no life signs Commander."

"Thank you, Justice. Job well done."

28

We went to the ready room and stepped out of our armor. I had no idea just how badly abused my battle suit was, until I got out and walked around it. I had my bell rung several times while in close combat with the Scrun. The large star shaped dents on the suit, indicated I had taken some direct hits from the Scrun rocket propelled munitions. Glancing over at Klutch's armor, I saw his looked worse than mine. If the impact dents were any deeper, they would have penetrated into our nanite reservoirs. The Scrun weapons were a step above any we had encountered before. In past engagements, the Scrun weapons were easily detectable by our suit sensors and they damn sure weren't as destructive as what these guys used on us. They knew we had cloaking, and now they have it as well. It seems the Scrun have taken an unexplained leap in technological advancements. The weapon strikes also took away our cloaking advantage within the first minute of our encounter, making Klutch and I easy targets in the confines of the freighter's corridor. Whoever selected the new weapons for the Scrun knew what they were doing. I couldn't help but think they were chosen to specifically target my crew and I.

"Justice, what is the status of the prisoners."

"Commander, one of the prisoner's life signs flat lined, and I was unable to revive him. The other two are in critical but stable condition. When I removed the armored exoskeleton from one of your prisoners, he had adornments typically worn by Scrun officers on his suit liner. It would only be speculation on my part, but there is a better than average chance, you may have captured Ortulla."

I was sure hoping something good would come out of this. Good probably wasn't the proper term, but I would take this as such. Turning the ring leader of the terrorist attack over to Pasta once we got the information we wanted, would be my pleasure.

"Justice, inform Pasta we have killed the last of the Scrun on the outpost and took two prisoners. Make him aware of the condition they are in, and that when we are done with our interrogation, we will turn them over to him."

"Affirmative Commander, message sent. Do you still want to return to Alpha base and give our Grawl passengers a chance to cohabitate with our scientific staff? They have been confined in the crew quarters for more than twenty-four hours."

After all that has happened in the past several hours, I had forgotten all about my promises to the Grawl we rescued.

"Roger that Justice, go ahead and make a DEHD core jump back to Alpha Base. I no longer think we have to hide the Legacy's capabilities from our guest. Once they meet others of their own kind and see the freedoms they have, I don't believe they will want to return to their former employers."

"Acknowledged. DEHD core transition in one-minute Commander."

Tria took me by the hand. "Nathan, I need a hot shower and some sleep."

That was all the encouragement I needed. I was tired and felt like an old rug that just got the dust beat out of it. As I walked out of the ready room with Tria, I called to Coonts and Klutch. They were already picking at each other over some nonsense or another and I didn't want to hear it.

"Hey!" I said, pointing my finger at them. "Knock that scat off! Since you two seem to have so much energy, I want you to get our Grawl guests introduced to Jaran and make sure they are squared away. Then I advise you to get some rest because we will be having a crew meeting in ten hours. I will see you then."

The two blockheads quit bickering, and gave me a positive shake of their heads, but failed to hide the grimaces on their faces. I knew they were waiting for Tria and I to get out of sight, so they could continue conspiring over whatever they were up to. Tria gave me a tug to turn me around, and we headed for the lifts. Our surroundings started fading to a brilliant white. When we returned to normal space time, Justice reported nothing unusual on his scanners. We made a direct approach to Alpha Base, and landed in the hangar in the time it took to get out of my shower. Tria and I had just laid down when Justice called to me.

"Commander, I am holding an IST transmission from the Principle Investigator. She is aware of the terrorist attack on Outpost 9765 and urgently wants to speak with you about it."

I rolled my eyes and rubbed my temples. I really didn't want to hash it out for Sael right at the moment. I was beat, and no matter how I said it, it was going to piss Sael off. I decided to pass the buck.

"Justice, please inform Sael that the crew and I are suffering from battle fatigue and unavailable."

I thought that would be sufficient, but Tria gave me an elbow and one of those looks that said I needed to be a little more courteous. I wrinkled up my face and gritted my teeth at her. She tossed her blankets aside, and showed me a damn good reason why I should capitulate to her wishes.

"Justice, please rephrase my statement so it sounds like my nose is inserted the proper distance up Sael's ass, and add that we will be having a crew meeting in ten hours and she is invited."

I turned back to my lover with a smug look on my face. I was thinking she would find my sarcasm funny. I was wrong. Her covers were back on and she had rolled over. Crap!

I awoke almost exactly eight hours later and found myself alone, again. Lately that was becoming a regular event. I had several reasons why I really liked waking to find Tria close by. One of them was a big one. I climbed out of bed and got my morning constitutionals out of the way. I put on a fresh uniform and went to the galley where I would typically find the rest of my crew. I was surprised to find that wasn't the case this time.

I got a cup of Justice's take on coffee. "Justice, where is everybody?"

"Commander, Coonts and Klutch are still in their quarters, and Tria went to meet the Principle Investigator. She arrived in her shuttle more than an hour ago. Tria took it upon herself to brief the Principle Investigator on the events that took place on Outpost 9765. They are both currently in the artifact storage area."

I guess Tria thought I needed some extra sleep so I could face Sael with a better attitude. I could think of a lot of other ways to improve my attitude, sleeping in, wasn't one of them. I was now aware that Justice was involved, because I should have got a warning that Sael arrived. Apparently Tria was the only one to get the heads up.

"Justice, why didn't you alert me that Sael was here?"

"I was ordered by Tria to allow you an extended rest period. She felt you would be exhibiting the human emotion of crabbiness, if I were to wake you early."

"Why wasn't I part of that discussion?"

"Perhaps you should put your questions to Tria. She might be better prepared to answer them for you." The cagey AI answered.

My dishwater coffee was quickly souring in my stomach, and I decided I needed some fresh air. I marched out of the galley and off the Legacy. The further I distanced myself from the ships AI, the better I felt. My spirits got another lift when I saw Jaran and Graf giving Kevel and company a tour of the greatly expanded replicator facility. If the Grawl crew decided to stay on with us, I would reveal the information on our Containium mine. Since they were asteroid surveyors that topic might be of special interest to them.

Out of the corner of my eye, I saw Tria and Sael leaving the Artifact storage building. Tria was pointing toward the Legacy, but Sael spied me and turned in my direction. The coffee in my gut was going to eat its way to my anus. I turned around and was going to make a beeline for the Legacy.

"Commander Myers!" Sael called. "I would like to have a word with you!"

Crap! She was going all formal on me. Usually she wouldn't waste her breath on tact, at least not to me anyway. It had to be for the benefit of our Grawl guests. The only reason I stopped and turned around, was because I wanted Tria to think I deserved something better than just sleeping late. It also meant I would have to return the gentility.

"Yes, Principle Investigator, how might I be of service?"

Tria was just behind Sael and I saw her smile at my reply. Things were looking up. Sael of course, took the aggrandizement for what it really was, and rolled her eyes. When she was close enough to me that no one else could overhear our conversation, she dropped the military decorum.

"Nathan, I have some intel related to the outpost attack I think you should be aware of."

I was still scratching my head wondering why Sael would arrive well ahead of our planned meeting. The last time I saw her, she showed off her dexterity using all four of her middle fingers. One would have been sufficient to get her point across. My response reflected my appreciation of her recent symbolic gestures.

"Is it something you have already passed on to Captain Burlor? If so, she can brief me later."

She ignored the comment. "Nathan, Ortulla Corva was one of the most decorated Scrun commanding officers that I have records on. He was awarded the Scrun star of honor by King Lashmos himself. Usually in the Scrun hierarchy, awards are given out by senior generals. My intelligence network reported Ortulla was a close personal friend of the King. He has not been in active service since Lashmos's death."

"Sael, King Lashmos is old history, and I really don't care who his friends were. Our meeting is scheduled to take place in another hour and a half. If you still want to discuss your intel, we can take it up then."

"Nathan, Ortulla Corva returning to active duty and leading the attack on the outpost, was part of a well-coordinated effort to kill you, your crew, and anyone seen as your allies."

"Sael, that thought has already crossed my mind, and I am keenly aware, that a lot of innocent bystanders were killed in the attempt. Is there something else you want to go over before our meeting, or can it wait?"

"I can identify Ortulla if you will allow me to look at your prisoners." Sael said in a hushed voice.

I looked over Sael's shoulder at Tria. I suspected that was where she was taking the Principle Investigator before she decided to give me a lecture. I nodded my consent to Tria, and she took Sael by the arm and led her away. While Sael was giving me her intel dump, I saw Graf wave at me. He was sitting on a bench in front of the artifact building waiting for me to finish with Sael Nalen. I went over to him and he stood. I waved him back down and sat next to him.

"It seems that Sael Nalen is as impatient as ever." The Grawl said, stating the obvious.

I gave Graf a grin. "Yes, and I don't think that will ever change. Is there something you would like to speak with me about?"

"Yes, Commander, Kevel and his crew have expressed their desire to stay on with us. Jaran is making arrangements to get them personal quarters, but they have requested to stay in the bunking area so they can remain together. I think they will adapt to their new surroundings and will eventually want individual quarters."

"That is great news. When they are ready, integrate them into your work schedules so we can cut back on the workload for the rest of the scientists. You have been doing an excellent job, and I think everyone deserves more free time."

It was Graf's turn to smile. "Commander, it is not our nature to do nothing. I will let the other members of our clan know you have suggested that they take additional time in between work periods. Please do not be offended if they choose not to."

I clapped my hand on the Grawl's shoulder. "Graf, I don't know what I would do without out you and the other scientists.

If there is ever anything that you need, please don't hesitate to ask."

I got another big smile from the Grawl, and it wasn't a pleasant sight unless you knew what you were seeing. "Commander." Graf said. "Tria told me the Scrun you have captured had some advanced equipment. She also stated that you would like to find out the source of the technology. With your permission, we can do a thorough study, and try to determine its origin based on the design architecture."

"That's an excellent idea. Tell Justice you want one of the Scrun exoskeletons. I don't think he will mind sharing. I know he has to be tinkering with some of the tech already."

Graf left in the direction of the Legacy. I got up from the bench and decided to pay Ilam Pove a visit. His information, while not completely proven, did have a lot of credibility now. Cralmo was temporarily dethroned from the top of my hate list, by an even larger piece of scat, Canik. The Ilor was in cahoots with the Scrun and I know he was responsible for the terrorist attack on the outpost. If I ever got my hands on him, I was going to tear him apart limb by limb.

I heard a familiar commotion, and turned around to see my two favorite blockheads picking at each other as usual. I let out a shrill whistle that instantly silenced them. I waved them over.

Before they could make up some lame excuse for needing to be elsewhere, I told them I had a job for them. "I want you two to go get the Rugerian and the Murlak off the Legacy, and put them in the tunnel holding cells next to Pove."

I could see the wheels turning in both their eyes. The chore was going to turn into some kind of a wager before it was over with. I took a deep breath and exhaled. As long as it didn't involve antagonizing me, I would let it slide. Besides, I needed to make sure Coonts would get back some of his lost credits, so he wouldn't walk around with a king-sized chip on his shoulder all the time. His over muscled ego was bad enough, but when he was on a losing streak to Klutch, he was a genuine pain in the ass.

The two took off at a dead run. I wasn't going to wait in the lift for them to get back. Depending on their wager, the ride to the escape tunnel might be more than I cared to witness. I took the lift down to the tunnel and walked at a leisurely pace down the passage trying to compose the questions I had for Pove. When I arrived at his cell, I cleared the enclosure walls so they were transparent, and turned on the audio so Pove could hear me. He immediately stood up and came to the wall and faced me.

I stared stone faced into the eyes of the Murlak. He found my gaze unsettling and cast his eyes downward. "The information you gave us seems to be correct once again. As long as you continue being truthful, your future might not turn out to be as bleak as it currently is."

He quickly looked back up at me. "If you question the Ilor on his dealings with Eiger, I am sure that I will be able to verify the authenticity of the transactions I have been made aware of."

I gave the Murlak's statement careful consideration. I decided not to hide the fact Canik had made good his escape. "I would like to have a chance to question him, unfortunately his ruse worked to his advantage. The Sig decided he was a harmless dolt, and released him at an Ilor Guild. He disappeared soon afterwards."

Ilam Pove pushed his face against the enclosure wall. "The information he gained on you and your allies the Sig, will be used against you. Mark my words, he will make you regret your mistake! I told you he has lived in situations when many others have died. His ambitions were even greater than Eiger's. Eiger once told me, if the Ilor became any more influential, he was going to have to find a way to kill him before Canik could do the same to him."

The irritation of the Pove's statement was a bitter pill to swallow. He was right again. Canik did make us pay for our mistakes. The admission made me wonder what I could have done differently? At the time, Canik's moronic behavior was so convincing, even Sushi dismissed the Ilor as a threat. The deaths of so many innocent bystanders weighed heavy on my conscience. It hardened my resolve as I was sure it did to Sushi. It also made me revisit the Rugerian's offer. After all that has happened, I was now more convinced than ever, it was another trap designed to lead us to our deaths. Canik thought we were fools to fall for his simpleton act, and must have felt we would fall for another when he sent the Rugerian with his peace offering. There was no doubt in my mind that Canik would have made the terror attack on the outpost regardless of our decision. It was designed to punish the Sig as much as it was a trap to kill me and my crew. The pain he inflicted upon the innocent while trying to target me, was going to pale in comparison to the agony I was going to inflict upon him and his allies.

Ilam Pove was staring at me as I slowly swallowed the foulness of his truths. I looked into his eyes and knew he had information that could help me find Canik. He wanted his freedom and would use the information as a bargaining chip. I had to decide how I wanted to get it. We were already guilty of torturing him to find Eiger. It was something that would have bothered my younger self, but after seeing the horrors I have witnessed, my morals have been changed forever, and not for the better. It had dawned on me some time ago, that my morals were just leftover baggage from my Earthman past, and they hindered my ability to find the truth. I thought about something I had once overheard my grandfather tell a neighbor who owned a farm not far from us. He was bitter because he lost his crops to flooding. He had decided not to buy crop insurance because he thought it was a waste of money. My grandfather told him that life was an endless series of choices, and more than half of them would suck. I have been forced to make choices that I thought I would never have to make. The truth of my grandfather's statement would be forever etched in my mind.

29

Coonts and Klutch arrived with their prisoners. Coonts was shoving the Murlak we had captured out in front of him. Klutch was carrying the Rugerian over his shoulder. He was limp as a sack of potatoes.

"Klutch, what happened to the Rugerian?"

"Commander, the Throgg asked me if I wanted to be rich beyond all comprehension. I answered his question."

I looked into the Rugerian's face shield. The side of his head was swollen, and he was bleeding from his nose and mouth. When he came too, I doubted if he would ever ask the Tibor another question. Klutch threw the alien in the cell next to Ilam Pove. The unconscious Rugerian landed on his already damaged face. The Troop Master turned and looked over at Pove. He held up his hand to his mouth and made chomping motions with his teeth. Pove backed away to the far side of his cell with his arms extended out in front of him. The menace Klutch implied, loosened Ilam Pove's tongue. It saved me the trouble of deciding whether to bargain with him or not.

"I have information about Eiger's allies that no other can tell you!" Pove yelled.

Klutch shouted right back. "Either you or this Throgg that calls himself the Collector, is going to tell us what we want to know, one way or another."

I backed Klutch's threat with implications Pove could easily understand. "As you can see, we have more sources of information than just you. Unless you continue providing us with plausible intel, we will have to resort to making use of others. It shouldn't be hard to figure out what your future will be shortly after that."

Pove pushed his face and hands against the cell wall. He looked desperate. "There is a place where the most wealthy and powerful can hide, regardless of the crimes they have committed. If Eiger had not been granted amnesty by the royal family, he would have moved his operations there. It is called Frontier."

I looked over at Coonts and Klutch, they shook their heads in a negative response. I squinted my eyes at the Murlak. "Where is Frontier?"

Pove stepped back from the cell wall and looked down at his feet. "I do not know the location. Eiger would have known, but your female killed him."

My bullshit meter headed for the high end of the scale. I wasn't in the mood to have my time wasted by this prick. Pove could tell I was losing my patience.

Justice called to me and I stepped away from his cell. "Commander, I have an IST communication from Bond Connery."

I had Justice black out the cells and I waved to Coonts and Klutch. "We will let the prisoner's dwell on their fates. We have more important things to do."

They followed me up the tunnel and to the lifts. Once we were inside, I told Justice to give me Bond's report. "Commander, Bond has reported his credentials have passed close scrutiny, and he was allowed to rent temporary quarters at Hub eight. He further states, he will be executing the second phase of his plans, and will keep us informed on his progress."

That brought a big toothy smile to Klutch's face and a grimace from Coonts. "I knew his plan would work Commander. It's what I would have done." The Tibor declared.

I rolled my eyes but didn't comment on the Troop Master's statement. I could only hope he was right. The Coram's plan of getting drunk and laid until Genda Binar contacted him, seemed pretty farfetched. Admittedly, it wasn't the weirdest scenario I had ever heard. The door to the lift opened and we headed for the Legacy. It was time to get on with the crew meeting. I felt sure with Sael sitting in, I would end up more irritated than I already was.

"Justice." I called. "What is the condition of the prisoners in the med bay?"

"They are stable Commander. With the proper care, they would eventually make a complete recovery from their wounds."

"Did Sael know whether or not one of the prisoners was Ortulla?"

"Yes Commander, she has made a positive identification of the Scrun prisoner we suspected to be the leader of the attack on the outpost."

That was good news, and I asked the AI the next question that was nagging at me. "Is he in any condition to question?"

"We should allow the treatments I have prescribed another four hours to completely stabilize his condition. If his prognosis is as expected, I will introduce stimulants into his blood stream that will allow you to question him."

We walked into the briefing room and found Tria and the Principle Investigator already seated and waiting. Tria smiled and Sael just stared at me. The persistence of her gaze insinuated she was waiting for me to ask her to speak. This was a departure from past meetings where she had no problem butting into a briefing well before any input was required from her.

I decided to let her start in hopes she would remain silent afterwards. "Sael, if you would like to start our briefing with your intelligence report, please do so now."

Sael quickly stood. "Nathan as you already now by now, you have captured Ortulla Corva. I cannot begin to stress just how important it will be to keep him alive." Sael said, while looking at Tria out of the corner of her eyes.

I stifled the smile I was going to give Tria. Her reaction to Sael's statement showed me just how unexpected it was. She apparently thought she was getting along famously with Sael up to that point. A hint of a scowl crossed her pretty face and disappeared with a shake of her head.

Sael continued. "Ortulla might possibly have important information on the Scrun base of operations where the Heckler ships were discovered. In the event you decide to make an incursion at that location, any intel from your prisoner could prove to be the difference between a successful mission, or a failure that could end in the needless loss of lives."

For an alien, Sael seemed very adept at a human trait practiced by all political figures back on Earth. It was called grandstanding, and it appeared she was just getting warmed up. Why she just didn't come right out and mention the Fury, also had me scratching my head. I wondered if it was some kind of veiled ploy to make me breach the topic. This was supposed to be a briefing, not a lecture.

"Sael." I interrupted. "Unless you have pertinent information that we are unaware of, please sit down."

It was easy to see my statement pissed her off, but I already had my fill of bullshit for one day. The expectant stares she was getting from everyone around the table, made her promptly sit down.

I stood and everyone focused on me, including a sour faced Sael Nalen. What I had to say was more for Tria's benefit than Sael's, but would serve to enlighten them both on current events.

"Coonts, Klutch and I, just came from another interview with Ilam Pove. I placed our latest prisoners, the Rugerian that calls himself the Collector, and the Murlak mercenary, who headed the strike team that was sent to recover Keena from the pirates on Outpost 9765, in cells next to Pove's. I had hopes of getting some kind of recognition from him. That did not turn out to be the case. We instead used our new prisoners to leverage additional information from Pove. He now claims to know where Canik might possibly be hiding. According to him, there is a place called Frontier, were wealthy criminals can hide without fear of prosecution. He seems to think this place is the ultimate destination of the most wanted criminals in the galaxy. He couldn't however, provide us with the location. That makes me believe he is telling us bullshit to lengthen his lifelines."

When I scanned my crews faces, they looked on with interest. Sael's looked shocked. I figured it would be best to enquire before she butted right in after finding her tongue.

"Is there something you would like to say Principle Investigator?"

"Yes Nathan. I have heard of Frontier, and Pove was correct. It is supposed to be the pit of the galaxy, where the wealthiest and most accomplished offenders go to hide."

"Do you know it's location?"

"No Nathan, it seems that it is the one of the most closely guarded secrets in the galaxy. I obtained information similar to what you have just discovered, several years ago. I relentlessly pursued every possible lead to uncover its location. All my attempts failed. Every single piece of evidence that even remotely pointed to Frontier's location, ended at a corpse. I am absolutely convinced such a place exists, and personally believe it is located in the uncharted void. It would be the only way for it not to have been discovered by now."

"So, you are telling us, that is the only intel you have discovered since you learned of its existence?" I asked in a tone that clearly indicated my skepticism.

Sael pursed her lips. It was obvious she did not like discussing her failures as an Operative. After another minute of indecision, she answered. "I have a number of unsubstantiated statements that were obtained under conditions similar to Pove's. The most interesting, is a statement claiming Frontier is on a barren rocky planet whose only resources are located deep underground. It was also revealed under duress, that Frontier was a large subterranean city with only two entrances. They are said to be so heavily fortified; the planet would have to be destroyed to gain access."

It was exceptionally difficult to take statements like we were hearing, for facts. It was all hearsay, unless we could find a legitimate witness to verify the stories. This was the kind of crap myths were made of. It was common knowledge that when stories like this spread, people tend to embellish the original to unbelievable proportions. I had no reason to not believe that was the case for this one.

Sael paused and looked me in the eyes. "It might have been something Eiger could have shed light upon."

I wondered when she would get around to shoving that back in my face once again. I also hated that she was correct according to Ilam Pove. Sael's smug look made me compartmentalize the information. It was questionable whether the information needed to be divulged to Tria either. When Sael noticed the stink eye she was getting from Tria, she decided to abbreviate her report.

"I obtained other bits and pieces of information over the years. None of it I might add, can be verified." Sael said with a note of finality.

Now that she actually had something interesting to say, I wanted to hear everything she had, regardless of how or where it came from.

"Sael, I know you have more than that. Let's hear it all. You have our attention."

She stewed on it for another minute then relented. "I was told you had to be well established in the criminal underworld. The way it was put to me, was you had to be so well known as an elite criminal, there could be no questions concerning your past or your future. I guess it was a way to insure you were not a double agent working to undermine the security that has kept Frontier secret for so long. There was another source that stated you must have wealth well in excess of five-hundred billion credits to even be considered for residency. That requirement all by itself, would preclude almost ninety-nine percent of the regular criminals and pirates."

Sael had a point. Even if there was an agent trying to penetrate Frontier, the chances of having a financial background that could past muster with the criminals in charge, was debatable. Wealth like that doesn't happen overnight. It would come from a long and sordid history of corruption. The kind of corruption that one might find in the background of the biggest shipping magnate in the known galaxy. Numbers with that many zeros attached, made admission exclusive to the very top one percent, of the worst of the worst. A number of our past foes would have fit into that category. Unfortunately for us, it was not a topic we were aware of till now. It also made me wonder about another wealthy piece of scat, named Cralmo. If Canik was a candidate, then Cralmo would most certainly be one as well. We needed to start collecting the subordinates of the crime syndicates, and do whatever it takes to find someone that knows where Frontier is located. We were slowly working our way up the chains of command. At some point, someone will want to keep their life bad enough to divulge the information.

It was time to move on to other subjects, but first I would give Sael credit for her information. I didn't think Pove was giving me the straight dope, but Sael's intel gave his story a little more credibility.

"Thank you, Principle Investigator for your input. Your information will form the basis for future interrogations. We have a number of ongoing operations against high level targets in large criminal organizations. If we succeed in capturing some of them alive, they may yield information related to Frontier."

I filled everyone in on Bond Connery's mission status. Sael didn't know about the operation and ate up every word when I explained what we were up to. When she found it might lead to Genda Binar's capture, as well as new intel on Canik, she of course wanted in on the action.

"Commander Myers, I would like your permission to accompany you on your missions. I know there have been times I have questioned your leadership and some of your decisions in combat. Your successes have proven my judgement wrong on a number of occasions. I am formally apologizing for my actions and hope that you will consider my request."

To say the least, we were all a little shocked. That was something I thought I would never hear coming out of Sael's mouth. Yes, she had more or less said the same things to me on a number of times in private, but I knew she didn't mean it. Now, she got all official on me, and said it in front of my crew. Even going as far as publicly apologizing for her actions. This was something completely out of character for her. I knew she wanted to join us on the Scrun base mission, because there was a small possibility the Fury might be at that location. This was something different even for her. Just a hint of her old self was evident when I didn't immediately answer. A small scowl flashed across her face but quickly disappeared.

I looked at each of my crew. I wasn't the only one she rubbed the wrong way. I was just the one she spent the most time on. "Are you good with Sael working with us again?" I asked.

Tria gave her a positive nod, which took just a little of the apprehension out of Sael's eyes. Klutch on the other hand, gave me a goofy grin. "Can we be out voted?" He said while looking sideways at Sael.

Sael's jaw tightened as she tried to maintain a straight face. The looks Coonts and Klutch were giving each other, said they were just yanking Sael's chain. The two drama queens finally gave her a thumbs up.

"Okay Sael, you are in, but I am going to warn you ahead of time. If this is just a temporary reprieve from your normal behavior, I will have no qualms about kicking you out of the airlock mid-mission."

Sael nodded, and to my surprise held her tongue. Normally she would launch into a lecture on how she would run the mission. This time, she sat tight lipped waiting to hear what I had to say.

"Sael, the first order of business I would like to address, is the wealth we took from Shurmosk. It is now cataloged and with the exception of a few items that appear to be artifacts, we are ready to release the rest to your people so it can be donated to the Protective Planet Fund."

Sael's facial expression brightened. "I will see to it immediately Nath...Commander Myers."

I cocked an eyebrow at Sael. "You can skip the formalities while we are aboard the Legacy, but I expect you keep a civil tongue elsewhere."

That got me just a hint of a smile and a nod of agreement. I ended the meeting after giving her a brief on our desire to hunt down Glock at some future date. Sael stopped Tria and I outside of the conference room, and told us Glock was a known fugitive, and had a large bounty on his head. It was her understanding, that a lot of bounty hunters attempted to collect the reward, but none were ever heard from again. Sael wanted to know why we would waste our time on chasing a mercenary. It was her opinion some lucky bounty hunter would eventually solve that problem. She wanted to know if we had any undisclosed intel on the Prule.

"Nathan, I thought you might bring up the Prule Hivemind in your briefing. You have not mentioned it since you disclosed the location of the Scrun excavation site. Is there any fresh intel you can share with me?"

I wondered if telling her we killed the last of the Prule entities, would trigger a relapse to Sael's default abrasive behavior. The glance Tria gave me, said the same thing had crossed her mind as well. I was going to remain mum on the subject, but Tria decided to find out now, rather than later.

Tria stopped and turned to face Sael. "The Hivemind was given an ultimatum. When it failed to respond to any of our questions, we followed through with our promised threats. We are working on data retrieved at the Prule base we turned over to you. When we decipher the information, you will be briefed on our findings."

At first, Sael looked shocked. She opened her mouth like she had something to say about the disclosure, but snapped it shut and nodded. She turned and walked away without comment. It appeared she was going to abide by her word.

30

I took Tria by the hand and went to our cabin. I was tired and needed some down time. I made it a point to tell Justice to wake both of us in three hours. Not one of us, both of us.

I was startled awake by Justice. He was giving me my requested three hours wake up call. I could have sworn I just closed my eyes. I started groaning about it, but Tria promptly ravaged me to silence. She smothered my bitching by any means she felt necessary. When she was done with me, I was lying on the deck with a fine sheen of sweat covering my body. I would never again wonder how the females of her race became the dominant sex. I was going to crawl to the shower, but in a sudden bout of dignity, got up on my shaky legs and walked the rest of the way.

With our shower complete, and fresh uniforms in place, I asked Justice for a current info dump.

"Commander, Coonts and Klutch are in their cabins sleeping. The Grawl scientists just changed work shifts after helping the Principle Investigator load the last of the property seized from Shurmosk. She is preparing to make the final trip to the Chaalt frigate that is sheltering in the crevasse south of Alpha Base. Are there any additional orders you would like to pass on to her before she departs?"

It crossed my mind to send her a Bon Voyage, but nixed the idea because she was holding up her end of our bargain surprising well.

"Negative on the additional orders. What else have you got for me Justice?"

"Graf is in the research labs and wishes to speak with you concerning the equipment removed from our prisoners. We have corroborating evidence as to its origins."

"Speaking of our prisoners, is their condition stable enough to question them?"

"Yes, Commander. On your orders, I will introduce stimulants into their systems that should allow them to function for a brief period of time."

"How long is brief?"

"An hour would be a reasonable estimate Commander."

"Okay Justice, wait until Sael returns and give them the stimulants."

"Affirmative Commander." Justice replied.

Tria and I went to have a talk with Graf. I was sure he normally took his sleep period at the same shift change as the rest of the Grawl. He was no doubt working non-stop to get me some answers to who might have helped the Scrun with their attack on Outpost 9765.

As we entered the research lab, Graf greeted us with a morose look on his face. It wasn't hard to see he was troubled by something he found in the numerous pieces of disassembled equipment that was scattered on several tables.

"Nathan." Graf said. "It is with great sadness I must report that a number of the systems used by the mercenaries, has technology developed by, or altered by members of my race. The cloaking suit technology is a direct copy of the standard Grawl cloak suit. The power sources for the armor and robotics are upscaled versions of

Grawl designs. The suits were revised to fit the Scrun and have additional layers of artifact materials including 699 woven into the liners. After comparing my findings to your obsolete Zaen battle armor, I have concluded the proprietary artifact weave in the liner, as well as the exoskeleton actuators and weaponized frameworks, are close copies of Zaen designs. Not that it matters to the terrorist, much of the armor tech would be considered illegal patent infringements."

The information, while not completely surprising, did bring back memories of Drayen, and his syndicate of corrupt Grawl scientists and engineers. It was becoming clear that Bren Carsoon or Genda Binar had similar operations.

"Were you able to identify whose technology was used to build the weapons?" Tria asked.

"Yes Tria, the weapons are modified versions of exported Galactic military hardware. They are utilized by the Murlak and a number of other militaries. As you already know, they were chosen because they have no telltale energy signatures."

"Are you sure Graf?" I said. "I find it hard to believe those were Galactic Union weapons. The damage they inflicted on our armor was significantly more than any of the weapons the Murlak have ever used against us."

Graf handed me one on the eight-inch-long projectiles. "The munitions are the most interesting development. They appear to be highly modified versions of Quill penetrator darts. They lack the acid component added by the Quill themselves, but are amazingly similar. The tips have been enhanced with advanced hull alloys that are used in the construction of all modern Galactic Union warships. The high velocity solid propellant and explosive cores have the earmarks of cutting edge Rugerian chemistry. They are a close second to the technology we use for our shotgun slugs and minigun munitions. If it were not for the Oolaran explosive technology and exotic materials that Justice incorporates into your munitions, they would be the equal to our standard loadout."

I examined the small missile and hefted it in my hand. It felt like it weighed a couple of pounds. I no longer wondered why I had been knocked on my ass so many times during my firefight with the Scrun. I handed it to Tria. It was becoming obvious our enemies were making a combined effort to stop us. Their cooperation hinted they now had an alliance dedicated to our demise. So many against so few was disheartening. There was a chance the mercenaries just dragged the Sig into a war with the Scrun. When I got another chance to speak with Pasta, I would broach the subject. I was going to tell Graf to take a sleep period, but Tria insisted we let him make the decision on his own accord. We headed out the door towards the Legacy.

Justice interrupted my thoughts. "Commander, I have an IST message from Bond Connery."

"Put it through to us Justice."

Bond Connery came through on the channel he was whispering. "Mr. Myers, my ore sample has been tampered with. I believe things are going to happen much sooner than I predicted. My companion will be returning shortly and I will give you a more detailed report when he has left for the evening."

"Okay Bond, be careful and watch your back. The criminals we are dealing with are ruthless killers. If you think there is any chance you have been compromised, get out and we will evac you."

"I think I am safe for now Mr. Myers. They will want to find the rest of the ore, and they cannot do that without me."

"Roger that, we will move to a location near you and await your call.

"Bond out." The Coram replied.

Tria and I were shocked at how the mission was unfolding. It was going exactly as Bond said it would. Coonts would be eating his words when he found out.

"Justice, we have a change in plans. Don't bother with the prisoners. I am going to turn them over to Pasta. He can interrogate them and let us know his finding. I want you to prepare to get underway. What is Sael's status?"

"She is still aboard her frigate, Commander."

"Open an IST channel to her."

"Channel open, Commander."

Sael came on and was very cordial. Tria was listening in on the conversation. Sael's tone made her smile and nod her head in approval. The Principle Investigator exhibiting manners was a pleasant change from her norm, and I wondered how long the anomaly would last.

"Yes Nathan, what can I do for you?" She said.

"Bring you combat equipment and whatever else you might need for an extended deployment. Bond Connery is getting positive results, and we will be moving to back him up."

Sael promptly replied and she was all business. "Acknowledged Commander Myers. My ETA is twenty minutes."

"Justice, is my armor combat capable?"

"I am still in the process of making repairs Commander. Both yours and Klutch's armor suffered significant battle damage and I am replacing the outer armor shells. Felix has the parts manufactured and will have them aboard before we depart."

Justice's reply made me frown. We normally had a supply of replacement armor parts just for situations like this. "I thought we had replacement shells already manufactured?"

"Commander, it has been my desire to further upgrade the battle armor worn by my crewmembers. When the Containium billets were brought to Alpha Base, I took it upon myself to requisition two of them for manufacturing newly designed outer armor shells. I am also working on a new weapon that will fit the needle gun mount. It will utilize accelerator rails to launch a

499

Containium tipped spike to velocities in excess of thirty thousand feet per second. The spikes have a mixed payload capability. They can carry weaponized nanites, high explosives, molecular acids, or be inert ballistic projectiles when you are operating within an atmosphere. My subsystems in your battle suit can adjust the speed of the projectile to subsonic velocities. The streamlined design of the spike will make it a very effective method to silently kill lightly armored targets at ranges of one-hundred yards or less."

"Don't you think I should have been made aware of the projects you are working on? It was my intention to use all of our Containium on armor plating for the defensive drone program."

"Commander, I have run the numbers at our current production rate. By the time we deplete our existing stock of Containium, the mine will be online and producing quantities that will exceed our demands for drone production."

I guess I should have known he would have an excellent excuse for diverting the materials to other needs. What I wasn't hearing was a cost analysis for the upgrades. Each of the expendable spikes had an armor piercing tip worth several thousand credits. The cost of the new armor shells had to be well into the billions.

"Justice, have you considered what the cost of your projects will turn out to be?"

The AI was quiet for several seconds and I assumed he was adding up the cost for me. That's not what I got.

"Commander, the cost is irrelevant. Safety of my crew takes precedence over cost. The materials are superior to previous combinations of artifacts. Therefore, the new materials will be used accordingly to improve on the deficiencies of our current generation of battle armor."

Tria looked at me and nodded her head in agreement. It would be stupid to pursue the line of questioning any further. What's not to like about being safer while being shot at, regardless of cost. My Grandfather's words came to me once again. Easy come, easy go, boy!

"Okay Justice, your reasoning is without fault. Can you give me a departure time?"

"Yes Commander, our estimated time of departure is forty-seven minutes."

"Roger that, alert Coonts and Klutch."

"Message sent Commander."

"Are you including the upgrades on Tria's previous generation armor?"

"Yes Commander. The Principle Investigator will have the same armor upgrades as all members of the strike team."

I turned to Tria and gave her an evil smile. She cocked an eyebrow at me. "What is going on in that backwards thinking brain of yours?"

"Well, now that you ask, I was just wondering if I can bill Sael for the upgrades."

Tria gave me a shove toward the boarding ramp. "I am all the payment you will receive from my people, and as far as I am concerned, I have paid you well in advance. So, just to be sure we understand each other, Sael will not be paying you with currency or otherwise."

The look on Tria's face, said that the queen had spoken and her loyal subject better be listening. I was going to let her know another payment was required and I wanted it now. Justice changed the subject to one of my least favorite.

"Commander, The Principle Investigator's shuttle is inbound."

Damn, Sael was going to be early and that left very little time for amicable compensation. Perhaps a down payment wouldn't be out of the question. I gave Tria a questioning look.

She crossed her arms and shook her head. "Not likely Tarzan!"

I heard some bickering coming from behind me and knew all to well what that racket was. It wouldn't take very much of that crap to turn my mood into something less than favorable.

Coonts and Klutch pulled up short when they saw me eyeballing them. They both turned around, but it was too late. "Coonts, Klutch." I hollered. "The Principle Investigator will be here any minute. She will probably have a lot of gear with her. Give her a hand and see to it she gets it stowed in the ready room. We will be departing shortly."

Both gave me a grin through clenched teeth, but I didn't hear a word of the expected grumbling. As I turned around to face Tria again I looked past her at the gravity sled Felix was piloting toward the open cargo bay doors. It had several stacks of armor plates on it. The departure time Justice gave me was generous.

Sael Nalen's personal shuttle rapidly approached from the tunnel entrance and landed near the Legacy. She wasted no time barking orders to the crew. They double timed it over to the Legacy's cargo bay with several crates and weapons cases. They set them down and came to attention. Sael saluted them and they disappeared back into the shuttle and quickly departed. Sael saw Tria and I on the boarding ramp and marched up to us.

"Commander Myers, Captain Burlor. I have been granted an extended leave of ~~absents~~ absence. I am now formally under your command, but I am required to make regular reports on my activities. I will of course consult with you, prior to any reports to my superiors. I will also respect your wishes if you want me to refrain from disclosing information that you might consider sensitive."

This was a first. I never thought I would see the day that Sael would make an effort to suck up to me. She wanted me to accept her as part of my crew, and was browning the end of her nose to do it. It crossed my mind she was finally willing to do whatever it takes to find the Fury. Since we were her best chance of doing it, she was swallowing her pride and submitting to my command.

I stepped aside. "Welcome aboard Sael. Coonts and Klutch will help you get your gear stowed. We will be departing for Outpost 9765 in the next few minutes."

Sael looked surprised. "May I ask why we are not going directly to Hub eight?"

"I have decided to turn Ortulla and the other Scrun prisoner over to my Sig allies for questioning." I replied.

Sael stepped closer to Tria and I. "Nathan, can I speak freely?"

"You always have in the past Sael. Go ahead and tell me what is on your mind."

"The prisoners will most assuredly die at the hands of the Sig before we can gain useful information from them."

"Sael, I doubt that their fate would be any different if they stayed here."

Sael stared at me for a moment then nodded. "Can I have your permission to question Ortulla."

"Do you think he will tell you anything?"

"Ortulla will know of me. He will remember me as Kala Mor Dee. I do not know if it will make him talk or not, but it is worth a try." Sael said.

"Justice." I called. "Revive Ortulla so Sael can question him."

"Acknowledged Commander."

"Carry on Sael."

Sael took off at a brisk pace, calling to me over her shoulder. "I will brief you on my finding, if any Commander."

"Justice, are we ready to launch."

"Yes Commander, all necessary supplies are aboard and the cargo hatches are secure."

Tria and I walked up the boarding ramp and the hatch closed behind us. "Roger that Justice. Take us out and make a DEHD core jump to our previous holding point near Outpost 9765."

"Launching now Commander."

It took Justice less than three minutes to get us into open space. Tria gripped my hand as our surroundings flared to a bright white. I was watching her pretty face as she faded from reality.

31

We returned to normal space time very close to the outpost. The view dome on the bridge lit up with seventy-two new scan returns. They were all Sig military spacecraft. Justice put blue boxes around them and yellow boxes around the other spacecraft holding close to the atmospheric retention field. I had Justice put in a call to Tam Lin. There was no response, so I had Justice break into Pasta's personal comm link. He answered immediately and didn't seemed surprised this time around.

"Yes, Commander Myers, is there something I can do for you?"

"I hope we have not interrupted you at a bad time, but I wanted to tell you that I am here to turn Ortulla and the other Scrun Prisoner over to you."

"Were you able to interrogate them?" Pasta asked.

"We have news from Bond and he may be on to something. I decided it would be best to let you interrogate the prisoners while we pursued the leads that Bond is uncovering."

"Thank you, Commander Myers. I can assure you we would be more than happy to take the prisoners off your hands."

"If you have the time, and I am not keeping you from more pressing matters, could you give me an update on the damage to the outpost?"

"Now that the relief fleet is here to aid us, we are in a better position to take a rest period from the rescue operations. We are fortunate that the civilian deaths were not nearly as high as we initially thought. We have eleven hundred-seventy dead, and forty-seven still missing. We feared that we had lost more than twice that number and to our relief, that is not the case."

"What about your garrison and General Bonaparte?" I asked.

"I lost two-hundred and nine troops in the attack. We have another seventeen unaccounted for. If you had not sent out your warning, the death toll would have been much higher. We managed to disperse a large number of troops just prior to the attack. For that, we owe you a debt of gratitude. As for General Bonaparte, his condition is stable, and he will make a full recovery. At some point in the future, he would like to personally speak with you Commander Myers."

"I tried to contact Tam Lin before I had my AI comm you on your personal link. I did not get an answer."

"Tam Lin worked tirelessly on the wounded for more than thirty-six hours. She became so exhausted, she almost collapsed. I had her relieved, and left orders she was not to be disturbed for twenty-four hours. She will be fine, but if you need to urgently speak with her, I will have someone wake her."

"That won't be necessary Pasta. We will comm you with the results of our mission, and keep you posted on our hunt for those responsible for the attack. I have one other question I wanted to ask you and I would understand if you declined to answer. I wanted to know if your people were going to war over the terrorist attack."

"As much as I would like to tell you yes Commander Myers, brighter minds than mine have decided it would not be in our best interest to go to war. We have on many occasions made attacks on the Scrun that have gone unanswered. The powers that be, have wrote the attack off as retribution for our past transgressions. That doesn't mean we will not do the same to them on a date of our choosing. I will tell you, that any revenge we will take, will not include the deaths of civilians."

"Thank you for your time Pasta, where would you like me to deliver the prisoners?"

"I have made Tam Lin's private dock available. Please be aware of the large number of spacecrafts aiding us in rescue operations. I am ordering a fifteen-minute hold on vessel traffic directly above the dock."

"Thank you, Pasta, Legacy out."

Justice nosed the Legacy over and made a high-speed maneuver that put us directly over the docking area. He dropped straight down and landed. We were met by Pasta and a security team of six Sig soldiers. Our prisoners were strapped onto evac gurneys and both were lucid as they floated off the Legacy. When they saw the Sig coming forward to take them, they both started thrashing at their bonds. Pasta's troopers pulled their restraints free and dragged them by their feet to an open hatch where more troops stood waiting. Pasta saluted me and I returned his gesture with a bow. I closed the hatch and Justice rapidly departed the outpost airspace.

Once we were well clear of the outpost, Justice made a standard transition in the direction of Carsoon shipping Hub eight. Sael joined us on the bridge.

"Did you get them to talk?" I asked Sael.

"Talk would not be exactly how I would describe what was said. They made a statement and nothing more."

Sael had our attention. "What was their statement?" I asked.

"They said they are the Legion of the Chosen. They will not stop until they have avenged the death of King Lashmos." Sael replied.

That made me frown because I thought the attack was orchestrated by Canik. If what Ortulla said was true, this was some kind of personal vendetta. From what I could gather from the information Graf discovered about the weapons, they came from several sources.

Coonts was scratching his bulbous head. "Commander, the evidence we have, suggests the Scrun enlisted the help of the other races we have been targeting. The

511

connection to Canik is somewhat vague, but I suspect he purposely funneled the information he had on us to the Scrun, and they in turn, gave it to the so-called Legion of the Chosen. It is a scenario my people favor over most others, when it comes to doing battle. I am sure you have not forgotten that Grawl prefer to leave the dying to someone else. Its not a stretch of the imagination to believe Canik would fully embrace that philosophy as well. I think that Canik, Genda Binar and possibly Bren Carsoon himself, were behind the attack. The freighter that brought the Scrun and the remote-controlled shuttles loaded with explosives would not have made it to the outpost if it were not for Carsoon shipping."

Sael was taking all the information in, and she finally held up a hand. "How did they know you were on the outpost?"

Tria filled in the blanks she had purposely left out the first time she briefed Sael on the attack. When Sael found out that Canik was masquerading as the buffoon Bolus, and he was a Sig prisoner they had released, I thought she was going to pop her cork. Her face took on an interesting hue and she ground her teeth in a very unladylike fashion. To her credit she kept her mouth shut.

"Justice." I called. "How long until the energy matrix is charged?"

"Forty-one minutes Commander." The AI replied.

"When the matrix is charged, DEHD core jump to the edge of the system where Hub eight is located."

"Affirmative Commander."

Sael still looked like she had something to say on the subject of Canik's escape. I suspected she had more than one rant directed at my Sig allies, and what she might perceive as their inept handling of the situation. Hindsight is always twenty-twenty. I don't think I would have done anything differently, so I didn't want to hear any suggestions from her on how she would have handled the Ilor. Sael's stare, told me she was thinking way too hard about events we could no longer change. I quickly thought of a way to occupy her mind.

"Sael, report to the ready room and Justice will outfit you with our combat armor. I recommend you take a refresher course on the suit systems and weapons."

That wiped the ugliness from Sael's face. She gave me a quick nod and disappeared

513

down the lift tubes. Coonts and Klutch slapped hands and followed her. I shook my head knowing they had just made some sort of wager. As long as Sael was the only target of their plots, I would not interfere with the games they endlessly played with each other.

The Troop Master would put Sael through a series of aptitude tests to ensure she was still current on our battle suit operation. If she passed, then both him and Coonts would make sure she was attuned to our tactics with test drills. The outcome of the tests would no doubt determine how the credits changed hands.

I wondered if Justice had added the spike launcher to our loadout. "Justice will we be making use of the new weapon you have been working on?"

"Yes Commander, I am in the final stages of updating your suit subsystem's targeting parameters."

"What about the payload selection?" I enquired.

"I have a limited supply of experimental spikes at this time. When we determine the most useful combination, I will have Felix put your final selections into production. You will each carry three nanite, three molecular acid, and three high explosive spikes. The remaining nine spikes in the magazine will be solid core penetrators."

"Do you have enough of the solid spikes we can get some practice in?"

"Affirmative Commander. Due to the unique qualities of Containium, the solid darts are reusable. I will make the Scrun armor available for practice in the hangar once the targeting software update is complete."

"Roger that Justice, please keep me posted."

"Acknowl… Commander! Both Guardian transponders have alerted me to a directional thread. They are still progressing and have stretched to beyond forty light years."

"Drop us from hyperspace so you can map the coordinates once they terminate."

"Terminating transition now Commander. The matrix will be charged in fourteen minutes, and DEHD core operations will be available."

My stomach did its flip-flop routine, and we were back in normal spacetime. Tria and I went to the bridge so we could watch Justice trace the transponder thread on the view dome. By the time we walked onto the bridge, Justice reported the thread terminated at ninety-one-point-four light years. That made the destination relatively close. It would only require a short transition to get us close to the termination point.

"Justice, go ahead and jump us to within scanner range of the termination point."

"Acknowledged Commander. Adjusting our course and engaging stealth systems. Jumping now."

We jumped and a comms window popped up on the view dome. Coonts face appeared in it. "Commander, I noticed the transitions, is there a problem?"

"We have an active transponder thread, and we are following it to its termination point."

"Roger that Commander. Klutch and I will continue with The Principle Investigator's weapons drills until further notice."

The window promptly disappeared from the view dome. The Guardian transponders were technology we had yet to completely disclose to Sael Nalen. She knew we had made references to the tech but never discussed it with her. Sael would be aware we were jumping around, but would not know the reasons why. I had a feeling she was trying to find out, but Justice was blocking her attempts to call me. Coonts would alert Klutch and the Troop Master would see to it that Sael stayed occupied with her training.

We transitioned back to normal spacetime and immediately got a warning from Justice. Red boxes started proliferating around a distant world in the dead star system. There was a lot of planetary debris filling the entire view dome. Justice highlighted the two planets that were visible in the starless mass of debris. The smaller of the two planets appeared to be missing a large chunk near one of its poles. The other planet was fully intact but had no atmosphere or other distinguishing features. It looked like a black lifeless orb floating among countless pieces of what may have been other planets in the distant past.

Justice identified the vessels surrounding the charcoal colored planet, and my stomach convulsed. It had nothing to do with jump sickness, and everything to do with the vessels he identified. They were Quill harvester ships. The Quill were a cannibalistic race of bugs. Bugs were commonly known in the Chaalt language as crits. They were a predatory race that preyed upon most everyone they encountered. There were some known and probably unknown exceptions. Our recent intelligence discoveries, gave us some sketchy evidence that suggested the Scrun somehow made it onto that list. For everyone else, the Crits were a generally despised enemy to all civilized races.

Justice's count stopped at twenty-eight ships and they were fully engaged in stripping materials from the planet. Both of our transponder threads terminated on the planet of the Quill's attention. I now needed to decide if I wanted to interrupt their party.

"Justice, can you pinpoint the origin of our thread?"

"Yes Commander. It is a location on the equator of the planet. My scanners indicate the area at that location, has no mining activity as of yet. The Quill appear to be concentrating their efforts on the poles of the planet. They have stripped huge swaths of ice from the polar caps and are extracting unknown materials from beneath."

I now had to make a choice. As I have already found on many occasions, there was a better than fifty-fifty chance it was going to suck. If I was not careful this was going to be one of them. I decided to get the rest of the crew, including Sael involved. If it turned out the decision was faulty, I could at least say the suck factor was shared by all.

"Justice, call Coonts and Klutch to the bridge, invite Sael as well."

"Message sent Commander."

Tria was standing close to me and surveying the view dome carefully. She had just a hint of a frown on her face. "Justice." Tria called out. "Do you think they somehow missed our transition? In the past they have always picked up a faint signature."

"I am curious as well Tria. Past experience has proven they have the ability to detect our distortion waves." Justice answered.

We observed no change in the Quill's mining operations and I was beginning to wonder if something in this area of space was hindering their scanning technology. Coonts and Klutch showed up on the bridge, and a scowling Sael Nalen was right behind them. One look at the view dome erased the look on her face and replaced it with surprise. She turned around several times taking in the entirety of our surroundings.

"Where are we?" Sael asked.

"We were in route to Hub eight when Justice detected something unusual. We dropped from hyperspace to investigate."

Sael knitted her eyebrows and gawked at the red boxes highlighting the Quill ships. She turned to me and asked a question that would be hard to avoid answering.

"May I ask how Justice managed to make the detection while we were in hyperspace?"

My answers would involve more choices, and of course, they would suck as well. Did I ignore her and piss her off, or do I answer without giving her the details, which would also piss her off. All three of my crew members were watching me closely to see if I would divulge one of our most closely guarded secrets. If it came down to it, the truth would be a lot less hassle than making up some bullshit. If I was going to trust Sael to have our backs, then I needed to trust her now. I would attempt to be vague, and hope that I could skirt the details.

"Sael, remember when Tria's patriarch told me your people had ways of detecting certain exotic transition waves."

Sael was squinting at me. "Yes Nathan, but that had to do with your DEHD core transitions. How could that possibly correlate to the question I just asked you?"

My ability to be vague was sucking worse than I thought. "Well Sael, this is kind of like that."

Sael crossed all four of her arms and her face darkened. She no doubt saw the looks I got from my crew. They were being mum on the subject and no help at all.

"Nathan." Sael said through clenched teeth. "Why did you bother to invite me to the bridge?"

"Because I usually discuss tactical options with my crew members before I make a decision on whether to do battle or not. If you are not interested in being part of that discussion, you can leave at any time."

The expression on Sael's face changed and she nodded. It was the first time I had actually implied she was now part of my crew. She stepped closer to the view dome and touched one of the red boxes. Justice magnified it so she could clearly identify the ship through the debris clouds floating away the planet's surface. She turned back to us with a look of anger on her face.

"Quill!" she said in disgust.

"Yes, the crits are stripping a barren planet of some unknown resource." I confirmed.

"If you are asking for my opinion, I say kill them all." Sael spat.

32

The Principle Investigator's statement closely aligned with my thoughts on the Quill. I had seen firsthand the atrocities they perpetrated on other races. The fact they collected all the dead after their battles, both theirs and any others, for a food source, made my skin crawl. It would be a tossup between them and the Prule as to who was the most loathsome.

Sael voiced her observations. "Since it appears they have not detected us, they would be very vulnerable to a surprise attack."

Coonts made her aware of our concerns. "Principle Investigator, we have had several encounters with the Quill. In every instance where we made transitions in systems they occupied; they detected the distortion waves. Depending on our proximity to their vessels, they have also detected our DEHD core transitions as well.

They were unable to locate the Legacy, but the detections always resulted in an immediate response and change of defensive posture. For reasons unknown to us, they have not acknowledged our presence."

Sael narrowed her eyes and studied the view dome carefully. "Yes, you have a very valid point. I should have thought of that before I spoke. They have always detected my people's warship transitions. Do you think they are intentionally ignoring the detection in hopes of luring you out of stealth mode?"

The Troop Master commented before I could. "If you had lost several capital ships and a habitat ship to an unknown aggressor, what would you do?"

Sael turned to me and shook her head. "So, it is a trap, and the mining ships are the bait."

Tria called to Justice. "Do you have any additional detections?"

"Negative Tria, I have noted the distinct lack of any communications between the mining vessels. That has never been the case in past engagements. They have a very unique communication system. They use high frequency sounds of varying scales, and they are usually always present when we encounter them. I have yet to decipher the codes but suspect that different sounds identify different ships and commanders. In any case, they typically flood the battlespace with the cacophony of their comms."

The void surrounding the two planets was loaded with debris, some of which were the size of planetoids. The Quill could hide several fleets in the mess and we would have to closely scan each piece to determine if a ship was hidden on it.

"Justice, do you have a hypothesis on their behavior?"

"Commander, I speculate we are seeing tactics designed to draw potential adversaries into a false sense of superiority and advantage. This phenomenon may very well represent a change of command within the Quill forces. I speculate it is a direct result of destroying a habitat ship."

"They couldn't possibly know we would be at this location. So, you are telling me this is something we can expect to see from all Quill forces?"

"Yes Commander, that is my theory."

I could see the wheels turning in Sael's head. She suddenly looked up at me.

"Since we are here, I am assuming you have a way to detect the Quill while traveling in hyperspace. This would be an incredibly valuable tool to my people. Why would you not want to share this technology with me? I think we have been more than generous with our tech. I know several instances where I have gone against my superiors wishes, and revealed some of my people's most closely guarded secrets to you."

Sael did not get the title of Principle Investigator because she was slow witted. I now had to make the choice I was attempting to skirt.

I looked at each of my crew mates. Coonts and Klutch just shrugged their shoulders in a show of indifference. Tria was leaning in favor of her people, at least as far as information went. Her nod was for full disclosure. Sael was watching both Tria and I closely.

"Sael, we don't have the means to detect the Quill, they just happened to be here."

A flash of anger crossed Sael's face then quickly faded with her next question. "Nathan, if you are saying you cannot detect the Quill, then what exactly did you detect that made you stop at this location."

I took a deep breath and let it out. "Artifacts."

"I knew it!" Sael blurted. "You have been making unprecedented discoveries, and my people and I, have always wondered how you have had such success."

The cat was finally out of the bag, and for some reason, the truth felt like a burden that had been lifted from my shoulders.

Sael looked like she could bust. She had told me she would withhold information from her superiors if I made such a request. I was contemplating just that, when she asked another question.

"Are the artifacts located on the planet the Quill are in the process of mining?" Sael asked with wide eyes?

"Yes. I called the crew together as a sounding board as to what we should do about it. Knowingly letting a race like the Quill, get their hands on what could possibly be a technological advancement for them, is not in anybody's best interest. Now that we have one less secret between us, I want to hear your thoughts as well."

Sael studied the view dome once more. "We should trigger the trap and see what their tactics turn out to be."

Coonts quickly commented on Sael's plan of action. "Principle Investigator, a false positive may trigger further changes in the Quill's tactics. This may be a case for stealth and caution. If this is a trap, we should attempt to find their planned response."

Klutch eyeballed Coonts nodding shaking his head. I could tell he was onboard with Sael's plans. He gave us his usual blasters and blood scenario. "I say a hundred stealth missiles from every point on the compass. We will bloody them and find out what the Throggs are up to at the same time. A trap is a trap, how much could it change their tactics?"

I could see the frown on Coonts face getting darker by the second. Rather than wait for the two to start bickering over their scenarios, I intervened. "What are your thoughts Tria?"

"I am going to have to agree with Coonts on this one. Stealth is the better option. Let the Quill believe they have an advantage. We should attempt to make a covert insertion to investigate the cache. If we find materials that would give the Quill a military advantage, we either try to remove them, or destroy them in place."

I was leaning toward the missile attack until I heard Tria's idea. Now I was thinking her plan made more sense. There was one more voice to be heard and I was sure he was crunching the numbers on the odds of success.

"Justice, do you have an alternative plan?"

"Commander, I concur with Tria's assessment, but must caution you that Bond Connery's situation can change at a moment's notice. To get involved with an alternate operation before ensuring his security, could compromise both missions."

Bond's security and the apprehension of Canik was our primary mission. The Quill situation was admittedly a distraction. Leaving the possibility of advanced tech falling into the hands of a sworn enemy, was a danger to all, not just for us. I couldn't come up with a plan, that wouldn't go to hell in a handcart, if we got a call from Bond saying he needed an immediate evac.

"I know you have a recommendation Justice, please enlighten us."

"I recommend targeting the cache with a torpedo and destroy it in place. Since we will not be targeting the Quill in our attack, it will sow uncertainty as to what exactly is happening. There is a very small chance the Quill will detect the weapon launch, and an even smaller chance it can be traced back to the Legacy once it transitions. There is more than a ninety percent chance that a number of the Quill ships will be damaged by debris from the detonation. There is also the same percentage of probability that the detonation will trigger a Quill response that will reveal their deception."

I looked at everyone to see if they had anything to add. Tria and Sael were both shaking their heads in a positive manner. It must have been a no-go for Coonts. He was giving the Troop Master a very sour look. Klutch however, was smiling ear to ear and held his hands up at the Grawl. He flashed all his fingers at him twice. It didn't take a genius to figure out Coonts just lost a bet. When they noticed I was giving them the stink eye, their expressions quickly turned neutral.

"Justice, prep the torpedo for launch and make the DEHD core ready for a transition."

"Affirmative Commander, I recommend a subsurface detonation at the cache's coordinates. A depth of one-thousand feet should ensure that any hidden subterranean passages will be subjected to catastrophic damage."

Justice had moved us well away from our entry point into the system. We were drifting at moderate velocity at an angle to the target planet, and would be passing within a million miles of it in a matter of minutes.

"Launch when you are ready Justice."

"Launching in three minutes Commander." Justice acknowledged.

We sat quietly watching as we closed with the planet. As was expected, Justice launched as we were just passing the target. A red circle appeared at the bottom of the view dome and disappeared from the screen. Justice veered sharply away from the planet. Seconds later a large portion of the planet bulged upward from the surface and blew violently out into the void. A hellish glow was flaring out from a crater that looked like it covered a quarter of the small planet. An explosion of that magnitude would have doomed all life on a planet with an atmosphere. Eleven of the twenty-eight mining ships were no longer visible.

I was going to comment on the results of the attack, when Justice called out an alert. "Commander, I am detecting numerous Quill star drives coming online. The number has surpassed three hundred and is continuing to climb!"

The view dome around us was lighting up with hundreds of red boxes. Almost every piece of planetary debris floating in the system, had one or more target boxes on them.

Justice commented on his observations. "Commander, there is dust and rocky plumes coming from the detection sites. The data indicates the Quill ships were buried under the materials prior to our attack. My scanners are picking up a massive spike in communications, and my power source detections have ceased at eight hundred."

The view dome was a mass of red boxes and they were swarming from every possible direction in toward the planet. We were quickly being hemmed in as Justice maneuvered in an attempt to get us clear.

Justice called out another warning. "Multiple missile launches Commander! All detected vessels have launched a salvo of missiles. I am now picking up the telltale emissions of high yield fusion warheads."

The view dome became impossibly cluttered with additional small red triangles, and all had lines extending from their launch points.

"Has any of the ships been able to get a target lock on us?"

"Negative Commander. The more likely scenario, will be inadvertently colliding with a missile if we continue to linger."

I had seen enough to know; it was time to bugout. No pun intended.

"Jump us out of here Justice!"

The giant display disappeared in a whitewash of brilliance. When we returned to normal spacetime. We were greeted by an overly bright white central star, and a system free of hostile ships. We breathed a collective sigh of relief.

A small yellow blinking box appeared high up on the view dome. Underneath it was the words Hub eight. Justice made a course correction, centering it on the screen in front of us. The box stopped blinking and was slowly growing larger. The local ship traffic started populating the screen. There were seventeen freighters stacked in a holding pattern and twelve on outbound courses. An assortment of small spacecraft was coming and going from the far end of the hub.

"Justice open a secure channel to Bond."

That got me a sideways look from Sael. The inquiring look implied she had questions about Bond's comms.

"Channel open Commander."

"Bond, we are near your location. Can you give me a sitrep?"

In a low voice Bond replied. "Wait one."

We heard him raise his voice and he was purposely slurring his speech. He yelled at someone, asking them what they were staring at. We heard a noise that sounded like something breaking. An unknown voice speaking in Galactic Standard was yelling at him, saying he would have to pay for that. Bond's slurred voice yelled back that he didn't care, he was going to be wealthy enough to buy this scat hole. We heard what sounded like a scuffle and Bond was yelling again, telling someone to unhand him. The unknown voice told him not to come back if he was intoxicated. Bond cursed his detractor, and said he was not intoxicated. We heard a thump and a grunt from Bond. It wasn't hard to decipher what happened. He got himself thrown out of whatever establishment he was in. Bond's voice came back on our comms and it was no longer slurred. "I am being watched and followed, so I will make this brief. My companion has not returned to my apartment, so I am pretending to search for him. I wanted to be somewhere public so I could message you with an update. I am glad you called first. I found listening devices in my residence that were left by my former companion. I believe Genda Binar is going to make his move very soon. I…"

A voice speaking Grawl said get him off the ground. We heard Bond groan. The Grawl voice said to hurry up. Bond slurred his speech again. He yelled out that he had payed a week in advance and that whoever had accosted him should pleasure him now. The response was a loud smack that must have been a blow to Bond's head close to where his IST was implanted. The Grawl voice could be heard again. He was calling someone a fool and not to kill him. We were hearing Bond's abduction in real time.

"Justice, do you have a hard lock on Bond's location?"

"Affirmative Commander. I have mapped the traffic patterns of all vessels, and have a holding point close to the shipping hub where we can take up surveillance, and monitor Bond's movements. Do you wish to close with the outpost?"

"Roger that Justice, move in now."

I turned to my crew, with the exception of Sael Nalen they looked at me with anticipation.

"Nathan! You told me you would keep my people's IST technology secret and not share it with others!" Sael hissed in anger.

"Sael, I have kept my word to you, and have not shared your technology with anyone. I have however, shared our IST tech with select allies."

Sael squinted her eyes. "What do you mean by that? My people developed the tech and you obviously pirated it for your own purposes!"

"Sael, I will give you credit where it is due, and the tech we developed is similar to yours. Yes, we did pirate your ideas, but our designs are different. We made many improvements in signal strength and range. We have also made use of the higher levels of interdimensional space encountered when using DEHD core technology. That is a shortcoming with Chaalt designs, and something Justice and our Grawl engineers discovered on their own."

Sael was momentarily speechless and then regained her composure. "Our scientists have been working on the same ideas. They have been utilizing the technology that came from the development of our dark energy hyper drive. We have yet to make a breakthrough. I now believe, that it may have to do with the tech related to the Oolaran design, and not the hybrid my people developed. There are a number of scholars on my people's home worlds, who believe our designs are superior to the dated tech incorporated in Oolaran architecture. We are failing, because we are guilty of only looking forward, rather than back at something we know to be hundreds of years old. With your permission, I would like to make our scholars aware of their mistake."

The Chaalt were learning the hard way. New is not always better. When it comes to utilizing shortcuts, you really need to look at what you are cutting out of the bigger picture. Setting your sights on a single goal, can blind you to the consolation prizes that may yield much larger rewards.

"Sael, we can discuss this later." I said. "For now, we have a mission, and that is to protect our asset. We are going to the ready room. If you want to stay behind and ruminate, feel free. We are going after Genda Binar."

Tria, Coonts and Klutch were already heading for the down tube. I turned my back on Sael, and ran to catch up with them. As I stepped into the tube I turned and saw Sael three steps behind me.

Justice called out a sitrep on Bond. "Commander, I have overheard Bond's captors state they are going to put him on a shuttle and take him off world. I am moving to the civilian traffic portal, and will attempt to identify the outbound vessel."

"Roger that Justice, follow them as close as possible. We need to know where they are going?"

We put our armor on and hustled to the hangar. We were going over each other's kit, when Justice called to us. "Commander, I have identified the shuttle Bond is on, and we are pursuing it at a safe distance to avoid other ship traffic. It appears to be heading for the commercial shipping lanes."

"Stay on them Justice, they may try to pull some funny stuff to make sure they are not being followed!"

I knew Justice was doing just that. I always got a little overamped every time we got ready for a mission. I just felt the need to voice it. Justice let me know he was listening regardless of the need to.

"Acknowledged Commander."

33

Justice put a viewscreen up on the bulkhead next to the hangar doors. It showed a shuttle with a yellow blinking box around it. The viewscreen wasn't showing a magnified view. The shuttle filled the screen. Justice was a lot closer than he was previously disclosing.

He gave us a heads up. "Commander, a freighter is moving out and away from the traffic holding pattern. The shuttle has made a small course correction that appears to be aligning for an intercept of the freighter."

Justice highlighted the freighter. It was a very modern looking skeletal design, and lacked the full load of cargo containers the rest of the freighters in the holding pattern were carrying. It also had some unusually large star drives. Just in front of the massive drives was a large square boxy looking structure with eight large hangar doors on it. One of the doors was opening.

Justice confirmed the target. "Commander, the freighter has cut its drives and the shuttle is headed directly for it."

"Justice, I want to board the freighter the same time as the shuttle!"

The AI surmised that, but acknowledged me anyway. "Affirmative Commander, I advise going out of the boarding hatch to minimize detection."

We ran to the hatch and lined up behind Klutch. Justice purged the atmosphere and gave us a pre-jump no shitter. "Commander, the strike team must depart the boarding hatch at maximum boost. If the hatch is open for more than six seconds, it may trigger a detection with the freighter's anti-collision systems."

We engaged our stealth systems and stacked at the hatch. We grabbed each other by the ammo pack and nervously waited. I could already feel the push of my gravity drives.

"I called to Sael. "When we get aboard that freighter you are to maintain comms silence at all times. No BS or IST, you got that?"

She sent back a terse reply. "Yes Commander! No comms!"

The hatch suddenly popped open and we went out in four seconds. The freighter loomed massive in front of us. The open hanger door seemed like it was leaping out to meet us at break neck speed. I still had my hand on Klutch's backpack. He leaned back into me and kicked his feet out in front of him to retro brake. We followed his lead and slowed enough not to collide with the side of the freighter. The shuttle was coming up quickly behind us. It undoubtedly had the assistance of a tow beam. We waited at the edge of the hangar door for it to break through the atmospheric retention field, then boosted along side of it as it was brought down for a landing. This was nothing new to us and Klutch rapidly led us up into the overhead machinery. The hangar door quickly closed and we came to terms with the Deja Vue of being trapped in another hostile filled transport, headed to an unknown destination.

Klutch led us to the top of the large ducts that supplied the atmosphere for the hangar. We laid down on top of them and peered down over the edge at the shuttle below us. The machinery around us roared to life, and started cycling to refresh the atmosphere lost when the shuttle penetrated the retention field. Within minutes the pressure readings monitored in our HUDs were back to normal.

I was beginning to wonder if Bond was unconscious or faking it to avoid another beating. The cargo ramp at the back of the shuttle dropped and a Grawl stepped out. He was followed by three Tibor in full body armor. The Grawl called to one of the Tibor and we used our external microphones to listen.

"Harmak." The Grawl called. "Let me know when the Coram wakes."

"We can wake him now, and not waste any more of your time." The Tibor answered.

"No!" The Grawl replied. "His intoxication makes him useless. Let him wake on his own, and I will assess his condition."

The Grawl and his two Tibor escorts walked to a hatch and left their remaining comrade behind, quietly grumbling. The Tibors were probably mercenaries, and I was hoping one of them would use the Grawl's title so we would know who he was. For all we knew, he could be Genda Binar.

Four Murlak walked out of the back of the shuttle and stopped in front of Harmak. One of them pointed back inside. "If that Throgg vomits in my shuttle, you make sure it gets cleaned up!"

The Murlaks were obviously the flight crew, and they were now snickering at the Tibor. Their faces became pinched and they rapidly stepped away from Harmak. The Murlak who appeared to be in charge, berated the Tibor. "Do not foul my ship with your stench!"

The Tibor drew a fighting knife from his armored breast plate. "Or what Plomo! Are you going to threaten me to death?"

Yep! I hit the nail on the head first try. The Tibors were definitely mercenaries. The Murlaks quickly moved on, casting disparaging words over their shoulders at the Tibor. Harmak laughed at them and made a show of grabbing at his genitals.

"I hope your females have not given me the Fusra Pus Virus!" He shouted.

It was nice to know there was little harmony within the ranks of the wicked. If we started shooting the place up, it would probably be every man for himself. When the Murlaks were a safe distance, the leader of the Murlaks shouted back at the Tibor.

"I am going to report your insubordination to the Overmaster! We will see how much humor he finds in your actions!"

The Tibor fired right back. "Go ahead! I have already told Elsin that you are cowards. Your neonate whining, will only prove that I am correct."

Bingo! We now knew the Grawl was not Binar. He might have information that could lead us to him, so we would not make him a priority target if any shooting started. The Tibor went into the back of the shuttle and after a couple of minutes came back out carrying Bond. This may prove to be good news, because it possibly indicated Bond was going to stay on the freighter, and they would not take him to another location. It might also mean that Genda could be meeting up with the freighter sometime in the near future.

We saw some movement from Bond as he was being carried down the ramp. I used the magnification in my helmet to verify what I was seeing. Bond was putting his hand in his mouth and I was at a loss as to why. My confusion was quickly cleared up when we heard him wretch loudly and puke down the back of the Tibor's armor. Harmak yelled out in anger, and threw Bond onto the ramp. He rolled to the bottom and pushed himself upright. His wasn't slurring his speech as badly as before.

545

"If you are Zimon's replacement you will have to learn to be gentler. Pleasure me now, and show me you are worthy of my attention." Bond declared.

The Tibor drew his fighting knife and stalked down the ramp toward Bond. I put my arm up and targeted the Tibor with my spike weapon. My strike team followed suit. I had no idea why Bond would purposely piss the Tibor off. All his years of living in filth must have made him immune to the Tibor's scent. If he kept it up, he was going to get himself killed.

Harmak stood over Bond waving his fighting knife in his face. "We were told you to had to be alive so you could answer questions. That makes your appendages expendable as far as I am concerned." The Tibor raged down at the Coram.

None of the Tibor's behavior phased Bond. "If you continue your abuse, I will forego any additional incentives and will report you and Zimon's breach of contract!"

The Tibor started yelling non-stop curse words and drew back his fighting knife to strike. Just when I thought I would have to shoot the Tibor, a hatch opened and the Grawl Elsin, charged through yelling at Harmak to stop. The Tibor froze and then promptly put his weapon away. Bond must have known he was being observed. If his gamble had turned out to be wrong, he would have suffered the consequences. He was pushing his luck and I wished he would tone down his act.

"You fool!" Elsin yelled. "What are you doing? The Coram must remain alive. Are you trying to get us all executed?"

Harmak tried to explain he was only going to cut the Coram's hands off, but Elsin would have none of it. He told the other two Tibor to go with Harmak, and not show their faces unless he called for them. They must not have been moving fast enough because Elsin yelled after them.

"If I have to smell your stench for another second, I will have all three of you thrown out of the airlock!"

The Tibor mercs quickly disappeared through the hatch. Elsin had to be in a secure position of power to throw his weight around like that. His comment about execution hinted he still wasn't high enough up the power ladder to avoid judgement by Genda. Bond was still playing his part and was blubbering nonsense to Elsin and asking for more intoxicants.

Elsin finally had his fill when Bond started pawing at the Grawl's feet, and asking if he was his new companion.

"Silence!" Elsin demanded. "I have no idea why Genda Binar would waste his time on a pathetic wretch such as you. If you touch me again, I will have Harmak come back and make good on his threat!"

Elsin finally confirmed we were on the right path to finding Genda Binar. It also vindicated the Coram's methods. Bond continued his act, and curled up on the deck pretending to cry. I suspected he had done this very same thing when he was being abused by Eiger's pirates. The Murlak flight crew came back through the hatch and had a med pod floating along behind them.

Elsin waved at them. "Hurry up and get this sniveling Throgg out of my sight before I kill him myself!"

The Murlaks thought that was funny, and were laughing it up. Elsin pulled a pistol from his cloak suit and pointed it at the shuttle crew. "I can always hire another shuttle crew!"

That comment quickly stifled the Murlaks snickering. They jerked Bond off the deck and locked him in the med pod.

Elsin waved his pistol at the pod. "Take this worthless piece of scat to shuttle bay three. Find that fool Harmak, and tell him to stand watch over the him. A shuttle will be arriving soon to take him away. Make sure those slow witted Tibors know that if anything happens to the Coram between now and then, I will see to it, the three of them are roasted alive. When you are sure they understand the situation, get back here and return me to Hub eight."

The Murlaks hurriedly escorted the pod out of the shuttle bay. They turned left as they exited. We couldn't immediately follow, and were stuck waiting. We didn't want to risk using our suit scanners to locate Bond. Elsin stood on the shuttle's ramp and watched as the Murlaks went through the hatch and it closed behind them. Our cloaking was cutting edge, but we couldn't take the chance our sudden movements toward the hatch might be detected by Elsin. We held tight until he went into the shuttle. We rapidly descended to the deck and plastered ourselves to the bulkhead on each side of the hatch. I used my implants to put a countdown timer in my HUD. I wanted to know how long it took the Murlaks to return. It would give me a rough idea how far away Bond was. I would divide the time in half and we would start searching when we reached that distance. My timer reached one-hundred and ninety-two and the big hatch opened. Plomo, and the flight crew walked through. They could not have taken Bond very far.

It was clear there was no love lost between the Murlak mercenaries and Elsin. All four were mumbling deprecating statements about Elsin, and complained they were not being paid enough. We rushed through the open freight hatch behind them, making just enough noise, the last member of the flight crew stopped and turned around. We heard Plomo call to him to hurry up as the hatch closed behind us. Klutch took us to the overheard and we froze in place amongst the ductwork to see if an alarm would be raised. The hatch opened and the Murlak leaned out and looked in all directions. We heard Plomo yell again, and this time it was a threat. The Murlak shook his head and muttered under his breath. He turned around and the hatch closed. We were in a huge corridor filled with stacked crates and transports. There were several different races busily going about their business. We moved along the overhead machinery at a pace that I hoped mirrored that of the Murlak flight crew.

My timer counted down from ninety-six. There were four large freight hatches in front of us and six behind us. None were marked with a number we could see. We had to assume one of the two doors closest to us was door three. The two against the bulkhead had to be one and two. I tapped on Coonts and Sael's armor and pointed to the overhead above the door across the way. They moved to the door and took up a position so they could see inside if it opened. Klutch, Tria and I did the same with the opposite one. It would now be a waiting game. As busy as things were below us, someone would have to open one of the doors sooner or later.

A klaxon blared three times behind us and we turned to see an orange light blinking beside the shuttle bay where Elsin's shuttle was docked. I took a leap of faith, and guessed that Elsin and the Murlaks just departed. The klaxon blared a single warning five minutes later and the light disappeared.

I was growing impatience, and wanted to know where Bond was being held. We heard a low pitch whine in the background noise that wasn't noticeable before. It was slowly gaining in volume. It was accompanied by vibration that was running throughout the freighter's hull. It wasn't a stretch to figure out the ship was accelerating. The whine and vibration leveled off and my stomach started churning like an old Earth washing machine. Damn! We were jumping out of the system. It was unknown if Justice could track the distortion waves created by the huge ship. If not, the Legacy would have to remain behind until we could send an IST transmission.

We stayed in our positions for forty minutes. The other hatches in front and behind us were opened numerous times. Cargo containers and pallets loaded with goods came and went. I was growing frustrated because neither of the freight hatches we were holding over opened. If there wasn't so much traffic below us, I would consider having Klutch make us a portal. Another eleven minutes slowly creeped by and the ever-present whine and vibration rapidly tapered off. Our stomachs suddenly got another good twisting. The freighter had reached its destination. It was hard to speculate as to how far we had traveled. The unusually large star drives on the freighter, could no doubt achieve much higher than normal velocities as compared to a normal freight hauler. To our surprise, the door Coonts and Sael were holding over opened. They took a quick look through the top of the door as a cargo transport carried its load inside. Coonts and Sael joined back up with us. Coonts hand signaled me a negative on Bond. He had to be in the bay on our side, we just needed a way to get inside.

To make my growing anxiety worse, a klaxon right above us signaled three times and the orange light to the side of the hatch started blinking. A ship was arriving and I had to assume it would be Genda Binar's or whoever was sent to retrieve Bond. Since no one was going to open the hatch for us, it was time to take a calculated risk. I rapped Klutch on the shoulder and pointed at the portal device. He gave me a thumbs up and pointed at the bulkhead between two big pipes that intersected with the ductwork we were hiding behind. I returned his thumbs up and crossed my fingers in hopes no one would notice the flash of the portal. Klutch got a good hole and we quickly boosted through. The Troop Master was the last through and immediately closed the portal. We froze in place as we watched a shuttle slowly turning to point it's nose out at the void. For a second, I thought it was going to leave, but was relieved to see the rear cargo ramp lowering and the big hangar door closing.

Down below us and to our left was a control room with clear view screens. We could see the three Tibor mercenaries standing around Bond's med pod. There was a lot of cargo containers stacked around the perimeter of the room and they would make great cover. I pointed downward to my strike team and we descended to the deck behind them. I had every one spread out and find a vantage point to surveille the shuttle and the entry hatch. We still didn't know if we had alerted someone out in the corridor with the flash of the portal device activating.

The tow beam set the shuttle on the deck and we could see six heavily armed Tibor standing just inside. They were apparently waiting for the ramp to finally touch down. A klaxon sounded a single sharp report and a green light on the side of the control room flashed on. Harmak and his two cohorts led Bond's med pod out of the airlock of the control room. The six Tibor in the back of the shuttle took this as their cue to march off the ramp and form a perimeter at it's base.

Harmak yelled out a greeting to one of the Tibor. "Sprag! Long time, no see! The word around the Guild, is you got a cushy job inspecting latrines."

Harmak's two comrades burst into laughter. Sprag frowned and was all business. "Stow that scat Harmak! Keep your mouth shut unless you want to forfeit your credits."

That put a stop to the mirth coming from the Tibor mercenaries. Sprag pointed to one of his troopers and then at the med pod. The Tibor pulled a wand from his kit and went to the pod. He waved it over the surfaces of the pod. Harmak and his men now had frowns on their faces. The Trooper with the wand shook his head negative and went back to his place in the perimeter.

"What is this Sprag?" Harmak called. "Do you think we would rig the pod with explosives?"

"I told you to shut up Harmak! I have my orders and I intend to carry them out. Open the pod, I need to inspect the merchandise."

Harmak grumbled something under his breath and unlocked the pod. He reached inside and jerked Bond upright and shook him.

"Wake up you Throgg!" He shouted.

Bond acted like he had been sleeping, and for all we knew he might have been. He looked around at his surroundings and started asking what going on, and where he was at.

Harmak shoved him back down and slammed the lid of the pod. He locked it and looked up at Sprag. "Are you satisfied?"

34

Sprag and his troops turned their heads and looked up into the back of the shuttle. A Grawl walked out onto the ramp. He was wearing a suit similar to our first generation Zaen battle armor. It was shiny black and reflected the overhead lighting. It had a blacked-out bubble style helmet hiding his features. He was also sporting a rather large pistol in a holster on his side. He had his hand on the downsized grip. There was a bad vibe in the air. These guys weren't just being cautious, they were getting ready for something else.

The Grawl in the fancy armor called to Harmak. "You have done well. Bring the pod into the shuttle and I will pay you."

While this was going on, my strike team and I were working our way around the cargo containers. We were now on either side of the ramp holding tight against the rear of the shuttle. As Harmak and his sidekicks approached the ramp with the med pod, everyone's focus was on them. It was our chance to make our move and we took it. We boosted up behind the Grawl and into the back of the shuttle. The shuttle had equipment crates and a mobile weapons platform in the back. It was going to get crowded real fast with the med pod and six Tibor inside. The overhead was about twelve feet off the deck and save for the numerous tiedown points, it lacked any cover. We couldn't all crowd around against the ceiling without blocking the light strips that lit the cargo bay. I was trying to decide who I would have to stuff behind the gun platform when we heard Harmak shout at Sprag.

The mercenary had stopped in the middle of the ramp with the med pod. He had his hands on his pistols. The two mercs with him were facing down the ramp and their hands on their on their weapons as well.

"Sprag, I don't like the way this is looking, and I don't like your crew pointing their weapons at our backs!"

The Grawl again told Harmak to bring the med pod and he would pay him. Harmak must have felt the same vibes as I did. He shoved the med pod at Sprag with his foot.

Sprag tried to stop it from careening off the ramp. Harmak drew his pistol in the blink of an eye, and shot him in the face. Sprag toppled headless over the side of the shuttle ramp and the pod went with him.

The Grawl yelled out. "Kill them!"

Everyone started shooting. Harmak and his team may have been clowns, but when it came to killing, they were lightening quick. As soon as Harmak drew his weapon and fired, his cohorts used the surprise of the attack to their advantage and did the same. They each shot down one of Sprag's crew and all three jumped over the side of the shuttle ramp. An errant shot from one of the Tibor weapons went into the shuttle's hold and hit Sael in the legs. The blast knocked her into Coonts and dumped them both on the deck. Sael inadvertently knocked the Grawl to the deck when she went down. The blast from the capacitive discharge pistol severely damaged the cloaking capability of Sael's armor, and her legs were now visible. The Grawl saw this and started screaming non-stop. He swung his pistol up trying to shoot Sael and she knocked it away as he pulled the trigger. The shot hit my weapons pack, blasting me into the shuttle's bulkhead.

Tria kicked the Grawl's weapon from his hand and called out over our comms. "Nathan are you hurt?"

"No! I want that Grawl alive!" I called over the comms.

Sael yelled out. "I have him! Look out behind you!"

The shuttle crew were Tibor, and there was four of them. They came running out of the flight deck hatch with their weapons up and ready. Coonts hit them with a burst of anti-personnel rounds from his tube launcher, knocking three of the four to the deck. The fourth tried to return fire, but Tria shot him in the faceplate with a penetrator spike. It pierced the Tibor's helmet and pinned his head to the bulkhead. He convulsed several times before he died, and each was accompanied by a squeeze of his trigger finger. His random shots blasted equipment and crates to pieces, causing a flash fire.

I tried to send an IST to Justice. "Justice do you have a copy? We are going to need an evac Justice."

The shielding on the freighter's outer hull was not your standard off the shelf equipment. I still managed to get a weak and garbled reply.

"I have a lock on your location Commander, and I am transitioning now." Justice replied.

Coonts put a long burst of minigun slugs into the downed flight crew tearing them apart. He managed to wreck the hatch to the cockpit and smoke started rolling out of it. Sael had the Grawl wrapped up with her legs and was firing down the ramp at one of Sprag's mercs with her minigun. She switched to her launcher and gave him an explosive round. The jarring detonation sent the remains of the trooper in all directions, splattering the rear of the shuttle and us as well.

I was wondering how Harmak and his crew faired in the gunfight. The ballsy bastard was nowhere to be seen. I looked at the carnage around the shuttle's ramp. To my relief the med pod was intact and laying on its side underneath the tail of the shuttle. One of Harmak's team was down next to the pod. He was gut shot and bleeding out. He managed to take two of Sprag's goons with him to meet his maker. Harmak and his remaining teammate were either dead or hiding in cargo crates stacked around the bay. I did a quick head count and couldn't account for all of Sprag's crew. I stepped to the edge of the ramp and looked over the side. My curiosity was rewarded with a pistol shot that just missed my head and struck the tail of the shuttle. I ducked down, and the bushwhacking Tibor jumped up from the side of the ramp, and ran toward the dock hatch. I hit him dead center of the back with a high explosive round from my launcher, blowing his torso to shreds. Tria and Coonts took up firing positions on each side of me. Klutch waded through the bodies of the flight crew and went into the cockpit.

"All clear Commander. We have a fire spreading in the cockpit and the suppression systems have malfunctioned. I recommend we abandon the shuttle." The Troop Master reported.

I looked around the cargo hold and it wasn't hard to see why the shuttle's safety systems were not functioning. Most of the control panels and other machinery around us were shot to shit. Smoke was boiling out of the back of the shuttle and an eerie silence fell over the docking bay. The calm was interrupted by Sael smashing her pistol into the Grawl's helmet multiple times. It was either a test to see how well the helmet would hold up, or she was just wanting to get the Grawl's attention. It turned out to be the latter. She finally got the Grawl to hold still when she jammed her pistol against the Grawl's face shield.

"If you make another move, I will blow your head off!" Sael yelled at the Grawl.

Just when I thought things might settle down, the dock entry hatch slid open and two combat mechs came rushing in with their shields up and scanning for targets. There were eight heavily armed mixed-race troops behind them. Tria and Coonts didn't hesitate. They opened fire, sending multiple shots from their beam weapons into the mechs. The mech's shields failed and they were blasted backwards into the following troops. The follow up shots blew the mechs to scrap and the troops into a gory mess. The cargo that was stacked near the hatch was shredded and burning. The hatch that once sealed the dock, was ripped from its track and laying in the outer corridor. Fire was rapidly spreading out into the corridor, and I doubted if anyone would make another attempt to investigate dock number three.

Above the din of the warning sirens, we heard someone calling to us. It was

Harmak, he had survived the shootout after all.

"You in the shuttle!" He called. "I have no quarrel with you. We just want to get out of here alive. We cannot stay here much longer. All I ask, is for you to let me and my comrade get out before we are cooked alive!"

I walked out on the ramp. My armor suffered enough battle damage it was pointless to stay cloaked. In the darkest corners of my mind the beast was whispering to me. It was reminding me that every time I had shown someone mercy it had come back to bite me in the ass. I pushed the monster from my thoughts. I admired the merc for his guts, and not backing down in the face of treachery and lousy odds. As much as I wanted to tie up any loose ends, I could not harbor ill will against them.

I uncloaked and shouted out in Tibor over my external mic. "Get out now, before I change my mind!"

Off to my right, some shipping crates tumbled aside. Harmak stepped out of the smoldering rubble. He had his arm around his remaining trooper and helping him walk. They were both wounded. They stopped at the bottom of the ramp and he looked up at me. "I hope you killed the Throgg that double-crossed me!"

"He will wish I had." I replied.

The Tibor nodded and they hobbled out through the burning wreckage and clouds of fire suppression spray.

Tria and Coonts ran to the bottom of the ramp and took up defensive positions I jumped down to help Klutch get Bond's med pod upright, and re-engaged its gravity lift. I could see Bond through the view port. He was smiling. He gave me two thumbs down until Klutch shook his head. Then he turned them upward and shrugged his narrow shoulders.

"Coonts, Tria, see if you can get the outer door open. Justice should be here any time."

They ran to the control room and leaped through the shattered view screens. Coonts commed me back. "Commander, the atmospheric retention field is inoperable. The emergency controls have the hull doors locked out because the inner hatch is no longer in place. We are going to have to make our own exit.

The fire in the cockpit of the shuttle took on a life of its own and started burning with a vengeance. The entire dock was now filled with thick dark smoke and the fire suppression systems went to work spraying a foam that completely buried the burning shuttle. Tria and Coonts rejoined us, and Sael jerked the Grawl off the deck where she was holding him down with her armored boot. I pointed to the corner of the bulkhead near the outer dock door.

"Klutch, make a hole and get us the hell out of here!"

The Troop Master ran to the bulkhead and faced the exterior hull. I steered Bond's pod along in front of me while Sael carried the Grawl like a ragdoll under two of her arms. Tria and Coonts covered our rear as we made our way to the corner of the dock. Klutch made a hole and I shoved Bond's pod through and went out behind it. I corralled the pod and held it in check with my gravity drives. When I turned around, I saw the Grawl come flying out end over end. I gave my drives a burp and moved out of the way. He smashed head first into the pod. It was a perfect field goal if I ever saw one. Sael came through and caught the little prick on the rebound. Tria, Coonts and Klutch came through, and the Troop Master terminated the portal. We put some distance between us and the monstrous freighter. It was dead in the void and had bright red emergency beacons flashing down the entire length of its spine. There were several rows of vents on the top of the large boxy looking hangar dock, and all were venting smoke. If this was another of Bren Carsoon's freighter's, he was going to have a meltdown when he got the news.

I thought sure Justice would be waiting to scoop us up, but that was not the case. We were drifting away from the stricken freighter and I was starting to think our destination was going to be the endless void.

I sent an IST message to the Legacy. "Justice, we have abandoned the freighter and I need an ETA."

"I encountered a small delay Commander, and I am forty seconds out." The AI quickly replied.

"What kind of delay?" I called back.

"When I transitioned into the system, my scanners detected a Galactic Union gunship. When I investigated its location, it was blacked out and running on minimal power. It also had its hangar doors in the open position. Its proximity to the freighter made it a threat to my recovery operations.

My actions were based on our past experiences. I disabled the gunship's star drive as well as its main weapons turrets and comms antennas."

That gave me something to think about. There was a better than good chance, the shuttle that came to pick up Bond was from the gunship.

"Justice, was there any shuttle's in the gunship's hangar?"

"Negative Commander, the bay was vacant."

"Did they launch comm buoys?" Tria asked.

"Yes Tria, they launched two, and I destroyed them both. I took the precaution of disabling the buoy launch tube. The odds are low, that they will be able to broadcast a distress call with sufficient signal strength to summon additional forces."

The Legacy's hangar bay suddenly appeared and Justice pulled us aboard with the tow beam. Sael took the Grawl to the brig and Klutch immediately freed Bond from the med pod and shoved it into the void. Justice closed the hangar door and made a turn that would take us toward the gunship.

Bond looked as thankful as the day we took him from Outpost 655. "I was concerned that your tracking device might be unable to disclose my whereabouts once I was removed from Hub Eight. It crossed my mind when the mercenaries started shooting at each other, that I might be killed before you could intervene."

I wasn't going to confirm just how close to the truth his statement was. "Bond, I told you we had you covered. Unlike others, when we give someone our word, we do not go back on it."

Bond cleared his throat and cast his eyes down at the deck. "Yes, Commander Myers, I will never doubt you again."

We needed to find out who we had in the brig before I made a decision on boarding the gunship. If it was Genda Binar we would jump out of the system and leave the ship to its own means. If not, it would be worth a look to see for ourselves who might be aboard.

We went to the brig and to our surprise Sael was in the cell with the Grawl. She was telling the Grawl to step out of his armor suit and identify himself. She was not getting any response from the prisoner. Sael kicked the Grawl hard enough to drive him into the wall of the cell. He collapsed to the deck then slowly got back to his feet. The armor was of a good design but he was still going to feel that shot in the morning.

I called to Sael over her comms channel. "That will be enough for now. Let him have a chance to consider his fate."

Sael stalked to the cell door without comment. She was staying true to her word. She has obeyed all of my orders without throwing a fit. I looked at the Grawl, studying his armor suit. I was curious if it came from the Zaens.

"Justice, can you tell me if that suit is of Zaen design?"

"Commander, my scans reveal it has several qualities that could be from Zaen designs. It also appears to have attributes that point to materials prevalent in Grawl cloak suit designs. The data leads me to believe that it is a Grawl copy of the Zaen's architecture. The suit has no integrated weapons systems, but does have excellent resiliency as well as a cloaking capability. My review of your data recorders, show that the Grawl never engaged the stealth qualities of the suit. I speculate it was intentional, and the capability will be used at some point to aid in the Grawl's escape attempt."

I asked the AI the next logical question. "Can we get him out of the suit without killing him in the process?"

"Yes Commander, the suit sustained several microscopic abrasions during the firefight with the Tibor mercenaries. A controlled nanite intrusion into the abrasion sites will allow penetration of the artifact weave. Once inside the weave, it will only take minutes to find any flaws in the interior liner and compromise them. The Grawl will want to abandon the suit shortly after that event takes place."

"He doesn't act like he intends to follow our orders, and must have it in his thick skull we cannot make him. Please show him that is not the case." I commented.

Justice extruded an arm from the overhead. When the Grawl noticed it, he jumped back against the enclosure wall and slid down it into the corner. Justice's arm came down level with the Grawl's helmet. He had the prisoner's undivided attention. A black tar like goo shot from the end of the arm and impacted the Grawl's helmet with enough force to bounce his head off the wall. He started wiping at the substance trying to get it off the helmet. He didn't need to bother. It undulated from his helmet and spread out on the armor suit. That finally got us a response.

"What is this scat! What are you doing?" The Grawl yelled out.

The Grawl ran to the front of the enclosure and pressed his helmet to it. "What have you done!" He yelled with terror in his voice.

"We asked you to remove your armor and you failed to comply. Now you will suffer the consequences." I scoffed.

The Grawl started rubbing at his armor but the residue was gone. It finally dawned on him what we had done. "You have committed a high crime! Weaponized nanites are forbidden!"

Bond looked over at me with wide eyes. He was just as surprised as the Grawl was. The Grawl's exclamation got a round of laughter from Coonts and Klutch.

Klutch yelled back at him. "So is abduction and murder!"

The nanites were deadly efficient. It took them less time than I thought it would to penetrate the Grawl's suit. He started screaming and collapsed to the deck. His helmet flipped forward and the back of the suit popped open. He was screaming louder now, than over his external mic. He rolled out onto the deck clawing at his face and head. Bond was staring at the Grawl in horror and was physically shaken by what he was seeing. He turned to me and looked like he was going to say something. The Grawl suddenly ceased his shrill screams. Bond tore his gaze from me and looked back at the Grawl, wondering if he was dead.

The Grawl rolled over and sat up moaning. Justice had neutralized the nanites. He had puffy splotches on most of his body and they were weeping bloody fluids.

I had Justice open the cell door and I went inside and stood over the Grawl. "I am going to ask you some questions and if I feel you are not being truthful, I will have the nanites start on your appendages and eat them away until I get the answers I am seeking."

The Grawl was almost pleading when he looked up at me. "What do you want to know?"

35

Now that the Grawl and I were on speaking terms, I asked him my first question. "What is your name?"

Without hesitation the Grawl replied. "Narren Breen."

"Who sent you to retrieve the Coram?" The Grawl stiffened at my question, and he hesitated. "Justice!" I called.

An arm came down from the overhead. The Grawl's eye bugged out and he curled up into a fetal position. "Genda Binar!" He yelled.

"Where can we find Genda, I would like to speak with him."

"He is aboard his personal transport." The Grawl whined.

"There is a Galactic Union gunship not far from here. Is that Genda's transport?"

The Grawl looked up at me in surprise, and nodded his head affirmative. I picked up the Grawl's armor suit and carried out of the cell with me. Justice closed the door and blacked out the enclosure.

I called to my strike team. "Top off your munitions. We are going to pay Genda Binar a visit."

Justice moved us close to the location of the gunship. He put a viewscreen up on the wall of the ready room. What we saw made us ᶍ stop momentarily to look at Justice's handywork. Justice's saying that he had disabled the ship was an understatement. The truth was, he had all but shredded it. I doubted if the gunship detected the Legacy until Justice opened fire. By the look of it, the AI was in close when he started shooting. An orbit of the wreck revealed that most of the rail cannon rounds went right through both sides of the ship. If justice would have hit them from a distance, there wouldn't be so many exit holes.

There was a large debris field drifting slowly along with the ship and it only contained a few bodies. A vessel the size of the gunship would have more than one hundred fifty crew members. It was likely a certain number of the crew would have been caught without pressure suits and died in the initial attack. Unless Justice got lucky, and managed to kill more, we would still be facing something in the neighborhood of twenty-five to one odds. While that made it a little more likely that Genda Binar was still alive, I had no illusions we would have to kill a lot of people before they would consider giving him up.

Justice made his final orbit of the gunship and came to a stop just behind the bridge. The damage the Legacy inflicted, was so severe, the ship's Captain jettisoned the anti-matter containment vessels to prevent a catastrophic detonation. Smoke, atmosphere and liquids were still leeching from the hull in numerous places. The gunship used to have four forward and two rear main weapon's turrets. All were gaping ragged holes marring the appearance of the once sleek hull. The antenna farms that used to dot the spine and belly of the ship were either missing our twisted broken protrusions. I couldn't see any telltale lights indicating the backup power sources were operating. There was a good chance the surviving crew decided they would all die if they were emanating any signs of a power source.

The damage was a testament to the Oolaran AI programming that dealt with the scenario of a pilotless ship still capable of combat operations. Justice apparently had no problem falling back on his default primordial directives when he felt it was necessary. I had nothing to say on the subject. The AI put our safety first. I went back to dumping my empty magazines and getting a fresh ammo pack. I looked over at Sael to see what her reaction was. To my surprise, she had just a hint of a smile on her face. I suspected she was reminiscing on how the Kala Mor Dee of old, used to operate. When she saw me looking, whatever her thoughts may have been, they faded away along with the smile.

We headed out of the ready room with Klutch in the lead. We stopped long enough to check each other's gear. The cloaking qualities of all our suits had been degraded in our last engagement. Unless we were moving against dark backgrounds we could be easily detected. There was not a lot we could do about it now, and we formed up at the hangar door. I turned to Tria and blew her a kiss. She gave me a smile and returned the gesture.

I rapped Klutch on the ammo pack. "We are ready when you are Troop Master."

"Roger that Commander. Union gunships of this design, have lift tubes just aft of the bridge that will take us down to the combat information center. I recommend we start our search for Binar at that location."

Klutch stepped out the hangar door and we quickly followed. We formed up into our combat formation and Klutch weaved us through the debris field. We touched down on the hull and the Troop Master pulled a grenade.

"They have had more than enough time to prepare for a boarding. Hold here Commander."

Klutch boosted about a hundred yards aft and stopped again on the hull. He made a hole and threw a couple of grenades in, then quickly terminated the portal. He boosted back to our position.

"Let's give them time to rally the troops." Klutch said.

We waited for more than four minutes, which was three more than I had patience for. Klutch leaned over and made a hole. We dropped through in a tight circle with our backs to each other and our weapons out and ready. Chaos would be the only way to describe what happened next. We dropped right onto the heads of a massed group of troops. All were firing down the corridor toward the area Klutch had dropped his grenades. We smashed down on several heads. Klutch was the only one that kept his footing. The rest of us toppled to the deck on top of the troops unlucky enough to be our landing pads. A brawl ensued and everyone started shooting. We were being hit by wild un-aimed fire. I was hit several times but so was the hostile forces around us. When our shotguns ran dry, we dropped them and extended our climbing hooks. We slashed and smashed anyone near us. There was a mounted weapons platform that was trying to turn around to fire at us. Klutch blasted the crew with antipersonnel rounds from his launcher. We were pelted by the high velocity fragments and the wild shooting lulled slightly.

Sael was the closest to the mounted gun and had her back to it. She must have got more than her fair share of the shrapnel. "Check your fire!" She yelled over our comms.

The blast doors on the bridge suddenly opened and it wasn't for a welcoming committee. Fire poured out, raking everyone in the corridor. Someone on the bridge threw a grenade out. Tria saw it coming and batted it away before it could land in our midst. The explosion flattened everyone, friends and foes alike. I pushed a body off of me, and fired a three-round burst of high explosive rounds into the bridge. Bodies and debris blasted back out into the corridor. There was survivors of my barrage and they managed to close the blast doors.

Our armor gave us the superior advantage over our opponents. We took a brutal beating but were not seriously injured. Several of the downed troops were still moving and some attempted to turn their weapons on us. We killed them all with penetrator spikes at point blank range. The smoke-filled corridor was finally silent. We were up to our knees in corpses. We rooted through the carnage and gathered up our weapons.

Slapping fresh magazines onto my shotgun. I pointed at the blast doors. "Klutch! Make a hole!"

Klutch kicked and shoved the bodies aside and went to the bridge doors. We stacked behind him with our weapons up and ready. He activated the portal device and we boosted through. There were four badly mutilated Tibor bodies on the deck in front of us. They must have caught the brunt of my HE rounds. Just behind them was two Murlaks kneeling behind an instrument station. They had pistols pointed at us but didn't fire. Their eyes were wide and staring. They were shocked to see how we passed through the blast door. We quickly spread out with our weapons pointed at them. Our HUDs gave us a warning. Our suit scanners were detecting three low output power sources. The detections were grouped together behind a console.

Klutch yelled out at them. "Tell us where we can find Genda Binar and we will let you live!"

Both of the Murlaks balked at the question. One of them glanced nervously over his shoulder to where the power sources were gathered. They should have spoken up or dropped their weapons. Klutch was still pretty pissed off about the meat grinder we were put through out in the corridor, and decided the Murlaks just gave him all the confirmation he needed. He unloaded both barrels of his shotgun into the them. The horrific mess would give the cloaked Grawl something to think about. We had at least three candidates that might possibly be Genda Binar. We moved to the console they were hiding behind.

Coonts called to them in his native language. He was appealing to their inherent self-preservation. "Uncloak and surrender. We want answers, not more corpses."

The three Grawl uncloaked and went prone face down on the deck with their arms extended. "We are unarmed!" One of them said.

Tria, Sael and Coonts snatched them off the deck and I called to Justice. "We are ready to evac."

I pointed at the bulkhead near the viewscreens. "Klutch, get us out of here."

The Troop Master made a hole and we stepped into the void. Justice was waiting and pulled us aboard the Legacy with the tow beam. My strike team dumped the Grawl on the deck and they got to their feet in front of me.

"Which of you is Genda Binar?"

What happened next almost made me laugh. Almost, being the key word. The Grawl were looking back and forth at each other and then at my strike team surrounding them. I was thinking we were going to do things the hard way all over again. To our surprise, two of the Grawl suddenly took a step backwards, leaving the one on the end standing by himself in front of me.

Genda Binar yelled out in rage. "You traitorous Throggs!"

I jerked Binar off the deck by his cloak suit and shook him like a ragdoll, then pulled him to within inches of my war mask.

"Where is Canik?" I yelled at the Grawl.

"I do not know anyone by that name!" Binar blurted.

I knew for a fact the Grawl was lying, and I damn sure wasn't in the mood for it. I grabbed his hand in my gauntlet and squeezed till the bones sounded like popcorn popping. The Grawl let out a bloodcurdling scream.

"I am going to ask nicely one more time, then I am going to get mean! Where can I find Canik?" I menaced.

He again hesitated. I crushed his other hand without the slightest thought of how wrong torturing him would have been back on my home planet. I was going to get my hands on Canik no matter how many criminals I had to kill or maim to do it. Binar's shrieks of agony were echoing throughout the hangar. My crew stood like statues and watched without pity. I dropped Binar on the deck and raised my armored boot over his foot.

The Grawl stifled his screams long enough to put together some coherent words. "He is on a planet called Frontier!"

Damn! There it was again. The mythical hideout of the worst criminals the galaxy had to offer. Someone had to know its whereabouts and I had a sinking feeling Binar wouldn't be one of them.

"Where is Frontier?" I demanded.

"I swear to you on the life of my sibling's I do not know!" The Grawl pleaded.

"Give me the name of someone who can!"

Genda Binar did not hesitate with his reply. "My employer, Bren Carsoon!"

"Tell me where I can find Bren Carsoon."

The Grawl tried to push himself upright from the deck but collapsed when he tried to make use of his hands. "No one knows how to find Bren Carsoon. He never spends more than a few hours at any one place. If he is not on Frontier, he is on his personal transport somewhere deep in the void. Those are the only places he feels safe." The Grawl ground out.

I turned on the other two Grawl that had exposed Binar's identity to me. "Does he speak the truth?"

They both immediately responded. "As far as we know, yes!"

I had my doubts but had to ask. "Do you know anything about Frontier?"

I could see their faces through their face shields. They were looking back and forth at each other. The blank looks told me the answer before it came out of their mouths.

One of them finally answered. "This is the first time we have ever heard of such a place."

"Coonts, Klutch, put them in the brig. Separate cells."

I was once again frustrated. We had climbed another rung higher up the ladder of the criminal hierarchy, only to fall back two. Genda Binar may yet prove to have valuable information, but we were no closer to finding Canik or where Frontier was located. We did learn something important. Our enemies have taken note of our successes and were changing their tactics to try and stop us. Combining forces was something new, and it showed they were growing a little smarter every day.

It was pointless to remain in this sector any longer. I called to Justice. "Destroy the remains of the gunship and take us back to Outpost 9765."

"Affirmative Commander." Justice replied.

Sael approached me. Her formal address made the corners of my mouth twitch upwards in a small smile.

"Commander Myers, I would like permission to question the prisoners."

I saw no problem with her request. At some point we were going to have a question and answer session that would determine the fates of all three.

"Carry on Sael. Keep me posted on your findings. I will leave it up to you whether or not Binar will be treated for the damage I inflicted on him."

Sael nodded and turned away. She stopped in front of the entrance to the brig and called back to me. "Are the two Grawl we captured with Genda Binar expendable?"

"Unless they can tell you something Binar can't, yes. I was going to turn them over to the Sig. Their life expectancy will be very short after that."

Justice transitioned the Legacy as Tria and I walked to the ready room. Our reality faded to a brilliant white. When we returned to normal space time, we found Coonts and Klutch putting on fresh uniforms. As they walked by Tria and I, Coonts stopped.

"Commander." Coonts said. "I sense you think we have wasted our time going after Genda Binar. Time will prove your apprehension wrong. While Genda's statements concerning Canik and Bren Carsoon helps us very little, I still think he has much more to offer in the way of useful information. I hope that he remains alive long enough to prove my theory correct."

I didn't know if Coonts was hinting to Tria and I not to kill them out of anger, or not to turn them over to the Sig who surely would. Coonts did have a point and arguably he was correct. Recent lapses in judgement by both Tria and I, had led to the deaths of important sources of information.

"I will take your recommendation under advisement." I responded.

Tria and I stepped out of our armor. I gave the suits a once over and determined they were a mess. They both had pock marks, blast abrasions and blood all over them. Justice was going to have to work overtime to get them back to combat status.

Justice called to us. "Commander, there are one hundred and twenty Sig military vessels in very low orbit over the outpost. The comms traffic I am intercepting, indicates the Sig are making ready to abandon the outpost."

"What? Have you picked up any indication why they would do that?"

"Unknown Commander. The comms network that we use to contact Tam Lin is now operational. Would you like me to open a channel to Tam Lin?"

"Yes Justice."

"Channel open Commander."

Tam Lin immediately came on the comms channel. "Nathan! I have been trying to contact you. Are you close to the outpost?"

"Yes. What is going on Tam? My AI has determined the Sig are leaving the outpost. Is that true?"

"Nathan, my private dock is available to you. Please land and come to my office. We have a lot to talk about."

"Roger that, we are on our way. We will see you in fifteen minutes."

"Nathan." Tam Lin said. Please forget what I said about Klutch being banned from the outpost. At one time, I felt it was necessary to help hide your identities and your presence on the outpost. That is no longer a concern. Please bring Bond Connery with you if he is available. What I have to say involves him as well."

I was left reeling at the implications of Tam Lin's statements. Something has drastically changed since the attack on the outpost. It couldn't be good if the Sig were leaving.

"Justice, alert the crew, and Bond Connery, we will be having a group meeting on the outpost with Tam Lin."

"Acknowledged Commander, message sent."

36

Justice engaged the Legacy's stealth systems and weaved us in and out of the dense Sig ship traffic. Justice put a view screen on the bulkhead and highlighted the shuttles moving around us. There were hundreds of Sig shuttles coming and going from the surface. Justice turned the view downward to the outpost. We were amazed to see thousands of Sig troops hard at work restoring the horrific damage we had witnessed more than a week ago.

We landed and Tam Lin met us. She was not accompanied by Sushi or Pasta. She hugged both Tria and I. "It is good to see you are back in one piece. Let's go to my office and I will tell you all that has transpired."

My crew and I followed and she gave me a sitrep on the mine. "Nathan, the shake down at the mine was a success, and we are moving forward with full time mining operations. We have processed all the ore rich materials that were present when you made the discovery. It yielded seventy-one tons of pure Containium. Now that we are prepared to start excavating new ore materials, I have come up with a number on the share split that was agreeable with both myself and the Sig.

"Okay Tam, what are the numbers."

We entered her conference room and she turned to face me. "The Sig have agreed to thirty percent and I am asking for fifteen. That leaves you with a fifty-five percent majority stake. If that is agreeable with you, I can have a long-term contract drawn up for all to sign."

I looked at the pretty young Earth girl and smiled, then held out my hand. "This is how my grandfather made a deal. It is good enough for me, if it is good enough for you."

Tam Lin smiled back and we shook. She led us in to her large ornate conference table and we took a seat. When Bond tried to sit at the far end, Tam Lin took him by the hand, and led him to the head of the table where she typically sat. She took a seat next to him. This got our attention. Bond had a huge smile on his face showing off his new pearly white teeth.

"Nathan." Tam Lin said. "General Bonaparte has ordered the evacuation of all Sig forces from the outpost. The interrogation of Ortulla has revealed that if the Sig remain on the outpost there would be more attacks. In order to avoid further collateral damage, and losses to the civilian population, the General ordered the withdrawal"

I frowned at Tam Lin's statement. "It is our mindset, the terrorist attack was triggered because of the search for Bolus, who we now know to be Canik. Since the Sig were the ones who released him, it would be logical for Canik to assume I was the one trying to find his whereabouts."

"Yes Nathan." Tam Lin said. "The information that you might be on the outpost coordinating the investigation on the whereabouts of Bolus, was passed directly to Ortulla and his Legion of the Chosen, by Canik."

"That was our thoughts as well." I replied. "Our intel indicates this is a coordinated effort by several races to put a stop to our interference in their illicit activities. Since the Scrun already have a serious grievance against us, the other criminal organizations are giving them the tech and support they need to stop us. The Legion of the Chosen, just happened to be a readily available tool to use against us and the Sig, for our affiliations."

"General Bonaparte is also convinced the terrorist attack served more than one purpose. The other being, retaliation for the losses of several well established Scrun bases that are now occupied by Sig forces." Tam Lin added.

Sael held up a hand. "Nathan, we already know the Scrun have associated those victories to you, as well as the Sig. They also have information that links you to the death of their most revered ruler, King Lashmos. My interrogation of Ortulla has revealed they formed the Legion of the Chosen to specifically target you and your crew for revenge."

That got me a surprised look from Bond. He wasn't privy to our past adventures. He was just now learning how extensive our list of enemies was turning out to be.

"Sael, we are aware of the Scrun's motives, what is your point?" I said with just a hint of annoyance.

"Nathan, perhaps it is time to coordinate with all your allies, and strike back at the Scrun. You should send them a message that you are not in this alone. You already know the location of a large Scrun installation. Taking the base, and killing every Scrun on it, would send a very powerful message of unity. I think it would make them rethink their terrorist strategies."

All eyes were on Sael. We knew she had ulterior motives for wanting to strike the Scrun base. There was a small possibility the Fury might be hidden somewhere at that location. Sael wasn't going to rest until she found it. The truth be told, I really couldn't find any fault with her reasoning. Maybe it was time to show the Scrun our resolve. I definitely wanted to show them what will happen if they choose to make another attack on a civilian target.

"Okay Sael, how soon can your people assemble a fleet?"

Sael looked genuinely surprised but quickly regained her composer. "I can have the battlecruisers in orbit above the salvage operation at the former Prule base move immediately. I can muster another sixty from the exclusion zone around my home worlds. That will give us eighty-two front line combat vessels and at least, two thousand troops. Sixty hours from now they could be within transition distance of the target and ready for combat operations."

I nodded to Sael then turned to Tam Lin. "Tam, can you get me a comms channel to General Bonaparte?"

"I don't have a direct channel to him right at the moment, but I can call Sushi and he will relay a message. Give me a few minutes so I can make the arrangements." Tam Lin answered.

Tam Lin got up and disappeared into her private office. I looked around the table at my crew members. "Any questions or comments? We need to wargame some likely scenarios before we decide on our order of battle."

Tria squeezed my hand. "My only concern is how effective the Heckler warships will be against our forces. They should be our primary targets. We need to overwhelm their defenses and destroy them before they can inflict serious damage to our fleets. We have very little in the way of intelligence on their full capabilities. We witnessed what may turn out to be only a small fraction of their arsenals."

That got Tria nods of agreement from all around the table. Klutch gave us a Troop Master's perspective. "There is bound to be a large Scrun presence in orbit, and that will significantly complicate the battlespace. We bloodied their noses the last time we were there. I think they will bolster their forces to make sure it doesn't happen again. We should also take the base's defensive batteries into consideration. If they are of Prule origin, they will be a danger to all vessels within their range."

Klutch was right, the stealth missiles we left in our wake when we made our strategic retreat, had to cause some serious damage. It was not just a blow to the Scrun fleet, it was a blow to their self-esteem as well. They would take steps to try and counter another attack.

I found myself trying to predict how General Bonaparte would respond if I told him about the Scrun base. Shaking my head, I decided it was a crap shoot at best. He has already proven he marches to no one's order's but his own. There was a chance he might order an immediate attack and suffer heavy losses. That was an outcome I couldn't come to grips with. I tried to clear my mind of all my doubts and uncertainties. The Sig have proven to be worthy allies in the past and I shouldn't discount them now.

"If General Bonaparte is willing to join our cause, and can bring a large enough battle fleet, we might get lucky and gain control of the orbitals fairly quickly. If that turns out to be the case, we can bombard the base until the Scrun are defenseless." I commented.

Sael Nalen gave us her thoughts, and as usual, they were from a point of superiority. "Once my people start teleporting troops down to the surface and establishing secure landing zones, there will be little the Scrun can do to stop us."

"Commander." Coonts said. "There is the very real possibility General Bonaparte might decide it would be a lot less risk for all involved, if we just turn the whole base into a crater. If that happens, we may never know if the Fury is hidden at that location."

I had not considered that scenario. The look on Sael's face said she hadn't either. "Nathan!" Sael said. "You must make sure you retain overall command of the operation."

"And what Sael? Order the Sig to stand down after we take the orbitals. Who do you think is going to take the most damage in a fleet on fleet conflict? We already know the Sig are no match for the Heckler warships. We can't guarantee those ships will be taken out early in the engagement. In a one on one with the Scrun, the Sig will have the advantage. If you add Klutch's scenario of a large Scrun fleet presence, the Sig could take some serious losses. If you were getting your ass kicked, what would you do if you were in Bonaparte's shoes?"

"Nathan, we have the technological advantage, I don't foresee…"

"Sael, giving me a best-case scenario, is not answering the question I asked you."

Tria answered for her. "She would marshal her forces and reduce the target to a pool of molten slag, then retreat with her surviving fleet out of the system."

Sael gritted her teeth and squinted her eyes at Tria. She did not make an attempt to dispute what was said. Tria stared back at her with a neutral expression.

"Principle Investigator." Tria said. "Kala Mor Dee's past history is well documented. Your scorched world policies are still used by our military to this day, unless I am mistaken."

Tam Lin returned to the table and the tension in the air eased considerably.

She saw the expression on Sael's face. "Did I miss something Nathan?"

"No Tam, we were just discussing some minor issues. Did Sushi get in contact with the General?"

"Yes, the general is indisposed due to the withdrawal. Sushi will be here shortly." Tam Lin replied.

Bond Connery was sitting quietly listening into our conversations but wisely refrained from discussing matters he knew nothing about. He cleared his throat loud enough to get our attention. All eyes shifted to him.

"Commander Myers, I am at a disadvantage, because I cannot truthfully enter into your conversation with helpful insight. Perhaps I should go back to the Legacy until you have finished your strategy meeting."

When Tam Lin heard his statement, she stood up next to him. "Bond, I am the one that requested your presence at this meeting. I wanted to tell you that the store we were preparing for your ownership, was completely destroyed by the Scrun terrorist attack."

The disappointment on Bonds face was easy to see. He was probably looking forward to espionage that wasn't quite as dangerous as his last mission. We would have to find him another secure location to run our covert operations.

I was going to comment on the unfortunate turn of events, but Tam Lin cut me off. "We have another location that needs very little in the way of preparation. As a matter of fact, it is ready for occupation as of right now."

Tam Lin's discloser changed Bond's expression for the better. He was now all smiles and looked up at her. "Do you mind if I inquire as to where I will be relocated too?"

You could have heard an ant fart when she replied. "Right here."

We were shocked to say the least. She looked at us all with a smile on her face, but only got the deer in the headlight's expressions in return. She cleared the air with her next revelation. "I am leaving with the Sig, and was thinking hard on who could fill my shoes. I think Bond would be the perfect candidate for the job. He already has experience running an outpost and his black-market credentials will serve him well when it comes to running the restaurant side of my covert operations. I will become his silent partner, and will share the profits from the business fifty-fifty."

Bond got up and looked around at the opulence of his surroundings. His eyes grew large and a big toothy smiled locked onto his face. I doubt if you could have wiped it off with a truncheon.

"I accept!" Bond blurted.

That brought us out of our shocked silence. "Tam." I said. "Where are you going?"

"I am moving with the Sig garrison to Venture. General Bonaparte has decided to move rather than have civilians suffer the consequences if the garrison remained on the outpost. I am still going to run my slave liberation, and intelligence gathering operations. It will just be from a more secure location. I also plan to take charge of operating the Containium mine as well. The location of Venture in proximity to El Dorado make it perfect for overseeing the shipping, as well as the day to day processes involved with managing the business side of mining. I have done all I can do here on the outpost, and I am ready for a change in scenery. Bond can oversee the operations here, and hopefully, take it to the next level."

Bond finally came back to the table and stood next to me. "Commander Myers, I would not be here if it were not for you. I feel the need to ask for your permission before I consent to the task Tam Lin has laid at my feet."

"Bond, as long as you do not return to the ways of your former life, I agree with Tam Lin. You are the perfect candidate for this job. We will stay in contact and expect to hear from you with regular intelligence reports. There is also the matter of our exports. You will be responsible for marketing our artifacts and exotic minerals. This is a win-win situation. You will be making honest profits from Tam Lin's business as well as ours. Who knows, maybe one day soon, you will be the owner of Carsoon shipping."

My last comment netted me laughter from my crew. Bond not so much. Tam Lin took Bond by the hand. "Come with me and I will show you around. There are a number of security measures that you will need to be briefed on. Once you are familiar with your new office, I will take you down to the restaurant and introduce you to the staff."

Bond looked back at me and I waved him on. "We will be leaving shortly and I am sure you are going to be very busy right up until Tam Lin leaves. I will be in touch if we need you."

Bond gave me a big smile. "I will not let you down Commander Myers!"

While my face sported a smile, my inner self had a frown. I needed to make a decision on whether or not to include the Sig on the Scrun raid. Sael had made a convincing argument for going without them. In my heart I didn't want to see them lose any more personnel to a war I had started.

Sushi came walking into the room with a grim look on his face. He tried to greet us with a smile, but you could tell he was forcing it. He got right down to business.

"Commander Myers, it is good to see you again. Tam Lin told me you have an urgent matter to discuss with me. How can I be of service?"

It was decision time and I was having difficulty making it. We had planned at one point to go it alone, with no support from any of our allies. We were going to nose around, and then cause as much havoc as possible on the way out. I was brought out of my contemplations by an expectant looking Sushi.

"Commander Myers, are you well?"

"Ah… yes Sushi, I'm sorry, I have a lot on my mind. We captured Genda Binar and two other Grawl we believe to be his gunship pilots. He is one of the criminals responsible for aiding Ortulla and his terrorist. He is an associate of Canik, and I would appreciate if you shared any intel you might obtain from them."

Sushi wrinkled up his brow. "Of course, Commander Myers. We have always shared our intel with you."

I called to Coonts and Klutch. "Get the prisoners from the brig and transfer them into Sushi's custody."

Now my crew was eyeing me as well. Coonts and Klutch got up and left but Sushi stood by for another moment.

"Commander Myers, if there is something you want to tell me in confidence, please do."

"No Sushi, its been a long day and we have to get going. I am sorry that we were the reason you and your garrison were attacked. When you get settled in at Venture, we will get together and discuss the Glock mission."

"I look forward to it Commander. Thank you on behalf of my people for apprehending the criminals responsible for the attack. I realize you are under no obligation to turn them over to us, and I personally appreciate your gesture of good will."

Sushi gave me a bow and I returned it. He turned and walked away, stopping once more at the door and looking back at me. He knew something else was on my mind, but wasn't going to badger me about it. He bowed once more and was gone.

37

I walked back to the table and sat down next to Tria. She grabbed my hand and held it. I thought she might have something to say, but she didn't comment. When I came here, I did not intend to turn Binar over to the Sig. After having Tam Lin call Sushi, I wasn't about to let him leave empty handed. I just hope I made the right decision.

I looked over at Sael and she was staring at me. "Principle Investigator, just remember, this is what you wanted, and it will be your people dying if the raid goes sideways."

Her gaze never wavered. "I am keenly aware of that Commander. For what it's worth, you made the right choice. You may have saved thousands of lives."

"That can go two ways Sael. I may have just sealed our fates."

"I will petition my leadership council for additional warships. We will have the technological advantage. It will more than make up for our lack of numbers." Sael responded.

"Sael, there is no guarantee the Fury will be there. As far as I am concerned, we will be going to investigate the Prule connection to the site. If it turns out the Fury is at the base, we will attempt to recover it intact. If it looks like that is not possible, we will destroy it to prevent the Scrun or the Prule from gaining the technology. I want to make sure we are absolutely clear on that subject before we go."

"I understand Commander Myers, and I agree with you."

We headed back to the Legacy. Stopping just long enough to bid Tam Lin and Bond farewell. We boarded and Justice took us out on a course that didn't conflict with the Sig shuttle traffic. Once we were well clear of the outpost, Justice DEHD core jumped us back to Alpha Base. While making our usual recon of our star system, Justice called to me.

"Commander I have an incoming IST transmission from Xul."

"Thank you, Justice, put it through."

Justice put the message on the bridge PA system. "Commander." Xul said. "I am pleased to report the modifications to our new Sig freighter are complete and all have been tested. We are ready to make our maiden voyage and are awaiting your orders."

"That is great news Xul, you first order of business, will be to take the freighter to the Sig storage facility and load raw materials they have been stockpiling for us. Once you are done there, jump to El Dorado and pick up all the available Containium, and transition back to Alpha base."

"Acknowledged Commander. I will alert you when we are preparing to depart El Dorado." Xul answered.

"Thank you, Captain, Legacy out." I responded using Xul's new title.

It was now official; we were a full-fledged mining operation. With the help of our Sig partners, we were also the sole shippers of our materials. If Bond effectively fills the shoes Tam Lin left behind, we should control most of the Containium market.

Sael Nalen interrupted my thoughts. She stepped close to me. "Nathan, my frigate is on its way to Alpha Base. I am going to return to my home worlds to brief the ruling council on my intelligence findings. It is my intention to petition them for additional fleet assets. The link between the Prule and the base, as well as the Scrun presence, should more than convince them of our need for an overwhelming show of force."

I looked Sael in the eyes. "I am counting on it. I left the Sig out of the mission plan on your recommendation. If you fail to produce a substantial fleet presence, I will scrub you and your people from the mission and make alternate plans."

Sael gave me a solemn nod. "I will try to not let you down Commander Myers."

Justice landed the Legacy and we debarked to the usual fanfare of our scientists and engineers. Everyone including Sael Nalen, made hand contact with the members of my clan. As everyone started going back to their workstations, the self-appointed senior level members of my staff stood waiting with expectant looks on their faces. Coonts and Klutch started their usual bickering at each other and walked off toward the lifts. The two were smart enough not to do it in front of me, so they took their sideshow elsewhere. Tria lingered with me to hear the operational reports.

Felix was the first to come forward. "Commander Myers, Justice alerted me to the damage sustained to your armor's cloaking systems. We know it has been an ongoing issue, and are doing our best to keep enough spare parts available to rapidly repair the damage. Myself as well as a number of our scientists and engineers, are working on shielding to protect the cloaking emitters. The task is formidable, but I am pleased to report we are making some progress. I will transfer the parts Justice requires to make repairs to your battle suits, and will assess the condition of the new Containium armor plates we installed prior to your last mission."

"Thank you, Felix. I want you to know how much we appreciate your hard work and dedication. Your tireless efforts are the reason we have not suffered serious battle damage while in combat."

The young Zaen beamed at me. He seemed to cherish praise more than the wealth he has accumulated while working for me. He hurried off to help Justice with the repairs to our armor.

Jaren came forward next with Graf at his side. "Commander Myers, production on the defensive drones has now peaked at eighteen units per day, with nine coming from each of their respective weapons groups. Our raw materials stockpile continues to slow our production levels. If we can replenish at a faster rate and maintain a surplus, our production numbers will increase. Justice has informed me that our new freighter will be remedying the current shortage situation within the next two days. We currently have one hundred and eleven of each design on hand for testing. With your permission, I would like to include twenty of each design in the Legacy's loadout. Our best testing data has always come from your battle assessment reports."

"Roger that Jaren. Load the drones and keep me posted on the resupply."

Jaren moved aside and Graf gave me his report. "Commander, the Grawl crew you freed from the pirates, are now back to good health and in equally good spirits. They are adapting well to their new surroundings and have requested permission to build individual quarters for themselves, which I have allowed. They are also proving very useful in our day to day operations and it has permitted me to shorten the work periods for everyone."

"What about our prisoners?"

"Now that Eiger no longer taunts him, and he is eating rations other than Pungo, Ilam

Pove is no longer acting irrational. He spends his days quietly laying in his bunk. I surmise he is waiting to have further discussions with you on how he can win his freedom."

"Admittedly, the information he has given us, has turned out to be truthful. That doesn't mean he is somehow absolved of the crimes he has committed against his countless victims."

Graf nodded in agreement and brought up the subject of the Rugerian prisoner. "The other prisoner has made daily requests to speak to you. His tone of voice sounds more like a threat than a request. When I tell him you are unavailable, his responses seem to indicate he would normally kill someone who fails to answer him with a favorable reply."

"Yeah, I got that impression as well. I will take the matter up with him when I have the time. If you still have a supply of Pungo, lets see if that tones down his arrogance a notch or two."

Graf smiled. "As a matter of fact, Commander, we still have a generous supply that was intended for Ilam Pove. I will see to it the Collector, collects his fair share of it."

"Have you come up with any information on his sidearm?"

"No Commander, it appears to be manufactured in the same unique manner as the Guardian Transponders and the portal device. We have come to the conclusion it is an artifact, and can only speculate on how the Rugerian came into possession of it."

The two Grawl made hand contact with me and turned away. Tria put her hand in mine and suggested a shower and some sleep. I was good with both or anything else she might have in mind. Out of the corner of my eye, I saw Sael Nalen walking in our direction.

Justice gave me a heads up. "Commander a Chaalt frigate has transitioned into our star system and has launched a shuttle. They are requesting access, and permission to land."

"Give them access Justice."

Tria and I turned to meet Sael as she stopped in front of us. "Nathan I will contact you within twenty-four hours and report the outcome of my meeting with the council. As you know, I must make a report on my activities and observations. If there is something specific you would like me to omit, I need to know now."

I stewed on Sael's question and glanced at Tria to see if she had any input for me. She left her pretty face blank to my obvious inquiry. If I told Sael to omit the IST data, it could lead to discrepancies in her report that might not pass scrutiny. The trouble with lying is that you can rarely tell just one. They tend to proliferate, and their deception is usually harder to hide than the truth you were trying to avoid.

"No Sael, I don't want either of us to be caught up in fruitless inaccuracies. I want you to tell your council that I excluded one of my closest allies from a military operation that could have benefited them technologically. I did so on your recommendation."

"Nathan, you will be saving…"

"Bullshit Sael! Neither you nor I, can predict whether or not we saved anyone's lives. If the Sig joined us with a large enough fleet, the Scrun might have jumped out of the system rather than lose a large number of capital ships. They might also abandon the base rather than risk an all-out war with the Sig. The terrorist attack on Outpost 9765 already have the Sig on a war footing. I know you and your people have a personal stake in the investigation of the base, and I understand that. You just need to make sure you bring the numbers to win any conflict decisively, because I believe that is what the Sig would have done. A protracted engagement will only encourage the enemy to send for reinforcements."

The entrance tunnel lighting flared to life as a Chaalt combat shuttle silently glided to a halt near the Legacy. It set down and extended its boarding ramp. Sael had nothing else to say, and left Tria and I watching her back as she walked away. She stopped just short of the shuttle hatch and turned to face us.

"If I fail to live up to both our expectations, I will warn you in enough time to make other arrangements." With that said, Sael entered her shuttle and it rapidly departed.

Sael's comment didn't impart all the confidence I would have liked to hear. It told me she may have concerns that she could not discuss with me. She said she would call, and I guess I couldn't ask for anything more than that.

After some much needed rest, Tria and I put on our recon armor and went to the galley for a light breakfast. A boisterous conversation from out in the corridor told us Coonts and Klutch were on their way. Tria and I wisely finished our meals as the two walked into the galley. They promptly quieted, but we knew it was just a temporary truce. The forced smiles I received from the pair indicated neither of them was interested in another meal of Pungo.

Tria and I wore our recon armor because we decided it was time to oblige the Rugerian and give him an audience. We went to the large cargo lift that takes you to the escape tunnel. When we exited, we found a surprise waiting for us? Most of our Grawl engineers and scientist were hard at work assembling a conveyor system. It ran all the way to the hidden shuttle bay on the back side of the mountain Alpha base was under. Graf saw Tria and I walk out of the cargo lift and quickly approached us.

Graf gave us a big Grawl smile. "We had hopes that we might have this project completed before you made your next visit."

It wasn't hard to figure out the conveyor was for the raw materials Xul would be bringing for the drone project. The Grawl previously brought the materials through the entrance tunnel a shuttle at a time. It was an inefficient and tedious process.

I put my hand on the Grawl's shoulder. "This is quite a surprise."

"As it was intended to be Commander Myers. It was decided to withhold the project from our operational reports until it was complete. If you are disappointed by our lack of transparency, I apologize on behalf of all responsible for the less than forthcoming information."

"I am not disappointed Graf. Of all the things that could be withheld from me, this wouldn't cause me any irritation. Can I ask whose idea it was, so I might commend them for their ingenuity?"

"Of course, Commander Myers. It was a collaboration between Felix and Jaran. When the subject of production came up in our daily meetings, it became clear to us all, that streamlining the material supply process would give us the most significant boost in production output. The conveyor system also proved to be the simplest solution to manufacture as well."

"Do you happen to have the revised production numbers?" I asked out of curiosity.

"It would be untruthful if I were to tell you no. I would greatly appreciate if you were to direct the question to Felix or Jaran, since the project was heavily influenced by their ideas and direction."

Tria and I looked at each other and then gave the Grawl a nod of acknowledgement. Graf was a lot of things, but glory hog would never be on that list.

"Thank you for your hard work Graf. Please carry on, and pass along my appreciation to all involved in the project. If there is something I can do to help, let me know."

We skirted the construction area and made our way to the prison enclosures. We closed up our helmets and Justice opened the door to the Rugerian's cell. When Tria and I entered, the alien that called himself the Collector, leaped up from his bunk and took a defensive stance with his back in a corner. He must have though he was going to get an ass kicking. I would reserve that option in case he felt the need to jerk us around.

"You have been very vocal in your demand to speak with me. It is my understanding that your tone sounds more like threat than a request. If my staff should mention it again, your current state of affairs will take a turn for the worse. You might find yourself in a situation where it will be difficult to speak at all, possibly for the rest of eternity. Do I make myself clear?" I menaced.

The Rugerian gave me a barely discernable nod. "You have stated your terms for a cessation of hostilities between you and my employers. I am requesting you release me so I can give them your reply."

I gave the Collector a barking laugh. He was already starting off on the wrong foot. He was obviously still clinging to his garbage cover story. It was time to give him a reality check.

"You know as well as I, that the offer was nothing more than an attempt to lure me into the open, so the criminals you work for, can try to kill me."

"I have no knowledge of their intent. I am just the messenger. If you have a reply, I will take it to them personally, and make sure they understand your demands."

I again laughed. "I don't need you to tell them anything. They have already given me their answer, and I am going to personally give them a reply they will never forget."

The look on the Rugerian's face conveyed his shock. His voice took on a desperate edge. "I can tell you how to find Genda Binar. He was the one who offered me this mission."

It was Tria's turn to laugh. "Genda Binar will not be sending any more fools on suicide missions. We turned him over to the Sig, who by the way, are extremely angry over the civilian deaths caused by an attack he masterminded. It shouldn't be hard, even for a Throgg like you, to guess the treatment he is receiving."

The Rugerian's eyes went wide then narrowed to slits as he stared at Tria. I could tell he was thinking the same thing Eiger did, just before Tria killed him.

I warned the Rugerian. "Before you do something really stupid, I should warn you, my mate killed Eiger with her bare hands and she wasn't wearing armor when she did it."

That revelation completely changed the Rugerian's body language. He sat back on his bunk with his hands at his sides.

"There have been a lot of rumors concerning Eiger's disappearance." The Rugerian said. "You just validated the one I gave the least credibility."

"Oh really, and which rumor might that be?" I asked out of curiosity.

"That Eiger was captured and killed by a small band of mercenaries. Myself and a number of others, believe he was betrayed by members of his pirate crew, and killed while he slept. To tell the truth, I didn't believe there was a Demon Warrior either, until the bodies started stacking up at my feet."

38

Since the Rugerian was trying to be truthful, I had other questions I wanted answers to. "I am going to ask you some questions. If you do not give me prompt accurate answers, I am going to make you wish you did."

The Rugerian stood up and backed into the corner once more. For the first time, he had genuine fear in his eyes.

"Who has been supplying Galactic warships to the pirates and others?"

The Collector looked me in the eyes and answered without hesitation. "I do not know, other than to say someone in a position of great power on the Galactic Union Council. Bren Carsoon's clan sibling Warla Carsoon is a level six council member and would be the one to ask such a question. He would be the only one I have knowledge of, with enough influence to know the answer to your question."

"Do you know how to find Warla Carsoon?"

"You already know that I am a third-party messenger. Genda Binar would have a better idea how to find him, and I doubt very much that he would know. Warla Carsoon has many enemies. Some sit with him on the Galactic Council, some are pirates, and others are former partners and business associates. My point is, that if he was careless, he would have died a long time ago. He is a very careful and calculating individual. The information on his location would only be known to Warla's inner circle, and their identities are as secret as Warla's whereabouts."

I had a feeling this would be another waste of time. We were picking the lowest fruits from a very tall tree. There was a good chance the criminals that wielded the real power, may never be found. I still had more questions and I might as well ask them while I was here.

"Do you know how to find Frontier?"

The question made the Rugerian smirk and shake his head. "Ahh, the legendary planet of grandeur, where the wealthiest linchpins in the galaxy go to hide from persons such as yourself. There are rumors

623

of such a place, but as time has passed, I have grown to be pragmatic, and no longer believe that nonsense. In all the time I have practiced my trade, not a single legitimate clue on Frontier's location has ever been divulged to me. When I heard the whispers for the first time, I wasted part of my life looking. If you are doing the same, I wish you luck."

Tria could tell I was getting frustrated with the ambiguous answers I was receiving. She threw one of her own at the Rugerian. "Where did your sidearm come from? We know it is not a product of your people's manufacturing skills."

The Rugerian hesitated for the first time. It may have something to do with him wishing it was currently in his possession, rather than a lack of clarity. He saw my eyes narrowing and answered.

"I recovered it while carrying out my assigned duties. It was in the possession of a Rossi pirate who made the mistake of cheating Genda Binar. I was allowed to keep it after successfully completing all aspects of the mission. I cannot begin to tell you how much I miss it."

Justice pinged my implants. "Commander, Xul is departing El Dorado and is enquiring if you have additional orders?"

"Negative Justice." I silently sent back. "Tell him to come home, and to give the new star drives a workout on the way."

"Message sent Commander."

I was going to tell Tria we were done with the Rugerian for now, but she had another question for him. "Do you know a Kasulla named Cralmo?"

The Rugerian stiffened at the question. "My my, you continue to amaze me." The Rugerian answered. "Your knowledge of the names of some of the most treacherous aliens I have ever encountered is quite extraordinary. If that Throgg has made it on to your target list, I will applaud your efforts if you are fortunate enough to find him." He said with disdain.

The Collector's answer piqued my interest. "How do you know Cralmo?" I asked.

"I never like to sound as if I am self-deprecating but, in this case, I will make an exception." The Rugerian said. "Before I came into Genda Binar's employ, I was a freelancer. I often teamed up with others in my profession. If the percentages were lucrative enough to keep my expenses paid,

I rarely turned down the business. I had made the acquaintance of a Tibor mercenary named Caspian. He always had a job that paid well, and I had gone on a number of them with him. He took a job that was supposed to be an abduction for ramson. The word was, once the ramson was paid, he would release the hostages unharmed and would get fifty percent of the take. Caspian was a careful operator and hired me to watch his back because his employer was an unknown entity. As with all mercenaries, the lure of substantial credits was the deciding factor on taking the job. I took up an overwatch as Caspian abducted a female and her three offspring. They were the siblings of a wealthy Zaen mining industrialist. He held them incommunicado for most of a rotation. Caspian and I, had a secure comms transmitter that kept the two of us in contact should he need me. After sitting in silence for an extended period of time and not hearing from Caspian, I decided to do a comms check. I got no answer, and after several attempts, went into the residence. What I found, horrified even me. The female and her offspring were butchered and horribly mutilated along with an unidentified male who I assumed was the patriarch. I found Caspian on the floor with the other bodies. His fighting knife was in his hand and it was covered in the blood of the Zaen victims. When I examined his body, I found his throat had been cut and he was left to bleed out."

I was appalled at the story, but it did not seem to have much in the way of evidence pointing at Cralmo. "That is a morbid tale, but does little to tie Cralmo to the crime or answer my question."

The Rugerian looked up at me with eyes that told me his next statement was true. "Before Caspian died, he left me a name scrawled in his own blood. It said Cralmo. At the time, I had never heard of him. It didn't take long to find out he was feared by most and loathed by all others who knew of him. The stories I heard, had one thing in common, no one wanted to be an enemy of Cralmo. At the time, I was not nearly as experienced as I am now, based on what I found out about Cralmo, I still have not made an attempt to avenge Caspian."

The Rugerian's story verified what we already knew. Cralmo was one evil bastard and he needed to be put down. The tale was a waste of our time and did little in the way of getting us any closer to catching him.

I had heard enough and needed to start prepping for the next mission.

I took Tria by the hand and we headed for the door. I looked back at the Rugerian. "Unless you can give us information other than stories from your criminal past, we will be turning you over to the Sig. You will share the same fate as your fellow Rugerian, Juda."

The Collector stood up in surprise. "You should know that Genda Binar told me he was ordered by Bren Carsoon to locate Juda. Bren doesn't give a scat for Juda or anyone else. He would only do that if his clan sibling Warla, told him he must be found. If Juda is that important to Warla Carsoon, you can use that to your advantage. If it were to become known that Juda is in Sig custody, then Warla Carsoon will want him released immediately. In case you do not know it yet, Juda is a nineth level council member and as such, has diplomatic immunity."

Tria looked over her shoulder at the Rugerian. "We know that, and in case you are not aware of it yet, we don't care."

The Carsoon clan was up to their eyeballs in corruption. Finding them, and proving it, was going to be extremely difficult. The Rugerian did have a valid point. We might be able to use Juda to somehow lure one or both of the Carsoon siblings out into the open. It wasn't like Juda was going anywhere, so I had time to think about it.

My mind was slipping back to battle mode and I was ready to concentrate on the Scrun mission. The terrorist attack on outpost 9765 was a coordinated attack against us. It was our turn to return the hate. Our incursion into that star system was several months ago. Even if they suspected it was our doings, their readiness for an imminent attack would have to be seriously degraded by now. The base's connection to the Prule was pretty sketchy. Justice has yet to uncover further evidence indicating how exactly it was connected to the Prule. For all we knew, it may have been a target of the Hivemind and not a base of operations.

I called to Justice. "Have you or the Overseer decoded additional information from the Hivemind data?"

"Negative Commander. The information collected from the Prule base appears to have encryption unique to that location. The information collected from the Hivemind uses an encryption algorithm that is similar, but still differs enough to make it exclusive to the Hivemind. I surmise it is how the Prule identify one Hivemind from the others. The coordinates of our current target were a shared factor in both encryption algorithms and was our basis for determining the base's location. It is our hopes that data can be recovered from the new location that will lead us to a common key. If such a key exists, it will establish a foundation for decrypting the various bio machine codes."

"Are we ready to go up against the Heckler ships in combat?"

"Yes Commander, I have formulated contingencies based on our previous encounter. It will require the extensive use of the new combat drones. In addition to the twenty we were initially going to test for defensive purposes; I have requisitioned another thirty for offensive operations."

We had a long history of using untested equipment in combat. In most cases we experienced a high rate of success. Justice's plan to use the new drones was an excellent idea. Proving their worth over a planet other than Earth had my unconditional approval. Now we just needed to hear from the Principle Investigator. I was still just a little concerned with her parting comments.

As usual, Tria had some uncanny way of determining what I was thinking. "Nathan, Sael will do everything in her power to bring a force capable of ending any conflict with the Scrun quickly. It is in all of our interest to keep the slavers from acquiring superior technology. It is also in our best interest to prevent the Scrun from coming into contact with the Prule. A large-scale subjugation by the Prule, could lead to a widespread machine infection that could put the entire galaxy in peril."

When Tria and I stepped out of the lift, we saw Coonts and Klutch leading gravity jacks in the direction of the Legacy. Each had a large pallet on them and from a distance it looked like they had ammo packs stacked on them. Tria and I increased our pace to intercept them. When the two saw our approach, they slowed their progress so we could catch up.

"Coonts, Klutch, I wasn't aware we had expended enough ordnance to require a replenishment?"

The two had excited looks on their faces. "That is not the circumstance Commander." Coonts said. "We are restocking the armory

631

with munitions of a new design. Justice has removed the hull alloy penetrator tips from our ammunition and replaced them with Containium. The lighter more durable apex has allowed Justice to make a small increase in the explosive cores. He says it equates to a twenty-one percent increase in destructive force and a thirty-eight percent increase in penetration capability over the previous design. He tested the new designs on the same materials that were used to make our old Zaen battle armor. The results were significant. Depending on the angle of attack, and number of hits to the same area, concentrated fire penetrated the materials in seventy-eight percent of the tests."

I nodded to the two and waved them on. It was nice to know Justice was still wargaming all our missions. The AI never missed a chance to make an improvement on our equipment, no matter what it may cost. If our next mission turned into the shooting war I thought it would be, we would expend a large quantity of the priciest munitions in the galaxy. The size of the loads on Coonts and Klutch's carts, insinuated Justice had already taken that scenario into consideration.

I took Tria by the hand and made a detour toward the replicator building. "Justice." I called. "I thought we were going to use our remaining supplies of Containium for the drone project?"

"Commander, drone production has increased and is currently above my initial expectations. Xul will be arriving in eleven hours with additional Containium and the other raw materials to further increase production. I carefully calculated our production rate and materials consumption and found that diverting nine percent of our current stockpile of Containium to munition manufacturing would have no adverse effect on the increasing production levels. Now that El Dorado is producing more Containium than our production capability requires, it was a logical decision to use the excess for munition upgrades."

Since I was never a hard numbers guy, stuff like the logistical percentages of our materials inventory, escaped my scrutiny. Justice did what Justice always does. He gives us every possible tactical advantage when it comes time to put our lives on the line. I could only say one thing to that.

"Thank you, Justice. Please carry on."

"Of course, Commander, I always do." The AI said with a sarcastic tone.

I was going to give the AI a little vocal return fire, but Tria slapped me on the ass and pushed me toward the doorway on the replicator building.

"Nathan, we should speak to Felix and Jaran about the new production numbers." Tria said with a smile.

Tria was right. Verbally sparing with an intellect of greater capacity would be a losing proposition. It also had me thinking it could lead to some other degrading mind game in the future. We entered the replicator building to find our new Grawl recruits busily feeding the five Chaalt manufacturing machines. Felix was orchestrating the supply lines that determined the order in which what materials went where. The next thing we noticed was that rear of the facility was stacked all the way to the ceiling with racks of battle drones. The racks each held five drones and there had to be more than a hundred stacked against the back wall. Jaran was standing near one of the machines and hurried over to us.

"Nathan Myers, Tria Burlor, I am glad that you have time to see the improvements we have made to the production facility. With contributions from our staff as well as the new additions to our team, we are making improvements on a daily basis. It is with great pleasure that I can tell you we have increased drone production. We can now produce twenty-four drones per work period. That is one drone for every working hour the four dedicated replicators are functioning. At our current production levels, we will meet Justice's target number of six thousand in just over eight months. If we further streamline the manufacturing process, the time line will decrease accordingly."

"Thank you, Jaran. I want you to make everyone aware that I am awarding all my clan including the new members, a one million credit bonus for their hard work and dedication to our cause."

The drone program was moving forward quickly. Seeing the growing stockpile made up my mind, I would be going back to Earth. I would take all the drones we had built and start seeding the star system of my birth, with the fruits of our labors. The galaxy was becoming more complex and dangerous every day. It was no longer a matter of if a predatory race stumbled across Earth, it was a matter of when. I was going to make sure my home world had a fighting chance. Leaving the defense of Earth to others was no longer going to be the final solution. It was time the powers that be, were given a no shitter on just how precarious Earth's future was.

I was going to personally commend each of my clan members, but was interrupted by Justice. "Commander, I have an incoming IST message from Sael Nalen."

"Put her through Justice."

Sael came on and got right to business. "Commander Myers, the military council has given the go ahead for a three hundred ship strike force. Two hundred of which will be frontline battleships and the remainder will be gunships. Each battleship has two hundred heavy combat troops aboard. We will need the coordinates of a rendezvous point so we can exchange IFF codes for both our ships and troops. I propose we meet thirty hours from now at a location of your choosing."

"Acknowledged Principle Investigator, we are currently prepping for the mission and I will have Justice send you a rally point within the hour. We will be at that location thirty hours from now and I will contact you to go over the order of battle. Am I correct in assuming that you will be in overall command of the Chaalt battle group?"

"Yes, Commander Myers. I will be waiting to hear from Justice."

Sael abruptly signed off. I thought she might elaborate on the extent of her command, and how we would fit in. That not being the case, I wondered if three hundred warships were what she had asked for, or was it all the council would send. Either way, I hoped it was enough to get the job done. I still had reservations about not inviting the Sig. Agonizing over the future, was almost as bad as reliving the mistakes of your past. It was time to move forward.

39

The Scrun were about to find out the true cost of their attack on Outpost 9765. When I meet up with Sael, I was going to let her know that it would only take a single Scrun to deliver our reply message. All the rest were expendable.

I called to Justice. "What is the status of our battle armor?"

"I have completed the repairs Commander, but will require additional time to install the newly designed blast shields for the cloaking emitters. It is by no means a perfect system, but they will extend the life of the emitters. As always, I recommend you avoid direct fire if at all possible."

No matter how many times the AI cautioned me on that subject, I always had an extremely difficult time convincing my adversaries to not ding up my hardware.

I looked over at Tria and winked at her. "You hear that lover; Justice thinks you are doing a lousy job of keeping me from being shot."

Tria scoffed at my comment. "Your habit of drumming on your chest and grunting at our enemies, has a tendency to draw an inordinate amount of fire. I have suggested on numerous occasions you should abandon the practice all together, but it seems you will not listen to reason."

My expression soured. I was being tag teamed and could think of a thousand other things I would rather be doing. I grabbed Tria by the hand and pulled her toward the Legacy. I would take them one at a time. We boarded the Legacy and on our way to the lifts, we heard Coonts and Klutch having an argument in the science lab. I was going to pass them by, but Coonts spied us as we went by the hatch.

"Commander!" Coonts yelled. "Can I have a moment of your time?"

Tria pulled me up short. I grimaced because I intended to ignore them and continue on to the lifts. I took a step back and looked in at them. Klutch was holding the pistol he had claimed from the Rugerian and was twirling it like a six gun in an old western movie. On the lab table in front of the two was the Tibor's prized plasma caster.

"If this has anything to do with a bet, you can count me out!" I stated with obvious aggravation.

Knowing that I found their wagers more than just a little irritating, Coonts quickly tried to redirect some of my shade onto Klutch. "Commander, this has nothing to do with Klutch's annoying habit of constantly betting on the outcome of almost everything."

Now the over muscled Grawl was getting the stink eye from everyone. He couldn't possibly expect us to believe that crap. You can't make a wager without a willing participant to accept the bet.

"You have another thirty seconds of my time, and it better not sound like the load of scat you just tried to serve us." I warned the Grawl.

"Commander, since Klutch is already in possession on one sentinel race weapon, I was thinking he should let me have the Rugerian's sidearm." Coonts reasoned.

I rolled my eyes and looked over at Tria. She just shook her head. She didn't want anything to do with the petty squabble the two were having. I didn't either, but Coonts wanted a command decision, and it was my place to make it. I could see Klutch wanted one as well. He spun the pistol around and handed it to me grip first. I took it from him and gave the weapon a cursory inspection. It was light for its size, but still large for a sidearm. The grip was equally large. While it was an okay fit for someone with hands as large as Klutch's and mine, it would be a two-handed grip for Coonts. The Grawl always had a thing for large weapons. I guess it had something to do with his short stature. I held it out to Coonts and it did indeed require him to grip it with both hands. His finger was barely long enough to reach the trigger button. This got Klutch to snickering, and Coonts to grit his teeth and squint his eyes at the Troop Master. This was ridiculous, and I was starting to think there was more to the this than meets the eye. Tria must have felt the same way. She reached out and snatched the pistol away from Coonts and stalked out of the lab with it. It was doubtful if either one of my favorite stooges had considered that consequence. I shrugged my shoulders at the two, and made a beeline for the lifts. The issue was settled as far as I was concerned.

I caught up to Tria on the bridge. She was quizzing Justice on the origin and attributes of the weapon.

"Tria, I have concluded the weapon is a Guardian design based on its similarities to the transponders and portal device." Justice said.

"Does it have an advantage over our Tibor capacitive discharge weapons?" Tria asked?

"Both weapons have advantages as well as disadvantages Tria. The Tibor weapon has impressive explosive damage but a shorter range. It is also prone to overheating with continuous fire. The Guardian weapon has greater range but has little effect on shielded targets. It does have a marked advantage on unshielded solid surfaces. The beam emitted by the weapon disrupts the molecules of solids by forcing them apart. The heat generated by this process approaches the temperatures of a star."

The question of who would have the weapon was a done deal as far as I was concerned. It was now Tria's. If my other crew members had an issue with that, they could take it up with her. I was ready to move on to another subject.

"Justice, have you selected a rally point for the Chaalt task force?"

"Yes Commander. I have a location that is far enough from the target to avoid any possibility of detection."

"Please send it to the Principle Investigator."

"Message sent Commander."

"What is the status of our torpedo stockpile?"

"We have two fully functional weapons and the materials to assemble one additional unit Commander."

"Put the two we have available aboard the Legacy. If the stealth missile magazines are at capacity, what are your thoughts on using some of the cargo hold to store additional missiles? If we come up against a large Scrun presence, I do not want to run out of weapons when we may need them most."

"I have anticipated that scenario Commander, and have one-hundred missiles already stored in the hold. I also took the liberty of having Jaran load our entire inventory of rail cannon munitions as well. With the addition of the combat drones, the hold is now at its working capacity. The Legacy is ready in all aspects for an extended combat mission."

I was glad to hear Justice had already ran the scenarios and addressed the problems that were troubling me the most. The only one the AI couldn't predict, was how the Principle Investigator was going to conduct her end of the operation. Before Justice transferred the coordinates to the base, I would have a heart to heart with Sael. In the past, she has shown a tendency to do whatever the hell she wanted, including marginalizing our roll in a combat operation. If she wanted our IFF codes and the Heckler telemetry, she had to give me some assurances she would not pull that crap on us.

Tria could tell I was agonizing over the variables. She grabbed the front of my uniform and pulled me off the bridge in the direction of our cabin. It was about that time that Coonts and Klutch stepped out of the lift trading barbs with each other.

Coonts called out to me. "Commander, I have…"

Without missing a beat, Tria jerked me to a stop and turned to face the two. They both looked like they had something to say right up until Tria spun the pistol around and pointed it over their heads. All thoughts of a conversation were immediately forgotten. They both turned around and jumped back into the down tube. When she turned back to me, she must not have liked the look on my face.

She squinted her eyes. "Don't make me use this!"

I awoke seven hours later, and for the most part, was well rested and rejuvenated. What aches and pains that were inflicted upon me, would be gone with a hot shower? Tria was still asleep and I managed to get out of bed without waking her. When I saw the pistol laying on her night stand, I quietly retrieved it and put in on my safe in the closet. The damned thing was cursed. Most would laugh at such nonsense, but I knew bad mojo when I felt it.

I showered and went to the galley for a bite to eat and some coffee. My crew was not present and I sat alone thinking about the upcoming mission. The price the Scrun were going to pay for their terrorist attack was going to be high. Those who helped orchestrate the attack were going to feel the pain as well. I was going to hunt them down no matter how long it took. We were going to take extreme measures to insure they get the message loud and clear. Attacking civilian targets was going to cost them dearly. Terror was their weapon of choice, and it would be what they would get in return.

I pushed my half-eaten meal aside and finished the dregs of my tepid coffee. There were other things to occupy my mind besides brooding over the consequences of my future actions.

Justice broke the spell of my preoccupation. "Commander, Xul has transitioned into the system. I have directed him to the new materials handling facility at the end of the escape tunnel. Kevel and his crew have taken it on as part of their duties to offload the freighter. Xul has made inquiries about your upcoming mission and wishes to speak with you."

"Roger that Justice, I will meet him at the materials handling facility."

"Message sent Commander."

I walked out of the galley and met Tria on her way in. I was glad she didn't have the Rugerian assassin's pistol with her. Coonts and Klutch probably hadn't noticed that yet, because they were following her at a respectable distance. For a change, neither one had a thing to say.

I gave Tria a peck on the cheek, and pointed down the corridor. "You sure got those two spooked."

She gave me a smile. "Yes, and as long as it keeps them from bickering at each other, I'm all for it."

She suddenly turned to face down the corridor. Coonts and Klutch froze in the passage. I don't know what was going through their minds at the moment, but they both turned and went back the way they had come. I couldn't blame them. The Chaalt warrior could be very intimidating when she wanted to be.

"Where are you off to?" Tria asked

"Xul has returned with our new freighter. I was going to have him give me a tour of his new command."

Tria gave me another ravishing smile, and hooked her arm in mine. "Lead on Tarzan."

Going to the ready room, we put on our recon armor. The freighter was in near vacuum conditions and would require a short trip outside of the retention field. When we debarked the Legacy, we found it was necessary to take the lifts in the Grawl living spaces. The freight elevators were filled to capacity with materials for the replicators.

We stepped out of the lift and into the tunnel that led to the materials facility. We walked alongside the enclosed conveyor system and was surprised by how quiet it was. We could easily carry on a discussion without raising our voices.

I put my arm around Tria. "Xul has been asking Justice about our next mission. I am sure he wants to be our combat shuttle pilot. What are your thoughts on the subject?"

"He has proven he can do the job, and it does free up Klutch for offensive operations. Poncho and Lefty can handle the freighter without a designated captain. Considering the scope of the upcoming mission, if it comes to needing a dust off, I can think of no one better for the slot." Tria replied.

Tria was correct. Once the Heckler warships have been dealt with, it would also free up the Legacy so Justice could fly high cover. It would enable him to pursue the Scrun or any other targets of opportunity while we investigated the Prule connection to the base.

We had finally reached the end of the tunnel and the large atmospheric locks that sealed it. Closing up our helmets, we stepped through the retention field. We walked to the gravity beam that would lift us up into the belly of the gigantic freighter stationary over our heads. The sixty plus foot trip up into the freighter only took seconds. We stepped out into an atmosphere and retracted our helmets. Xul was there to meet us.

"Commander, it is a pleasure to see you and Captain Burlor. I am happy to report that the freighter's systems performed flawlessly and the trip to Alpha base was without incidence."

"That is great news Xul, could you give us a quick tour?"

"Of course, Commander, please follow me." Xul said with enthusiasm."

The tour didn't take long. The freighter was mostly a huge hollow shell. Due to the unique size of the Sig, the bridge and other temporary living spaces were cavernous compared to our Chaalt freighter. Xul wrapped up the tour and turned to us with a serious look on his face.

"Commander, the Sig informed me about the attack on the outpost. It is also my understanding you are going to raid the Scrun base we discovered several months ago. I am formally asking permission to join you on the mission."

With the input from Tria, I had already made up my mind. I would give Xul a reasonable chance to back out, but was confident he would not take it.

"Are you sure Xul? Is there something about being the captain of our new freighter that you find unappealing?"

"Not at all Commander. It's just that Poncho and Lefty don't need my supervision. They handle the ship like they were born in it. Since it is a Sig design, the crew is familiar with all the equipment. If anything, I am the one behind the learning curve."

"Okay Xul, if you are sure you want to go into harms way again, gather your gear and get it aboard the Legacy."

The words were barely out of my mouth and Xul was headed for the supply tunnel. For a Grawl with no combat modifications, he sure was eager to get shot at. We said our goodbyes to Poncho and his crew. I gave them orders to return to Chief when the freighter was unloaded, and pick up all the available materials. It would be their regular route until we had more Containium from El Dorado to transport.

Tria and I made our way back to Alpha base. Everything that I could think of that needed my attention was done. It was now time for us to make our final preparations for departure. We would be leaving in six hours to meet with Sael and her task force. Hopefully, everything would go as planned. When we returned, it was my intention to make our next mission, a trip back to Earth. I was going to show the leaders of their respective countries, what was going on in the galaxy. Like it or not, they would have to work together to overcome the challenges that Earth was facing. The consequences for their failure to heed my warnings, were unthinkable.

"Justice." I called. Pull the Daggers out of the hangar and load the Eagles."

"Affirmative Commander. Do you have a preference on the munitions loadout?"

"I thought about it for a moment, and a better safe than sorry scenario played out in my brain. "Split the missile loadout with nanite weapons."

"Acknowledged Commander."

By the Time Tria and I got back to the Legacy, our clan was already gathering around the boarding hatch. Coonts, Klutch and Xul were mingling among them and making our customary hand contact. I didn't know if aliens believed in luck, but the send off they always gave us, made me feel it was their intention to impart it to us. The gathering parted as we approached, then closed ranks around us. We touched each of their hands as they gave us words of encouragement. When we made it to the boarding ramp where my crew waited, we turned as a group and waved our final farewells.

As the hatch closed behind me, I called to Justice. "If we are ready, take us out to the jump point."

"Affirmative Commander."

We took our seats on the bridge and Justice rapidly exited Alpha Base. When we were well clear of our moon base, Justice made a DEHD core jump to a location very close to our designated rendezvous point. I had a feeling Sael would be several hours early. I was not disappointed. Justice quickly populated the view dome with three-hundred green circles showing the location of Sael Nalen and her task force. They were cloaked and hiding in the edge of a large dust nebula.

"Commander." Justice called. "I have incoming IST traffic from the Principle Investigator."

"Put her on Justice."

Sael's voice filled the bridge. "Commander Myers, we have detected your transition. I am requesting a face to face meeting with you before we start the mission."

"Acknowledged, Principle Investigator."

The Legacy was quickly closing the distance to the Chaalt fleet. I queried Justice. "What is our ETA Justice?"

"Seventeen minutes Commander."

I sent the transmission to Sael. "We will be alongside your flagship in seventeen minutes. Legacy out."

Justice killed the connection and increased the Legacy's speed to maximum.

40

The Legacy entered the edge of the dust nebula and Justice highlighted Sael's flag ship. We closed the final distance and came alongside the monstrous Chaalt battleship. As was expected, we could see Sael Nalen standing alone in the center of the hangar door. Tria and I went to meet her. When we were standing at the hangar door, Justice opened it. Sael Nalen wasted no time closing her helmet and leaping the short distance to the Legacy's hangar deck.

She made a graceful landing and opened her helmet. "Nathan, Tria, it is good to see you again. My fleet is prepped and ready and I am ready to discuss the order of battle."

Tria gave me a sideways glance out of the corner of her eye. In all the times we have ever met with Sael Nalen, she had never stated it was good to see us. The more I thought about it, I don't think I have ever heard her say that to anyone, including her own leadership council. I was now wondering if this was a prelude to a screwing that didn't involve kissing.

Sael noticed the looks we were giving her and frowned. "Is there a problem that I am not aware of?"

I couldn't actually think of anything to say about the very unexpected civilities and did the next best thing. I stepped forward and gave her an embrace. One of those, I have been waiting to hold my body against you deals. "It is so good to see you too Sael."

Her eyes bugged out and she pushed me off with all four of her hands. "What are you doing?" She said in a loud voice.

Tria never missed a beat and pulled me aside. She latched on as well. "Nathan is correct. It is so nice to see you again."

Sael pushed Tria off and squinted her eyes at us. "Okay, I get it! I will dispense with the exaggerated pleasantries."

"Sael." I said. "Where I come from, people would only take that tact if they were trying to perpetrate some type of bullshit on someone."

"I am not perpetrating anything on anyone!" Sael declared.

"Then what is it you are trying to hide?"

"I am not hiding anything. You have yet to let me brief you, and you are already jumping to conclusions." Sael stammered.

I gave her a no-nonsense stare. "Then brief me… on everything!"

Sael's mouth became a thin flat line. We had her in a corner and she knew it. She was obviously very uncomfortable with something, and I wanted to get to the bottom of it now, rather than later. She wisely decided to come clean.

"Interspersed within the ranks of my ground troops are scientific scholars. Their sole purpose for being here is to secure technology as it is encountered. They have been ordered to immediately put items of interest aboard any available transport and return to the closest capital ship. It is my understanding, that they have been ordered to do it in secrecy if possible."

I rolled my eyes. While I did find her disclosure irritating, it wasn't totally unexpected. When we destroyed the Chaalt research center, it effectively wiped out all the collective artifacts and knowledge they had on the Prule. It was a huge blow to the scientific community. We were also guilty of the same "finders, keepers" mentality when we stumbled across the Prule lifeboat. We stripped everything of interest from the derelict ship and then let the Chaalt have the remaining junk. The council must have decided they were not going to shed the blood of their troops for the same paltry rewards. I knew the Sig would have lost a lot of lives if the coming conflict turned out to be a worst-case scenario. It was debatable if they would have resorted to the same tactic.

"Is that all?" I asked.

When I didn't pop my cork, Sael seemed to relax. "Yes."

"Okay, lets move on and clarify a few things. Our first order of business when we enter the area of operation, is to locate the Heckler warships. It may prove unnecessary because they may want to find us first. No matter how this unfolds, we need to neutralize those ships. Unless the Scrun have made some significant strides in warship development, they will be more of an annoyance than a serious threat. Of course, that could always change if they have moved a large number of ships near to the base. They have decent weapons but they can't shoot what they can't see, so we have a marked advantage in that aspect. Are we on the same page so far?"

"Yes, the only difference is that we will try to recover as much data and tech from the Heckler ships as possible. If we are fortunate enough to disable one of them during the conflict, we have orders to board and capture them if possible."

"This is where I am going to draw a defining line. If the Legacy disables one or more of the Heckler ships, they are ours to keep. I want you to wave off any attempts by your people to board them. The same goes for any discoveries we make while on the base as well. This is going to be a case of what you find is yours, and what we find is ours, are we clear?"

Sael did not take more that s few seconds to agree. I suspected she had orders to not interfere with any of our recovery efforts, as long as we did not interfere with theirs.

"Yes Nathan." Sael said with just a hint of a smile. "Is there anything else you wish to discuss before I depart?"

"There is just one more thing. I want any Scrun ship that does not manage to escape, destroyed. I want them to feel the same pain they inflicted on the civilians at Outpost

9765. I am going to make sure they understand this is a message they should take seriously."

The hint of the smile Sael had on her face moments earlier, turned into something sinister. "That was my plan from the start." She said.

Sael turned to leave and Tria pulled me close, whispering in my ear. Before Sael could jump across to her flagship, I called to her. "Principle Investigator, there is something else."

The Principle Investigator turned to us with a frown. "And what would that be Commander Myers?"

"Captain Burlor would like you to have her old combat armor since it is no longer anatomically correct."

Sael's frown was replaced by a look of surprise. When she could not come up with a prompt reply, I told her to report to the ready room. As she walked back toward us, she stopped. "Why would you want to do that after I disclosed my people's ulterior motives?"

"I guess that is a question you should ask Captain Burlor, it was her idea not mine, I just agreed with her."

Sael shifted her gaze to Tria and gave her a nod. Tria just shrugged her shoulders and threw a thumb in the direction of the ready room. "Justice will have the battle suit prepped with a full load out in the ready room. It will include twenty rounds of our anti-matter munitions." Tria glanced over at me. "I strongly urge you to heed all of the suit's warnings, before you decide to use them."

Sael disappeared down the corridor. I reached over and pulled Tria against me, and started mocking her in a childish voice. "I strongly urge you to heed all…"

I abruptly shut up when Tria grabbed me in such a way the last words out of my mouth were at a very squeaky pitch. She again whispered in my ear, and it had nothing to do with Sael Nalen. "If you want to make use of these sometime in the near future, I advise you to stow that scat."

Since I had every intention of doing just that, I smiled and nodded in agreement. Sael walked up behind us in Tria's armor. She must have taken exception to our rather close proximity.

"Is it not in your disposition to at least wait until I am off this relic before you start acting like a primate?" Sael said as she made her way to the open hangar door.

"Just remember who the AI is that operates that hardware, and what he will be doing while you are wearing it." I shot right back.

Sael stiffened as if she was frozen in front of the atmospheric retention field. She slowly turned and scowled at me. "I will be returning your spy when the mission is concluded!"

Sael closed up her helmet and jumped back across to her flagship. I called to Justice. "When you send the jump coordinates to Sael's flagship, make sure they are about a hundred lightyears off of our true destination. That should give us enough time to locate and engage the Heckler warships before they detect our true jump location."

"Affirmative Commander. Stealth systems are optimal and the energy matrix is charged and ready for DEHD Core operations once we are clear of the Chaalt fleet."

"Roger that Justice, jump at your discretion."

Tria and I went to the bridge to join Coonts, Klutch and Xul. We took our seats as our reality faded away. Even before the whitewash of our transition had completely dissipated, I heard Justice call out a startling warning.

"Commander! I am detecting a very large number of Prule encrypted communications among thousands of Scrun distress calls."

The alert was so shocking, we sat speechless as Justice populated the view dome. What we were seeing turned the blood in my veins to ice. Our view of the target planet was almost obscured by the wreckage of starships. What did stand out, was the considerable number of very large bogies Justice had highlighted with red boxes. I knew what they were, because it was not that long ago my crew and I had destroyed one. They were Prule Destroyer class warships. They exactly matched the profile of the one we found in the underground Prule base. How they got here, and their numbers, was a question I could not comprehend an answer too.

"Commander." Justice called again. I have accounted for all the powerplant signatures visible to my scans. There are seventy-three Prule Destroyers and three-hundred and eighty-four Scrun warships of various designs. I am only detecting one active Heckler star drive. All detected ships are engaged in combat. The Scrun are attempting to single out the Prule Destroyers and overwhelm their shields. The Heckler warship then attacks the target. The tactic has just reduced the number of Prule assets to seventy-two. The Scrun are taking a lot of damage. They just lost another forty ships in the attack. They are countering the Prule weapons advantage by staying close to their targets. It appears the point defensive weapons on the Prule Destroyers are only moderately damaging to the Scrun's defensive shields. The Scrun cannot continue to lose ships at the current attrition rate, or they will be wiped out in just over six hours. I have detected more than two-hundred and forty-one heavily damaged or destroyed Scrun spacecraft in orbit above the planet. The Prule have sustained twenty-seven losses and I have what I believe to be one Heckler warship destroyed as well. The scanned fragments that remain are small, but I believe they are of Heckler design.

"Open an IST channel to Sael, Justice."

"IST comms available Commander."

The Principle Investigator came on the channel and she was pissed. "Nathan! If you think running some kind of game on me is funny, you would be mistaken! I…"

"Sael, shut up and listen! The Prule have the target planet under siege. The Scrun have the numbers and are trying to hold them off, but they are slowly being wiped out."

"WHAT!" Sael yelled. "Are you telling me the Prule have a fleet?"

"Yes. Justice has a positive ID on seventy-two Prule heavy destroyers."

"What about the Heckler ships?" Sael demanded.

"Justice has only identified a single Heckler ship that is still operational. He has identified what might possible be the scattered remains of another. One is still unaccounted for."

There was a momentary silence on the Principle Investigators end. Then she finally spoke. "How do you want to proceed with this operation?"

It was my turn to ingest and process everything I was seeing on the view dome. My crew was silently watching me. It was easy to see they were wondering what I was going to do. They knew we were not about to help the Prule in any way, shape, or form. This was not an easy decision and it definitely was not a case where the enemy of my enemy, was my friend.

Sael could no longer stand my silence. "Commander Myers, we need to take action now!"

"Sael, Justice is going to be sending you our current data and some very precise attack vectors. Divide your task force up into three attack groups and stand by. When Justice sends the execute order, I want you to jump in and hit the Prule destroyers with everything you've' got!"

"I want to make sure I am absolutely clear on the rules of engagement Commander Myers. We are to ignore the Scrun fleet, and only engage the Prule."

"Yes. Unless the Scrun fire on your ships, or blunder into your attack envelope, they are to be ignored until further notice."

"Acknowledged Commander, we are standing by." Sael replied.

"Okay Justice, what have you got for me?"

"Commander my scans of the planet have revealed the location of another Heckler warship. The wreckage lies in the ocean, six point two miles off the coast of the continent. It is accompanied by the wrecks of two Prule resource gathering platforms and a destroyer. I speculate it may have been a Prule invasion force that was trying breach the bases defenses undetected."

"Still no location on the third ship?"

"Negative Commander. There is a small probability it's remains may be intermingled with the wreckage that is accumulating in orbit above the planet."

"You have a single Prule destroyer highlighted in low orbit. What is it doing?"

"I surmise the Scrun have left the target alone because it is heavily damaged and no longer maneuvering. It does however have several operational weapons and is using them to bombard the base's defenses. Because of the deflection angle, the Prule are only striking the fringes of the base and the elevated weapons towers. They have managed to set the forest surrounding the peninsula ablaze. The heavy smoke and heat have obstructed my visual and infrared scans. My other sensors are detecting shuttle size craft sporadically departing the damaged destroyer. Those that have not been shot down by the Scrun defenses, are approaching the base at a very low altitude."

"Do you have attack vectors for the Chaalt strike force?"

"Yes Commander, my plan, if executed properly, will result in the Prule fleet being pinned against the planets gravity well and what remains of the Scrun fleet. Because of the close proximity of the Scrun warships, there will be considerable collateral damage."

A small part of me felt sorry for what was about to happen to the Scrun. They were, after all, standing their ground against the Prule. The rest of me thought they were getting exactly what they deserved.

"Okay Justice, send the data package and our IFF codes to the Principle Investigator, and get them moving."

Coonts called to me and pointed out something that I had not considered yet. "Commander, the Prule would have to have a very good reason to assemble a fleet and move it to this location."

Tria chimed in as well. "There must be something here that is of great importance to the Prule. The ships in their strike force would have been in hiding somewhere in the galaxy for more than two hundred years. To bring them out of hiding now, means they are protecting something extremely valuable."

Both Xul and Klutch were shaking their heads in agreement. Something big was going down, and the Scrun had made the mistake of stumbling on to it.

"Justice, take us down to the planet and let's finish off the Destroyer. We need to take a look and see what the Scrun have uncovered."

"Affirmative Commander, jumping now." Justice called.

The Legacy made an intersystem jump, that was just a couple blinks of an eye, and a single churn of my stomach. The giant hulk of the Prule Destroyer filled the view dome. Its shields were still active but weak. The large number of debris surrounding the ship indicated the Scrun did all they could to take it out before they were destroyed for their attempt.

The Legacy's main beam weapons lanced out into the Prule ship's aft shields, flaring them to a brilliant milky white. Justice quickly followed it up with a point-blank shot from our anomaly weapon. The blinding ball of energy made contact with the destroyers depleted shields. The milky white translucence of the failing aft shields, was sucked into the energy ball as it passed through them. When the anomaly made contact with the hull, it looked like the rear of the ship was sucked into it. The ship's spaces just forward of the strike, started wrapping themselves around the anomaly. It ate its way into the target then suddenly flared so brightly, the view dome blacked out. When the dome reset, the massive hole in the rear of the Prule ship was gushing its guts out into the void. The remains of the wreck started skipping through the upper reaches of the planet's atmosphere. The derelict's progress was marked by a trail of fire and sparks. Soon, it would be nothing more than another fiery streak lighting up the planet's horizon. If any of the remains made it to the surface, they would splash down somewhere in the massive ocean that covered most of the planet.

Justice turned the Legacy away and put target boxes on several Prule transports that were headed for the surface. He closed the distance and sent multiple bursts from our rail cannons into them. The basketball sized rounds rapidly depleted their shields, and turned the hulls into ballistic scrap.

I called to my crew. "Armor up!"

41

We ran to the lifts and went down to the hangar level. Stepping out of the lift, I told Xul to get his armor on and prep Eagle One for a combat sortie. Xul's Zaen armor was not the complicated affairs ours had grown to be. He quickly donned his armor and headed out the hatch for Eagle One. We went through our ritual of going over each other's armor. Once were had checked and double checked our gear, we moved to the hangar. I could see Xul sitting in the cockpit of Eagle One. He was head down, and going over his check lists. When he noticed our approach, he threw us a thumbs up and dropped the rear boarding ramp.

Xul gave us a sitrep. "We will be ready for departure in five minutes Commander. Justice is still working to find an LZ that isn't covered by Scrun heavy weapons or overrun by Prule Hunters."

I opened a group comms channel to Justice. "Show us what we are up against."

Our HUDs flickered, and switched to a sensor feed from the Legacy. The heavy smoke from the burning forest obscured normal vision. Justice's scanning sensors gave us a surreal black and white picture of the target. Right in the middle of the base was an enormous pit. The last time we had investigated this place it was a hell of a lot smaller. Now it was more than a mile long and at least a quarter wide. Why the Scrun would open up an excavation this large, indicated they might be wanting to take something out of it, equally as large. I was now thinking it might be where the other Heckler ship was hidden. If not, it might also mean they had found another ship.

"Justice." I commed on the group net. "Why are we not seeing any data from the excavation?"

"My scans indicate that sixty feet below the rim of the excavation, there is a mesh stretched over the entire opening. It is effectively blocking my attempts to scan deeper."

After studying the picture thoroughly, it became painfully obvious, I had grossly underestimated the Scrun. While I assumed they would bolster their defenses in answer to our incursion several months ago, I could not have been more wrong in my theory that they would become complacent. From what I was observing, they have been improving their defenses non-stop since our last visit. The excavation was completely ringed by pill boxes, covered trenches, and heavy anti-air defenses. That was just the stuff that was visible to our scans. I was willing to bet all the credits I had ever pillaged from the pirates, there was a crap load more that we couldn't see. Whoever was in charge, knew what they were doing. Even the Prule were going to have their work cut out for them if they thought they could jump in and retake the base.

My crew was also studying the sensor feed. Klutch gave me a no-shitter.

"Commander, I will go anywhere you tell me to, including the place you so fondly call hell. I want you to know up front, if we fly into that meat grinder, our chances are slim to none of getting out in one piece."

I gave the Troop Master a solemn nod. I had no doubts he was right. The debris on the outer edges of the base was the visible proof of his statement. The Prule had made several tries at landing on the base. Their attempts were scattered all the way to the edge of the burning forest. The Hunters that had managed to crawl from the wreckage, lay in shattered heaps several hundred yards from the outer defensive circle. The interlocking shields of the Scrun heavy weapons platforms, had very few holes in it. Even now, we could observe new weapons being moved into place while under fire from the waves of charging Hunters. The Scrun had no intention of ever abandoning the base. Whatever they unearthed, they planned to keep at all cost.

Justice gave us another sitrep. "Commander, I have detected seven new transition signatures. All the new contacts are broadcasting encrypted Prule machine language."

"How is the Chaalt task force doing?"

"Their initial attack destroyed eleven Prule Destroyers. The Scrun lost seventy-one ships in the attack because of their close proximity to the targets. The Chaalt lost two battle ships when Prule Destroyers jumped into their attack group ramming the lead elements. Three Chaalt ships have broken ranks with the task force and will be over the base in four minutes. One of the ships is the Principle Investigator's flagship.

I surmise it is her intention to teleport ground troops onto the base."

"Give me her IST channel Justice."

"Channel open Commander."

"Principle Investigator, you have no doubt seen the same sensor feeds I have. The Scrun have a deathtrap waiting for anyone who attempts a landing. You are going to lose a lot of good people if those defenses are not suppressed. I am sure you know by now, if you blast your way in, you are opening the door for a flood of Prule Hunters to follow you."

"Commander Myers, we have a contingency for this scenario. We did not come here with the intention of leaving empty handed."

"Sael, as soon as your troops start landing it won't take long for the Scrun to figure out they have cloaked ships overhead. When that happens, they are going to shoot at you with everything they have got. I want you to know, I am seriously considering destroying the entire site from orbit."

"No Nathan!" Sael shouted. "I have to know if the Fury is here. I am going to do this with or without your help, but one way or another, I am going to find out."

Sael killed the connection. I looked at my crew and threw my hands in the air. Sael's obsession with finding the Fury was going to get her killed.

"Justice, deploy our attack drones around the target. Make sure we have cover when we launch."

"Affirmative Commander. Moving into the atmosphere, and launching drones."

"Xul, are you ready?"

"Yes Commander, just give me a destination."

As far as I knew, our Guardian cloaking technology was the best around, and undetectable by the Scrun. If Justice opened fire that would change. The Scrun would blind fire everything they had to light up our shields. Once that happened, there would be no hiding, and we would be the center of their targeting envelope.

"Xul, on my mark take us out and directly into the excavation."

"Ready on your mark Commander." Xul replied.

Justice took the Legacy down to fifty-thousand feet and put us in a tight circle around the base. He launched the drones and moved further out when the Chaalt ships started bombarding the perimeter around the excavated pit. As was expected, the return fire from the base was intense. The shields of the cloaked Chaalt ships became visible under the withering counter fire. It gave the Scrun a target to concentrate on.

"Justice, have the drones open fire on those anti-ship batteries."

The view in our HUDs changed to a close up of the excavation. Anti-ship fire from around its perimeter was tapering off as more of the weapons were targeted. The respite was short lived as missiles poured out of the middle of the pit. The shields on one of Sael's troop ships flickered under the tremendous pounding, and took four missile strikes to the hull. It veered off and climbed away from the planet. Three of the Prule Destroyers doing battle in orbit above the planet, took notice of the damaged ship. They turned away from their fleet engagements and pursued the wounded battleship. One of the Chaalt attack groups concentrated their fire on the ships, destroying one and dissuading the other two from following. The damaged Chaalt battleship finally jumped out of the system to safety.

Justice called out another warning, two more Prule resource gathering ships just jumped into the system near the planet. They were making a high-speed run for the base. The Chaalt were forced to divide their forces once again to chase the ships and attempt to engage them. I wasn't sure where the Prule were coming from, but they were jumping in from all points of the compass. The Scrun were now down to one-hundred and ninety-seven ships. It had me wondering if they would bail on their comrades, leaving those trapped on the base to their own means.

Sael must have been having a hell of a time getting troops down on the perimeter of the excavation. The main batteries on her flagship suddenly opened fire, sending blinding bolts of energy down into the pit. Gigantic plumes of fire and debris belched out from the excavation. Sael would not have fired her main weapons danger close to her troops unless things were going poorly. Her choice of weapons did manage to solve the missile problem. The missile fire abruptly ceased after her bombardment.

"Justice open an IST channel to Sael."

"Channel open Commander."

Sael didn't let me get a word in edgewise. "Nathan! I do not have time for another of your lectures."

"Stow that scat Sael! I am calling you to say I am taking my team into the excavation! Do not, I repeat, do not, fire into the excavation. Have you got that!"

There was a momentary silence. "I understand Commander Myers, we will continue to land troops around the perimeter of the excavation. I ask that you secure an LZ and IST its location, so I can teleport down with a fire team."

I had no problem with that. As far as I was concerned the more the merrier. I don't know what was down in that hole, but I was going to feel a whole lot better with someone watching our backs while we found out.

"Roger that Principle Investigator, stand by for my transmission."

"Sael's reply came out in a whisper. "Hurry Nathan, our shields are at fifty percent and falling. We cannot stay here much longer."

Justice was listening to my transmission and dove for the base. He opened the hangar door when we were ten-thousand feet above the base.

I called to Xul. "Mark!"

Justice spit us out of the hangar and Xul hit the thrusters shoving us back in our jump seats. I looked around at my crew as we dove for the hard deck. They all gave me a thumbs up and it put a smile on my face. I felt heavy Gs as Xul pulled us horizontal and headed for the target. We stood up and cloaked when the G-load eased off. The Troop Master stood at the hatch and we took our positions behind him.

Xul called from the cockpit. "Thirty seconds Commander!"

"Roger that Xul. As soon as we jump, stay low and start taking out the Prule trying to invade the base."

"Acknowledged Commander, shoot the Prule, and leave the rest for the Chaalt."

At twenty-seven seconds Xul yelled over our comms as the cargo ramp dropped open. "Going vertical Commander, good hunting!"

Xul pulled the nose of the shuttle abruptly up, and we were jettisoned out the back. Our suit AIs quickly oriented us, and we dove headlong into the smoke-filled abyss. My suit sensors revealed the excavation was more than six thousand feet deep. They also revealed what we thought was blind fire on the part of Sael's flagship, was precisely aimed fire that took out the missile launchers that once sat on outcroppings that ringed the monstrous pit. The further we dropped the more it became apparent, there were two subsurface levels and the balance of the pit was an access hole to a massive tunnel. The mesh that was blasted away from the opening, hid the tunnel from overhead sensors.

We finally touched down and took a knee with our weapons up and ready. The roar of the pitched battle above us was barely audible at this depth. We were facing outwards in a defensive perimeter and had no movement. The rubble and debris from the surface levels was the only prominent features of an otherwise vacant tunnel.

I called to Sael. "Principle Investigator, we are down in the excavation and for the moment, have no opposition or movement."

"Acknowledged Commander Myers. Move away from your current location, we are teleporting down in fifteen seconds."

"Roger that, moving now." I replied.

Klutch looked back at me and I pointed to the slagged debris of a missile launcher that had been blasted from its perch. He moved out using his gravity drives. We rapidly followed in our combat formation, and sheltered under the edge of the warped and fused launcher tube.

There was no point just sitting here with our thumbs up our asses. "Klutch, Tria, find out where the tunnel behind us leads to. Coonts and I will wait for Sael and her troops. If you run into trouble get back here on the double."

They both gave me a thumbs up and silently disappeared into the blackness of the tunnel. My suit sensors showed me the tunnel in the opposite direction, dropped off about a quarter mile from our entry point. There was a loud report from the front of our hide. A circle of twenty shiny pulsating columns appeared. The molten metal like appearance faded away, and the Principle Investigator appeared with nineteen members of her fireteam. I uncloaked and flashed my suit lights at them. They ran in our direction, encircling us and going prone. Another report echoed down the passage, and another fireteam materialized. They rapidly joined the rest of Sael's team and all cloaked.

Sael moved to my side and used her Backscatter Transmitter to comm me.

"Commander Myers, my ships could no longer remain over the base, they were taking to much damage. We managed to get four hundred and sixty troops down around the rim above us. They have taken heavy casualties but have cleared the Scrun from most of the perimeter. Our biggest problem now is holding back the Prule Hunters that are making wave attacks from the edge of the forest. Thinning the Scrun herd, may have helped the Prule more than we would have liked, but it was the only way to get boots on the ground."

Tria interrupted Sael's briefing with a sitrep. I held a finger up to the Principle Investigator, making her frown. "Nathan." Tria called. "We are more than a mile from your position. We encountered two Scrun patrols on mounted weapons coming up the tunnel from an unknown location. They have been neutralized, but there is a good chance they will be missed."

I commed Tria back. "Roger that, hold in place. We will move to your location."

"Copy." She replied.

I relayed the message to Sael. "Tria and Klutch have taken down two Scrun patrols. If you have additional troops coming, you need to get them here now, or we will leave without them. We need to move to their location and back them up. There is a good chance they have triggered an alert."

"We are your only backup. The rest of my troops are tasked with taking the base and holding off the Prule."

I nodded to Sael and had my battle suit AI transfer Tria and Klutch's location to her HUD. As a precaution against losing our comms from the surface, I had my suit AI bring a drone down from over the base and into the excavation. Our comms would be relayed from Justice or Xul in the event something major changed on the surface. I did a quick comms check with Justice before we went further down the tunnel.

"Justice give me a sitrep."

"Commander, there have been thirty-nine new transition signatures from Prule ships. Thirty-two are Destroyers and the balance are of a design that appears to be heavily armed troop carriers. Several of the carriers dropped low into the atmosphere and landed at different locations in the forest that surrounds the base. The forest fires and heavy smoke have done little to hinder their attacks. If anything, it is helping to mask their rally points. With the help of our drones, the Scrun have managed to keep the base perimeter intact. I do not know how much longer that will be the case. The Chaalt have destroyed a large percentage of the anti-ship batteries when they secured the perimeter of the tunnel entrance. The Prule will no doubt exploit that weakness when they discover the vulnerability."

"How is the battle going against the Prule fleet?" I inquired.

"The ninety-seven surviving Scrun warships have abandoned the battle, and are attempting rescue operations. Many have already jumped out of the system. The ships that remain, are so heavily damaged they can no longer maneuver. The Scrun losses more than doubled when they were caught in the crossfire between the Chaalt fleet and the Prule."

"What about the Heckler warship?"

"It is severely damaged and drifting. The Chaalt have the ship surrounded and are attempting to board it. The rest of the Chaalt fleet is engaging the ever-growing number of Prule ships that are still randomly jumping into the system. I have intercepted a transmission from the Principle Investigator's fleet commander. She is requesting additional warships to secure the system. The Chaalt have come to the same conclusion I have, whatever the Prule are hiding on the planet, must be of monumental importance. There is no other acceptable reason for them to expose their remaining assets in this galaxy."

"Roger that Justice, we are going to find out one way or another."

42

I gave an audible for all to hear. "Let's move out Principle Investigator."

I cloaked and boosted down the tunnel in Tria and Klutch's direction. Sael commed me on a discreet channel. "Commander Myers, while I am under your command, I would prefer if you addressed me as Senior Operative in front of my troops. A Principle Investigator is a leadership role that I am not currently fulfilling. The members of my fireteams, understand that unless I have orders for them, they are to follow your commands."

"That works for me Sael. As soon as we arrive at Tria and Klutch's position, I want you to leave a portion of your team behind as a rear guard. If we have to retreat under fire, I want to make sure we are not trapped between two forces."

"Acknowledged Commander." The Senior Operative signed off.

Tria and Klutch appeared in my HUD as two blue circles. They were sheltered in the wreckage of the Scrun weapons platforms they had destroyed. We touched down and the Senior Operative immediately chose a dozen of her strike team members to stay behind to cover our six. Four separated from the group and went back down the tunnel a short distance to place stealth mines and other devices to secure our route of retreat if it was necessary.

I uncloaked and huddled with Tria and Klutch. The Senior Operative had her fire team surround us. "What have you got Troop Master?"

"Commander, I am sure you have noticed the tracks under our feet. I think this is some kind of service tunnel. It goes downhill another hundred feet, eight-hundred yards in front of our position. There is some kind of scrapyard down there, and the Scrun have snipers and heavy weapons deployed throughout it. My suit sensors detected several mines and triggering devices set on all the obvious approaches. They have to know by now they are cut off from the surface. Tria and I should have let the gun platforms pass, but did not want them on your flank if you were engaged by a pursuing force. Now that the gun crews are missing, it will not take them long to know they have company. If we are going to hit them, we should get on with it before they set up additional defenses."

It would have been nice to make a stealth approach, but that was not going to be the case with a full-blown war going on the surface. The Scrun knew something was going to happen, and they had to be preparing for the worse. Its what I would be doing if I was in their shoes.

I held a finger up to Klutch and Tria, then turned to the Operative. "Have your team take cover, we are going to blast our way in."

Sael turned to her troops and signaled for them to go prone and cover. Turning back to Klutch, I commed him permission to do his favorite thing. "Klutch, two rounds anti-matter. Fifty percent yield, thirty second delay. As soon as you fire, get back here on the double."

The Troop Master's face lit up with a big goofy smile. His war mask reappeared on his face shield and he cloaked, then disappeared up the tunnel. Tria and I cloaked and joined the Operative with her troops on the deck. My HUD lit up with a yellow warning light, and the words "Anti-matter" flashed across my display. The Scrun ambush teams didn't know it yet, but they were about to meet their maker.

Klutch was coming in hot, and hit the deck well ahead of us. He slid down the metal track to our position with sparks flying from his armor. My countdown timer dropped to zero, and the tunnel heaved under us in almost simultaneous explosions. Debris were blasted up the incline of the tunnel with many raining down around us. A pressure wave of smoke, dust and heat washed over us, and headed down the tunnel at considerable velocity. When that mess went belching out the excavation, the Scrun were going to know their woes were growing exponentially.

My theory proved correct when I got a call relayed to me from Xul. "Commander, the Scrun forces are abandoning their positions. They are leaving the barricades and heavy weapons unmanned. The Prule Hunters are slaughtering them as they attempt to retreat to the forest. Even with the help of the drones, I am not going to be able to keep the Prule from overrunning the outer walls of the base. I am recommending you let me evac you from the base."

"Negative Xul. Get back to the Legacy and bombard the perimeter of the base from orbit."

The Senior Operative commed me over our group channel. "Commander Myers, I have ordered all available assault shuttles to land troops on the base. My remaining forces that secured the excavation, are moving to the barricades to man the heavy weapons."

The way things were moving, I was hoping it was not too little, too late. Dividing my attention was not going to change what was happening on the surface. We had no choice but to carry on and hope that the Chaalt could land enough troops to keep the Prule ground forces out of the base.

"Klutch, take the lead, let's move out!"

The Chaalt strike team got up and formed up on both side of us. Klutch saw that we were ready, and boosted down the smoke and dust filled tunnel. There was a lot of movement in front of us, and we started firing at the pop-up targets. The survivors of the blast quickly threw down their weapons. Those that did not run, held their hands out in front of them with their fingers splayed upwards. We flew past the retreating Scrun and headed deeper into the tunnel. Klutch was right, the tunnel was filled with pieces of ships. The track was lined with massive cradles. They were filled with several types of large weapons that might have been mounted on warships. I had growing anxiety, because I had seen things like this before, onboard a Prule life boat.

Klutch led us down to the tunnel tracks and behind a massive cradle that was holding what appeared to be the aft section of a starship. "Commander, there are massed Scrun troops ahead of us, and they have nowhere to go. They are backed up against a gigantic door."

Klutch shared his video feed with the rest of the team. I did not like what I was seeing. The last time we had seen a door like that, it had a Prule Hivemind on the other side of it. To make matters worse, this door was at least ten times bigger.

The Senior Operative voiced what was going through my mind. "Commander Myers, that looks a lot like a door we have encountered before. If the Prule have brought their fleet here to protect what's on the other side, what are the chances of it being another Hivemind?"

"I would say they are good, especially if they know what we did to the last Hivemind." I answered.

The Scrun that were holed up with their backs against the massive door, were hunkered down behind their weapons waiting to see what was going to transpire. I came here to kill every Scrun that I could find, but now it was hard for me to continue thinking that way. They had lost countless thousands of personnel, and hundreds of warships. The payback I was wanting to give them, happened well before we got here. It had me believing in Karma. It also put a lot of fact behind my grandfather once telling me, "What comes around goes around." The death they had inflicted on innocent others, has come back on them a thousand-fold.

I turned up the volume on my external PA system, and called out in the Scrun language. "I am the one you call the Demon Warrior. Those of you that want to die, stay where you are and I will grant your wish. Those of you wanting to take your chances trying to escape, should start running now. You can keep your weapons, because you are going to need them. The Bio-machines are not likely to give you the same concession!"

What started as a trickle of Scrun soldiers running up the tunnel, turned to a mass exodus. They abandoned their heavy weapons and only took what they could carry. We took up positions in the wreckage of our anti-matter attack, and waited to see if they would try to turn on us. They ran by our defensive positions without even looking to see if we would take them under fire. My suit AI made sure the drone hovering at the tunnel entrance did not attack the retreating troops. The Operative was on her IST transmitter alerting the fire team we had left behind, and her troops on the surface, unless they were fired upon, let the Scrun come up the lifts out of the tunnel.

Klutch reconnoitered the vacated Scrun positions, then called me on our group comms. "Commander, you need to take a look at this."

"We are on our way Troop Master."

The Senior Operative gathered her strike team and we moved out to where Klutch was waiting. He was standing at a makeshift building against the face of the massive door. As I touched down with Tria and Coonts, he reached out and pulled a heavy tarp aside. Inside was a large machine with an operator's booth on the rear of it. It had a single barrel protruding from the front, and two large arms that looked like something you would see on a backhoe.

"What have you got Troop Master?" I asked.

"It's a boring machine Commander. The Scrun have been trying to cut an opening in the door. By the looks of it, they were not having much luck."

I stepped to the front of the machine and looked at the face of the door. It had a four-foot ragged opening burned into it. It was about the same depth as it was large. The arms on the boring machine were for dragging the molten slag from the edges of the hole. I don't know how long the Scrun were working on the door, but Klutch was right, they weren't making very good progress. Whatever the massive door was made of, it had excellent resistance to burning through it. My guess, is that it was made of the same materials as the hulls of the Prule battleships.

Justice interrupted my thoughts with a dire warning. "Commander! The Prule have divided their remaining fleet and nine destroyers are in a tight formation protecting

694

three resource gathering platforms. All twelve are headed directly at the planet. We are attempting to stop them, but there is a high probability some of the formation will make it to the surface."

"Are the Chaalt still bringing down shuttles?"

"Yes Commander. It may have been what triggered the change in the Prule's tactics. As they approach the planet, they are taking the Chaalt shuttles under fire."

I looked over at the Senior Operative and I could see she was carrying on a discussion over her IST. She looked up at me shaking her head. "Commander Myers, the Prule are pursuing our shuttles and shooting them down. We are taking heavy losses. The seventeen shuttles that have already touched down, bolstered our numbers by more than a thousand. The surviving shuttles are flying close air support and we are holding the perimeter. Another sixty Chaalt battleships have entered the system and have joined up with my task force. I have called on them to try and intercept the incoming ships, but I am afraid they are too late. The Prule ships have already entered the atmosphere just over the horizon and will be here in another four minutes."

It has always been my experience, that every time I thought things were going our way, they weren't. My illusion of good fortune was just that. Now we were going to get a bad dose of reality. The ground suddenly started shaking under our feet and clouds of dust and dirt rained down from the tunnel ceiling. We didn't know what the hell was happening, but I knew it had to involve the Prule, and it wasn't going to be good. I got another unexpected call. "Commander! Two Chaalt battleships just jumped into the atmosphere directly in the path of a Prule assault force. There was a collision, and a number of ships just went down in the ocean!"

"Xul, what are you doing? You are supposed to be aboard the Legacy!"

"Commander, the perimeter would have been breeched before the Chaalt relief force could have touched down. With the help of the drones, we have kept the Prule Hunters at bay."

I was going to order Xul to get aboard the Legacy. Before I could get the words out of my mouth, he yelled over the comms link.

"Incoming Prule ship!"

It felt like the planet heaved in revulsion. We were knocked off our feet and the air in the tunnel thickened with even more dust and smoke. My premonition of bad mojo was coming true.

"Commander." Xul called. "I owe you two apologies."

"Xul, what the hell just happened?"

"A Prule ship just crashed into the base and is now blocking the entrance to the excavation."

"Are you headed back to the Legacy?"

"Negative Commander. That is the reason for my first apology."

"Xul! You are not making sense! Where are you?"

"I am sorry to report I am in what appears to be a tunnel Commander. I am assuming it is the same one you are presently located in."

"Xul, if I am understanding what you are telling me, you landed in the tunnel before the Prule ship crashed. Is that correct?"

"That is the grounds for my second apology Commander. It wasn't exactly a landing. Judging by the angle of the port side weapons pod, which is not normally viewable from the cockpit, I would say that I have crashed. I would also like to report a large number of armed Scrun running past my location."

"Are you injured?"

"No Commander, but I am pinned in the cockpit and cannot free myself."

"Hold tight, we are on our way." I replied.

"Commander, there is one more thing I would like to report." Xul commed. "There is a considerable number of Prule Hunters jumping into the tunnel from the wreckage of the ship."

"Roger that, we are moving now!"

The Senior Operative overheard my discussion and had her troops ready to move. We boosted up at the tunnel at maximum velocity. The gravity drives in our battle suits were more efficient and faster than the Chaalt design. We left them to our rear. Since the Senior Operative was wearing Tria's third generation armor, she easily kept pace with us. We heard her call back to her troops. She ordered them to set up a defensive perimeter around the shuttle, as soon as they rejoined us.

My HUD highlighted the shuttle in the distance. Xul's admission that he had crashed was an understatement of the facts. The nose of Eagle One was crushed flat on one side and the whole flight deck was bent backwards over the top of the ship. His dive into the excavation was apparently followed by an unnegotiable pull up to horizontal flight. I looked into the distance and could see a lot of weapons fire. The next thing I noticed, is that it looked like it was raining Prule Hunters from the wreck above us. I used the magnification in my HUD to get a closer look. Hundreds of the bio-machines were pouring out of several rends in the ship's hull. The Scrun we had given a free pass, were now engaging the Prule. They were being slaughtered by the ever-increasing number of Hunters. Finding out if we could escape out the other end of the tunnel was no longer a viable option. We only had one avenue of escape, and it was back in the direction of the door.

"Klutch, make a hole in the cockpit, we need to get Xul out of there now!"

Klutch did not hesitate, and we boosted up onto the wreck of Eagle One. He crawled over to the shuttle's view screen and peered inside at Xul. It looked like the instrument panel was bent over the top of his legs. Klutch moved to the side of the cockpit and activated the portal device. He got a good hole on the first attempt. Tria, Coonts and I jumped through, landing on what used to be the cockpit overhead. Xul was just above us, pinned in his seat upside down. Klutch came through behind us, and closed the portal.

"Commander." Xul said. "It was my intention to protect your flank. I have instead endangered your lives. I recommend that you leave me here, and retreat down the tunnel before the Prule forces can reach this location."

I cleared my war mask so the Grawl could see my look of disapproval. "Xul, under the circumstances, I am going to ignore your request. I don't want to hear anymore of that defeatist scat coming out of your mouth. That's an order!"

Tria and Klutch reached over their heads and grabbed the bottom of the instrument panel on both sides of Xul's legs. Coonts and I got a good grip on each side of his chair.

"On the count of three." I called. "One…two…three!"

We all pulled at the same time. The instrument panel ripped loose as Coonts and I bent the back of the command seat over. Xul slid free of the wreckage with a grimace on his face. His suit telemetry indicated he had two broken ankles. If he wasn't going to point it out, I wasn't going to make note of it either. The Zaen Armor would stabilize it as much as possible.

The Senior Operative rained a little piss on our achievement. "Commander Myers, the Prule have killed the remaining Scrun and are moving this way in force."

"Then I suggest you give them a demonstration of your battle suit's weapons capability." I shot back.

Klutch made a hole and we pulled Xul out of the wrecked shuttle. Tria was attempting to communicate with the Legacy, but we were now cut off from the surface. The Senior Operative raised all four of the tube launchers on her battle suit. With a sweeping motion, she fired a four second burst of high explosives at the oncoming Prule. The results were gratifying when we saw their front ranks scattered into pieces and blown into the air. The Chaalt soldiers sent the Prule Hunters a barrage of aimed fire from their anti-ship rifles. Our combat drone retreated deeper into the tunnel before the Prule ship crashed into the excavation. The drone's onboard AI decided it was time to reveal its presence. It opened fire with its main beam weapon. The weapon was designed to defeat the shields on starships. It sliced through the Hunter's shields like they were non-existent, turning the Bio-machines into plumes of molten sparks. A torrent of Prule return fire flared on the shields of the cloaked drone. It quickly reversed course and moved down the tunnel toward our position.

Not wanting to leave without sending the enemy of all, a parting gift. I raised my launcher up at the wreck. An orange warning flashed in my HUD when I selected a full yield anti-matter round. The Senior Operative yelled at her troops to retreat at maximum speed back to the scrap yard. I told my strike team to do the same, but they stood their ground. I put a two-minute delay on the round and fired up into the belly of the Prule ship.

"Take the lead Troop Master, maximum velocity!"

43

We flew low down the tunnel with our drone following closely behind. My countdown timer was at fourteen seconds. The warning in my HUD was now flashing yellow and green. We took refuge behind a cradle loaded with hull plates. My HUD showed the Senior Operative and her fire team had already gone to ground.

There was a blinding flash, and a jarring thump that was felt through our armored boots. Seconds later, our audio pickups were momentarily shut down by the high decibel blast. The pressure wave that followed, blew a hurricane of dust and debris over our positions. I was thinking it sucked to be a Prule right after the blast, then thought better of it, deciding they just plain sucked anyway. I seriously disliked the Scrun, but hated the Prule with a passion.

We led the Chaalt team back to the gigantic door and they set up a perimeter.

Thinking that it would be nice to know just how bad we hurt the Prule, I sent the drone on a fast recon mission. It would only have to clear the gradual incline of the tunnel to use its sensors to give me a view of what the Prule were doing. I had a small smile on my face thinking I might have wiped them out, leaving just a handful of stragglers for us to mop up. It was the second time I was completely wrong about something. The wreckage of the Prule ship was hanging lower into the tunnel. What used to be several rends in its carcass, was now a huge hole, and the Prule were pouring out like water.

"Senior Operative." I called. "Gather your team and be ready to move. We are going through the door. This position is about to become untenable. Klutch, we don't have a lot of time, so find a spot on that door and make a hole on my command. Tria, set an anti-matter charge in the Scrun's drill shack. When the Prule fail to find us, I am sure they will search it. Coonts I want you to take command of the drone. As soon as Klutch gets a good hole, send it through and make sure we are not jumping from the frying pan into the fire."

I got confirmations from everyone. Klutch chose the center of the door because the tracks were located there. He figured there was always the possibility a cradle similar to the ones on the track behind us, might be sitting on the other side of the door. If that turned out to be the case, it would make excellent cover. I looked back up the tunnel using my HUD to magnify my view. The slowly settling dust was being whipped back up into a growing cloud by the advancing wave of Prule.

"Make a hole Troop Master!"

Klutch activated the portal device and got a good hole. Coonts immediately sent the drone through only to find its view was obstructed. He released it for autonomous reconnaissance. It climbed straight up and moved to one side of the large obstruction. My heart skipped a beat at the picture in my HUD. The track we had followed to the door, was lined with cradles. They all held huge pieces of starships. Further up the line, some even held whole ships the size of the Legacy. I was having a hard time comprehending what we were seeing, but couldn't take the time to study it.

I turned and waved to Sael. "Move out Senior Operative, the portal will close in three minutes!"

She didn't hesitate because she saw my video feed of the oncoming wave of Hunters. She ran into the portal with her troops following closely behind her. I got a red flashing anti-matter warning in my HUD. Coonts had his launcher raised to our rear.

He commed me on our group channel. "I will be right behind you Commander." Tria grabbed me by my ammo pack and pulled me into the portal as the last of the Chaalt troops entered. The last thing I saw was Coonts firing his launcher, and Klutch reaching out to grab him. Tria and I stepped out of the portal inside a defensive perimeter of Chaalt soldiers. Klutch and Coonts came barreling into us because we had failed to move out of the way in time. Klutch killed the portal as it started to flash.

The drone sensor feed did not give us the true magnitude of what we were seeing. We were in the shadow of the what I could only guess was the forward section of a starship, and it looked vaguely familiar.

I was getting back to my feet when the Senior Operative commed me.

"Commander Myers, that is a front section from a Heckler warship."

I was going to blurt out an expletive, but the ground under our feet seemed to jump up at me as I stumbled back to the ground. The thump was followed by a loud metallic clang from the massive door, and dirt raining down from the overhead.

We quickly got back to our feet and I called to the Senior Operative for a sitrep. "Have you got any movement?"

"Negative Commander." Sael replied. "But they could change at any time. We should use the drone sensor feed to determine our next move."

I commandeered the drone's video feed and transferred it to my HUD. My crew and Sael did the same. Stretching into the distance was an endless line of materials, ships, and large pieces of ships, that would not fit on the monstrous cradles. That was a stunning sight, but not what I was now focusing on at the moment. On either side of the heavily laden cradles, were thousands of Prule maintenance machines. Moving around them like ants in a hive were re-animated life forms of every description. They had electrodes protruding from their bodies and the crazy lighting like electricity dancing among them. I could not have painted a more horrific picture if I had tried.

My crew and I had seen this before, but this was new to Senior Operative's strike team. They were all staring back at me, and the anxiety on their faces was obvious. No one wanted that to be their fate.

"Nathan." Sael whispered over a discreet comms channel. "What are we going to do?"

Tria broke the spell the morbid scene had cast over us all. "Where are they taking all these ship parts? Is this how they assemble a lifeboat?"

It was a damn good question, but I didn't have a clue as to how to answer it. "I don't Know Tria, the only way to find out, is to work our way to the other end of the tunnel."

Coonts was studying the section of ship on the cradle in front of us. "Commander, the Senior Operative is correct. This is indeed the forward section of a Heckler ship. We can now account for the three that we had observed on our previous visit to this star system. The question that I now find troubling, is how did the Prule take possession of it, and how did it end up in here?"

I genuinely hated it when people asked me questions, I could not truthfully answer.

An old slang Earth adage crossed my mind, but never made it to my lips. We were flattened by a shockwave that bowed the corner of the giant door behind us. We were all dazed, and I had to shake my head several times to clear the fog from my brain. I would have never thought the Prule could recover that quickly from the anti-matter shell, Coonts had dropped on their heads. Tria set her charge for proximity detonation. I had a feeling what just happened could only mean one thing, the tunnel was filled with Prule. I tried to call Justice again, but there was still no reply. I got back to my feet and helped Tria up. My audio pickups were picking up a piercing alarm that had a very annoying cycle to it. It was hard to say whether it was an automated response, or triggered by a Bio-machine. Either way, we now had everyone's attention. My drone feed showed a mass of Prule maintainers, and more than a thousand of the energy charged zombies, turn in our direction. To make matters worse, the giant cradle holding the nose section of the Heckler ship started moving down the track away from us.

Klutch called out a warning that was more for the Chaalt fire team, than it was for me.

"The Prule have sensors that detect cloaked targets. We need to find cover now!"

Klutch always had a way to light a fire under my ass when he thought I might not be up to speed, and now was no exception. "I think it would be advisable to take cover on the cradle Commander!"

"We will follow your lead Troop Master!" I called back.

Klutch boosted up onto the ship fragment and worked his way to the top. There were several exposed corridors and hatches we could hide in. "We can shelter here for now, but I recommend we find a more defensible location."

I tapped Sael on the ammo pack and pointed up at the ship fragment. She nodded and pulled her fire team back in. Coonts was standing over Xul like a mother hen, and helped him to his feet. The little Grawl was in pain, but wasn't going to slow us down by showing it. We boosted up onto the ship section, and moved to the top. Klutch was laying prone against the hull and surveying our surroundings. The Senior Operative's team spread out around us and did the same. Tria, Sael and I crawled to Klutch's side.

He pointed down the tunnel. "Commander, the heavy haze is obscuring my view. My sensors indicate the tunnel splits off to the right. At the cradles present pace, we will reach that point in twenty-one minutes. We don't know what could be waiting for us there. I think we should find out now, rather than wait until we get that far. It might be worth risking our combat drone to find out."

I didn't want to take the chance of our drone being discovered. It was currently holding tight against the ceiling of the tunnel just in front of the massive door. If it came down to a shootout, it was our only backup. I was going to give the Troop Master my recommendation, but it caught in my throat. The cradle we were riding on, suddenly lurched to a stop. We were about three hundred yards from the door, and I wondered if we should take our chances going back in that direction. The Prule and their surrogate soldiers were now on either side of the cradle, and would have us completely surrounded in another couple of minutes. It was doubtful if they had detected our presence, but they were definitely looking. If, and when they did, everybody was going to have a bad day. Glancing over at Tria, I could see the expectant look on her face. It was a look that I seldom ever saw from her. I winked and blew her a kiss. Her face lit up with a smile and she turned away so she would not laugh at my silly antics. I hadn't noticed, but the Senior Operative was also watching me. When I glanced in her direction, she looked like she might have sucked some wind from Klutch's suit vents.

"Troop Master." I called over our group comms. "Keep moving up the tunnel. We are going to jump from cradle to cradle. Take the lead and move out!"

The Troop Master was an alien of action, and didn't like sitting around with his thumb up his ass. He boosted the hundred or so feet across to the next cradle. He paused to see if his movement garnered a reaction from the mass of hostiles below us. Nothing changed, and they continued to move toward the massive door behind us. Klutch disappeared into the maze of protrusions sticking out from the ship fragments.

"All clear Commander, it does not seem as if the Prule are interested in the cradles."

I waved the Senior Operative and her fire team across. They wasted no time and boosted forward. When they were out of sight, Tria, Coonts, Xul and I boosted across behind them. We worked our way through the severed machinery and deck plates until we came up on Klutch's position. So far, so good. I knew thoughts like that fell into the category of things going our way. It had proven to be faulty thinking in the past, but I was hoping to catch a break from that scat. The gods of war must have heard me. The siren that was blaring out an alert ever since our anti-matter charge detonated, suddenly ceased. I switched my HUD view to the drone's video feed. The wave of hostiles stopped about twenty feet from the door. If they were expecting someone to come for a visit, they would be waiting a long time.

I called to Klutch. "Move to the next cradle Troop Master."

He gave me a thumbs up and started to move, but froze in place when we heard a loud groaning noise that was accompanied by equally loud metallic pops. The Prule were opening the damn door. By the sound of it, our anti-matter charge had severely tweaked it. The groan grew louder as did the metallic popping noises. I looked at my drone video feed and could see the door had opened about a foot, then stalled. The bow in the left side of the door had the gigantic cross bolts in a bind. The mechanisms were straining to get it open. The Prule Hunters were sticking their appendages through the opening and trying to assist. They climbed on top of each other until they were stacked all the way to the top of the narrow opening. There had to be several thousand of them on the other side of the door, and all of them were trying to pry it open. My Earthman brain finally came to the conclusion the base was overrun, and the Prule had nothing better to do, than search for last thorn still sticking them in the ass.

I waved Klutch on. "Get moving Troop Master. I will be along shortly."

He gave me a look, that another ranking officer among us would consider insubordinate. I pulled an anti-matter charge from my storage pack. It was all that was needed to get the Tibor to change his mind about arguing with me. The other ranking officer I was referencing, saw what I was up to, and wasted no time getting her team up and moving. Coonts and Xul followed close behind them. Tria was the exception, and stayed at my side as I wedged the charge between two hull plates. We each carried four, and the way things were starting to look, I may not get another chance to use them.

Tria grabbed me by the arm. "Nathan! We need to move now! The maintenance machines are helping the Hunters pry the door open."

My drone feed confirmed Tria's exclamation. The Prule on this side of the door, had all of their appendages wedged in with the Hunter's on the other side. There was another loud metallic pop and right side of the door opened another couple of inches. We boosted across to the next cradle and my anxiously waiting teammates. I commed Klutch to leapfrog ten of the cradles, and find a place to set another charge. He should have acknowledged my order, but I was getting nothing. We were completely hemmed in by the worst enemy our galaxy has ever known, with no clear escape route, and my point man wasn't returning my calls. I was starting to get a really bad feeling that was playing hell with my lower intestine.

Coonts must have had the same reaction, and called out on our group comms. "Klutch, have you got a copy?"

Something changed the demeanor of the Bio-machines around us. The ones that were working on unknown pieces of machinery, stopped what they were doing. The reanimated soldiers that were carrying materials to large shipping crates, suddenly stopped as well. With a sudden jerk, the train of cradles started to move again, and now they were moving faster.

"Commander." Coonts called. "I request permission to check on the Troop Master."

"Negative, we move as a group or not at all. The Prule know we are here, and are trying to figure out where. We have to assume Klutch would not answer our hails if it would give away his position. I will take point, and we will try to locate him. I don't need to remind anyone, that stealth is the only thing protecting us. No unnecessary noise or comms from this point forward. Hand signals only, and keep your eyes moving. We need to be aware of our surroundings at all times. We don't want to make a mistake, and stumble into the hands of our enemies."

Tria, Coonts and Xul gave me a thumbs up. The Senior Operative acknowledged the signal and turned to her fire team doing the same. They all held a thumb up to me. I circled my finger over my head and pointed to the next cradle. We boosted over to it and momentarily stopped to see if we had attracted attention. The Prule bio-machines and their surrogates were now standing at both sides of the three-hundred-foot-wide tracks as the cradles passed by. The massive door to our rear gave off another metallic pop, marking the Bio-machines progress as they worked to make the opening larger. I had no idea what Justice and the Chaalt fleet were doing, but knew they would not abandon the base. Unless another large fleet of Prule jumped into the system, they should be landing addition troops to retake it. Time was running out for us, and I hoped it turned out to be the latter of the two scenarios.

The haze in the tunnel grew thicker as we worked our way forward. We leap frogged seven more cradles, crawling carefully among the ship parts and hull plates. I got a pop-up warning in my HUD. Three cradles in front of us, two faint pulsating glows appeared. Our cradle was almost to the fork in the tunnel when it suddenly stopped. The two events happening at the same time was no coincidence. I looked back at the power sources, they were about three feet apart and the pulse was reciprocating perfectly with its twin. They rose up from between the cradles and moved in our direction. I held up a fist and splayed my fingers. Everyone went prone weapons out and ready. I was not getting a visual, so the target was cloaked and moving directly at us. The glows flared brighter in intensity. A blue circle popped up in my HUD with Klutch's ID under it.

"Commander! It can see our power sources!" Klutch yelled over our comms.

The glow of the power sources immediately turned toward Klutch. A bright blue white beam of energy lanced out at him, striking the ship section he was sheltering behind. There was an enormous blast of heat and flying shrapnel. Klutch was blown from his perch, and sent flying off into the throngs of hostiles.

"Weapons free!" I called over our group comms.

All hell broke loose when the Senior Operative and her fireteam opened up on the power sources directly to our front. The repeated blasts wrecked the cloaking of the power sources, revealing a grotesque abomination that could only be described as a bizarre mutation of a scorpion. It had eight long metallic legs similar to a Hunter, and a short fat stubby tail with an oversized weapon on the end. Its two large front arms had six fingered hands with razor sharp tips. It was clawing and ripping at the hull section it was clinging to, trying to flee the barrage that was wrecking its appendages. Tria hit it with a beam shot that blew its stubby tail off, and sent it sprawling into the frenzied crowd of hostiles swelling up the sides of the cradles.

Coonts boosted over the side and into the ocean of waiting hostiles. "Klutch! I am coming." He yelled over our comms.

Tria and I opened up with our miniguns, mowing down huge swaths of Prule coming up the sides of the cradle.

The Senior Operative called out a warning. "Commander!" She yelled. "They are charging from the fork in the tunnel!"

I looked over my shoulder, and saw three of the machines that vaguely resembled scorpions, come out of the of the junction of the tunnel. They had shields and were plowing over their own kind, in a mad rush at our position. Xul and the Senior Operative opened up on them with their beam weapons. Their shields flared and flickered but they still kept coming. From

719

somewhere behind me, there was a blinding flash and two of the machines were blown to molten slag. Our cloaked combat drone was active and coming up the tunnel firing as fast as its main weapon could cycle. We needed all the help we could get, but I didn't think it was going to be enough.

44

My HUD picked Coonts out of the hordes of hostiles, wanting a piece of our asses. He had cleared a path in front of him with his launcher. He was firing anti-personnel rounds point blank into the surrounding crowd. Just when I thought it couldn't get any worse, the combat drone's AI gave me a sitrep I was hoping I wouldn't hear.

"Commander Myers, the Prule have widened the opening in the door large enough to allow the Hunters passage into the tunnel."

I took a quick look at the drone feed. The Prule were popping out of the gap in the doors like toast out of a toaster. Two simultaneous blasts hit the ship fragment we were on, ripping it from the cradle. As it tipped over the side, we jumped clear to keep from being crushed along with the Prule and their surrogate slaves. I had no idea what they were shooting at us, but it was blowing our cover to pieces. The Prule just upped the ante, and all our cards were already on the table.

Klutch's voice suddenly yelled over our comms. "Eat scat you Throggs!"

A pink glow illuminated the crowd of hostiles to our front. A glob of plasma spurted out from his last known position. A burning hellfire enveloped all who were splattered by star hot plasma. The Prule maintainers wisely decided to leave the reanimated slaves behind, and move away from the burning inferno that was consuming their fellow minions. It was a reckless display of weapon discipline, but it cut us an ever-expanding path in his direction.

I called to the Troop Master. "Klutch, check you fire, we are moving in your direction!"

The Senior Operative commed me and the news wasn't good. We were taking casualties, and still didn't know where we were running to.

"Commander Myers, I lost six in the explosion, and we are retreating with four wounded. Xul stayed behind to cover our retreat, and I don't think he can hold his position much longer."

I looked at Xul's location in my HUD. He was back on top of the burning remains of the ship fragment, firing on the Prule attacking out of the side tunnel. The drone had moved away from his position and back down the tunnel. It was firing nonstop to our rear. The return fire coming from the ever-growing numbers of Prule Hunters was flaring brightly on its shields.

"Xul, have you got a copy?" I called. "Xul, we need to fall back to the Senior Operatives rally point."

I wasn't getting an answer and turned to Tria. "Get everyone together and rally on Klutch's position, I am going after Xul. We have to get away from the junction of the tunnel. We can't afford to keep expending munitions at our current rate."

Tria refused to leave my side. "The Senior Operative, and the remains of her team are with Coonts. They are not far from the Troop Master."

The fire was intensifying and I wasn't going to stand around and argue the point. We boosted up on the ship fragment and worked our way toward Xul. A hail of incoming fire was coming from our rear and left flank. Tria and I stayed low, but I was knocked off my feet by a lucky shot from the

Hunters that were climbing on the tops of the cradles. Tria took a knee beside me and raised her launcher tube. She fired two long bursts of high explosive rounds back at the pursuing Hunters. The smoke and dust filling the tunnel, completely obscured our vision. Tria's barrage only registered as small dull orange flashes. It managed to slow the counterfire, and she pulled me to my feet.

"Xul!" I called. "Its time to move out. Let's go soldier!"

I pumped out twenty rounds of high explosive over his head and down the arm of the tunnel. Xul was trying to get to his feet and collapsed. He raised his hand and wave us off. There was a brilliant white flash that blacked out my face shield. I don't remember being blown off the top of the ship fragment. When the fog cleared in my head and my vision returned to normal, I was in the grips of at least a dozen of the Prule surrogate soldiers, they were trying to carry me back down the tunnel.

The beast I had shuttered away somewhere deep in my consciousness, ripped free of the Earthman bonds I had placed around it. The pain from the concussive blast faded away as a hunger for death and destruction took its place. I extruded my climbing hooks and twisted my body violently, wrenching my arms free from the hostiles gripping me. I chopped, kicked and punched until the reanimated soldiers were forced to drop me. I located Tria in my HUD and opened fire with my minigun into the endless mass of legs and appendages surrounding me. It ran dry, and I pulled my shotgun from its clip, emptying a full magazine of explosive buckshot into the gap I had created. Switching to slugs, I fired until the gun was empty. Grabbing the barrel like a club, I ran into the parting horde, smashing, ripping, and breaking everything I touched.

I caught sight of Tria and her captors, they were closer now, but the path I had opened, was quickly closing. I extended my spray nozzles and emptied my battle suit's nanite reservoir onto the throngs of maintainers trying to drag Tria down the tunnel. A Hunter leaped down from the overturned cradle and landed on the reanimated soldiers, crushing them under its weight. Its power whip glowed and fired a bolt of energy at me that struck my oncoming attackers. I was knocked to the ground by the pressure wave. The Hunters weapon had opened up a break that led directly to it. I raised my arm and sent a beam shot into the oncoming machine. The blast flattened the Hunter and everything around it. Its shield was flickering, and I was going to give it another shot when a ball of plasma splashed down onto it. You could hear its warbling screech above the din of the non-stop weapons fire.

"Commander!" Coonts yelled. "Klutch and I have your flank, check your fire!"

Coonts and Klutch pulled me from the pile of machine carcasses and back onto my feet. The insanity of the beast quickly faded, and I looked around for my life mate. "We have to get Tria!" I yelled. There was another tremendous blast above us and our combat drone went down in the surging ranks of hostiles. The Hunters seized on the opportunity. They massed together and dove onto it. The drone fired one last time into the hundreds of Hunters pinning it to the ground. The point-blank blast slagged the drone along with a large number of Hunters.

The nanites I sprayed onto the Prule, had finally penetrated their armor. Those who came into contact with the mist, were now thrashing wildly on the ground. Those that were carrying Tria, dropped her on the ground and were flailing away at everything around them. I rushed in and hoisted her onto my shoulder. Her suit telemetry told me she was alive, but unconscious.

Klutch gave me a shove trying to get me moving. "Commander, we need to move now!"

He emphasized his exclamation by firing his plasma caster, sending ball after ball of burning death onto the massed Prule trying to overtake us. A desperate voice called to me. It was the Senior Operative. I don't know how long she had tried to hail me. I had shutout everything but the thought of getting to Tria.

"Nathan, you must pull back to our position now! My nanite weapon is depleted, and we cannot hold the Prule back much longer!"

Klutch grabbed my ammo pack and turned me around. I wasn't sure if I was hit by incoming fire, or the Troop Master kicked me in the ass. Either way, I was moving in the right direction. My HUD marked Sael's location and she only had three members of her fireteam with her. I could not locate Xul.

I called to the Senior Operative. "We are going after Xul!"

Coonts commed me. "Commander, Xul died in the line of duty, his body was not recoverable."

I felt like a knife just stabbed me in the heart. I did not want to believe what Coonts just told me. The rage inside of me was building once more, and the beast was crying out for revenge. I clenched my teeth in anger and my vision was blacking in and out. I wanted to scream out so the Prule would know, I was going to kill them all.

"Nathan." Tria yelled. "Put me down!"

Tria's voice was like water on a wildfire. The hate and rage I was feeling, dropped to a slow simmer. I let her down off my shoulder and she wasted no time pulling me along.

"We will avenge Xul's death, but we will do it together! We need to reach the Senior Operative, and we have to do it now!"

The shit storm only grew worse. Sael Nalen called out another warning over our group comms. "Commander Myers! A gunship is forcing its way into the tunnel from the junction."

I no longer wondered what kind of heavy weapons the Prule had brought to bear against us. I knew it was something big, but had no idea it was a ship mounted main battery. That explained why Coonts said Xul's body was unrecoverable. We boosted low over the top of the hostiles between us and the Senior Operative's rapidly shrinking defensive position. Tria was draining her nanite reservoir along our path of retreat, it would slow the Prule but not stop them. Klutch was hitting anything moving to our front with penetrator slugs from his shotgun. Coonts was sending rapid fire shots from his beam weapon to our rear. When it overheated and shut down, he switched to the last of his explosive buckshot rounds. I was using the last of my explosive rounds judiciously to our flanks. Our expendable munitions were getting dangerously low. We started dropping our Chaalt grenades along our escape route. They would have little effect on the shields of Hunters, but could wreak havoc on the other Prule minions.

Before we could reach the Senior Operative, she had lost another of her team to a Hunter that had jumped into their midst. It unknowingly blundered into the weaponized nanites she had spread over her own position. When the Bio-machine's shields faltered, they blasted it to pieces.

"Commander Myers, we are about to be overrun, we can't hold much longer." Sael said urgently.

I knew we were screwed, but I wasn't going to let Sael know that. "We are close Senior Operative, don't give up on us yet."

An anti-matter warning flashed in my HUD next to Tria's name. She had taken control of the charge I had set, and was about to take some extreme measures to slow the oncoming Prule. The warning was flashing orange to yellow. That put our location in the detonation danger zone, but considering the circumstances, that was the least of our worries. I was just glad it was not blinking from red to orange. We landed in the Senior Operative's defensive perimeter, taking cover behind the piles of mangled machines and twice dead aliens. We went prone beside Sael, and her two remaining strike team members. Tria detonated the charge, and it felt like the floor of the tunnel reached up and slapped us for being such a nuisance. The shockwave hammered us back to the ground, and a blast of heat and debris blew over us at sonic speeds. The bodily remains we had sheltered behind, pummeled us as they were blown away. Something huge crashed down in front of us with a jarring thud, and then there was sudden silence. Directly to our front, shielding us from direct fire, was a giant piece of ship hull sticking up from the tunnel floor. It gave us a small window of opportunity that we could not afford to waste.

"Klutch, lets get moving! I don't care where you take us, as long as it is not here!"

The Troop master tossed his last two Chaalt grenades behind the protruding hull plate, and boosted down the tunnel at a pace the remaining Chaalt soldiers could maintain. We followed close behind, wondering where the tunnel would lead us. The relentless pursuit, and unwavering resistance, told me we have yet to discover what the Prule were so desperately trying to protect.

The Bio-machines and reanimated soldiers not damaged by our blast, were closing ranks in front of us. They were climbing up onto the cradles trying to form an impenetrable wall. We were not going to be able to pass without a fight. The passage was making a gradual turn to our left. My suit sensors were being blotted out by a sea of red hostile indicators surging from around the bend. I also detected something I hadn't noticed before. Up ahead, the smoke and dust filling the tunnel's atmosphere, was being illuminated by an eerie pulsating glow.

Coonts was covering our rear and called a warning. "Commander, the gunship has made it into the tunnel. It is using its shields and hull to shove the cradles and ship fragments aside."

We had no choice but to push on. Going back was not a viable option. I armed my launcher with an anti-matter round and dialed back the yield to fifty percent. I got looks from everyone, when they got the warning in their HUDs. It was still going to be danger close, but we had to break up the Prule blockade. The alternative would be to perish where we stood when the gunship got a clear shot at us.

I called out on our group comms. "One round each, with a five second delay into the heaviest concentrations of troops to our front. As soon as you fire, turn and fire two more to our rear, with no delay. Troop Master, as soon as the scat stops falling, you lead us forward and don't stop."

I got acknowledgments from everyone. They knew we were going to die if we stayed. Our only choice was to move forward no matter the consequences.

I held up my arm and pointed the launcher tube down range at the Prule gathering into a solid wall in front of us. "On the count of three, fire on my mark."

My team chose their targets. "One… two… three. Mark!"

We fired in unison, then rapidly fired to our rear and went prone. Five seconds was just about perfect. There was no noticeable ripple to the blasts as we felt the punishing blow of the sucker punch, we just gave our enemies. The stunning concussion was more than the lighter Chaalt armor could withstand. Sael's two remaining soldiers suffered trauma that rendered them unconscious. The Senior Operative dropped her weapon and tried to pull them both off the ground. Tria grabbed one of the soldiers from Sael's grasp before I could do it.

She hoisted the trooper onto her shoulder and pushed me toward Klutch. "I have got her, let's go!" She yelled.

Klutch waited till I was at his side, and we boosted up the tunnel through the wreckage of our attack. Tria and Sael were having difficulty with the extra weight of their loads, and moving at a dangerously slow pace. The clouds of dust and debris were giving my suit sensors a workout. The information they deciphered from the shitstorm around us, made my heart skip a beat. It was the end of the line. The tunnel terminated into the bright glare of huge power sources, several thousand yards in front of us. There was a flash quickly followed by a tremendous blast to our rear. The Prule commanding the gunship, was slaughtering their own in a gambit to stop us.

Coonts called out another warning, and his voice was an octave higher than normal. "Commander! The gunship is blasting the cradles from its path. If it can negotiate the turn in the tunnel, it will have a firing solution."

Klutch's answer to the report was to take us lower. There were large ships sitting on cradles just in front of us and Klutch used them for cover. Another blast from our rear, sent pieces of ships and hull plates crashing down around us. As we neared the end of the tunnel, what we discovered shocked us beyond comprehension. Klutch guided us to cover behind a ship of an unknown design. The respite was short lived, and we were forced to move when the cradles lurched forward. We went to ground against the tunnel wall and gawked at the sight in front of us. At the terminus of the tunnel was a massive shimmering portal, and it was in the process of consuming a ship. The portal was pulling the ship in, along with the noxious clouds of atmosphere around it. It was picking up momentum and would be gone in another minute.

Just when I thought I could not be any more surprised, the Senior Operative yelled out over our comms. She had lost all of her usual military correctness. "Nathan!" She screamed. "It's the Fury!"

I looked to where Sael was frantically pointing, and my mouth fell open. The missing ship was sitting on one of the giant cradles, and it was moving toward the shimmering portal. I tried to stand, but Klutch jerked my feet out from under me as something exploded on the tunnel wall above us. We were showered by high velocity fragments from the wall. I wasn't sure who fired the shot, but knew it came from our front. As I regained my senses, I saw movement near the portal. It was a silhouette I knew from past memories; one I had come to despise. It was a Prule Hivemind and it spooling up its energy weapon for another shot. The Troop Master fired first. His beam shot flared on its shields and disrupted its aim. The Prule's return shot went wide and hit one of the cradles behind us. Tria and I fired almost as one, and the Hivemind's shields flickered then failed. The Senior Operative's shot passed through the failing shield and struck the Hivemind a glancing blow to its bulbous entity reservoir. It was blasted to the ground and rolled to the side of the portal. The Troop Master and I took careful aim, but were suddenly knocked violently to the ground by a blast that blacked out our HUDs. I don't now how Coonts managed to shake off the concussion, but he was pulling on my leg. The ringing in my ears finally cleared enough to hear him.

"Commander!" he yelled over our comms. "We are being targeted by the gunship, if we do not find cover, we are going to die!"

The beast imprinted into my brain was raging at me. It was not wanting blood or revenge; it was wanting me to survive. I rolled up on my knees and looked back behind us. My view of the gunship was blocked by the vessel it had blown off the cradle beside us. If it had rolled any farther, it would have crushed us all. One of the Senior Operatives soldiers was lying next to me. I tried to pull her up on my shoulder but saw a jagged piece of hull plate sticking out of her side. Tria and Sael grabbed me by the arms and pulled me to my feet.

"They are dead Nathan!" Sael yelled. "If you don't get moving, we are going to join them!"

My brain started hitting on all cylinders, and I knew what needed to be done. "Klutch where is the Hivemind? They will not attack us if we use it as a shield."

The Troop Master grabbed the front of my armor and pulled me along. Tria, Sael and Coonts crowded in close to me. "Commander, it dragged itself into the portal and disappeared."

The Troop Master's statement threatened to give the sanitary qualities of my armor a thorough testing. The situation was dire, and inaction would spell doom for us all. I don't know how it came to me, but it was an epiphany. I looked up at the Fury as its nose entered the portal.

"Throw all your anti-matter charges onto the power generators!"

My teammates looked at me like I was insane. They were probably correct in their thinking, but quickly complied.

"Klutch make a hole on the Fury, we are going aboard"

That got me a crooked smile and a thumbs up from the Tibor. The anti-matter warning flashed a solid red in our HUDs as I set the charges for one minute. It would be cutting it close. When the charges detonated, I hoped the machinery would cease functioning a split second after we disappeared into the portal. If I was wrong, we would be explaining ourselves to our maker, sixty seconds from now. We boosted to the side of the Fury and Klutch activated the Guardian device. We got a good hole and piled inside just as the ship we were sheltering behind, blew apart. The Fury shook violently, knocking us to the deck. I rolled over on Tria and held her tight. We had no way of knowing where we were going, or what would be waiting for us when we got there. I was praying to my maker it would not be somewhere in Andromeda. One way or another, our destiny was going to be determined in the next thirty seconds.

To be continued…

Other Books in this Series.

First of my Kind Second Edition

For the Good of All

The Deadliest of Intentions

Made in the USA
Columbia, SC
04 August 2020

15505101R10450

'La.. Mc....................................empting-to-
in...te v................................e so smooth
an.. mellow you can almost hear the ice clink against the glass as he
talks'   Max Byrd, *New York Times Book Review*

'Those who enjoy McMurtry's rueful humor and understated tone of
elegiac melancholy will devour the book in one setting'
                              Michael Lindgren, *Washington Post*

'A deftly narrated, often comically subversive work of fiction . . . If
Lonesome Dove is a chronicle of the cattle-driving West that contains
within its vast, broad ranges a small but heartrending intimate tragedy
of paternal neglect, *The Last Kind Words Saloon* is a dark post-
modernist modernist comedy'
                              Joyce Carol Oates, *New York Review of Books*

'By turns droll, stark, wry, or raunchy, this peripatetic novel . . . will
satisfy many readers who long for more from literary icon McMurtry'
                              Keddy Ann Outlaw, *Library Journal*

'[*The Last Kind Words Saloon*] is never dull, and it's also very funny.
As always, McMurtry's characters are plain-spoken but subtle and
full of dry humour . . . Moseying along with McMurtry is always
worthwhile'   Adam Wong, *Seattle Times*

'In this "ballad in prose", as McMurtry describes his latest book, he
paints the familiar historical characters in unfamiliar ways . . .
lovely'   Richard Eisenberg, *People*

Praise for *Dead Man's Walk*

'McMurtry has crafted a tale of love, fear and sacrifice in the face of Wild West adversity. With his vibrant, dynamic landscapes and language that springs from the page, this book captures the heart until the last word'
The Times

'A well-told novel, undemonstrative in its depiction of violence, and it offers a fascinating lesson on the realities of life in the mythical Wild West'
Sunday Times

'In *Dead Man's Walk*, McMurtry uses a simple, wry, immensely accessible storyteller's voice to ponder the same questions that Melville and Conrad did. This is a great book . . . Larry McMurtry, at his best here, is one of the finest American novelists, ever'
Los Angeles Times

'Succeeds marvellously . . . resurrecting two brilliantly conceived characters and delivering a rousing tale of the Wild West'
San Francisco Chronicle

'Gee-haw! Larry McMurtry is back in the yarn-slinging business – with a vengeance . . . Readers will gobble up *Dead Man's Walk* – a wild and woolly read – from cover to cover'
Denver Post

'McMurtry spins some scary, bloodthirsty tall tales and peoples them with remarkably vivid characters'
New York Daily News

'McMurtry remains a good storyteller, and he remains a master of dialogue, doing a sort of frontier version of Oscar Wilde'
Washington Post